SILVER KEY

ALYSSA L. BERTINATO

ISBN 978-1-7781512-0-0 (paperback)

ISBN 978-1-7781512-2-4 (hardcover)

First edition published 2022

To Matteo, the best brother ever.

SILVER KEY

CHAPTER ONE

I wake up with a silver key tattooed on my wrist.

After staring at it in the bathroom mirror, I jam my wrist under the tap, scrubbing until my skin turns red. The tattoo doesn't wash off.

My mom's going to kill me.

She's always been adamant about her disapproval of me getting a tattoo. But I've never given her a reason to worry, because I'd never spontaneously get one. In fact, spontaneity is overrated. Taking risk, winging it, playing it by ear... none of it is for me. I'm a planner. Sometimes I plan days in advance. Sometimes weeks. Sometimes I plan out my entire day, broken neatly into steps:

1. Get ready and eat breakfast
2. School (8:30 a.m. to 3 p.m.)
3. Homework

For as long as I can remember, I've needed structure, rules, and schedules. So a tattoo I don't remember getting? It sits on my wrist like a problem with no solution.

Once I'm ready, I pull my sleeve down as far as it will go and head downstairs. The kitchen smells like toast and coffee. My parents are already seated at the table when I join them.

"Ash, get down here and eat some breakfast!" Mom calls.

Footsteps thunder down the stairs, and my little brother bursts into the room wearing his favourite Superman T-shirt, dirty-blond hair neatly parted to the side.

"Morning," I say.

He steals the piece of toast right out of my hand and takes a huge bite. "Morning."

I snort. "Asshole."

"Aria, watch your language around your brother," my dad says from behind his newspaper.

I grab another piece of toast and butter it, forcing myself to eat even though my stomach feels hollow. The silver key on my wrist makes my arm feel heavy. I tug my sleeve down again.

My mom comes up behind me, her familiar scent drifting over my shoulders—fresh peony mixed with honey and caramel. She rests her hands on me gently. "Honey, after school, your dad and I would like to talk to you about something, okay?"

4. Talk with parents

... And then my mind immediately starts scrambling—*did I forget to do the dishes last night?*

I turn in my chair to look up at her. "Why can't you tell me now?"

"Not enough time. You need to get going." She kisses the top of my head. "Don't worry, you're not in trouble."

The relief is brief. I can't shake the feeling that something isn't right.

I arrive at school, grab my textbooks, binder, and pencil case, and slam my locker shut.

"So my mom was on the phone last night and I overheard her talking to Katie's mom about Br—"

"Jesus Christ, Violet!" I jump, nearly dropping everything in my arms.

I still remember the day Violet Miller became my best friend. Some jerk had called me an "uptight bitch" in the cafeteria. Before I could respond, Violet stepped in, calling *him* a "low-life jackass whose only realistic career path is dealing drugs on the side of the street".

We've stuck together ever since.

"Sorry," she says. "But did you hear about Bryan? He's going to ask you out."

She runs a hand through her long, straight hair, twirling one of her many purple highlights around her finger as we head to class.

I cringe. "Are you serious? Oh, please no."

"Why? He's hot."

I shrug. "Not my type."

"Right," she says dramatically. "You're into sweet, romantic guys with charming smiles. *You're so beautiful, Aria. I love you so much—*"

"Are you done?" I cut in. "You've been reading too much fanfiction."

"Actually, I've been reading just the right amount," she says.

I snicker. "I'm not interested in dating right now. I don't have time for it. It would be too distracting."

The only boyfriend I ever had was a guy from my freshman year history class. We barely saw each other, and most people didn't even know we were dating. Eventually, I realized it wasn't worth the effort. Between homework, clubs, and everything else, I could barely keep track of myself, let alone someone else.

"You need to find time," Violet says. "It could be good for you."

I sigh, but before I can argue, the bell rings. I've never been so grateful to hear that sound.

We take our usual seats near the back of the classroom. Outside the window, cars rush past and an oak tree sways in the wind. As I unzip my pencil case, my sleeve slides up. The reminder on my wrist makes my stomach twist.

"What's that?" Violet asks. "Did you get a tattoo and not tell me? Aria! Your mom is gonna kill you!"

I rub at the key, like that might help. "No. I don't know. It was there when I woke up this morning, I—"

"Good morning, class," Mr. Smith says. "Today we're starting our new unit on quadratic functions. Page 210."

And so it begins.

Another day. Same as the one before.

Sometimes I feel like a robot, programmed to follow rules and stay in line. And I'm not even mad about it. Yes, life has its ups and downs, but at the end of the day, life is normal and boring, and that won't change because that's how the world works. I don't hate that I know pretty well what I'll be doing tomorrow, and the day after that, and the day after that... It gives me control. Spontaneity is not for me, and I hate the unexpected.

There's a knock at the door and Mr. Smith opens it. After a brief exchange with a teacher, he turns to me.

"Aria, please go to the principal's office. Your parents are on their way to pick you up."

"Lucky," Violet whispers. "Why are you leaving?"

I shrug and exit the classroom.

As I walk, the key on my wrist shimmers in the light pouring in through the windows of the hallway. The bow of the key is shaped in odd swirls and curves that connect to the purple gem in the centre. The key itself is quite ancient looking, like an antique.

I grab my bag from my locker. As I head to the principal's office, I pull out my phone and call my mom.

"Hello?" My brother picks up.

"Ashton? Is Mom there?"

"She's driving."

"Can you put me on speaker?"

A moment later, my mom says, "Hello, honey. Everything okay?"

I reach the principal's office and grab the door handle. It's cold in my hand. For a split second, I think it's glowing, but as quickly as I see the glow, it's gone. Things like this have been happening all the time lately. I stopped believing I imagined it a while ago.

"You tell me," I said. "Are you coming to pick me up? The principal said you're taking me out of school today."

"No, I'm driving Ashton to school. Why would I..."

"Mom?"

"I'm pulling over. Ashton, give me the phone, please." There's rustling on the other end of the line, and then, "Aria, listen to me carefully. Today is the day. They told us it would happen soon, but I wasn't sure when—I wanted to prepare you—you're going to be confused, but everything will be okay." There's a sense of panic and urgency in her tone.

"Mom, what are you talking about? You're scaring me," I say, as her words strike up a panic in me as well.

I twist the doorknob and step through—

I'm standing in an office, but it's nothing like Principal Anderson's.

"What—Mom, are you there?"

No answer. My phone screen is black and refuses to turn on. My heart hammers in my chest.

I force a deep breath. The air smells sharply of burning incense. Paintings and portraits adorn the walls—scenes of rose fields framed by clouds, a woman with pin-straight hair and a shy smile. They feel priceless. The couch and desk face each other, and decorating one corner of the desk is a framed photo of a little girl. Upon further inspection, a long black chalkboard centred on one wall captures my attention. The other surrounding walls are made of mahogany so smooth I'm tempted to run my hands against it, but my feet feel glued to the floor, and I realize there's nothing logical about how I got here.

"Hello! You must be Aria," a short blond woman says. An overwhelming scent of lavender fills the air as she enters the room. "I'm Moreen Patrickson. You must be terribly confused. Take a seat."

I don't take a seat.

"Where am I?"

"You're at Silver Key Manor."

The words settle heavily in my chest.

Silver Key.

The tattoo on my wrist tingles, faintly warm. And all I can think is that whatever this is, it certainly wasn't on my schedule.

CHAPTER TWO

"How am I here right now?" I say, hands trembling.

"This will be a lot to process," Mrs. Patrickson says. "There's no easy way of saying it."

I stare, wide-eyed, at the woman in front of me. She closes the door with a casual wave of her hand, then pulls a glass out of thin air and fills it with water.

My mind must be playing tricks on me. There's no way that just happened.

I raise my eyebrows, waiting for an explanation.

"The first thing you should know," she says, settling back in her chair, "is that magic is real."

"Come again?"

She chuckles. "I know you're feeling a bit disoriented. You're in a unique situation."

Disoriented is an understatement. I still can't bring myself to move, afraid that if I so much as inhale, it'll make this more real than it already is.

"Please tell me what's going on," I say. "Is this some kind of joke?"

"Instead of being raised by your biological parents and growing up in the world of magic, you were given to your adoptive parents when—"

"Adoptive parents?" I say. "No. There must be a mistake. I'm not adopted. And magic? There's no way—how—"

Tears pool in my eyes as I lean against the wall for support, my legs suddenly unsteady. It hits me all at once. This isn't a misunderstanding. This is happening. It's *real*. The realization shakes me to my core.

"Oh, darling," Mrs. Patrickson says. I barely register her moving closer until she places a hand on my shoulder. "I know this is hard to hear. I hate being the one to tell you."

She pauses. "You're going to meet many other kids here. Witches, wizards, sorcerers— I don't know what they like to call themselves these days—who are just like you, except they've grown up with magic. They've been trained by their families their entire lives. Trained for this moment."

I blink.

"Since you haven't tapped into your magical potential yet, we'll meet every day for lessons. I'll teach you as much as I can before the first trial—"

"Trial?" I interrupt, my voice barely holding together.

"The Silver Key Tournament has three trials. Points are accumulated as you compete. You'll live here, along with the other sorcerers, until the trials are completed—"

"This is crazy," I say. "I need to go home. I have school. My friend is going to be worried. My parents are going to be worried. I—"

"We've already notified your parents," Mrs. Patrickson says gently. "And you'll be able to write to them. Don't worry."

She smiles, like that's supposed to help.

"This is a good thing, Aria. Every teenager and young adult dreams of this moment. You'll meet new people, make new friends, and learn incredible things."

I turn away. They say lavender is supposed to be calming, but right now, the smell is so strong it makes my head spin.

Or maybe that's just my thoughts colliding, one on top of the other.

"What if I don't want this?" I ask. "Can I leave?"

"I suppose you could. But there would be an unfortunate consequence. Any sorcerer who refuses to take part in the tournament is permanently stripped of their magic."

The room tilts. I'm lightheaded, unable to speak, my pulse roaring in my ears.

Maybe this is a dream. I'll wake up any second.

But I don't.

"You have five days to make your decision. The choice is yours, Aria."

My head is spinning, the only clear thought being: *Why, of all people, is this happening to me?*

"I'll take you to your dorm room, where you'll be sleeping. We've laid out some clothes on your bed," Mrs. Patrickson says.

As we walk through long halls and up several flights of stairs, I try to clear my head and process everything I've been told. If I'm adopted, who are my biological parents? Why did they give me up? Why hadn't my parents ever told me?

"Here we are. Room 22 of the girls' dormitories. The male dormitories are one floor down and off-limits to women past 7 p.m.," Mrs. Patrickson emphasizes. "Your roommate, Celie, is inside. She's a sweet girl and can help you get settled. Take this and read it over. It's a list of rules you must follow if you decide to stay at the manor."

She hands me a small piece of paper, and it's like I can breathe again as the list enters my grasp.

Finally, something I'm used to.

"I'll see you in my office tomorrow at 9 a.m. for our first lesson." She smiles, then walks away.

Standing alone in front of my dorm room, I'm very tempted to run. But even if I could find my way out of this giant mansion, I have no idea where I am. Besides, if what Mrs. Patrickson told me is true, I *can* return home. I've been happy living as I was, without magic. Would losing this ability I supposedly have really be so bad?

With a deep breath, I open the door.

A girl with long, dark-brown hair looks up at me, a bubbly smile lighting her face. Setting her thick book on the bedside table, she glides over, yellow sundress swaying with each step. Her tan skin shines in the sunlight, and her chestnut eyes sparkle with curiosity.

"You're Aria, right? I'm Celie Solano, your new roommate. It's so great to meet you!"

"It's nice to meet you too... Sorry, this is a lot to take in, I—"

"Oh my gosh, of course! They told me about your whole *predicament,* and I'm here to help. I'll do everything I can to make you feel comfortable. This is an exciting experience for all of us. Once it all sinks in, I'm sure you'll have a fantastic time."

I don't know how to respond.

"Where even are we?"

"Honestly? None of us know. Only the staff do. But that just makes it cooler, right?" She tilts her head. "Some people swear we're in Canada. Others think somewhere in Europe. And then there are the conspiracy theorists..." She leans in like she's sharing a secret. "They say we might be in a whole other realm. I like that theory best."

I stare at her with a blank expression.

Celie's smile doesn't falter. "How about I give you a minute. Come down when you're ready, and I'll introduce you to my friends." She waves cheerfully, then slips out of the room, the door clicking softly behind her.

I toss my school backpack onto the floor. My math, history, and biology textbooks will be of no use to me here. Through the small clear pocket of the bag, a family photo peeks out: Ashton, Mom, Dad, and me, all smiling at the camera. We took it on Ashton's first day of school. I can't help but smile at the memory.

I pull out my phone to call my parents. The screen stays stubbornly black. No matter what I try, it won't turn on. My jaw aches from clenching it so tightly.

1. Get ready and eat breakfast
~~*2. School (8:30 a.m. to 3 p.m.)*~~
~~*3. Homework*~~
~~*4. Talk with parents*~~
2. Write to parents
3. Meet up with Celie

I glance around the room. It's surprisingly spacious, with two beds and a small bedside table tucked next to each. Sunlight streams through the window, warming the space, and two dark wooden dressers sit in the corners.

I dig through a drawer, find a pen and a scrap of paper, and start writing.

Mom and Dad,

Where do I even begin? One second I'm at school, and the next I'm in this huge mansion in... I don't even know where. Somewhere far away. There's a woman here telling me that magic exists—and that I have it too. Apparently, I'm supposed to compete in these trials.

They said I can go home, but if I do, they'll strip me of my magic.
I don't know what's real anymore, or what I'm supposed to believe.

They also told me something else. They said you knew. That you've
always known. Why didn't you tell me? I keep thinking about it, and
I don't understand.

I'm confused. I'm scared. But I think I'm okay, at least for now. I'll
figure it out... somehow.

I love you.
— Aria

I fold the paper and slip it into the front pocket of my jeans.

Closing my eyes, I exhale. I feel so... lost. For the first time in my life, I have no idea what's coming next. No plan. No clues. Just this strange new world I'm being forced to navigate.

I don't like it.

There's this huge decision I'm supposed to make, but my thoughts are all tangled. I can't think clearly for more than a few seconds. I don't even know if I believe them—that I have magic. Maybe they got the wrong person.

I pull out the paper Mrs. Patrickson gave me and stare at the list of rules.

1. **No leaving the manor.** Doing so will result in the removal of your magic for a determined period.

2. **No using your magic or personal combat skills to fight another sorcerer or staff member.** Challenges aren't encouraged, but students may defend themselves if one is called for.

3. **Boys and girls are not allowed in each other's dormitories past 7 p.m.**

4. **Any disrespect toward teachers or staff will not be tolerated.**

5. **In desperate need of aid, contact the Emergency Sorcerers' Authorities.** Only as a last resort.

Note: Silver Key Manor is not a typical school but an institution to practice for the tournament. Classes are not mandatory, though they are recommended. Teachers are here to help as much as possible. If you have questions, do not hesitate to ask.

By competing in the Silver Key Tournament, you agree to abide by the above rules.

I refold the sheet of paper and set it on the table beside what I assume is my bed, my fingers lingering for a moment before letting go.

Taking a deep breath, I leave the dorm room.

CHAPTER THREE

Following the sounds of noisy teenagers, I pause for a moment to take in my surroundings. Arched windows line the walls, framing a picturesque view of an open backyard that stretches toward a nearby forest and glimmering lake. Not a single building breaks the horizon. *We really are in the middle of nowhere.*

The staircases seem to stretch on forever, but eventually I reach the final step. The chatter and laughter grow louder with each movement. Rounding a corner, I step into a room packed with at least two hundred people, all seemingly around my age. Most are clustered in groups, deep in conversation. My eyes catch a dirty-blond haired girl. She's talking to a few others, though a brown wooden pillar partially blocks my view. To my left, another circle of friends laughs and jostles each other.

As I weave through the crowd, fragments of conversation reach me. One girl recounts how her teacher once caught her using a spell to cheat on a test. She had her magic taken away for a week. Nearby, a man in his twenties bursts into laughter at something the girl across from him just said, the sound cutting through the hum of chatter around us.

I can't seem to find Celie among the crowd, so I awkwardly slide into an empty chair.

Not even a minute passes before I'm no longer alone.

"Aria! I'm so happy you came down," Celie says, appearing out of nowhere. "This is Lukas Prince." She gestures to the boy at her left. His brown skin and dark, curly hair catch the light, and he offers me a friendly wave. When he smiles, his whole face seems to light up, and just like that, a small slice of the fear I felt in this place melts away.

"And this is Mykel Griffin," Celie says, nodding toward the boy on her right. Mykel is tall with hazel eyes and dark eyebrows that frame them perfectly. His brown hair is slightly wavy at the top, and I can't help but watch as he runs a hand through it. He's beautiful—like a sculpture shaped from clay, every feature carefully carved and balanced. But there's something more—something hidden behind his gaze as he looks at me. His soft lips curl into a small, teasing smile, and I catch the faintest glimpse of his charm.

"Nice to meet you guys," I say, my voice a little steadier than I feel.

Celie slides into the empty chair next to me. "They're great. No need to be intimidated."

The boys sit too, closing the circle and making the space feel a bit less overwhelming.

"If you need anything or want someone to hang out with, we're here," Lukas says.

"Thank you. This is... pretty crazy," I admit.

Mykel chuckles. "Yeah, it must be a lot to take in."

I nod, grateful they get how difficult this is for me. Feeling a bit more at ease, I decide now's the time to ask some questions that have been swirling in my mind.

"My phone doesn't work here," I say. "Do people with magic not use them?"

Celie grins. "We do, but they're prohibited at Silver Key."

"Something about being immersed in the experience, away from distractions," Mykel adds.

"What about social media, movies, video games..." I trail off.

"We have those," Mykel says.

"But isn't magic supposed to be a secret? If you post something magic-related online, anyone could discover it."

"There are spells that keep it hidden," Celie explains.

"Huh, cool," I murmur. "And these trials... what exactly are they?"

"They're part of the Silver Key Tournament," Celie says.

"Alatar will explain it in the meeting," Lukas says, "Basically, we compete in three trials, and the winner gets a magical prize."

I nod, though my stomach clenches at the thought of competing in a magic tournament I never trained for.

Still, talking to Celie, Mykel, and Lukas eases the tightness in my chest, their easy warmth like a small anchor in this overwhelming room.

"So, how did you all meet?" I ask, steering the conversation toward something a little more normal.

"Lukas and I have been best friends since we were kids," Celie says. "Our parents were close, so that's how we first met."

"And I've known these two for a while since we attend the same school, but we really became friends after meeting at a party a few years ago," Mykel says.

"That's nice," I say.

Violet's face pops into my mind—my best friend. And now, if I decide to stay, I won't see her for who knows how long. What will she think? What will they tell her? Do I even want to know?

Celie frowns. "What's wrong?"

"Nothing. It's nothing."

"Thinking about someone back home?" Mykel says.

"Kinda... Sorry. I just—I know you guys are excited to be here, but everything's moving so fast, and..."

"It's okay," Lukas says gently.

"Are you thinking of leaving?" Celie asks. "I know you'll need to make a decision soon."

"I have no idea what I'm going to do," I say. "Anyway... I was actually wondering where I should bring this letter I wrote to my parents?"

"You should give it to Mr. Johnson. I can walk you to his office," Mykel says.

I stand. "Thanks."

"We'll catch up with you later," Mykel tells Celie and Lukas. They respond with two thumbs up.

I follow Mykel out of the room.

"This place is huge, right? I had a picture in my head of what it would look like, but it's even crazier in person," he says.

I nod. "Definitely big. You've never been here before?"

"Nope, first time. It's pretty much exclusive to people in the Silver Key Tournament," Mykel says. "Students can only come here once it's their turn to compete. From what I've heard, the manor closes down when the tournament isn't happening."

We walk a little further, and I can't help but admire the manor's Victorian elegance. Opulent furniture lines the hallways, plush, velvety couches tempt anyone to pause and linger, and tables hold antique vases overflowing with white tulips. Sunlight streams through open, silk-lined curtains, brightening the rooms. Mykel guides me past ornate frames adorning the walls, my footsteps echoing on the dark hardwood floor.

"Hey, so... are these permanent magical tattoos?" I break the silence, holding up my wrist to reveal the silver key.

"Silver Key uses that symbol to tag people before teleporting them here," he says. "It also links you to the manor. You could remove it with magic after the tournament, or if you decide not to stay, it'll disappear on its own."

"I kinda like it," I say. "Where's yours?"

Mykel lifts the bottom of his shirt to reveal a silver key tattooed on the right side of his lower stomach. "I like it too."

We walk on in silence, my mind racing with everything I've seen so far.

"This is insane," I mutter. "How is magic actually real?"

Mykel chuckles. "Yeah... it's a lot to wrap your head around." He pauses, then adds, "Let me show you something."

He curls his right hand into a fist, closes his eyes, and mutters under his breath. When he opens his eyes and unclenches his fist, a handful of dark red rose petals hover above his palm, circling.

I stare, completely mesmerized.

Mykel notices my wide-eyed expression and smiles. I can't help but smile back, and for a single, suspended moment, we lock eyes. He lets the petals fall back into his palm, and I take one before he tosses the rest onto a nearby table.

"That was... so cool," I breathe, holding the delicate petal.

"That's not even half of what we can do," he says, grinning. "I could teach you sometime?"

"I'd like that."

We reach Mr. Johnson's office, which looks like a classroom in an upscale boarding school—long wooden desks in neat rows, a chalkboard stretching across the front. I knock before stepping inside.

"I brought this letter I wrote to my parents. Where should I put it?" I ask.

"Aria Knight, right?" Mr. Johnson says, taking the letter.

"Yeah."

He reaches into the top drawer of his desk and pulls out another letter. He hands it to me.

I furrow my brows. "What's this?"

"It's from your parents. They weren't sure they'd have a chance to tell you everything before you arrived, so they wrote this about a month ago. I was told to give it to you when you got here."

Mykel moves closer, standing behind me. I feel his presence as I stare at the letter. It's wrapped neatly with my name in cursive. My mother's handwriting, instantly recognizable, makes my chest tighten. Time seems to slow as I let Mr. Johnson's words sink in. *They wrote this a month ago.*

"You can go into the hall and read it," Mr. Johnson says, holding up the letter I wrote to my parents. A moment later, a small, shimmering pink-and-blue creature swoops in, grabbing the letter. It flies away, leaving a faint trail of glitter behind.

My jaw drops involuntarily.

"Pixies," Mr. Johnson says. "Faster delivery."

I nod, feeling a little numb, and leave the office, Mykel following with concern.

"You gonna be okay?" he asks. "You look a little pale. I can stay if you want."

I force a smile. "No, it's fine."

He hesitates, then says, "Have lunch with us?"

"Yeah, thanks," I manage.

And then I'm alone.

Leaning against the wall, my heart racing, I take a deep, shaky breath and open the letter.

Aria,

Before you read any further, we want you to know this above all else: we love you with all our hearts, and nothing—now or ever—will change that.

We never told you that we aren't your birth parents. Not because we wanted to lie to you, but because we never wanted you to believe, even for a moment, that we loved you any less. The truth is, a week before you were born, your biological mother came to see us. We had met her before—she lived in the neighbourhood, and we'd even had her over for dinner once.

She told us she was going to give you up for adoption. She wanted us to raise you as our own, so you could have a good life. That night, she told us about magic—that it was real. It was overwhelming and difficult to believe at first, but she convinced us she was telling the truth. She never explained why she needed us to take you, only that it was urgent. And because we'd already been talking about having a child together, we agreed.

If you're reading this now, it means we didn't get the chance to tell you any of this before you were taken to Silver Key, and for that, we are so deeply sorry. We always knew this truth would come out someday, especially as we began to suspect that you may have inherited magical abilities from your biological parents. We planned to tell you. We just never knew when the right time would be.

We know you must feel hurt, confused, and maybe even betrayed. We wish more than anything that we could be having this conver-sation with you face to face. While your dad and I are worried about you being away at some magical tournament, we've been assured that you're safe. Please don't worry about us—or about Violet. We've come up with a believable story to explain your absence.

We understand that learning about your birth parents and your true background may feel important to you. As your parents, we support you completely if you choose to explore that part of your history.

Write to us anytime. No matter what you decide, no matter where this path takes you, you are our daughter, and we love you.

Love always,
Mom and Dad

CHAPTER FOUR

I want to curl up in a ball and cry. My entire life feels like a lie. I don't know what to believe anymore, and the uncertainty is terrifying.

Eventually, I muster the courage to go to the dining hall (I only get lost twice). The scent of freshly baked bread and hot apple strudel reaches me before I even make it inside. My stomach rumbles.

The dining hall is long, its high ceiling lit by countless flickering candles. Dark wooden walls tower above me, complementing the oak-brown tables that stretch across the room. At the far end stands a dais, a tall podium resting atop it.

I walk farther in and spot Celie, Lukas, and Mykel waving me over from a nearby table. I pause for a moment to compose myself.

Breathe in and out.

Anger, sadness, confusion, fear—everything twists together into a sharp sense of betrayal. I push the feeling aside for now.

As I make my way toward my new friends, I accidentally bump into someone's chest.

"Oh, crap. Sorry!"

I look up, and a pair of cold blue eyes meets my green ones. He's handsome, with messy silver hair and a faint scar above his left eyebrow. He smells dangerous, like cologne mixed with a hint of heartbreak.

Surprise flashes across his face, gone too quickly for me to be sure I didn't imagine it. I pull my hands away from his chest and step back.

"Watch where you're going," he says, shoving past me.

"Aria!" Celie calls, but her voice feels distant, drowned out by my thoughts.

Who does this guy think he is?

"Hey!" I say. "No need to be rude."

He turns around, a—frustratingly attractive—grin on his face. "Do you know who I am?"

"No, actually, I don't. And I don't really care."

"Cute," he says, stepping closer. A spark of amused curiosity lights his eyes. "I didn't catch your name."

"I didn't throw it."

The corner of his mouth lifts into a devilish smirk. "Well, you should."

Did he really just say that?

I shove down the unwelcome thoughts his obnoxious response stirs and open my mouth to reply, but Mykel and Lukas step in front of me, cutting me off.

"Heyyy, Blade," Lukas says. "Aria's had a crazy day so far—y'know, finding out about magic and all that—so maybe you can leave her alone."

Blade's gaze stays locked on me, sharp with intrigue. "So you're the new girl..." He tilts his head. "Maybe you should hang out with me. Trust me, you'd have a lot more fun." He punctuates the offer with a confident wink.

"I think I'll pass."

"You sure?" he says. "With that attitude, you'd fit right in."

"Not gonna happen, Blade," Mykel says.

"Whatever," Blade replies, shooting Mykel a venomous look—one Mykel is more than happy to return.

They scowl at each other, both tall and evenly matched in height. But where Blade's face is all sharp angles and piercing eyes, Mykel's features are softer—a smooth-edged jaw, a gentler curve to his mouth. Watching them, I get the strange feeling I'm intruding on something personal.

With his jaw clenched, Blade finally turns away. He walks off with arrogant confidence, a subtle swagger in his step, and drops onto a bench at the far end of the room beside a group of friends. That's when I notice how quiet the dining hall has become. All eyes are on us as we walk over to our table.

"Who the hell is that guy?" I ask, sliding into the seat beside Celie.

"Blade Casteel," she says, handing me a glass of orange juice, which I accept. "His father won the tournament in his generation, and his grandfather won the one before that. They're some of the most powerful sorcerers alive."

I take a sip as Lukas adds, "Blade's basically famous. Super rich."

"And a complete dick," Mykel mutters.

"Such a waste of good looks," Lukas says, taking a bite of his jam-smeared bread.

Across the room, Blade laughs with his friends as they watch a boy's can of soda explode in his face. I roll my eyes and look away.

"Attention everyone," Mrs. Patrickson says from the podium. "Alatar Blight would like to make an announcement regarding this generation's tournament kent."

Quiet whispers ripple through the room before my gaze lands on the man who must be Alatar Blight. I can't quite pinpoint his age. A rugged face and sharply groomed facial hair contrast with the strands of grey peppered through his raven-black hair.

He wears a tailored black suit that accentuates the breadth of his shoulders, and his presence alone seems to press the noise from the room until silence settles.

"I'm sure you all know why you've been gathered here," Alatar begins, his deep, gravelly voice echoing through the hall. "To compete in the Silver Key Tournament." He pauses. "But before I discuss the trials, I'd like you to welcome our newest sorcerer, Aria Knight."

He points directly at me.

I want to sink into the floor and disappear. Heat rushes to my face as every head in the dining hall turns my way. Some people clap. Others offer curious smiles. A few don't bother hiding their displeasure.

Celie bumps my shoulder as she applauds, Lukas lets out an enthusiastic whoop, and Mykel smiles at me. I try to return it, but it feels stiff. Unconvincing.

After what feels like an eternity, Alatar continues, and I force myself to breathe. Being the centre of attention has never felt worse.

"These three trials will test your strength, bravery, magic, and your ability to think on your feet," he says.

I shoot a worried glance at Celie, but she doesn't notice as she's practically vibrating with excitement.

"You'll earn points based on how you overcome obstacles and how fast you do it," Alatar says. "At the end of the third trial, the individual with the highest score will win."

He steps away from the podium, extends his hand, and murmurs something under his breath.

The dining hall falls utterly silent.

Seconds later, a book appears in his grasp. It's a deep, unusual shade of purple, with a silver key set at its centre—the same symbol tattooed on my wrist.

Alatar grins. "The prize, as many of you know, is this grimoire. It contains every spell, potion, incantation, and magical herb imaginable, surpassing the spellbooks of generations past."

The key on the cover shimmers, and the purple gem at its centre pulses with light.

"Beautiful, isn't it?" Alatar says, setting the grimoire atop the podium. "And that's not all. The winner will also be granted the power of the Sight."

Excited murmurs ripple through the room.

"The Sight," Alatar continues, "allows its wielder to see magical energy in the air when magic is about to be used, and when it has recently been used—an advantage in any fight."

A flicker of curiosity stirs in me at his words. Across the room, Blade smirks at his friends, confidence written plainly on his face, as if the prize already belongs to him.

"The first trial will take place in a few months," Alatar says. "Until then, I suggest you train hard. This is not a game. It's to be taken seriously. We've raised the stakes this year, so expect the trials to be far more complex, with much higher stakes. Any questions or concerns can be brought to my office."

Before anyone can so much as raise their hand, he steps down from the dais and strides out of the dining hall.

The moment he's gone, the room erupts back into noise.

"That was so cool," Lukas says, still staring at the spot where Alatar stood moments ago.

"I'm so excited," Celie says. "I wonder what the first trial's going to be. I need to start studying."

Mykel laughs. "Slow down there, Celie."

I let out a shaky breath. "I am so unprepared for this."

The thought of everything I'd need to learn sends stress coiling in my chest. It feels daunting—almost impossible—and I'm not sure I want to put myself through it at all.

"Hey," Mykel says gently, reaching for my hand. "We're going to help you as much as we can."

His fingers wrap around mine. His soft touch and that small, kind gesture send a flutter of butterflies through my stomach.

"Yeah," Celie adds. "There are still a couple of months before the first trial. You've got this."

"He doesn't seem worried at all," I murmur, glancing across the room at Blade, surrounded by his circle of admirers.

"Of course he isn't," Mykel says. "He's way too cocky to be worried."

Mrs. Patrickson steps back onto the dais. "Thank you, Alatar. We're incredibly lucky to have you as headmaster of Silver Key for this generation's tournament. Now, everyone, please get into groups so we can begin the tours of the manor."

Celie, Mykel, Lukas, and I join Mrs. Patrickson's tour group along with several other sorcerers. Once everyone has gathered, she claps her hands, practically buzzing with excitement, and leads us out of the dining hall.

"Now, if you'll follow me down this hallway..." she says, guiding us through a long, narrow corridor I recognize from earlier. "Most of the teachers' and senior staff offices are located here. Alatar's office is on the right."

I glance inside as we pass. Unsurprisingly, it's immaculate, everything in its place.

Mrs. Patrickson continues through the manor and brings us to the library. It's impossibly vast. Though part of the same building, it somehow feels larger than the manor itself.

The library spans at least three stories and smells faintly of wood and vanilla. Spiral staircases with glowing silver railings curl upward to a balcony that rounds the second story, and towering shelves packed with what must be millions of books loom over us.

As we walk through, a librarian aggressively stamps a few books before flicking her hand, sending them flying neatly back to their shelves. Tall windows line the walls, framed in even panels that mirror the design of the domed glass ceiling above. Both are accented with the same silvery tint as the railings.

On our way out, we pass a cluster of plush couches draped with fuzzy blankets, a fireplace crackling warmly along the wall.

Next are the male dormitories, followed by the female dorms after Mrs. Patrickson leads us up a flight of stairs. We continue on to the communal bathrooms, which sounds awful, but they're surprisingly pristine—bright and spacious—with not a speck of dust to be found under the glaring lights.

She then shows us the practice room, which somehow manages to be even more overwhelming than anything I've seen so far. The walls are deep navy, flecked with shimmering black, and don't look solid—like I'd fall straight through if I leaned on them. In the centre of the room, ten doors are spaced evenly in a wide circle. Each door is white, with a bright, framed image on its front that illuminates the dim room.

"Each of these doors will teleport anyone who steps through it to a different location," Mrs. Patrickson explains. "It allows you to practice spells and combat in field-like settings, heightening the quality of your training."

Across the room, Mr. Johnson guides another tour group. I peek over as one person opens a door, revealing a vast forest. I'm in awe and have to pinch myself to make sure it's real.

The door closest to me bears the image of a sparkling blue wave. Lukas opens it, and a group of people steps out, startling me, before walking away. Once they've cleared, the sight calms my racing heart. I smell salty water and feel a gentle wind brush against my face. Mykel shuts the door, and the soft caress of the breeze vanishes as if it were never there.

It feels almost too crazy to process, and I wonder if I'll ever get used to things like this. I manage only a whispered, "Whoa," as we move on.

Beyond the practice room, there's a sparring room and a gym. We then move on to the grand kitchen, filled with wooden cabinets and neatly arranged appliances. A long walnut table sits in the centre, a bowl brimming with bananas, oranges, and apples atop it. The scent of freshly baked cookies hangs in the air, making my mouth water. Lukas and I each grab a cookie from a plate on the counter before exiting the kitchen. I take a giant bite and sigh in delight as the chocolate chips melt in my mouth.

When we reach the medical wing of the manor, I'm struck by how quiet it is—no beeping machines, no sterile alarms. It's a long room, with dozens of beds lined up neatly. Several gurneys are parked at one end, and at the opposite end, a giant window frames a tranquil view of a pond.

We continue through many empty classrooms as we wind our way through the manor. Tiny specks of green, yellow, blue, and pink glittering lights zip past in the halls—I'm told they're pixies, like the ones that delivered my letter.

Next, we arrive at what may be my favourite place in the manor so far: the back garden. It's breathtaking. Trees are spread across the freshly cut, bright green grass, their leaves not only green, red, and yellow but also shades of hot pink, royal purple, and cobalt blue, all dancing in the breeze. A pebbled pathway winds through the garden, lined with dozens of flowers. Mixed among the familiar lilacs and lavenders are peculiar petunia-like flowers whose petals seem to breathe in and out softly.

I hear the gentle trickle of water as we turn a corner. A pond, shaded by a large willow tree, shimmers before me. Its inhabitants look like fish but are clearly magical creatures, flashing different colours as they leap in and out of the water.

As we head back inside, descending a few flights of stairs, Mrs. Patrickson stops at the start of an empty hallway. "Now, down this hall is a door that is off-limits to all of you."

I find myself inexplicably drawn to the door, staring at its ornate design. The bright silver accents catch the light, and I can't tear my eyes away.

"The only reason I'm showing it to you is so you don't stumble upon it yourself," Mrs. Patrickson says. "There are wards on the door and hallway to prevent entry. If you try, there will be severe consequences."

I share a curious look with Celie. From the corner of my eye, I notice Blade. His features soften as he stares at the door, captivated. But the moment he catches my gaze, his expression hardens, and I quickly look away.

"And so you are all aware," Mrs. Patrickson continues, "if a dire emergency occurs and you cannot reach Alatar or any of us teachers, you can call the ESA: Emergency Sorcerers' Authorities. Trace the number 829 on your palm, clench your fist, and say '*Subitis.*' Officers will teleport to your aid. Do this only in genuine emergencies. Using this for a prank or minor inconvenience will result in trial."

I suck in a shaky breath of air and pray I never have to contact the ESA. Honestly, none of this is making me any less anxious. If anything, it's worrying me into thinking maybe I should stay out of this entirely. Why put myself in such danger if I don't have to?

"Aria Knight," a deep voice says from behind me. I spin around—and freeze. Alatar Blight stands there.

"Hi, sir," I manage.

He grins, eyes crinkling at the corners. "Please, call me Alatar."

"Okay... sir..." I cringe as the words leave my mouth.

Next to me, Lukas chuckles. Celie elbows him in the side.

Alatar smiles again. "I'd like to speak with you in my office, if that's alright."

"Um... okay," I reply.

I feel Mykel, Celie, and Lukas close by, their presence comforting, but I can tell they're as shocked as I am. It's like talking to the school principal, except he's a famous sorcerer who rarely addresses students unless it's by appointment and *urgent*.

"Blade," Alatar calls. Blade steps forward. "How's your father?"

"He's doing well, Alatar," Blade says.

"Tell him I said hello. Enjoy what's left of your tour, ladies and gentlemen."

Alatar walks away. Celie shoves me to remind me I'm supposed to follow. Alatar and I ascend a flight of stairs and turn left.

"Is everything okay?" I ask, keeping pace behind him.

"Oh yes," he says. "I wanted to welcome you—to Silver Key and to the world of magic as well."

"Wow... thank you," I say as he opens the door to his office. He holds it for me, and I notice the ring on his right index finger as I pass: a round emerald set in gold, exquisite.

As I enter his office, an enormous ball of flame in the corner of the room catches my attention. My heart skips as the flame bursts, and like a butterfly emerging from its cocoon, a creature materializes. I stumble back, and Alatar chuckles softly.

"It's alright," he says. The fiery butterfly flutters to him, resting above his shoulder. "This is Hestia."

I once again find myself speechless.

"She's an emppeta," Alatar explains, "my companion. You'll learn about creatures like her in time. Please, have a seat." He gestures toward a black velvet couch in front of his desk.

I sink into the seat as if I'm about to be swallowed whole by the cushions. Once composed, I let my eyes wander. The office is dark, furniture matching the grey walls. There are no family photos like in Mrs. Patrickson's room. Not even so much as a decorative plant. The most decoration he has is a meticulously alphabetized bookshelf and a small statue of a man with wings, and even that seems to be there solely for the purpose of filling up the empty space.

I'm not sure what to make of the man before me. He's like an incomplete puzzle, and as I search for the remaining pieces, it's as if the most important ones are missing.

"I knew your birth parents, you know," Alatar says, snapping me back to reality. He sits behind his desk, studying me as intently as I had studied his office—with curiosity and intrigue.

"You did?"

"Yes. We competed in the trials together. They were brilliant people. Your parents always made a charming couple." His eyes soften, and only then do I realize just how intently he was looking at me before.

My birth parents.

"Do you know why they gave me up for adoption?" My heartbeat accelerates in anticipation.

"I'm sorry, Aria. I don't. We lost touch over the years."

I slump back onto the couch in disappointment.

"What I *can* tell you is this: when I knew them, they were both powerful sorcerers. Especially your mother. Their blood runs through your veins, and I believe you have the potential to be just as great as they were."

"But I'm so new to this," I say. "I'm not even sure I want to stay. And if I did... how could I learn enough before the first trial?"

He smiles. "You'll work hard. If you're determined, it's not impossible. You strike me as a quick learner, like your mother."

I stay quiet, absorbing his words.

"You have so much potential, Aria," Alatar says. "Truthfully, I think you could even win."

"*Really?*" I don't bother hiding my surprise.

"Really," he says. "I trust that you'll make the right decision."

I nod, unsure what else to say.

Alatar stands. "Well, Aria, thank you for speaking with me. If you need anything, or have questions, my door is always open."

I step out of Alatar's office, and for the first time since arriving, feel a flicker of motivation to compete in this tournament.

CHAPTER FIVE

That night, I find myself unable to sleep.

I'd received a letter from my parents earlier. Pages filled with apologies and regret for not telling me sooner. They wrote that they wouldn't be upset if I chose to stay at Silver Key. That magic is a part of me. That I should learn to control it and compete in the tournament, if that's what I want.

The problem is, I don't know what I want.

I toss and turn as moonlight slips through the curtain beside my bed. Owls hoot in the distance. There's no honking traffic, no rush of cars outside my window. Instead, I'm pretty sure I hear a wolf howl somewhere beyond the grounds.

I roll onto my stomach and bury my face in the pillow—but it isn't *my* pillow. It doesn't feel the same. Smell the same.

Celie is asleep in the bed next to me. Her breathing is slow and even, but my thoughts keep me wide awake. With nothing else to do, I try to make sense of everything the only way I know how: by weighing my options, even though this decision is unlike any I've ever faced.

Pros and cons of staying at the manor and competing in the tournament:

Pro: I'm learning magic. That's... kind of incredible.

Con: I'm learning magic—and that's terrifying.

Pro: I'll be with Celie, Mykel, and Lukas.
Con: I'll be away from my family, Violet, and home.
Pro: This could be life-changing—a chance to step out of my comfort zone.
Con: I'm not sure I want to; I was fine and comfortable before.
Pro: This could be the most fun I've ever had.
Con: I won't be in control of what comes next.

Eventually, frustration seeps in and forces me to sleep.

I wake the next morning in a haze, bracing myself for the shrill blare of my alarm, but it never comes.

When I open my eyes, I see wooden dressers, curtains drawn over a sunlit window, and a girl asleep in the bed beside me.

Lying there in the pale morning light, the previous day rushes back all at once. Silver Key. Magic. Alatar. The tournament.

I stare at the ceiling and let it sink in.

"For your first lesson, I'll be introducing you to some basic spells," Mrs. Patrickson says as she tidies her desk. "I know you're still deciding whether you'd like to stay, but we should at least get you doing a bit of magic so you know how it feels. We'll start easy."

I sit in an empty chair at a small wooden table. A candle and feather rest in front of me. I have a pretty good idea where this is going.

"Ready?" she says.

I'm *really* nervous. Part of me doesn't believe I can do the things these people say I can do. This feels like a defining moment—like everything hinges on what happens next—and I can't stop my hands from shaking. If I can do magic, then all of this becomes real. And I'm not sure how I'll handle that.

But I'll never know if I don't try.

"I'm ready," I say.

"Good. Let's start with the candle. This is one of the easiest spells to learn. Focus on the wick. Imagine a flame igniting at its tip. As you concentrate, say the incantation *'Incendo.'*"

I do as she says, narrowing my focus on the wick and speaking the word.

Nothing. Not even a flicker.

"It's alright," she says gently. "Try again. This time, look for a warm sensation in your chest. Let it build until you're ready, then allow the magic to ignite through you and say the spell."

I try again, searching for the warmth she described, but I feel nothing.

"Magic is personal to every sorcerer," Mrs. Patrickson says. "You have to find the emotion, the feeling, that opens the door to your abilities."

I close my eyes and stop fighting what I'm feeling. I let it all surface—the emotions I've been trying to bury since yesterday. Frustration. Anger. Confusion. Fear. Sadness. Doubt.

Doubt that I can do this at all.

Then a different feeling slips in. A quiet, stubborn spark of motivation. Alatar's voice echoes in my memory, his certainty.

Celie. Lukas. Mykel. Their faces form clearly in my mind. They believe in me. They're willing to help me learn, if it's what I choose.

I *can* do this.

I focus on that determination. I've never been someone who gives up easily. Violet and my parents have told me that my whole life. When I commit to something, I give it everything I have.

Mykel's voice rises to the surface of my thoughts—telling me not to worry, promising they'd help me through this. And then the memory of his hand in mine flashes through me, the sudden flutter of butterflies in my stomach.

And there it is.

Warmth blooms in my chest, spreading outward. I hold onto it, letting it grow, letting the magic rise to the surface.

"*Incendo.*"

Heat surges through my body, rushing down my arms and bursting from my fingertips. A spark jumps—alive, electric—and a small flame catches at the tip of the wick.

"Holy shit," I breathe.

How is this possible? How is this happening to me?

Every lingering doubt, every thought that this might not be real, vanishes. In its place is something new. Something powerful.

I feel powerful in a way I don't have words for.

"Amazing," Mrs. Patrickson says, awe flickering in her eyes. "See? Easy. You'll be excellent at this."

The rest of the lesson passes in a blur of flames and focus. I light candle after candle and even manage to lift a single feather into the air. It's beginner magic, but I'm proud of it anyway.

Definitely better than learning how to graph quadratic functions.

I never imagined I could do anything like this. Yet the more I think about it, the more it makes sense. All those strange moments in my life—losing something only to find it minutes later, my lamp flickering on just as darkness settled in.

I always felt like something in me was waiting. Like there was untapped potential I couldn't quite reach. Maybe all of that was my magic trying to wake me up. Trying to tell me it was there.

Maybe staying at Silver Key wouldn't be so bad after all.

Ready to meet Celie, Mykel, and Lukas in the back garden, I make my way through the manor, doing my best not to get lost.

I end up in the sparring room.

A long black folding mat stretches across one side of the space. A large crate filled with punching bags and boxing gloves sits against the wall, and above it, a neat row of bo staffs hangs in place. The room smells faintly of sweat and rubber.

"Make a wrong turn?" a voice says behind me.

I spin, startled. Two guys stand there. One is tall and lanky, thin brown hair falling into his eyes, shoulders slumped as if he's trying to take up less space despite his height. The other is shorter and stockier, with spiky black hair and a round face. An ugly smirk curls his lips.

"Well?" the shorter one says.

"I'm sorry," I say. "I got lost. I was heading to the back garden."

The tall one snorts. "Entrance is on the other side of the manor."

"Oh. Okay." I step forward to pass them.

They block my path.

Before I can react, the door opens again. Blade steps inside and shuts it behind him.

"Aria, right?" he says.

In the dining hall, we were surrounded by people. Here, I'm alone. Still, I square my shoulders. "Aria Knight. Now, if you don't mind, I have somewhere to be."

"Come on, Knight," Blade says. "Why don't you stay and hang out with us for a bit?"

"I'm good," I reply. "Or do you need a reminder that I'm not interested?"

Blade laughs, and the other two join in.

"What should we do with her?" the tall one asks.

"Nothing," Blade says. "Let her go."

Relief barely has time to register before he continues.

"If Aria would rather hang out with Mykel and his friends, let her. She's the one missing out." His mouth curves into something unreadable. "We've got the practice room reserved anyway. Let's go."

He leaves without another glance. I mentally curse him for abandoning me with his friends.

"Hm," the shorter one muses. "Should we let her go, Nathan?"

"I don't know, Rex," the tall one replies. "I'm leaning toward no."

"I don't want trouble," I say, keeping my voice steady. "I haven't done anything. Just let me leave."

"We heard you might not be staying at Silver Key," Nathan says. "That you're planning to give up your magic and go live a boring normal life."

"Where did you hear that?" I ask.

He shrugs. "Word travels fast."

"We're here to encourage you to leave," Rex says. "We don't need another competitor, especially one so ungrateful for her power."

"I haven't decided," I say. "And I definitely won't let two assholes decide for me."

Nathan steps closer, invading my space. His face is inches from mine. My pulse hammers, but I don't move.

"You're weak, Aria," he says quietly. "You don't know any-thing. You'll get yourself killed in the tournament." He smiles. "So go ahead. Compete. We won't stop you."

"I told you to let her go," Blade says, standing in the doorway.

"Why?" Rex scoffs. "She's a pathetic, ungrateful bitch—"

"Excuse me?"

The anger hits fast and hot, surging through my chest before I can stop it.

"You heard me—"

I punch him.

My fist connects with his cheekbone, and the shock on his face makes it worth it.

Blade's eyebrows shoot up. Then—infuriatingly—he smirks.

"You son of a—"

"Enough, Nathan," Blade says, failing to hide his amusement as he eyes the reddening mark on Nathan's face. He turns to me. "Go."

I move to leave, but Blade grabs my wrist.

I face him, heart pounding. For a moment, it looks like he's about to say something. But he doesn't.

I yank my arm free and storm out of the room.

"They did *what*?" Mykel says once I finish explaining why I look so shaken.

"I'm fine," I insist. "Blade came back and made them stop. He let me leave."

"The fact that he left you alone with them—" Mykel runs a hand through his hair. "He knew what would happen."

"Dude, breathe," Lukas says. "At least he stepped in before things got worse."

"Nathan and Rex are the real assholes," Celie says. "They, of all people, have no right to call you weak." She turns to Lukas.

"Remember fifth grade, when we had to perform an attack spell for the first time?"

Lukas snorts. "Rex could barely get his spell to hit the dummy, never mind an actual person."

"I remember that," Mykel says. "Everyone got it on the first try except him."

"And Nathan *did* manage it," Celie says, smirking, "but it backfired and hit him in the face. He was in the hospital for a week."

"That honestly makes me feel a lot better," I admit, grinning.

Celie rests a hand on my shoulder. "Don't let Blade—or those two idiots—affect your decision. They might make you feel like you don't belong here, but you do, Aria. You're a sorcerer."

"Yeah," Mykel says firmly. "Fuck what anyone else thinks. We want you here."

The next few days blur together, and I still haven't made my decision. I go back and forth constantly, stuck in the same loop.

Part of me wants to go home. I've never been away from my family for more than a day, and missing them hurts more than I expected. And the sparring room incident won't leave my mind, no matter how much Celie, Mykel, and Lukas tell me not to listen to Nathan and Rex.

What if they're right? What if I really do get myself killed because I'm not prepared? I have no idea what the tournament will demand of me.

On the other hand, so many people here have been welcoming—especially Celie, Mykel, and Lukas. And while the special attention from the teachers makes me uncomfortable, it's also reassuring to know they believe I'm worth the effort.

Most of all, there's the magic.

That first time—feeling it surge through me, bending to my will—was unlike anything I've ever experienced. I haven't been able to do it again since Mrs. Patrickson paused my lessons until I made my choice, but the memory lingers. The control. The release. The thrill of it. I don't know if I'm willing to give that up.

I find myself back in the library, seated at a long wooden table tucked into a quiet corner. A stack of heavy books towers in front of me. The crackle of the fireplace and the soft turn of pages nearby are the only sounds.

I open the first book—a thick red volume titled *A History of Silver Key*, the letters stamped in silver—and read over paragraphs of history. The manor was built in 1860 as Ellfire's School of Sorcery, founded by Astalon Ellfire, one of the most powerful sorcerers in history.

I stare at the image of him. He has dark, hooded eyes and looks to have been about forty years old when this photo was taken. An inexplicable chill crawls down my spine.

I continue reading. Ten years after the school's founding, the Silver Key Tournament was created to push young sorcerers to their limits, preparing them for the dangers of a magical world. Eventually, the school became Silver Key Manor, a home and training ground for the tournament.

I set the book aside, letting it sink in, and pick up another. Skimming through, I land on a list of past tournament winners.

My gaze lands upon a man named Elyon Casteel, who is unmistakably Blade's father. A photo of him sits above his name, and I study his features as best as I can through the grainy photo. Blond hair, sharp jaw, striking blue eyes. Young. Confident. Powerful.

After reading about several Silver Key Tournament winners, I close the book and rub my eyes. How am I supposed to live up to *this*? Every winner was trained, experienced. I have none of that.

Truthfully, I think you could even win.

Alatar seems to believe that I can compete. That I could win. Maybe that means I should start believing in myself. The first trial is still months away. If I stay—if I train hard enough—I might have a chance.

Not quite ready to call it a night, I open another book, this one on the art of magic itself. It explains how magical energy is passed through bloodlines and amplified by the other realms. There is one primary source of magic in the universe, and whichever realm houses it holds the greatest power.

A source of magic...

A section on the Sight draws my attention. Alatar said the winner of the tournament will not only win a magical spellbook but will be gifted with the Sight. According to this book, the Sight is the most coveted ability a sorcerer can possess.

There are three forms: Strength, Emotion, and Agility. Each allows the wielder to see magic form in the air, anticipating spells, while also sensing recent magic use. Strength enhances your spells' power. Emotion grants you mastery over your own feelings. Agility sharpens reflexes and perception, especially useful in combat.

By the time I finish reading, it's dark outside. I barely noticed the hours pass. I yawn and look up—

The glass ceiling above reveals a sky filled with enormous, glittering stars. It's like looking at the view from an observatory, and I lean back, tilting my head further to take it all in.

So engrossed in the view, I don't hear Mykel coming until he says, "Find anything interesting?"

I lower my gaze as he takes the seat across from me, nudging the books aside.

"Pretty much everything," I say. "Did you know magic can make you invisible? *Invisible.* That's insane."

Mykel grins. "I've done it a few times."

My eyes widen. "Seriously?"

"Yeah. My dad taught me. Said it might come in handy someday. Mostly I just used it to mess with Lukas."

I laugh. "Add that to the list of things you're going to teach me."

"Gladly."

His smile makes *me* smile, and I can't help thinking of what Violet would say about Mykel.

Charming. Sweet. Incredibly attractive.

Yeah. I might need to rethink my stance on dating.

I'm back in Alatar's office. Mrs. Patrickson stands to his left as he watches me from behind his desk. I sit on the couch again, but this time I'm perched on the edge, nerves buzzing beneath my skin. Five days passed far too quickly.

I wipe my sweaty palms on my jeans.

Alatar clears his throat. "Aria Knight. If you choose to stay, you will train with Mrs. Patrickson daily. You will work harder than any other sorcerer here. You will compete in the tournament to the best of your ability—and you will not be permitted to leave the manor until the tournament concludes."

My heart pounds.

"If you choose to leave," he continues, "your magic will be stripped immediately, and you will be returned home."

Mrs. Patrickson meets my gaze. "So, Aria. Have you made your decision?"

"I have."

I straighten. Lift my chin. Gather every ounce of courage I can find.

"I want to stay."

CHAPTER SIX

It's been two weeks, and I'm exhausted.

I have lessons with Mrs. Patrickson every day. When I'm not with her, I'm training with Celie, Mykel, and Lukas. When I'm not training, I'm cramming as much information into my head as I possibly can.

Learning magic from scratch is overwhelming. Some days, the gap between what I know and what everyone else knows feels impossible to bridge. I take one step forward, and everyone else is fifteen steps ahead.

It's hard. But I want to do the best I can.

I still miss my family, but the ache in my chest has dulled. I almost feel guilty admitting it, but between lessons and training—and spending so much time with Celie, Mykel, and Lukas—I'm actually enjoying myself.

I'm glad I chose to stay.

Being roommates with Celie is... interesting. I love her, but I don't know if I'll ever get used to her staying up until three in the morning with her nose buried in a book—or setting an alarm for 7 a.m. so she can get a "head start on the day." My sleep schedule has suffered, but honestly, I wouldn't trade her for anyone else. Our late-night conversations have become something I look forward to. More than that, I've found comfort in hopping into my bed at night. I'm not sure when I started thinking of it as mine, but it feels right.

I didn't know how things would turn out when I decided to stay at Silver Key, but I'm starting to believe I made the right choice. The weight on my chest eases just a little.

"Good morning, Aria," Mrs. Patrickson says as she enters her office, closing the door behind her.

"Morning," I reply.

She's especially chipper—though, really, she's always a little cheery. It's something I've grown used to over the past two weeks.

She takes a seat and straightens a picture frame on her desk. The photo shows a little girl with brunette hair tied into pigtails.

"Is she your daughter?" I ask.

Mrs. Patrickson looks up, confused, then realizes what I mean. "Oh—no. Not biologically." Her voice softens. "But she's like a daughter to me."

The smile on her face fades, and I probably should leave it alone, but curiosity gets the better of me.

"Is she a sorcerer?"

Mrs. Patrickson shakes her head. "No, she's not." She hesitates, then forces a smile. "Probably for the best. She's enough trouble as it is."

I chuckle and drop the subject. Clearly, it's not something she wants to discuss.

"Ready to begin?" she asks brightly. "Today's lesson is a fun one. Familiars."

"Like magical pets?"

"Precisely," she says. "Most sorcerers bond with a familiar. Each species carries its own magical abilities, and once bonded, their loyalty belongs solely to you."

I think of Alatar's emppeta, the butterfly with wings of fire.

"Once bonded, you can summon your familiar. If it's nearby, it will come to you. If it's far away—or even in another realm—it will teleport. No matter where you are, your familiar will always find you."

Something stirs in my chest at that. The idea of a connection like that—constant, unbreakable—feels comforting in a way I hadn't realized I needed. From everything I've learned, the bond between a sorcerer and their familiar is unique. Irreplaceable.

"As long as you're in an environment your familiar can survive in," Mrs. Patrickson continues, "all you need to do to summon it is fold your hands like this"—she demonstrates, one hand over the other—"and, with intent, say the spell *cito*."

As if on cue, a bird flies through the open window. It's small but striking, its feathers a seamless blend of red, blue, yellow, purple, and green.

"Whoa," I breathe as it lands on Mrs. Patrickson's shoulder.

"This is Misty," she says fondly, stroking the bird's feathers. Misty lets out a soft, musical chirp. "She's a mellifluous. On my command, she can sing a tune that charms anyone within range. Those affected become... persuadable, for a short time."

"Okay," I say, "how do I get one?"

Mrs. Patrickson smiles. "Typically, you don't choose your familiar. The familiar chooses you. It can take time." She studies me for a moment. "But since everyone here already has one, and familiars can be a significant advantage, it's only fair that you find one as well. There are many unbonded familiars around Silver Key."

"So I just... wait?"

"Not quite. Spend time outside. Go on walks. Be open to it." She smiles knowingly. "Because once you carry the intent to find a familiar, one will find *you*."

After the lesson, Mykel, Celie, Lukas, and I meet in the dining hall for lunch.

"So?" Celie asks. "How did it go?"

I slide into the seat beside Mykel. "It was good! I learned about familiars. You guys have one already, right?"

"Yeah," Mykel says. "Mine's named Winter. He's an ice dragon."

He says it like having a pet ice dragon is normal.

"What the hell? An *ice dragon*?"

Celie grins. "Mine's an almiraj."

"What's an—"

"The unicorn bunny!" Lukas chimes in.

Celie rolls her eyes. "Her name is Daisy. And yes, she's a bunny with a unicorn horn, and she's cute as hell."

Of course Celie has a unicorn bunny.

"What about you, Lukas?" I ask.

Mykel and Celie snicker.

"What?" I say. "What am I missing?"

"He's got a sky swimmer," Mykel says, and Celie bursts into laughter.

"You guys are awful," Lukas says. "His name is Dot, and he's adorable." He turns to me. "He's a dolphin with wings. He can swim *and* fly."

"Sorry, you're right, Lukas. He is adorable. He's not the brightest, though," Mykel says.

"That's fair," Lukas agrees.

Celie perks up. "Want to meet Daisy? She's been hanging around the back garden."

"Is that even a question?" I say.

We make our way to the back garden. It's warm, with a perfect breeze that blows my long hair back and fills the air with the fresh scent of flowers. The sun is hot on my face, making the breeze feel even better as it kisses my skin.

I tuck my hair behind my ear as laughter drifts from a picnic set up near the lake.

Celie folds her hands together. "*Cito.*"

Seconds later, a small brown-and-white bunny hops toward us, floppy ears bouncing. A short unicorn horn protrudes from her forehead. Celie scoops her up, and Daisy immediately curls into her arms.

"She's adorable," I say, petting her head.

"I know," Celie says proudly.

"What can she do?"

"That's where it gets less adorable," Lukas mutters.

Celie rolls her eyes at Lukas before saying, "Her horn is razor-sharp, great in combat, and it fires rainbow magic."

"Which sounds cute," Lukas says, "until she nearly takes your leg off."

"That was a *training accident*," Celie says. "And you insisted on watching."

"I still have a scar!" Lukas says, rolling up his pant leg to reveal a faint line.

Mykel pets Daisy's ears. She lets out a strange, purring chirp. "Come on. Look at her. She's harmless."

"I almost died," Lukas says flatly.

I laugh. "So... how do I find my familiar? Mrs. Patrickson said if I'm looking, one might come to me."

"There's a practice room that opens into the forest," Mykel says. "A lot of familiars hang out around there."

"Good to know." I smooth my hair as the wind picks up. "We still on for training?"

"Of course," Mykel says.

"We'll catch up with you guys later," Lukas says.

Celie's familiar hops out of her hands and bounces away. Lukas winks in Mykel's direction before walking off with Celie.

Mykel leads me to a white bench beneath a tall, colourful tree.

"Let's try a summoning spell," he says. "Like the rose petals I showed you when you arrived. Have you learned those yet?"

"A little."

"Okay. Focus on the object you want to summon."

I close my eyes and do as he says.

"Now repeat after me. *Et Convoco.*"

I repeat the incantation, but nothing happens. I try a few times before getting frustrated.

"It's not working," I say, slightly embarrassed.

"That's normal," Mykel says. "Magic isn't just about saying the words. It's intent. Try folding your hands, it helps when you're learning."

I clasp my hands together, intertwining my fingers.

He smiles. "More like this." He reaches out, carefully adjusting my hands, one over the other. His touch lingers just a moment longer than necessary. "There," he says softly.

When he pulls away, I pretend I don't miss the warmth of his hands on mine.

Closing my eyes, I try again. "*Et Convoco.*"

I give this a few more attempts until I feel it. Magic pulses through my veins. I hold onto it, let it build, until something solid forms in my palms.

I open my eyes. "I did it!"

Mykel grins. "What did you summon?"

I look down at the wallet-sized family photo before handing it to him.

"My parents. And my little brother, Ashton."

He hesitates. "How *are* you... handling everything? The adoption?"

I swallow.

Since I found out, I've been doing my best to ignore the fact that I'm adopted. Every time I think about it, I either want to cry or send my fist through the wall. Yet at the same time, it sort of feels like I've finally gotten the answer to a question I didn't even know I had.

"At first, I was devastated. Then angry—at my parents for not telling me, at my birth parents for giving me up." I pause. "But I know my parents love me. And now... I'm curious."

"About your biological parents?"

"Yeah. And *why* they gave me up. My mom says there was a good reason, but... I don't know. It doesn't feel right."

Mykel studies me. I get the sense that if I asked, he wouldn't hesitate to help me find out more about my birth family.

His lips stretch into a smile. "Look at you, Aria. We've got ourselves a conspiracy theorist."

I snort. "It's just... I feel like I'm missing something."

"Well, why don't you look for them?"

"Part of me is afraid of what I'll find," I admit.

"I get that. But don't you owe it to yourself to find out?"

Silence falls as I turn over his words. Mykel is right. I can't let my fears hold me back. Whoever—and wherever—my biological parents are, I need answers.

I'm still lost in thought when a voice cuts in.

"Make a move yet, Griffin?" Blade says, sauntering over.

"Shut it, Casteel," Mykel says.

"What? Afraid she'll reject you? Can't blame her."

Mykel glares at him, jaw tight, fury darkening his expression.

Blade nods. "I guess you don't have it in you, huh?"

"Blade, enough," I say.

Mykel's hands clench into fists. I place a hand on his arm, and he eases slightly at my touch.

Blade's gaze drops to my hand on Mykel's arm. His lips curl. "Look at that. Aria Knight defending you?" He lets out a cold laugh. "You really are pathetic."

Mykel rips his arm away from me, and in one swift motion, slams his fist into Blade's face. Blood spills from Blade's nose as he looks up at Mykel, icy blue eyes blazing. When Mykel turns toward me, Blade lunges, punching him back and sending him crashing to the ground.

Mykel thrusts his hand forward. "*Obtundo!*"

A surge of bright blue magic explodes from his palm, rippling the air as Blade flies across the yard and skids several metres away. He groans, winded, but recovers quickly, pushing himself to his feet.

"*Impetus!*" Blade roars, punching the air. A crimson ripple shoots forward, slamming into Mykel like a blow to the gut. Mykel collapses, and Blade strides toward him, clearly intent on finishing this.

I stand frozen for half a second too long, shouting for them to stop. Right before Mykel swings again, I rush between them, pressing my hands to their chests.

They hesitate, glancing down at me—surprised—just as I say, "*Confuto.*"

They freeze mid-motion, locked in place.

"That is enough!" I snap, glancing at both of them.

I drop my hands, and the spell releases. For a moment, neither of them speaks. They just stare at me, breathing hard. Blade looks almost impressed. Mykel's expression is unreadable.

Then their scowls return as their focus shifts back to each other. Blade wipes the blood from his nose and storms off. Mykel stays where he is. Blood trickles from his split lip, and he presses a hand to his stomach as he catches his breath.

"What is up with you two?" I ask.

Mykel shakes his head. "Nothing."

"Uh-huh. Right. Because that was *nothing*."

He doesn't answer.

"Mykel, you can talk to me." I soften my tone. "Since my first day here, I could tell something was going on. I mean, the tension between the two of you is palpable. I didn't ask because I wanted to respect your privacy, but I think we're close enough now that you can tell me what the hell I'm missing."

There's another moment of silence before Mykel rakes his hand through his hair, lets out a frustrated sigh, and sits on the bench.

"Blade's dad, Elyon, is my mom's brother," he says.

Oh. *Oh.* Mykel and Blade are *cousins.*

"My dad and Elyon were neck and neck during the last tournament. My dad helped him countless times. But when it came time for Elyon to return the favour... he didn't. He sabotaged my dad at the end and took the win." Mykel exhales. "You can imagine how that went over."

"Family gatherings must be awkward," I say.

He lets out a breathy laugh. "You have no idea. Growing up, Blade and I never got along. Elyon puts a ton of pressure on him—to be perfect, to be powerful. Blade lets it consume him. His dad's his hero. And he's been taught that our side of the family is in the wrong."

"What about you and your dad?"

"That's the difference between Blade and me. My dad's a good man. He raised me to be respectful. To do the right thing. Make the right choices." His mouth tightens. "Blade's just... a bully."

"Do you feel pressured?" I ask. "Like you have to compete with him?"

"Yeah," he admits. "That pressure's always there. It's like a rivalry our parents built for us." He hesitates. "Before I left for Silver Key, my dad told me to do whatever it takes to win. He didn't say good luck. Didn't say he'd miss me. Just win. And I promised I would. Whatever it takes."

As he talks, I start to see it clearly: the weight he carries, the expectations pressing down on him. Almost like he and Blade are trapped in roles written by their parents.

Maybe Blade and Mykel are more similar than they'd let themselves believe.

Having misread my silence, Myke says, "I'm sorry, I shouldn't have said anything—"

"No," I say, placing my hand on his arm. "I'm glad you told me."

"I just... feel like I can tell you anything."

I smile. "You can."

"I don't want to let him down, you know?"

"You won't," I tell him. "Whether you win or not, you'll make him proud. From everything you've said, your dad loves you, and that won't change."

CHAPTER SEVEN

I've only been to the practice room a handful of times. Partly because the idea that each of those doors can teleport me to an entirely different place is still hard to wrap my head around, but mostly because I'm not sure I'm ready. What if something attacks me? These *are* practice rooms. They're designed for field experience.

I shove the thought aside and head there anyway.

As I step inside, the magic still steals my breath. Glowing doors form a wide circle in the centre of the room. The walls shimmer, alive with movement. The room is empty, so I take my time studying the images displayed on the doors.

There's the crashing wave I remember from the tour on my first day. Next to it, a twinkling rose-gold star floating above a white cloud. A tiny fairy with fluttering wings adorns another, followed by a door bubbling with underwater light. I pass one marked by a skull—lava dripping from its crown—looking like it leads straight into the fiery pits of Hell.

I quicken my pace until I reach the door Mykel mentioned. I'm a little nervous, but I need to find a familiar, and Mykel wouldn't send me here by myself if he thought I might get hurt.

A willow tree is etched into its surface, twisted and hunched. As I step closer, the tree straightens, its branches swaying in an unseen wind. The door glows beneath my hand as I turn the handle and step through.

My feet hit the ground on the other side of the door, crunching down on dead leaves and dry dirt. A forest looms ahead of me. I glance behind me, and there's just the door, standing alone among the trees.

A chill slides down my spine. Wind whispers through the branches, leaves rustling loudly in the silence. A clear path stretches ahead. I follow it.

The trail winds deeper into the forest. The air hums softly, as if the wind is speaking to the bushes and plants lining the path. Moss glimmers along the trees, crawling up their trunks in shades of deep purple and navy blue. I pass a few sorcerers along the way. They wave before casting a spell at a towering oak. The tree groans, splitting open as arms sprout from its trunk, grasping at invisible prey.

The farther I go, the dimmer the light becomes. Tiny pink, green, and blue lights begin to drift around me, illuminating the darkness. Fireflies. Hundreds of them.

It's colder here. My breath clouds in front of me as I exhale. The ground is damp, slick with moss-covered roots that force me to tread carefully.

Eventually, the forest opens up.

A park sits before me—abandoned, forgotten. The sight tugs at something in my chest, memories of the park near my childhood home. The swings were always my favourite.

These swings creak in the wind, neglected, their eerie squeal echoing through the trees. Across from them, a play structure slumps in disrepair, the slide coated in dirt. Everything about this place feels wrong. Unease coils in my stomach.

Before I can turn to leave, a hiss slices through the air behind me, low and sharp.

I turn—and freeze.

A massive snake towers over me, its yellow, slit-pupiled eyes locked onto me. Its scales are a sickly green, slick with grime, dirt clinging to its body. Its forked tongue flicks out as it hisses again, hunger burning in its gaze.

It slithers closer. Each slow, deliberate movement carries terrifying weight as its body slides across the ground of the forest.

My pulse hammers in my ears, my heart contracting with fear.

It's too big. I can't fight it.

Think, Aria. There has to be a spell—something—

I can't think straight. I don't know what to do. Running would be a bad idea. This thing would catch me in seconds.

Is this really how I die? Eaten by a giant magical snake?

The snake strikes before I have time to react, digging its knife-like teeth into my flesh. I scream. Pain explodes through my arm. My chest heaves violently, breath coming too fast, too shallow. I gasp as if the air itself has vanished—

A sound cuts through my panic.

A growl.

It comes from behind the snake. Low at first, then louder. Stronger. Fiercer.

The snake recoils, startled, and slithers away. Shaking, I search for whatever just saved my life.

That's when I see the wolf. White, and smaller than a normal-sized wolf. I'm actually stunned that such a powerful growl came from such an adorable creature. His eyes are aqua, bright and endless, like the ocean under a clear sky.

But it's the wings that steal my breath.

Two angelic wings rise from his fur. A wave of calm washes over me, like being pulled under a warm tide. For the first time since entering the forest, my fear melts away.

I move toward him slowly. He mirrors me, cautious but curious. We meet halfway, and I crouch until we're eye level.

Wincing, I extend my hand, careful despite the throbbing pain in my arm.

Somehow, I know that he would never hurt me.

He lowers his head, nudging his nose into my palm. His fur is warm, impossibly soft.

I grin. "Hi there."

He places a paw over the snake bite, now oozing an unsettling shade of lime green. I flinch as pressure and heat bloom beneath his touch. He lets out a smooth, melodic howl, wings spreading wide—

And then the pain disappears.

When he lifts his paw, my skin is unbroken. The wound is gone, as if it never existed.

The wolf presses closer until he's curled against my chest. I wrap my arms around him without thinking.

"I'm gonna name you Halo," I whisper. "Do you like that?"

He licks my cheek.

I laugh. "I'll take that as a yes."

Over the next few days, Halo follows me everywhere. I learned that newly bonded familiars need constant time with their owners at the start, and I'm not complaining. I love having him around.

I read up on his species in the Silver Key library. According to some thorough books, Halo is a pterolycus. There are many breeds, and Halo seems to be a healing type. His other abilities won't show up until he's older.

I also decided it's time to look into my birth parents. Celie helps by checking out stacks of books for me, and I'm grateful. Every night, Halo curled up nearby, we sift through volumes in our dorm room, searching for anything that might give me a lead. Most nights we come up empty-handed.

Until one night, when we find a book filled with names and portraits of sorcerers who competed in past tournaments. The only problem: I don't know my birth parents' names. I immediately sit down and write my mom and dad a letter, asking for the information.

"I'm gonna grab a snack while we wait for their response. Want anything?" I ask.

"No, I'm fine. Thanks," Celie says.

The manor is usually quiet in the evenings, but faint chatter echoes through the building as a few people make their way to the dining hall. Candles cast flickering shadows along the hallway as I turn a corner—and nearly collide with Blade.

"Blade?" I call.

He spins, a guilty look crossing his face, but he relaxes when he sees me.

"What do you want, Knight?"

I ignore his tone. "Where are you going?"

"None of your business."

"But—"

"Don't follow me," he warns. Then he walks away down the stairs, leaving me confused.

Until I realize I have an idea where he might be going.

I shouldn't go after him. Especially if I'm right about where he's headed. I shouldn't care what Blade does, even if it's reckless. But him telling me not to follow only makes me want to do it more.

"Blade?" I whisper.

"Goddammit, Knight! What the hell are you doing?" he snaps as I step up behind him.

"What the hell are *you* doing?"

"Isn't it obvious? I'm getting through that door," he says, pointing to the shimmering silver door at the end of the hall.

"Blade, you heard what Mrs. Patrickson said during the tour—"

He rolls his eyes with exaggeration. "Don't give me that lecture. You're just as curious as I am to see what they're hiding in there."

"Okay, maybe I'm curious. But I'm not going to—"

"I'm not asking for your help, Knight. *You* followed *me*."

"Yes, to stop you from doing something idiotic."

"I don't think it's idiotic. They're clearly hiding something important. I wanna know what it is. Now leave before you get us both in trouble."

I let out a frustrated breath. "Blade, why do you hate me so much? You barely even know me."

"I don't hate you."

Well, you sure have a funny way of showing it.

"Then why are you such a jerk?"

"That's just how I am, Knight. Better get used to it. Mykel, though... Yeah, I hate him," he says.

"I've noticed," I say, watching him edge down the hallway. "Why are you trying to mess things up this early? We just got here a few weeks ago."

"Why do you even care—"

"There are wards here, on the door. We don't know what could happen. You could get hurt."

He smirks. "Doesn't seem like you're leaving, so at least I've got you to help me."

That smirk is infuriating.

"Blade—"

"If you're not helping, leave. I don't have time for—why are you staring at me like that?"

"I'm hoping you spontaneously combust," I say.

We both pause. This is a terrible idea. If someone sees us, we could be expelled. Yet Blade is right. Curiosity is killing me. The hallway is empty; everyone else is either at dinner or in their rooms for the night.

Pre-Silver Key me would never even consider this. I have absolutely no idea what to expect. No planned course of action if something goes wrong.

"Alright," I say. "Let's say I entertain this. How are you getting past the wards?"

"Easy. I know some spells. You forget who taught me magic. You know, some of the most powerful sorcerers in the world?"

I roll my eyes. "Okay, smartass. Just do it."

I turn to keep watch while he mutters incantations. Vibrant gold orbs shoot from his palms, latching onto the wards, shining blindingly before vanishing. He moves quickly, disarming one after another. When he reaches the door, I think I hear footsteps—but no one comes.

"I did it," he says, satisfaction in his voice.

"What? How did you do that so fast? Why was that so easy?"

"Easy for *me*. I bet I'm the only student here who could do it."

I sigh. "Okay. Let's go."

We step through the door into a dark room, dimly lit by a gold glow on the ceiling. The door shuts behind us. At the far end of the room is another door, but it's locked.

"Try your magic thing you just did," I say.

He tries, but nothing happens.

"It's not working this time."

"Why not?"

"How the hell should I know?"

"Well, it looks like we need a key," I say, gesturing to a keyhole in the door. At least it looks like a keyhole, but it's sealed shut.

"I've seen this before," Blade mutters. "Enchanted doors. Needs a specific password or spell." He crosses the room, analyzing it. "There's usually a hint somewhere."

"What is this, an escape room?" I say.

"A what?"

"You don't know what an escape room is?"

"No. Shut up," he says, embarrassed.

I bite back a grin. "When the trials are over, we're going to an escape room together."

"That sounds like torture."

I scoff. "*Rude.*"

"Hey, Knight?" Blade says. "Less talking, more looking."

"Right," I say, looking around for any hints.

Blade casts some sort of spell on the wall, and symbols appear in a blue shimmer all over the room.

"Whoa. What are these?" I say.

"I don't know. I don't recognize them."

We fall into an uncomfortable silence.

"So... since we're here, can we talk about your fight with Mykel?" I ask.

"I'd rather not."

"He told me you don't get along because of your parents."

"Yeah. And because he's intolerable."

"Funny, he's said the same thing about you."

"Mykel and I have never gotten along. He hates me, and I hate him. Simple as that. Now, can we move on?"

Voices echo in the distance.

"Someone's coming," I whisper.

"Shit. Give me your hand," Blade orders. Hesitantly, I do. He places a hand on the wall and says, "*Lacus.*"

In a blink, I'm standing in a bedroom. The layout is the same as my room, only the walls are a darker grey. Blade flicks on the lamp sitting on a bedside table. This must be his dorm.

"Um. How did you do that? I thought we could only teleport through doors."

"My dad taught me," he says, slightly out of breath. "I'm not supposed to do it. It takes up too much energy. Especially taking someone with me. But better than getting caught."

"Are you okay?" I ask as a few drops of blood leak from his nose.

He swipes at it instinctively, then pauses when he sees the red smeared across his fingers. "Shit. Yeah, I just need to rest." He stumbles toward the bed. I move to help, but he waves me off. "I've got it."

I stand there, unsure of what to say. We were so close to finding out what's behind that door. Now I'm even more determined.

He stares at me. "You can leave now..."

"Right. Sorry."

I walk out of Blade's room and hear him release a long sigh as I shut the door behind me.

CHAPTER EIGHT

"Hit me with a spell, c'mon!"

"I don't know what I'm doing!" I say. "What if I hurt you?"

Mykel laughs. "You won't. Trust me."

"Someone's cocky," I say.

He stiffens, panic flashing across his face. It's... kind of adorable. "What? No—that's not what I meant—"

I grin. "Relax. I'm joking."

He exhales and rolls his eyes. "I put a protection spell on both of us. You physically can't hurt me. Now come on, just like I taught you."

I take a deep breath. Clench my fist. Close my eyes. Focus.

"*Scintillam,*" I say, and throw my hand forward.

A burst of golden sparks erupts from my palm, flying toward Mykel's chest. Just before they hit, an invisible barrier flares to life. The sparks explode like tiny bombs before fizzing out.

"Nice," he says, holding up his hand.

I high-five him, and our fingers intertwine. My lips curve upward as he looks at me, eyes bright with pride. Something warm and fuzzy spreads through my chest. And his smile—it's the best smile I've ever seen. Perfect teeth, soft dimples—

"Aria?"

"Sorry—what?" I blink, shaking myself back to reality.

Mykel laughs and steps back.

I briefly considered telling Mykel, Celie, and Lukas about Blade and the off-limits hallway... and immediately decided against it. If anyone found out, we'd be expelled. Not to mention the long lecture I'd get from Celie about recklessness, followed by Mykel's lecture about how I shouldn't be spending my spare time with Blade.

I'm honestly not sure which would be worse, their nagging or the expulsion. I've decided to do my best to avoid both.

"So," Mykel says, "we should try some hand-to-hand combat. What do you think?"

"Um, sure. I mean, I've never tried it before."

"That's why you've got me," he says with a grin. "Magic's great, but you never know what situation you'll end up in. You need to know how to defend yourself."

I nod, already bracing for my impending humiliation.

"Okay," he says, eyeing me critically. "First of all, your stance is terrible."

I snort with laughter.

He comes behind me and adjusts my body. "Now bend your knees a little."

I do, bringing my fists up.

"Good. Now jab with your right hand."

I follow his instructions, aware of his eyes on me as he demonstrates. Jab. Uppercut. Dodge. Left hook. How to block. How to read an opponent's movement.

"Alright," he says. "Come at me."

With absolutely zero confidence, I throw a punch. He catches my wrist before I even get close to his face and spins me around, pulling me back against his chest. My breath catches. His grip is firm but careful, his body warm against my back. His breath brushes my neck, just below my ear. It makes my brain foggy, and I close my eyes at the sensation.

"You have to be faster," he says, snapping me out of my daze.

Get it together, Aria.

He releases my wrist, and I step away. "Again."

I try, and miss.

Again.

Again.

Again.

He dodges easily at first, but as time passes, I start landing closer, moving quicker.

I'm still absolutely terrible. But slightly less terrible.

About an hour later, I'm drenched in sweat and so exhausted I have to lie on the floor to catch my breath.

"That's enough for today," he says with a smile. "You did really well. Let's go again tomorrow?"

I nod.

He offers his hand, and when I take it, he pulls me smoothly to my feet.

"God," I groan as we head for the door, "I need a shower."

That evening, I barge into my dorm room.

"Celie! Get the book!" I shout, clutching a letter in my hand. My parents finally wrote back.

You'd think their daughter—who somehow finds time to write despite learning magic and surviving near-death experiences—would rank a little higher on their priority list.

Okay, I'm being dramatic. It's only been a day, but I haven't stopped thinking about it. I even considered asking Alatar for my birth parents' names, before shutting the idea down, unsure if it's something I'm willing to bother him for. Especially since the answer was just one letter away.

Celie grabs the book from her desk as I tear the letter open.

I skim the page, my heart pounding. "Amelia Drake," I whisper. "My mother's name is Amelia. And my father is Peter Drake." I swallow and look up from the letter. "My middle name is Amelia."

Celie flips through the book, pages rustling quickly. "I found them," she says, tapping a photograph.

They're young here, maybe three or four years older than I am now. My father presses a kiss to my mother's cheek, and she's smiling wide, radiant.

She's beautiful.

"She looks just like you, Aria," Celie says.

We flip through every page of the book and don't find any other photos of them until we reach the last page. It's like they were always together, inseparable. My father's arms are wrapped around my mother, his grey eyes crinkled at the corners as he beams at the camera. They look so happy. So in love. Even trapped inside a faded photograph, their affection feels real, almost tangible.

My chest tightens. I want to meet them. Desperately.

My parents told me they had a good reason for giving me up. I cling to that. Whatever it was, I hope it mattered. I want to find my biological parents. I want to forgive them. Maybe even thank them. If they hadn't given me up, I wouldn't have the parents I have now, and despite everything, I couldn't ask for anyone better than them.

Maybe they wanted me to have a better life. Maybe—

I need to know.

"Who's that behind them?" I ask, noticing another figure leaning into the photo, hands resting on my parents' shoulders.

Celie squints, pulling the book closer. "I think... that's Alatar."

"Whoa. Really?"

I drag the book toward me. Now that she says it, there's no denying it. "He did say they were close."

"He looks so young," Celie murmurs.

Even with Alatar in the frame, my gaze drifts back to my parents. "I wonder where they are," I say. "Do you think I'll find them?"

"You will," Celie says without hesitation.

I let out a slow breath, brushing my fingers across the photo. *I hope she's right.*

CHAPTER NINE

T he library is packed with sorcerers when I settle into an
armchair near the unlit fireplace, a book resting in my
hands. Heavy clouds outside darken the room, so I've lit a few
candles on the table beside me. Their flames flicker softly.

Halo sleeps on my lap, and I run my fingers through his warm
fur as I turn the page. The book is about combat spellwork.
Dense, but surprisingly helpful. I'm about to start the next
chapter when Mykel, Celie, and Lukas appear.

I set the book aside, glad for the company. They've just come
from a lesson with Mr. Johnson. One I decided was a little too
advanced for me right now.

We talk for a while about spells, the trials, life at Silver Key,
and Lukas's questionable taste in men, until a girl approaches.
She carries herself with easy confidence, but as she nears Mykel,
a flicker of nerves breaks through. Halo stirs on my lap, lifting
his head to peer at her.

She smooths the front of her pale blue dress—that looks like
it was made solely for the purpose of being worn by her—and
says, "Can I speak with you for a minute, Mykel?" There's
something effortlessly magnetic in her voice.

Still, Mykel stiffens. "I don't think that's a good idea—"

"It'll be quick," she says.

I watch them, unsettled. There's history here, and I don't like how little I understand it.

Mykel exhales, resigned, and stands. He follows her out of the library, her strawberry-blond curls bouncing as she goes.

"How peculiar," Celie says.

"Peculiar?" I repeat, half amused, half distracted.

Lukas nods solemnly. "Celie likes to use big-girl words some-times."

Celie narrows her eyes. "I will beat your ass, Lukas Prince." She swings for his arm as he dramatically recoils.

Their bickering fades into background noise.

That was... strange. A random, stunning girl pulling Mykel aside—and he clearly didn't want to go with her.

"What was that about?" I ask. "Who is she?"

"Eliza," Lukas says. "Mykel's ex."

Something tightens in my chest. I ignore it immediately. I refuse to be that girl, getting jealous over nothing.

"They were together for a long time," Celie adds. "The breakup hit him hard."

Yup... definitely not jealous.

Halo glances up at me as if he senses it, and I narrow my eyes at him. He blinks back, unimpressed, then settles his head on my lap again.

A few minutes later, Mykel returns. He doesn't say anything, clearly not interested in explaining. His eyes flick to mine, then away just as quickly.

And just like that, we all move on as if nothing happened.

The thoughts that plague my mind make sleep difficult. After tossing and turning for what feels like hours, I finally drift into a deep slumber.

It's early morning, and I'm sitting in biology class with Violet. She twirls a strand of purple hair around her finger as the teacher drones on about the anatomy and functions of plants. I'm about to raise my hand and ask him to go over everything again when Alatar bursts into the room. My heart skips a beat. Panic claws at me. He's here. In my classroom. His eyebrows are furrowed, hair dishevelled, eyes darker than usual.

"Miss Knight, you are not supposed to leave the manor. Doing so is in violation of the Silver Key Tournament rules," he says, gaze fixed on me.

All eyes turn to me with curiosity and judgment, and I want to disappear. I sit in silent fear, unsure what to do in this impossible situation.

"You're a sorcerer now," Alatar continues. "You must take magic-related rules seriously. No excuses."

Violet's eyes widen, a mix of betrayal and hurt. "You're a *what*? And you never told me?"

"Violet—"

"How could you keep something like this from me?"

"I'm sorry," I plead, but she's furious, her words cutting off any explanation.

"I will never forgive you for this."

Before I can respond, Alatar yanks me from my seat and whisks me out of the classroom.

I step through a door, ready to teleport back to Silver Key, but instead, I land in my bedroom. Alatar is gone.

I collapse onto my bed, tears streaming down my face. The ache of losing my best friend feels unbearable. Then, the door bursts open. My birth mother, Amelia, stands there.

"Y-you're here?" I stammer, startled. She looks impossibly young, as if she stepped out of the photo Celie and I found. I summon every ounce of courage I can muster to ask the question that's been eating away at me, afraid that if I wait, she'll disappear and I'll have missed my chance. But when I open my mouth to speak, all I can say is, "Why?"

"We didn't want you, Aria," she says. "You... didn't show enough potential. We were ashamed to be the parents of a weak sorcerer."

"But... I was only a baby, I—"

She's gone before I can finish, replaced by my adoptive mother, the woman who raised me, who loves me unconditionally.

But she isn't smiling. She stands in the doorway with a suitcase in hand.

"I'm leaving, Aria," she says. "I can't raise a daughter with magical powers. I want nothing to do with your *world*." She says the last word with disgust. As if being a sorcerer is a disease, and she wants nothing to do with it.

"We can work through this, Mom—"

"We can't. You're not normal, Aria. I can't do it."

"Don't you love me enough to try?"

"No. Not enough."

I want to beg her to stay, but she slams the door, leaving me alone with my tears. I reach for a tissue on my side table, and suddenly—

I'm running. The halls of Silver Key blur past me. My heart pounds. I hear footsteps behind me and pick up the pace.

I burst through the double doors leading to the back garden, and a wave of pain and jealousy courses through my body.

Mykel and Eliza are locked in a passionate kiss beneath the colourful tree. The tree itself seems dimmer than I remember, as if the joy it once radiated is now twisted. My heart aches as their hands tangle, as petals fall from the branches, wilting as they touch the earth.

I want to look away, to speak, to do anything, but I'm frozen. Eliza's hand slides up Mykel's shirt, and—

I jolt awake.

Morning light filters through the dorm room window, brightening the room. Relief floods me; it was only a nightmare. It's like my brain picked out all my current worries and fears and tossed them together for my unconscious enjoyment.

Halo curls at the foot of my bed, and I stroke his back. Then I feel something sticking to my forehead.

I frown and pull it off. It's a pink sticky note. In Celie's handwriting, it reads: *Up early today, thought I'd let you rest. Meet you in the back garden later for training.*

I check the time. An hour until my lesson with Mrs. Patrickson. Skipping breakfast, I dress quickly and hurry to her office. She greets me cheerfully, and the lesson begins. She teaches me counterspells and protective spells. Confidence blooms as I master the basics, knowing I can defend myself if needed.

After the lesson, I rush to the dining hall, stomach rumbling. Without stopping to enjoy the scent of bread and butter that fills my senses, I grab a ham and cheese sandwich and take a seat at an empty table. The sandwich is an inch from my mouth before I'm interrupted by Blade sitting across from me.

"*Sure*, sit," I say, silently cursing the hell out of him and unceremoniously letting my sandwich flop back onto my plate.

"We need to sneak back to that room," he says.

I groan. "We almost got caught. Isn't it too soon?"

He pauses, thinking it over. "Fine. But come to the library with me so we can at least try to figure out what those symbols on the walls are."

"Can I finish my sandwich first?"

"Take it to go," he says, already standing and leaving the dining hall.

I sigh and wipe a hand across my face. Blade—bossy, arrogant Blade. I am not in the mood to deal with him.

Nonetheless, I head to the library.

When I get there, books are floating onto high shelves. A group of sorcerers chat in the sitting area near the fireplace. I search the room until my gaze lands on Blade, sitting at a table with a stack of books. I take a seat across from him, and he hands me one.

"These are most of the books I could find on magic symbols, languages, and runes. Whatever that writing was, we should be able to find it in one of these."

I begrudgingly open the first book and skim through the pages.

"Hey, what about this?" I ask, showing Blade the page. It looks pretty similar to my memory of the symbols on the walls, but I can't be sure.

"Let me see."

He walks around the table and sits next to me, pulling the book closer. "I don't think this is it," he says, flipping through the book.

He furrows his brows. His focus makes a small smile tug at my lips.

"Enjoying the view?"

"What?"

He grins. "I could feel you staring. Sorry, *admiring*."

"I was *not* admiring you," I say.

"Now you're blushing."

I shake my head and turn away, pulling the book back over to me and refocusing. I flip the page and read.

The same word.

Over and over again.

I feel his gaze on me, making concentration impossible.

"Yes, Blade?" I say, looking up at him.

He stares at me for a long moment before he shrugs and says, "Nothing."

Then he pulls another book from the stack and flips through it. He makes no move to return to his seat on the opposite end of the table, and as he flips through the book, his arm brushes against mine.

Okay...

We get back to work, reading about different ancient languages, common symbols, and runes that date back centuries. It's a lot of information, and we opt to take notes to keep our thoughts and information organized.

Finally, I decide I need a break. "It's been two hours," I say, resting my elbows on the table and pressing my face into my hands.

"Giving up so soon?" Blade says.

I give him an *are-you-crazy* look, and he chuckles.

"Okay, fine. Let's take a break." He sticks a bookmark into the book in front of him before closing it.

"I think we're close," I say.

"Same."

And then we fall into silence. I glance at the clock on the wall and—

"Oh shit! I need to meet Celie in like twenty minutes."

"Training?" he asks, and I nod. "Can't you skip just this once?"

"Enjoying my company, Casteel?"

"Of course not," he says.

"Good. Because working together is already too weird for me."

"Really? Cause I thought you were really growing to like me."

"And what could have possibly given you that idea?"

"Well, you *were* admiring my handsome face just two hours ago."

"Once again, I was *not* admiring," I say.

I rise to leave, but Blade grabs my wrist, pulling me back down. Our shoulders touch. I turn to him.

We're so close I can see every detail of his face. My eyes land on the scar above his eyebrow, but I quickly avert my gaze. Instead, I find myself looking into his eyes, just as he's looking into mine. They're so mesmerizing, it's hard to look away.

And then his eyes glance down to my lips, briefly, before meeting my eyes once more. He tucks a loose strand of hair behind my ear before letting his hand rest against my cheek.

"Blade..." I say, but it comes out as little more than a breath.

"You can stop me," he murmurs.

I don't think I can. I don't think I can speak. It's as if I'm in a trance.

But as he slowly leans in, as his lips are inches away from mine, I finally snap out of it and pull away.

"What the hell, Blade?" I say, flying out of my seat, face no doubt flushed as a tomato.

"What?" he says.

"You tried to kiss me!"

"You weren't doing much to stop me." He chuckles, but uncertainty flashes across his features. "I thought you wanted me to—"

"Why the *hell* would I want that? We just met, you barely know me, and you've been an asshole every encounter we've had!"

He says nothing, slightly stunned. A blow to his ego.
Good.

"You may think every girl here is in love with you, but they're not. I can't believe you'd think I'd want you to kiss me after how you've treated me. How you've treated *Mykel.*"

"Aria—"

"You're unbelievable."

I don't give him a chance to reply before storming out of the library.

I march straight to the back garden to meet Celie for our training. I try to shake that moment with Blade out of my head, and though it's a struggle, Celie's excited smile as I approach her brightens my mood a little.

"Did you get my note?" she says.

"Of course I got it. You stuck it to my forehead while I was sleeping."

An accomplished grin spreads across her face. "Good. You should be saying, '*Thank you, Celie, for letting me sleep in even though the first trial is alarmingly soon, and I should be practicing every chance I get.*' You're welcome, Aria."

I roll my eyes. "Oh, Celie. I love you."

"I know. Now let's train."

We train for hours, but all I can think about is Blade.

CHAPTER TEN

I'm starting to think Celie was right; I should have woken up at the crack of dawn every morning to train. The first trial is fast approaching, and my nerves are on edge. I bounce my knee anxiously, torturing myself with doubtful thoughts while I wait for Mrs. Patrickson to arrive.

Finally, she enters her office. "This lesson is important, so pay close attention."

I pull out my notebook, grateful for the distraction, and prepare to take notes.

"The first trial is only a few days away, and today's lesson may come in handy. The world of magic is full of creatures—demons, celestials, and aquatic beings, to name a few. It's important that you learn about them so you have some idea of what you might encounter," she says, jotting a few notes on the chalkboard.

I haven't spoken to Blade since the incident in the library. I've wanted to, but every time I try, he's with his friends, who hate me. I'm pretty sure he hates me now, too. I hope he knows I still want to find out what's in that room. And if he tries to figure it out without me, I'll be pissed. I'm invested now.

"Beginning with the demons," Mrs. Patrickson says, snapping me out of my thoughts. "An icolt is a species of demon that feeds on humans. They have sharp fangs and huge bat-like wings and are usually female. However, they can shape-shift into almost any living thing. Icolts are mischievous and very dangerous. The only way to kill one is with an enchanted golden dagger."

"Are there a lot of demon species?" I ask, marginally afraid of her answer.

"Oh yes, too many to describe to you today."

Fantastic.

"Icolts are common, but some demons are more difficult to find, rarer, like dothyes, kaldins, olagers, and doleons. Not all demons are ruthless or evil, though many are."

At least I have some idea of the kinds of demons I may encounter during this tournament.

"Another common one is the fidolus. They're manipulative, cunning, and smart. They take the form of someone you trust or love."

"How do they know whose form to take?"

"They don't. You do. You see who you want to see."

"So, no one's actually seen their true form?"

"Correct."

"What about creatures I've already heard about, like werewolves or mermaids?"

"I'm not sure about werewolves—at least not how you imagine them—but mermaids are very real," Mrs. Patrickson says.

"Really? That's amazing."

"Yes, though you don't want to mistake them for sirens. Mermaids are harmless, kind, and, as you would assume, beautiful. Sirens, on the other hand, are dangerous predators. They lure people in just to kill them."

"Well, looks like I'm never going into the ocean again," I say.

Mrs. Patrickson chuckles. "Not to worry. They rarely come close to the shore like some mermaids do."

I jot down a few more notes, and Mrs. Patrickson continues the lesson.

The next day, I'm sitting in the library with Lukas and Celie, as usual. The only difference is that Mykel isn't with us.

"Do you think they'll make us fight, like, an army of fairies or something during this trial?" Lukas says.

Celie flips a page in the book in front of her. "Maybe we'll have to journey through a mysterious forest. And we'll pass those hoax plants that emit a gas that plays tricks on you when you get too close. I need to find a counterspell for those..."

"They can't give us anything too dangerous though, right? They said we aren't at risk of dying," I say, not fully convinced even as the words leave my lips. I can't think of anything else to add, too distracted by my own thoughts.

I haven't seen Mykel all day. He's been holed up practicing spells. He said he works better alone, which makes sense. Still, I find myself missing him, even after only a short time apart.

As soon as I acknowledge this thought, Mykel enters the library, and it's like the room lights up. He smiles at us as he approaches, and it steals the air from my lungs. When he sits next to me, the warmth of his presence settles around me, comforting in a way I didn't expect.

"Did you hear about the party tonight?" he says. "It's in the ballroom. Starts at eight."

"That sounds fun," Lukas says.

"It does... but I don't know. I wanted to get some extra practice in before the trial. I may be good at magic now, but I'm still nowhere near as experienced as everyone else."

"Come on, Aria!" Celie says. "You've had plenty of practice today."

"If Celie's saying that, it must be true," Lukas says.

Mykel places his hand over mine. "Aria, you have to come. It won't be as fun without you there."

Those words from Mykel sell me instantly, but I pretend to mull it over a little longer as they all give me pleading looks.

"Fine! But tomorrow, you're all spending the entire day helping me practice."

"You know I will," Celie says. "But tonight... let's party."

That night, Celie and I put on nice outfits—Celie in a light pink cardigan and white skirt, me in ripped jeans and a black off-the-shoulder top—and make our way to the ballroom together.

Once we arrive, Celie uses a magical password on the door: four knocks, a pause, then two more. The door swings open, and immediately, loud music blares, overwhelming my senses. The room is huge, bathed in multicoloured lights streaming in every direction. People are everywhere: dancing on the dance floor, eating at the snack bar, chatting in corners. When I look up, the ceiling is gone, the star-strewn sky clouding my vision.

I've never been the partying type.

Shocking, I know.

I never went to those high school house parties. Only once, when Violet dragged me to her boyfriend's party sophomore year, where I was either being hit on by drunk teenagers, hiding in a corner with a bottle of water, or—lucky me—breaking up a fight between Violet and another girl who was so intoxicated

I'm surprised she was capable enough to stand, never mind try to claw Violet to death.

Needless to say, I never went to another party after that, but I'm almost certain they've never been anything close to this one.

"This is so cool. There's even a pegasus over there!" Lukas says as he and Mykel join us. He points to a beautiful white horse with large, outstretched wings. Jakson and Sherry are charging five gold coins per ride. I make a mental note to go over there later.

"This party is insane," Celie says as Mykel hands me a plastic cup.

I stare at the bubbly orange drink. "What is this?"

"It's a happy potion," Lukas says. "It makes you drunk... but on happiness."

"Trust us, drink it. You deserve it," Mykel says.

I shrug, and the four of us clink cups before downing the drinks. It burns a little as it goes down, but instantly, a weight lifts from my shoulders. A wave of euphoria washes over me. My worries—about the trial, my biological parents, missing home—drift away. In their place: pure elation. I've never felt so carefree.

Celie grabs my hand and pulls me onto the dance floor, Mykel and Lukas following. We dance and sing along to the music. Lukas lifts Celie off the ground, spinning her around as she bursts into laughter. Mykel takes my hands, and we jump in sync with the upbeat rhythm. Sweating, cheering, surrounded by people all having a great time. Even Blade is laughing and dancing with his friends. I think it's the first time I've seen him genuinely smile. It suits him.

"Hey, you're Aria, right?" a girl asks, dancing beside me. Her dirty-blond hair bounces in a smooth ponytail, her grey eyes lit up with a grin.

"Yeah," I say. "What's your name?"

"Sarah! And that's my friend Clarity," she says, pointing to a girl dancing wildly on a table.

"She looks like fun," I laugh.

"I thought I'd introduce myself. If you ever need a training buddy, come train with us anytime!"

And just like that, she dances back to Clarity, pulling her down from the table, presumably to grab her something to eat.

I keep dancing with Mykel, Celie, and Lukas for a while, and a warm realization hits me: I finally feel like I belong here.

"Okay, I need a break," I pant, stepping off the dance floor.

I wander to a quiet corner and grab some magic candies. One tastes like chocolate, but when I swallow it, I feel light, like I'm floating—because I am. Actually levitating a few inches off the ground. It only lasts a few seconds.

Leaning against a wall, I watch the starry sky and let tonight sink in. A regular party could never compare. Not with magical drinks, candies, and a *pegasus*.

"What are you doing all by yourself?" Blade asks. He has to project his voice over the music.

"I needed a break," I say. "What about you? You seemed pretty happy over there with your friends. I don't think I've ever seen you smile like that. Why are you here talking to me?"

"I thought I'd grace you with my presence," he jokes.

At least I think it's a joke.

"Right," I play along.

A few droplets of sweat drip down the side of his face. His silver hair is wet and sticks to his forehead messily.

"Are you just going to admire how good I look, or actually talk to me?"

"*Shut up*," I say, and he snickers. "Look, about what happened in the library—"

"We don't need to talk about it," he says. "I know you have a thing for my cousin, though I don't see why. You *have* met him, right?"

"How did you—"

"It's obvious. I see the way you look at him."

Is it that obvious?

Of course it is. I suck at hiding my feelings, especially around guys.

I shrug, smiling. "He's sweet and caring and romantic—"

"Gross," Blade cuts me off.

I roll my eyes.

"Blade! Get your ass back here!" Nathan shouts.

"Better go," I say.

A ghost of a smirk creeps onto Blade's face as he turns back to the dance floor. I don't understand him. One minute, he's a complete asshole and the next, he's actually tolerable.

Mykel joins me moments later, breaking me from my thoughts. "So, aren't you glad you came?"

I am. I *really* am.

"I don't think I've ever had this much fun," I say.

Mykel smiles at me. It's a soft, gentle smile that says so much without saying anything at all. We lock eyes like the day we met, but this time, neither of us looks away.

All thoughts of Blade flutter out of my mind as the world around us blurs. For a moment, it seems like he's leaning in, and I realize there's nothing I want more at this moment than for him to kiss me.

A loud sound interrupts us.

Multicoloured fireworks explode above. I search for the source and spot a guy on a table, shooting the sparks from his fingertips. Before I can process it, Mykel grabs my face and kisses me. I'm surprised at first, but then I relax, eyes fluttering closed. His lips are soft, almost teasing when he pulls away.

He looks deep into my eyes, searching for an answer. When my lips stretch into a grin, he smiles and brings his lips back down to mine. I instantly kiss him back this time.

We move in sync, my hand resting on his chest, his hands still pressed against my cheeks. I can't help but think about how perfectly his lips move against mine. The kiss deepens, and I grip his shirt in the palm of my hand with a burning desire to pull him closer.

This kiss is freeing. It's *perfect*. I never want it to end.

"Celie, you owe me ten silvers!" Lukas yells over the music.

Mykel and I pull away, laughing.

The party goes on for hours. Mykel gives me five gold coins, and Celie and I pay Jakson and Sherry before hopping onto the pegasus.

We fly high into the air, holding on to any part of the horse-like creature we can.

"This is amazing!" Celie shouts from behind me. "You have to open your eyes!"

Hesitantly, I do. When my eyes are fully open, I realize we're much higher than I thought. The wind blows my hair back as I look down at the world below. At flowing rivers and tops of bushy trees. At the moon that seems so unbelievably close. I let out a shout of excitement. Celie shouts too, and then both of us are laughing and cheering and flying through the night sky.

The pegasus dips down and skims along a lake. The cold water splashes at my feet, and the mist refreshes my face. We soar through the sky for a while longer, over the manor, and more forests and open clearings, before making our way back to the party and landing gently on the ground.

It's the most exhilarating thing I'll ever experience.

At around 11 p.m. the teachers arrive to enforce curfew. Celie and I return to our room and collapse on my bed.

"We are so drunk right now," Celie says.

I giggle, and once I start, I can't stop.

We laugh until we fall asleep, side by side. I can't imagine a single night that could ever top this one.

CHAPTER ELEVEN

I think I might throw up.

The day has come, and I'm a nervous wreck. The first trial begins at 11 a.m., and we're told to meet in the dining hall fifteen minutes early. I'm not sure I'm ready, but after twenty-four hours of reviewing notes and training, I feel a bit more confident. It's been... intense—in the coolest way possible.

Honestly, I'm having so much fun.

But at the thought of going into this trial, I want to run back to my dorm and lock myself in. I have no clue what to expect. It's the worst feeling ever.

Walking into the dining hall is tense. My footsteps echo along the polished floor. The usual clamor of teenagers is reduced to quiet whispers. I can almost feel the nerves in the air as I join Celie, Mykel, and Lukas at our table. Mykel tries to play calm, but fidgets with his fingers under the table. Celie and Lukas sit in silence, far from their usual bubbly selves.

After what feels like hours, Alatar Blight steps onto the dais. He wears a black cloak with the Silver Key emblem on the front and an intricate silver pattern stitched into the fabric.

"Good morning, everyone. As you know, today marks the start of your first trial. You have been working hard these last few months, and I am pleased to see your dedication," he begins. "The previous competitions had three trials, each lasting a few days. This year, you have two and a half weeks to complete your trials."

People whisper to each other. I panic.

Two and a half weeks?

What could be so difficult it takes that long?

"I know it seems like a lot," Alatar continues. "We want to test your abilities to the fullest. If you do not complete the trial in time, you will be exported out, and the points you've gathered will count toward your final score. I want to stress that if, at any time, you wish to leave the trial, simply send a flare into the air and you will be transported out.

"You will be split into groups and enter the trial from the room assigned to your group. You may work together or alone. This decision is yours. However, points are awarded individually and tallied magically. If no one has questions..." He pauses. Silence. "...please exit when you hear your name. A uniform will be provided to you. You will change into it before meeting at your assigned room."

My heart is going to beat out of my chest.

"Group one will meet in front of room 112." Alatar begins to read a list of names, and each one sends a jolt through me.

Once the first group leaves the room, he continues. "Group two, room 113. Sarah Belmont, Clarity Hearthfire, Aria Knight..."

At the sound of my name, I stand and amble to the door.

"Eve Stark, Celie Solano..." I let out a breath of relief. "Jakson Black, Lukas Prince, Sherry Light, Blade Casteel, Rex Davenport, Nathan Hale, Mykel Griffin," I stop listening after hearing my friends' names.

I head to the bathroom and change into my uniform: a pair of black cargo pants and a matching long-sleeve zip-up top. It's made of some sort of thick nylon fabric, with a silver *SK* pasted on the chest. I admire the outfit, pleased by how easy it is to move around, before realizing I should probably hurry.

Apparently, though, I didn't need to rush myself as I'm one of the first to arrive at room 113.

As I wait for Celie, Mykel, and Lukas, Blade walks over to me. His uniform is similar to mine. All black, with the *SK* on the front. We stand in silence as we wait for more people to arrive. Until I break the awkwardness.

"Good luck in there," I say.

"You too."

I open my mouth to say something else, but Rex pulls Blade away before I can.

"Was she bothering you?" he says, glancing back at me. When Blade doesn't respond, he continues. "Can't wait for her to get her ass kicked in this trial. If we're lucky, we'll get to watch."

I wait for Blade's response, but it doesn't come. He just laughs it off and changes the subject.

I'm confused by the pang in my chest. Why do I feel hurt? Because Blade didn't defend me? It's not like we're friends.

"You ready?" Celie asks, walking over to me with Mykel and Lukas.

"As ready as I can be," I say, letting out a shaky breath as Mykel slides a comforting arm around my shoulders.

Alatar arrives moments later.

"When I open this door, you will enter the first trial. Think of it like walking through a portal to another world or teleporting to another place, like in the practice rooms," he says. "Now for a hint: your first objective is to reach where the water flies."

I don't know how he says these things as if they're normal.

With a wave of his hand, Alatar opens the door. One by one, we step through.

Just like when I got teleported to Silver Key three months ago, I go from standing in the hallway of Silver Key Manor to entering an entirely different setting. Bright sunlight shines down on the lush green trees and bushes that surround us. I walk along a winding pathway, colourful flower beds decorating either side. Birds soar through the bright blue sky, singing between the fluffy clouds. A clear lake glistens nearby, with three white swans dipping their heads in the water. Breathing in the fresh air, the scent of flowers fills my lungs.

"This is amazing," Celie breathes.

"Look over there!" someone calls.

Vast green mountains stretch into the distance. On the highest peak, a massive white fountain sprays crystal-clear water that cascades down the hill.

I repeat Alatar's clue under my breath, "*Reach where the water flies.*" Then I turn to Mykel. "That's where we have to go first."

"We better get moving," Lukas says, pointing to the rest of the group who have dispersed in different directions, all pursuing the mountain. Blade, Rex, and Nathan are the last to disappear into the trees. We spot an entrance in the forest and begin our journey to the mountaintop.

But this isn't a normal forest. Flowers of every hue bloom from the ground. Trees and bushes bear fresh fruit. Specks of glitter drift from the air like autumn leaves, sparkling in the sunlight filtering through the trees. Pathways branch in different directions, and we struggle to choose which way to go.

As we walk, we pass many open clearings, perfect for picnics. Long rivers wind along the paths, so clean I can see the pebbled ground beneath. Small snakes slither through the trees above, hissing softly.

"Doesn't this place remind you of the Garden of Eden?" I say.

Celie hums in agreement. "Exactly what I was thinking."

"What, like, from the Bible?" Lukas says.

Mykel cracks a teasing grin. "Yes, dumbass, like the Bible."

Lukas rolls his eyes and shoves his middle finger in Mykel's face, and then we continue walking.

Mykel walks in front of me, and as he steps off a tall rock, he turns and offers me his hand. I take it and hop off the rock, landing inches in front of him. Our faces are almost touching as he looks down at me. If I got on my tiptoes and tilted my head up just the slightest, our lips would touch.

"Get a room," Lukas says as he passes us. Celie giggles.

Mykel doesn't let go of my hand as we continue our walk through the forest. Hours pass before a piercing scream slices through the air.

I whip my head toward it, searching.

"Did you hear that?" I say.

Mykel frowns. "Hear what?"

"You didn't hear that scream?"

"Scream?" Lukas questions.

I hear it again, and without thinking twice, sprint off in that direction.

CHAPTER TWELVE

"Aria, wait!" Celie calls, but I don't listen. I weave through the trees, scramble over jagged rocks, and find myself at the mouth of a cave.

I glance around. The dusty walls of the cave are etched with red symbols. Familiar, like the ones Blade and I discovered at Silver Key. As I lean in for a closer look, something—or some-one—shifts in the shadows.

"Hey, I heard screaming. Are you okay?" I say.

The figure emerges from the darkness. She's tall and alluring, with hair as black as night falling below her waist. As she rises, large bat-like wings unfurl from her back.

"Truth be told, I've been better, Aria."

I stumble back. An icolt. Just as Mrs. Patrickson described.

"You know my name?" I manage to ask.

"I know a lot about you. Tell me, how's your family do-ing? You know, your *real* family." She winks. Her voice is low, smooth, and seductive. Two fangs peek out of her mouth as she speaks, short but sharp enough to pierce flesh with ease.

"My family *is* my real family," I say.

"Oh, honey, you know what I mean."

"Who are you?"

"Irena," she says. "But my name is of little importance right now."

"What do you want?"

"Well, Aria, I require something. Or rather, someone." She creeps toward me, one slow step at a time. Her red eyes gleam like knives, almost as sharp as the tips of her wings. "See, creatures like me need to feed. If we don't, we weaken. And this place... I haven't fed in a while. But now, with you sorcerers here... I'm starving, Aria. The problem is, I can't feed willingly—part of the curse," she explains. "But I can give you the information you've been searching for."

"About my biological family?"

"Yes. I know everything—who they are, where they are, why they gave you up." She giggles, as if she already knows how the truth will hit me. "All I want from you is one of your little sorcerer friends."

"Absolutely not," I say. "You seriously think I'd give up one of my friends for information about a family that abandoned me? You overestimate how much I care."

"I thought you might say that. But just because I can't feed doesn't mean I can't kill. Who should it be... Celie? She seems like a ball of sunshine; it might be fun. But Mykel... he's so handsome—"

"Don't touch them."

"What are you going to do, Aria? Fight me? I think you're underestimating how powerful I am, even without feeding. Definitely more powerful than an amateur sorcerer like you."

"I don't know. I've been getting pretty good." I blast my hands forward, shouting, "*Obtundo!*"

Blue magic surges from my body, erupting from my palms. It hits Irena, sending her crashing into the cave wall. Dust and stones scatter as she hits the ground, but she recovers with frightening speed. Laughing, she twists in the air, her wing slamming into me.

Pain sears through me as I hit the cold floor, air knocked from my lungs. A fresh cut blooms across my arm from her wing, blood trailing to my wrist.

As I struggle to breathe, Irena kneels before me. Up close, I notice a faint scar that runs vertically from her brow, over her eye, down her cheek.

She leans in, her voice a dark, honeyed whisper in my ear: "I will take something from you, Aria. Something you care for. And there is nothing you can do to stop me."

"*Why?* Why me?"

She pulls back. "I'm a demon. It's in my nature." She winks before turning to leave.

"Wait!" I shout. "What are these symbols on the wall?"

Her evil laugh echoes through the cave as she leaps into the air and vanishes into the distance. I let out a long breath, pressing my back against the wall. The bad feeling in my chest that this isn't the last I'll see of her refuses to fade. Surely, she can't kill us. This tournament is monitored. We're meant to be safe. Yet the thought barely calms me as I close my eyes and try to steady my breathing.

My eyes snap open as footsteps approach the cave. I spring to my feet, but it's only Mykel, Celie, and Lukas running toward me.

"Oh my God, Aria," Mykel says.

I throw my arms around him, and he hugs me just as tightly.

"What happened?" he says, pulling away and scanning my body for injuries. "Are you hurt? What happened to your arm?"

"I'm okay."

"Are you sure?" Lukas says.

"Yeah... yeah, I'm fine. There was a woman—a demon. She threatened to kill one of you. We have to be careful."

"What the hell?" Mykel says. "Which way did she go?"

"She flew away. I don't know."

Celie grabs my hand. "I was worried, Aria. You can't run off like that. We don't know what's out here. We have to stick together."

"I'm sorry. You're right. It won't happen again."

"It's getting dark," Lukas says. "We should set up for the night."

"How about here?" Mykel suggests.

I shake my head. "Not here. It doesn't feel safe."

"Fair enough," Lukas says.

I glance at the cave walls. "Before we go... do you guys recognize these symbols?"

They each study the markings.

"They're ancient inscriptions, maybe Greek," Celie says, squinting. "I saw a book at Silver Key about them."

"What does it say?" I ask.

"Couldn't tell you. I'd need the book to translate."

We leave the cave and come across a waterfall. Its deep, steady roar soothes the tension in my chest. White water tinted with shimmering purples and pinks tumbles into the blue lake. Grey rocks line the shore, and stepping stones peek out of the water, leading to a small patch of grass beneath a tall tree. Perfect for camping.

Lukas and Celie gather fruits from nearby bushes, while Mykel conjures a fire with just his bare hands. Celie later summons several books out of thin air, stacking them beside her.

"What are those?" Mykel says.

"Books I borrowed from the manor," she says, holding up *The Book of Mythical Creatures*. "I thought they might come in handy."

"How did you do that?" I say, grabbing the book from Celie and flipping through the pages.

"I'm advanced in summoning spells. As long as I know exactly what I'm summoning, it's easy. Even with multiple items at a time."

We sit around the fire for hours, reading and planning the next day. As night deepens, I lie back on the grass and stare up at the twinkling stars. Lukas and Celie are already asleep.

I chuckle. "Lukas is snoring."

"I'm used to it," Mykel says, lying down next to me.

I turn onto my side to face him. He looks breathtaking under the moonlight.

He meets my gaze, then smiles softly. "Good night, Aria."

I smile back. "Good night."

CHAPTER THIRTEEN

I wake to a scream and Mykel's arm around my waist.
Carefully, I slip out from under it and look around, trying to pinpoint where the shout came from. The sun is already high above us, forcing me to squint as my eyes adjust. As I stand, Rex barrels past me without a word, nearly knocking me over.

"Mykel, wake up," I say, shaking him.

He doesn't stir.

"Mykel—"

Another scream pierces the air, followed by a red flare shooting into the sky.

I don't wait. I take off toward the sound, dirt flying as my feet pound against the ground. I duck beneath low branches and leap over tangled roots until I burst into a clearing.

Nathan is collapsed on the ground, unconscious—probably the one who fired the flare. My heart thuds as I scan for the source of the panic.

Then I see Blade.

He's fighting someone in the distance and crashes to the ground, blood dripping from the cuts along his face, but he forces himself back to his feet. I sprint toward him. As I get closer, I finally see who—or rather, what—he's fighting.

Long black hair. Bat-like wings.

Irena.

She laughs as she lands another blow to Blade's face, flashing her sharp fangs.

"*Pendulus!*" Blade shouts, thrusting his hand upward.

A translucent force of magic suspends Irena mid-air before he slams her back into the ground.

"Blade!" I yell.

"What are you doing here?" he says. "I'm handling this."

"I know her. I saw her yesterday. She said—"

"Leave me alone, Knight. I've got this."

With a sharp flick of his hands, Blade mutters another incantation. Irena's wings snap back into her body, and she freezes, unable to speak. Before she can react, Blade summons a golden dagger from thin air. It gleams in the sunlight filtering through the trees.

"Wait!" I shout.

Too late.

He drives the dagger into her chest.

Irena gasps once before collapsing onto the cold morning grass. Her body dissolves into a cloud of red ash that scatters in the wind.

"You killed her?" I say.

"I had to," Blade says, voice wavering. "She—she was going to kill me."

"Did she say why she attacked you?"

"No. She just did. I figured it was a test." He pauses. "Why?"

"No reason." I hesitate and then add, "I found her yesterday. In a cave. The walls were covered in symbols—like the ones in the room at Silver Key."

His eyes widen. "What? Really?"

I nod. "They're ancient Greek inscriptions. Celie said there's a book in the Silver Key library that can translate them."

"Did you tell them—"

"No, don't worry."

"Okay." He exhales. "When we get back, I'll translate them."

There's a beat of silence, filled only by the chirping of the birds above us, before I speak. "I should get back to Mykel and the others. I don't want them to be worried."

But when I return, they're still asleep. It takes a few firm shakes to wake them, but once they're up, I explain everything.

"You should've woken us before running into danger, Aria. Again," Mykel says.

"I was going to. It just felt urgent."

"It's alright," Celie says. "We're glad you're okay—"

A loud crackle from the sky cuts her off.

Lukas squints upward. "What the hell?"

It starts to rain. Except... it isn't rain.

"Is that—"

"*Blood?*" Mykel says.

Celie grabs my hand, and the four of us scramble into a nearby shelter. It resembles the cave where I found Irena.

"Guys," I groan, "it's in my hair."

Celie wipes her face with her sleeve. "That's disgusting."

The blood-rain slows after a few minutes and then stops entirely.

"Well," Lukas says, "that was terrifying."

"Definitely weird," Mykel agrees.

Celie peeks out of the cave and looks skyward. "I think it's over. We should be good."

We cautiously step onto the blood-soaked grass.

So gross.

"Now that that's done," Lukas says, "the plan for today is to start the hike up the mountain. And pray we don't get showered in blood again."

It's gonna be a long day.

Most of the walk through the garden is surprisingly calm. We steer clear of a few magical snakes, which is a relief—I have no desire to repeat my last encounter with one. We sneak past a lion that barely acknowledges us and get lost more times than I'd like to admit. At least an hour is wasted doubling back through dead ends. But other than that, this place is beautiful, and not much else has gotten in our way.

That is, until we reach the base of the mountain. We head for the trail that'll take us up, and slam straight into an invisible barrier. It's like walking into a translucent wall.

"What the hell?" Celie says.

Lukas stumbles back, rubbing his forehead. "Shit."

I reach out until my palm meets the unseen barrier.

"You cannot pass," a voice says behind us.

We spin around.

A short man stands there, green eyes shimmering beneath the hood of a navy-blue cloak.

"We need to get to the top of the mountain," Mykel says. "We have to pass."

"In order to do so," the man says, "you must each give me something of great value."

"Like what?" I ask.

"A memory."

Mykel folds his arms across his chest. "Absolutely not."

"That is my price. I quite enjoy stepping into people's memories. It is almost as fun as taking them."

"Any memory?" Lukas says.

The man laughs, harsh and ugly. "Happy memories only. Important ones. Personal ones." He licks his cracked lips, yellow teeth peeking through. "Those are... delicious."

I shudder. "What are you?"

"He's a memoram demon," Celie says.

The demon smirks. "Very clever, girl."

"I think this is a test," Lukas says. "They're testing us on how far we're willing to go to win this tournament."

The demon watches us with gleeful anticipation.

"I think we have to do it," I say.

"I do too," Lukas agrees.

Celie lets out an anxious breath and steps forward. "Fine. How do we do this?"

The demon grins and walks closer to her. "Think hard about the memory, and I will do the rest."

Celie closes her eyes and concentrates. A tear slides down her cheek as the demon cups her head, his long black nails digging into her hair. A moment later, he pulls away, satisfied.

"Touching," he says, licking his lips again.

I fight the urge to throw up and place a comforting hand on Celie's back. She opens her eyes and wipes away her tear, like she doesn't even remember why it's there.

Lukas is next. Then Mykel. I'm last.

I close my eyes.

I'm fifteen years old. We're at a theme park. My family and I have been planning this vacation for months. Ashton and I spent hours mapping out which rides we wanted to hit first, and now that we're here, it's hard to wipe the smile off our faces.

"I love it here," I say, breathing in the warm scent of popcorn and metal tracks baking in the sun.

"Me too!" Ashton says.

Dad pulls out his camera. "Give your sister a hug for the photo. Come on, Ash!"

We hug, and Mom cheers. "This place *is* magical."

"Don't worry, Mom. We love each other," I say, giving Ashton a small shove.

We lean in to look at the photo, but the screen is black.

I frown and look up.

Mom is gone. So are Dad and Ashton.

I turn in a slow circle. The amusement park—once bursting with people—is empty. Abandoned.

I blink, and the rides vanish one by one. The sky smears into grey. The memory unravels until I can't remember what it was at all. There's only endless darkness.

I open my eyes.

What just happened?

"How sweet," the demon says.

"Are you happy?" Mykel says. "Can we pass now?"

"I am a man of my word." The demon snaps his fingers and disappears.

Mykel reaches toward the barrier. A light breeze washes over his hand. "The barrier's down."

"Let's go," I say.

We follow the narrow trail winding up the steep mountain.

"That was weird, right?" Lukas says. "I can tell something's missing, but I can't remember what it is. There's just... this empty feeling."

I nod. "It's on the tip of my tongue, but I can't remember."

"I think mine was about me and my mom and dad," Mykel says. "Something happy."

"Mine was about my parents too," Lukas mumbles, and Celie gives him a look. Whatever that memory was, it clearly hurt to give away.

"My memory was about my younger sister," Celie says. "She's the most important person in my life." Her eyes fill with tears, and I take her hand as we walk. "I'm okay. I don't even know what the memory was. I have so many others of us together. I just miss her so much. She's only six. I'm missing so much time I could be spending with her. I miss waking up to her cute little face every day."

Ashton's face flashes through my mind. I'm missing out on so much with him too. I wonder if my parents told him the truth about where I've been.

"She's so young, Celie," Mykel says gently. "You'll be back before you know it. You'll have your whole life to watch her grow."

"I know. You're right." She scrubs at her eyes. "Sorry. Why am I such a mess?"

Lukas rubs slow circles on her back.

We walk the rest of the way in silence. Celie has only mentioned her sister once or twice before. I didn't realize how close they were. Maybe it hurts too much to talk about.

The path spirals higher and higher, and by the time the sun dips below the horizon, we're exhausted. We settle beneath two flowering trees, their petals drifting down around us. I fall asleep almost instantly.

CHAPTER FOURTEEN

We wake bright and early to birdsong and the sharp scent of morning dew. Droplets fall from the trees above us, and the blood that once stained the grass red has mostly vanished. It must have rained during the night. How I slept through it, I have no idea. I could've used a good rinse.

It takes what feels like hours of hiking before we finally reach the mountain's peak.

The view is stunning. The entire garden stretches out below us—countless shades of green layered together, broken by ribbons of blue water and bursts of pink and purple flowers. Colourful birds and strange little creatures glide through the sky as we head toward the fountain.

It's the largest fountain any of us have ever seen. An angel statue sits atop it, wings outstretched as water shoots from their tips and sprays in every direction. It cascades down the mountainside, forming a small waterfall that crashes into a blue river winding through the valley below.

I turn slowly, trying to take it all in. Everything is so... breathtaking.

I spot Jakson and Sherry talking near the edge, Kara and Eliza admiring the view, and Sarah and Clarity sitting on the ground, catching their breath.

I'm slightly annoyed to see Eliza with us. Mykel is clearly doing his best to pretend she doesn't exist. Just as I'm about to say something, Blade approaches from behind us. His hair is damp, clinging to his face.

"Is this all of us?" Celie asks. "Are we the only ones who made it?"

Mykel scans the area. "So far, looks like it."

"What do we do now?" Lukas says.

"I don't kno—" I start, but a thunderous roar cuts me off.

It's the same sound the sky made before it rained blood. I brace myself, searching for shelter—but no blood falls. Instead, grey clouds swallow the sun, draining the blue from the sky. The birds vanish, replaced by massive, bat-like creatures circling overhead.

"What's happening?" I say as Mykel takes a protective step closer to me.

"Oh my God!" Sherry screams.

Jakson is on the ground, his body convulsing violently. We rush to him. Sweat mats his raven-black hair to his forehead, and his eyes squeeze shut in agony.

"I don't know what happened!" Sherry cries. "We were just talking and then—what do I do?"

"Turn him on his side," Blade says.

"What the fuck *is* that?" Mykel says, staring at Jakson's neck.

His skin ripples—*moves*—like something is crawling beneath it, trying to escape.

"We have to get it out," Lukas says.

Blade pulls out a knife.

"Whoa—Blade, you don't know what you're doing," Mykel says. "You could kill him."

"I won't."

"It's okay," Celie says. "H-he can't die. They said we were safe."

"He doesn't look very safe," Lukas mutters.

"Should we send up a flare?" Eliza says.

"It'll pull him out of the trial!" Sherry protests. "He wants to win this so bad—I—"

"Sherry," I say gently, "I think he might die if we don't."

Clarity paces. "How is this even possible?"

"I don't know," Blade says grimly. "It'll take time for them to extract him after the flare. He might not have that long. But send it anyway."

Jakson stops seizing, instead gasping weakly for air. Sarah grabs his hand and looks at me. I nod.

She fires the flare.

"You need to cut it out," I tell Blade. "It's the only thing we can do right now."

Blade meets my gaze, fear flickering across his face. Then he looks back down and presses the knife to Jakson's neck. He cuts carefully. Blood wells as a black, worm-like creature writhes free. Blade jerks back as it launches itself onto the grass, slick and twitching, until Mykel stomps on it, crushing it into a smear of black sludge.

Celie kneels beside Jakson. "Is he okay?"

"I—I don't know," Sherry says.

Blade checks his pulse. "He's breathing. Pulse is weak."

Then Jakson vanishes.

Eliza rests a hand on Sherry's shoulder. "They'll save him."

Blade stands, dragging a hand through his hair. "What the fuck is going on?"

"We should spread out," Celie says. "There has to be a clue, some kind of objective."

Everyone agrees.

"Hey," Mykel says, grabbing Blade's arm as he passes.

Blade glares until Mykel releases him.

"I just wanted to say—you did well back there."

Blade scoffs. "It's not like you were going to do anything."

He starts to walk away.

"I'm just trying to be nice, man," Mykel says. "You don't have to be a dick."

Blade stops. "Mykel *fucking* Griffin." He turns, eyes sharp. "You try to make yourself seem so interesting by putting that *y* in there, but your name is still just *Michael* at the end of the day."

"Your name is *Blade*, dude."

"At least I don't pretend to be someone I'm not. Must be exhausting, trying to be perfect all the time."

Mykel says nothing. Blade shoves past him, bumping his chest. Mykel goes to retaliate, but I grab his hand and shake my head. Now is not the time. He exhales sharply, and together we head toward the forest at the mountain's edge.

The air here feels heavier, darker than the forest we crossed before. Wind whistles through the leaves as we step over roots and tree stumps. In the centre of a clearing stands a massive tree, its branches heavy with red-orange fruit. I reach out and press my palm against the trunk.

"Is this—"

A twig snaps. Then another. And another. All around the clearing.

"Stay close," Mykel whispers.

I step back from the tree and search the surrounding forest with my eyes. Finally, a figure makes its way out of hiding.

It's a man. At least that's what I thought until he sprouted two large, white-feathered wings from his back. His exposed chest glistens in the light, and he wears a white loincloth below his waist.

A woman appears, a little girl following close behind. They emerge from all directions until five or six of them surround us, all sporting those magnificent white wings.

The first one steps forward. His voice is melodic, warm. "Don't be afraid. We won't harm you. This place is our home, and it is being taken over by demons. We need your help to defeat them. You and your people must save us."

His eyes are mesmerizing, a shimmering gold, but there's a flicker of desperation in them. There's desperation in all their eyes.

"You must have seen what is happening to this world," he continues. "The sky fading. Blood falling from the clouds. Soon the sky will turn crimson. Water will remain blood. Plants will die. When that happens, it will be too late. The demons will not stop until our realm is destroyed—us along with it."

I look around at the celestials. Some of them are injured, I realize, with long gashes across their bodies and wings stained dark red with blood. The little girl clings to her mother's hips, and I notice a fresh cut across her face.

"We'll help you," I say.

Mykel grabs my arm and pulls me close. "Are you sure about this? What if it's a trick?"

"Look at them, Mykel. They're desperate."

"Or they're very talented actors."

I scoff. "This has to be our mission. What else would it be?"

"I don't know. But I don't think we should be so quick to trust them."

"Stay here and hide," I say to the celestials. "We'll talk to the others and come back."

"How do we know you will return?" the mother asks.

"Trust me," I say, before grabbing Mykel by the hand and dragging him off with me.

"Aria, I don't know about this."

"We'll talk to the others, think it through. Then we'll decide."

When we reach the others, they're pacing across the grass.

"Did you find anything?" Celie asks.

"We did—"

"Is it just me," Lukas says, "or is the sky turning red?"

We all look up. The sky definitely has a red tint now—one that wasn't there earlier.

That can't be good," Clarity says.

"It's not," Mykel says, before recounting our conversation with the celestials.

When he's finished, silence settles.

Celie is the first to speak up. "I don't know for sure, but I think this *is* what we're supposed to do. I think they want us to help the celestials. I mean, it makes sense, right? They said these trials would have higher stakes. I'd say this certainly qualifies."

"Yeah," Sherry says. "And the bad omens they mentioned are happening. There is truth to what they said."

"Maybe, but let's keep an eye out. I don't think it's a good idea to trust anyone completely," Blade says.

"So..." Lukas says. "What's the plan?"

CHAPTER FIFTEEN

Nothing. We come up with nothing.

We think and plan for hours, but none of it is good enough. We have no idea how we're supposed to save a group of celestials—and an entire *realm*—from demons on our own. There are only ten of us, and who knows how many demons. We're exhausted and frustrated. When it gets even darker—the sun presumably setting, though we can't see it through the greyish-red sky—we finally decide to call it a night.

In the morning, Mykel and I are the first ones awake. While everyone else is still asleep, we walk in silence, searching for anything that might give us information about the demons or how to stop them.

Mykel is the first to break the quiet. "What's that?"

I follow his gaze and spot a glowing red orb levitating in the distance. Drawn by curiosity, we follow it as it drifts toward the edge of the mountain—and disappears.

"What the hell?"

We peer over the edge, but the orb is gone. A split second later, a red-black mist coils into existence in front of us. It floats past, and when we turn, it shapes itself into a figure.

A woman.

My mother.

Not Amelia, but the mother I've known my entire life. Dirty-blond hair resting on her shoulders. Full lips. Light eyes.

"Mom?"

"Not exactly," she says.

My heart slams against my ribs. I don't know what to think. All I can see is my mom, and all I can feel is how much I miss her.

"Wait," Mykel says. "You see your mom? I see my dad."

"What—"

Then I remember... A fidolus. The demon Mrs. Patrickson taught me about. The one that takes the form of someone you love.

"What would you trust more," the demon asks, "a demon's face, or your own mother's? And for you, Mykel, your father's."

"What do you want from us?" Mykel says.

"I want you to join the demons. This realm is being reclaimed. It will belong to us once more, and we want your help. You are powerful. With sorcerers on our side, we would be unstoppable."

Her confidence is unsettling. The corner of her mouth lifts into a devilish smirk, and seeing that expression on my mother's face makes my stomach clench. It's nothing like her usual warm smile—the one she gives me when saying goodbye before school or saying good night before bed.

"Why would we do that?" Mykel says. "There are people—creatures—who live here. Why would we help you destroy their home?"

"They are not as innocent as they appear," the fidolus replies. "This realm was once ours. The celestials took it during the war between Heaven and Hell. We want it back, and we will do whatever it takes. We've grown stronger. With or without you, we will succeed. I only wanted to offer you a chance to survive. Especially you, Aria. You don't even know how valuable you are."

"I don't understand," I say. "Why would celestials take your home? They're angels. There has to be a reason."

"They feared us," she says, and for the first time her voice falters, just slightly. Anger and betrayal ripple beneath her smooth tone. "They saw how this realm united us and worried we would turn that power against humans. Some of us did. I won't deny that. But others, like me, only wanted a place to exist. A place to embrace the darkness within us without hurting innocents. The celestials attacked first. When we fought back, they banished us to Hell, where we've lived and trained for centuries. But now, Hell has been conquered by someone—something terrible. We cannot live under his rule any longer."

Mykel and I fall silent.

The celestials in the woods... their eyes were filled with despair, their white wings tainted red. But this demon sounds convincing. Too convincing. Still, something inside me resists. I can't help but feel like our goal in this trial isn't to help the demons.

"I'm sorry," I finally say. "We can't help you. We were put here for a reason. A test. I think we're meant to *save* this realm. To help the celestials." My voice falters. "I just don't know how they expect us to do that."

"This is not a simple test, Aria," the demon warns. "Your kind always has ulterior motives. This war goes far beyond demons and celestials. Lives—dark and light alike—are at stake. Be careful who you trust. Both of you."

Then she vanishes, as suddenly as she appeared.

I'm left confused. Angry. Uneasy.

"I don't know what to do," I say. "What if she's telling the truth? What if we're on the wrong side?"

Mykel shakes his head, as unsure as I am. "Should we tell the others?"

"We should. Everyone deserves to know."

We return to the sorcerers, wake up the ones still asleep, and fill everyone in.

"I don't get it," Lukas says. "Why would they throw us in here if we could actually get hurt? Isn't this just a trial?"

"They *are* demons," Clarity says. "It could have been lying."

"I agree," Mykel says, turning to me. "It's a demon. We can't trust a word it says. But I *do* trust Silver Key, Aria. This is a test of our strength, our judgment, our courage. Don't fall for their tricks."

Mykel is right. This is a trial, and I'm being too naive and gullible, falling for the tricks thrown in my path.

"I have a plan," Blade says, speaking up at last. "First of all, I think that fountain is the key to everything. Protecting it from the demons is the first step. We can't let them get too close to it. We might have to fight them off, but we have no idea how many of them there are. Knight and I will lead the charge by casting a protection spell over the fountain and summoning the demons. We've had the most encounters with them and will know how to handle them better. No matter how much we try to persuade them to change their minds and leave this realm alone, we know that probably won't happen. Knight and I will stall so all of you, along with the celestials, can get into your positions and prepare your spells. Once they attack, we trap them in a barrier and disarming spell. They won't be able to use their powers or escape. Then we figure out what comes next."

"That sounds like a great plan," I admit.

Blade smirks and winks in my direction.

Mykel rolls his eyes. "So many things could go wrong. What if the spells don't work? What if they're way more powerful than you expect?"

"You got a better idea?" Blade challenges.

Mykel begrudgingly shakes his head.

"Then shut up."

Mykel turns to me. "I want you to stay with me. I won't let you be alone with *him*. I need to make sure you're safe, and the best way I can do that is if you're with me."

"Mykel," I say, taking his hands, "Blade is right. I know you want to protect me, but I'll be okay. I've gotten better at magic. I can handle myself."

"You may have gotten better, but you still have the least experience. I can't let you put yourself in the front line of danger."

I drop his hands from mine. "Well, you're going to have to. I can do it. I'll be fine, I promise," I say, the slightest bit annoyed.

Mykel pulls me into a tight hug, and I let out a soft breath. We stay like this for a moment before pulling apart.

"I'll be okay," I say, and he reluctantly nods.

Stumbling through the forest an hour later, Mykel and I find the celestials we promised to help. They greet us and agree to follow Blade's plan.

As the days pass, we practice spells and refine the plan. Every night, we sit around the fire and talk. Not just about the tournament, but about life. Somewhere along the way, these people stop feeling like competitors and start feeling like friends.

The celestials visit us daily to thank us for our help. The demons haven't returned, but the fidolus's words linger in my mind. Though I believe helping the celestials is what we're meant to do for this trial, an inexplicable heaviness settles in the pit of my stomach and refuses to fade.

I find myself back in the forest with Blade, walking beside him in silence. It isn't uncomfortable; our thoughts simply leave no room for words. We've just placed the protection spell over the fountain. The rest of the sorcerers are moving into position, preparing for the inevitable attack. I try to reassure myself that the plan will work. We've practiced it relentlessly. But practice is nothing like execution. We can't afford to fail, and the unknowns press in on us as we walk.

How many creatures will we summon? What if we can't stall them long enough? What if the demons overpower us easily?

The walk is short, yet it feels endless. We stop at a small clearing shaped almost perfectly in a circle, trees closing in around it like a wall.

"We've got this," I say, forcing a soft, uncertain smile.

The corner of Blade's mouth lifts slightly in response. "*Praesidio,*" he murmurs.

A protective barrier settles over us.

We step into the centre of the clearing and face one another. My pulse is racing as Blade takes my hands. Together we speak the summoning spell.

"*Voco daemonium nunc. Nullam obesse illis qui advocant. Venerunt daemones. Vocamus te.*"

We speak the words in unison, just as they were written in one of the textbooks Celie summoned. As we do, demons materialize around us one by one.

The first, an icolt, emerges behind us. She carries herself like Irena, but her hair is cut just above her shoulders, her frame smaller. Another demon appears to my right. Then my left. Soon the clearing is filled with them—some vaguely human, others grotesque, with long black tails, razor-sharp teeth, and large, slitted eyes. At least twenty of them surround us.

The same demon as before, wearing my mother's face, appears. She seems to be the last one.

"What are we doing here?" she asks, her demonic voice echoing through the clearing.

Blade and I release each other's hands and turn to face the gathered creatures.

"We want you to retreat," Blade says.

Laughter ripples through the demons.

"You know we can't do that," the fidolus replies. "We're being tortured in Hell. This place is rightfully ours, and we're taking it back."

"Please, just consider leaving this place alone," I say. "The celestials live here now. Families, *children*... You can't do this to them."

"Aria," she says coolly, "you think we care? They stole this realm from us. The truth is simple—if you aren't with us, you're against us."

The demons move closer, tightening the circle around us. I back into Blade, our shoulders touching. Back to back, we watch them close in.

Suddenly, one of the demons lets out a piercing screech and charges. The moment it reaches us, the protection spell flares to life, hurling the demon backward through the air. I release a shaky breath of relief as it snarls from the ground before scrambling up and fleeing. The others follow, all racing toward the fountain. Toward the others. I can only hope we bought them enough time.

Once the demons vanish from sight, Blade and I break into a sprint, chasing after them. When we reach the fountain, relief crashes over me.

The demons are trapped inside an invisible barrier, unable to escape.

Blade's plan has worked.

CHAPTER SIXTEEN

"I have an idea," Celie says.

We all turn toward her as she lifts a book into view: *Creatures from Heaven to Hell.* "I've been reading this, and I think I found something." She hesitates for a second. "It might be a long shot, but we might as well try."

Blade raises a brow. "Try what, exactly?"

"In the book, there's a spell that can permanently banish demons to Hell. It's supposedly difficult and takes a massive amount of energy. There's also a potion we'd have to brew first." She flips a page. "It lists the ingredients."

"What are they?" I say.

Celie reads aloud. "Dandelion root, three rose petals, blackthorn, blood, an angelic feather, poison ivy, and holy water."

"Where are we supposed to get all of that?" Sarah asks as Celie hands me the book.

I scan the list again. "We'll have to split up. But I think we can find everything."

"Then let's get moving," Mykel says. "Sherry, Clarity—you stay here and keep an eye on the demons."

They nod, and moments later Mykel and I head into the forest together.

"So," I say, stepping over a thick root curling up from the ground, "this is... insane."

He huffs a quiet laugh. "Yeah. Never thought the trials would involve trapping a bunch of demons and banishing them to Hell."

"Are the trials always like this? From what you've heard?"

"No," he admits. "This one's different. The stakes are much higher."

"I hope we're not screwing this up."

"Me too."

I glance up at the sky. It's grown darker and redder over the past few days, like something bleeding out overhead. Soon, it'll be too late to save this realm, and the celestials within it.

We search in silence for a while, combing through bushes and empty clearings until we manage to find dandelion root and blackthorn.

"What's the deal with you and Eliza?" I ask. The question has been gnawing at me since I found out about her that day in the library.

"Nothing," Mykel says. When he sees that I'm unsatisfied with his answer, he blows out a hard breath and continues. "We dated for a little while, that's all. I don't really like talking about it."

"So there's nothing going on between you now?"

"What? *No*. Not at all," he says, and I think I believe him. "Are we good?"

"Yeah. Why?"

"We haven't really talked the past few days. I didn't realize you had questions about... Eliza."

"There's just been a lot going on."

Not entirely true. I've been distant—partly because of Eliza, partly because Mykel's been hovering lately. I know it comes from a good place, but I don't need protecting every second of the day.

He stops walking. "This is about when I didn't want you going with Blade, isn't it?"

"I know you were trying to help," I say carefully. "But I can handle Blade. And I *have* gotten better at protecting myself, magic or not."

"You're right. I'm sorry," he says. Then he smiles, playful again. "You must have a great teacher."

"Who, Mrs. Patrickson?" I tease.

He steps closer, and my heart stutters. For one reckless second, I want him to close the distance and kiss me.

Instead, he laughs—but there's something distant in his eyes. His demeanour completely changes. "It's getting dark. We should head back."

Disappointment sinks into my chest as we turn around.

By the time we regroup at the fountain, we have nearly all the ingredients. Celie and Lukas managed to get rose petals and an angelic feather. Blade somehow obtained poison ivy.

Eliza gestures to the fountain. "This counts as holy water, right?"

"Worth a shot," I say.

Celie picks up a rock. "*Verto.*"

It transforms into a small, dark-grey cauldron. Lukas reads from the book while Blade follows the steps. Celie fashions a rough mortar and pestle out of stone, and soon the ingredients are crushed and mixed into the water.

"Last step," Lukas says. "A few drops of blood. Then it needs to sit for ten minutes."

"I can—" I start.

"No," Mykel says, stepping forward. "I'll do it." He drags his finger across his palm. "*Segmentum.*"

An icy blue blade slices his skin. Blood wells instantly. He clenches his fist over the cauldron, letting several drops fall. The mixture steams.

"Now we wait," Celie says.

We disperse as Celie watches the potion. Mykel is talking to Sherry and Lukas, and I'm about to join them when Blade walks up to me. He says nothing, just gestures his head to the right, inviting me to follow him.

We reach a deserted area of the mountaintop, and when Blade still doesn't speak up, I break the silence. "What's up?"

"I don't know about this," he says.

"What do you mean? You don't think this is what we're supposed to do for the trial?"

"That's not it." He hesitates. "I just don't know if what they *want* us to do is the right thing."

I nod slowly. "What that demon said earlier... I've been thinking about it too. But maybe Mykel is right. Maybe we're overthinking it. They're demons. We shouldn't trust them."

Blade takes a step closer to me and lowers his voice. "Mykel does what he's told and doesn't ask questions."

I glance back toward Mykel. He's already watching me.

"I used to be like that," Blade continues. "But I've learned the hard way that people in power don't always tell the whole truth. I know firsthand how fucked up things can be once you peel back the layers."

I bring my focus back to Blade. "What's that supposed to mean—"

"Everything okay here?" Celie interrupts.

"Everything's fine," I say as Blade straightens, taking a step back.

Blade turns to Celie. "What do you think about all this?"

"About what?"

"Do you think we're doing the right thing?" I say, gesturing to the trapped demons.

Celie gives a half shrug. "I don't know. I think there's truth to both sides of the story. But we have the demons trapped, and we're ready to send them to Hell. The trial ends in a few days… It's too late to change our minds. Besides, the blood-rain, the sky… we've seen so many things—clues—that are pointing to getting rid of the demons and helping the celestials."

Blade thinks over her words before sighing. "Okay." Looking directly at Celie, he says, "I trust your judgment."

Celie smiles at him, and something unspoken passes between them. Then she turns toward the cauldron and announces, loud enough for everyone to hear, "Potion's ready!"

We gather around the cauldron again.

"What was that about?" Mykel asks as he reaches my side.

"Nothing," I say.

He doesn't press. Mykel is convinced we're doing the right thing, and maybe he's right. I don't want to cause any problems between him and Blade. We just need to get this over with.

"Now for the hard part," Celie says.

Eliza scoffs. "Making the potion *wasn't* the hard part?"

Above us, the crescent moon hangs low in the crimson sky. Inside their barrier, the demons snarl and claw, some of them shouting pleas, others hurling threats. Whatever they're saying, it doesn't matter.

We're doing this.

Sarah mutters a spell, and the demons quiet, their voices dropping to angry murmurs. As Mykel and I scan the incantation, I send her a grateful nod. She smiles back.

"It says this takes a lot of energy," Mykel says, lifting his eyes from the page. "We'll need all of our magic. We'll recite the incantation together. It may take more than one attempt to work."

No one speaks.

The celestials approach us, offering soft words of thanks. The little girl steps forward, her small wings fluttering behind her.

"What's your name?" I ask, crouching to her level.

"Angelica," she says.

"That's a lovely name."

"Thank you for saving our home." She hugs me, and warmth floods through my body—gentle, steady, powerful.

"Whoa," I breathe as she pulls away.

"Uh... guys?" Clarity says. "The fountain."

What was once holy water spurting out of the fountain has turned crimson. Blood bubbles violently to the surface.

"Shit," Sarah says. "We need to hurry."

"Then let's do it," Blade says.

Angelica runs back to her mother. I step toward the demons.

"First, we each take a sip," Celie says, lifting the cauldron. She grimaces after drinking. "That's horrific."

She passes it down the line. At last, Blade hands me the cauldron. I take a sip. It's warm and fizzing, the taste so foul it makes my eyes water, but I force it down.

"Oh my God," I laugh weakly, handing it to Mykel.

Once we're done, we form a line in front of the barrier, hands linked.

Mykel's grip is firm on my right. Blade's is warm on my left.

"Okay, the incantation is *expello daemonium infernum*," Celie says. "On the count of three, we'll repeat it."

She counts down, and we repeat the incantation. Mykel and Celie are on either end of the line, and they shoot their free hand out in front of them.

Nothing happens.

"Again," Blade says.

We repeat it.

This time, the demons scream. Smoke curls around the barrier. They slam against it, teeth bared, eyes blazing.

We chant again. And again. Until—one by one—they begin to vanish in bursts of red and black smoke.

"It's working!" Celie shouts.

A violent wind whips around us, yanking at my hair and clothes. Black light erupts from our hands, tearing toward the demons as their cries dissolve into the roar of the storm.

The last demon vanishes. The wind dies.

"Holy crap," Lukas pants. "We actually did it."

My knees buckle as exhaustion hits me all at once. I brace my hands against my thighs, lungs burning.

I blink—

And suddenly, we're standing in the dining hall of Silver Key Manor.

CHAPTER SEVENTEEN

I've slept for three days, and my head hasn't stopped throbbing.

The second the trial ended, exhaustion took over. We were all left with pounding headaches and an overwhelming need to sleep. Now, after doing nothing *but* that for three straight days, the sun has gone down and I'm wide awake.

My feet whisper against the polished floor as I descend the first flight of stairs toward the kitchen. When I reach the last step, I catch sight of someone in the hallway to my right. He's sitting on the floor, back against the wall, shoulders hunched.

"Blade?"

His head snaps up. It's dark, but I can still see the pain in his eyes. Once the surprise of my presence fades, something tortured clouds his expression.

"I'm fine. Leave me alone, Aria."

I don't answer. Instead, I walk over, slide down the wall, and sit beside him on the cold hardwood floor.

"Seriously, Knight. Leave me the fu—"

"Shut up," I say. I mimic his position, pulling my knees to my chest and folding my arms over them before resting my head down. "Just let me be nice to you."

He sighs and leans the back of his head against the wall a little too hard. A soft thud echoes in the quiet. Even without facing him directly, I catch a glimpse of how shockingly blue his eyes are and realize he's been crying.

"What's wrong?"

"I'd rather not talk about it. Especially with you."

"Why?"

"Because you're—" He stops himself. "Just go. I'll be fine."

"You want me to go? Just when I was starting to get comfy." I say. When he doesn't reply, I bump his shoulder lightly with mine.

He looks at me like I've done the strangest thing in the world, and I almost laugh. But the moment passes, and his face settles into something unreadable.

"Blade..."

"Knight..." His voice trails off. I wait. Finally, he exhales. "It's... family stuff."

Something is clenched in his fist, though I can't tell what it is.

"Family stuff," I repeat.

He doesn't respond. The sounds of owls hooting and crickets chirping fill the silence.

"I got a letter," he says at last. "My dad wrote me a letter."

I turn toward him, waiting.

"He was wondering if his teachings have been put to good use. Wants to know how the first trial went."

I remember hearing how most sorcerers are trained by their parents from a young age. He must be referring to the magic his father taught him.

Moonlight spills through the window, illuminating his face as he quietly says, "I don't want to be like him, Aria."

I nod slowly. A million thoughts rush through my head, but the only word I manage is, "Okay."

"He's just..." He buries his face into his elbow. He won't look at me. "He's not a good person."

A few pixies flutter past us, trailing blue and green glitter through the air.

"Looks like other people are getting letters too," I say.

He rubs the scar above his left eyebrow.

"Does it hurt?" I ask.

"Not anymore."

I hesitate. Maybe his father...

"Did he hurt—" I stop myself before finishing the question.

His jaw tightens. He glances at me without meeting my eyes. There's conflict there—anger, hesitation. Like he wants to defend his father and can't quite bring himself to. After a moment, his expression softens. "I wanted to be like him."

"Not anymore."

Silence settles comfortably between us, broken only by the occasional rush of wind outside.

"What about your mother?" I say. "Are you more like her?"

"Maybe." He looks like he wants to say more, then shrugs it off.

I don't push.

He finally unclenches his fist. A crumpled letter unfurls in his hand.

"What if I don't win?" he says.

"Do you want to win?"

"I have to." Another beat passes before he mutters, "And then there's fucking Mykel."

I let out a soft breath of air. "You know, you two are a lot more alike than I thought."

"I thought you said you were going to be nice to me?" he deadpans.

I roll my eyes, but I'm grateful some of the tension has eased.

"Everybody loves Mykel," he says, turning to face me. It's the first time he's made eye contact since I sat down. His eyes narrow playfully, lips curving into a teasing smirk.

I laugh. "You are so petty."

"Damn right, I'm pretty."

"I said *petty*, asshole," I say, shaking my head.

The ghost of a smile tugs at his mouth. "I don't really hate Mykel. I don't have the energy for that."

Then my stomach growls embarrassingly loudly, piercing the quiet. Blade stares at me, wide-eyed, before bursting into laughter. It's real—unrestrained.

"Have you eaten?" he says. "Like, ever?"

"I was on my way to the kitchen," I say, laughing. "Have you?"

"No."

I stand. "Wanna come?"

"I'm good."

"You should eat."

"Okay," he says. "I'll head over in a bit."

I nod, glancing out the window. "In spite of everything, it's a really beautiful night."

I turn to leave, but Blade stops me. "Good night, Aria."

"Good night, Blade."

I take the last flight of stairs to the kitchen, though it feels like my feet are moving on their own—my mind still sitting on the floor beside Blade. I grab bread, cheese, and salami, making myself a small sandwich.

I leave the supplies on the counter and head back to my room.

CHAPTER EIGHTEEN

I'm conflicted and confused—feelings I've grown quite familiar with since I first came to Silver Key.

I'm glad Blade and I had the chance to talk last night. What he said doesn't excuse his behaviour, but it does make it easier to understand. But then I remember everything Mykel has told me about Blade. All the cruel things he's done. Especially to Mykel.

What kind of friend does that make me? To sympathize with his biggest rival. Comforting Blade feels like a betrayal of Mykel. He'd be furious. He'd tell me I shouldn't have stayed with him. That Blade isn't worth my time.

But I can't bring myself to regret it.

As I make my way to the dining hall for breakfast, descending the long staircases, hands trailing along the polished railings, I try to shake the thoughts loose.

It's way too early in the morning for this.

A group of girls rush past me, giggling, as I enter the dining hall. I take a seat beside Mykel and don't mention my encounter with Blade.

"Good morning," I say, scooting closer and grabbing a waffle from the table.

Lukas gives us a knowing look. "It *is* a good morning, isn't it, you two?"

I roll my eyes, though I can't stop the small grin from forming.

"Ignore him," Mykel murmurs into my ear.

Then Celie says, "Can you two just date already?"

"See!" Lukas says. "Celie agrees. It's eight in the morning, and Mykel looks like he's ready to go back to bed. And take you with him."

Heat floods my face, and I turn away to hide my embarrassment.

"Shut up," Mykel says, though the smile in his voice is impossible to miss.

Lukas sighs dramatically. "Come on. Who are you kidding? You clearly like each other. Mykel's literally blushing."

"Dude," Mykel says, shaking his head, "now you're just making us both uncomfortable."

Lukas raises his arms in surrender. "I'm only stating the obvious."

I chuckle and look at Mykel. At first, he avoids my gaze, clearly hoping I won't notice the faint pink on his cheeks. But when our eyes meet, he relaxes.

"Jesus Christ, get a room," Lukas mutters.

Mykel closes his eyes and exhales slowly. Celie and I exchange a look and stifle a laugh.

"I'm just saying, you—"

"May I have everyone's attention, please," Alatar says, standing on the dais at the front of the room.

"Oh, thank God," I say.

Lukas rolls his eyes playfully, and I break off a piece of my waffle and throw it at him.

"Now that the first trial is over and you've had time to adjust back to your normal routines, I'd like to congratulate you all," Alatar says. "Very well done. There were some impressive performances during this trial."

His expression turns more serious. "However, some of you did not perform as well and have landed at the bottom of the leaderboard. The bottom ten can no longer catch up on points and will be sent home early. I will inform those individuals privately."

A hush falls over the hall.

"I'm sorry this journey has come to an end for some of you," Alatar continues, "but for the rest, keep practicing. Prepare yourselves for the second trial."

"People are leaving?" I whisper.

"I guess so," Celie says.

Despite feeling confident about my role in the first trial, anxiety twists in my stomach. I'm surprised by how badly I want to stay. A few months ago, I wasn't even sure I wanted magic in my life at all. I had considered walking away, pretending none of this existed. Now, I can't imagine leaving. I haven't known these people long, but I don't know how I spent the first seventeen years of my life without them. I don't even remember what it felt like to consider giving this up.

I don't want to leave.

More than that—I want to win.

"We're good," Mykel says, sensing my nerves. "Don't worry."

I nod, though uneasily.

"I know it's not going to happen," he adds, "but part of me wishes Blade would end up in the bottom. He's a jerk, but he's also an incredible sorcerer."

At the sound of his name, I glance across the room. Blade sits with Rex and Nathan, their voices animated, while he seems distant. As if sensing my gaze, he looks up.

I quickly look away.

"Before I let you go," Alatar says, "I have a surprise. I've invited the winner of the last Silver Key Tournament to demonstrate and speak to you about the Sight."

Murmurs ripple through the room.

Alatar grins. "I'm pleased he could join us today. Elyon Casteel, everyone."

Elyon's presence commands the room as he steps onto the dais. A long black jacket drapes over his broad shoulders, accentuating his imposing stature as it flows behind him.

My conversation with Blade echoes in my mind as Elyon smirks at the crowd. Blade stiffens in his seat as applause erupts for his father. Mykel says nothing when he sees his uncle, only shifts uncomfortably.

"Thank you, Alatar," Elyon says. "Winning the Silver Key Tournament changed my life. The Sight is a gift granted solely to the victor—or to those deemed worthy. I was gifted the Sight of Strength. Let me show you what I can do."

Elyon closes his eyes. When he opens them again, they're no longer a cold, pale blue but a shimmering gold.

"As many of you know," he continues, "sorcerers possess the power to do things unimaginable to ordinary humans. With the Sight of Strength, I can amplify any spell. I can make magic last for hours—days, even. I can cause ten times the usual damage to an opponent. Any spell you can do, I can do much better."

Another man walks onto the dais carrying two pots—one ceramic blue, the other matte black—and places them on two stools beside one another.

"What the hell?" Mykel mutters. "That's my father."

"Did you know he was coming?" Lukas asks.

Mykel shakes his head.

I turn my attention back to the dais. Mykel's father is tall, with dark brown hair, just like Mykel.

"Mr. Griffin will now perform a standard plant-growing spell," Elyon says.

Mykel's father steps in front of the blue pot. "This pot contains soil and buried cherry blossom seeds." He places his hands on either side and murmurs, "*Cresco.*"

At first, nothing happens. Then a root bursts through the soil. It grows rapidly, branches spreading, pale pink blossoms blooming at their tips, until the tree stands about a metre tall.

"Thank you, Jakob," Elyon says.

Jakob nods and takes a seat beside Alatar and the other instructors.

Elyon moves to the black pot. "The spell you just witnessed accelerates the growth of a planted seed. This pot contains only soil—no seeds at all. With the Sight of Strength, I can create any plant using nothing but power and intent."

He places his hands on the pot, gold eyes fixed. "*Cresco.*"

In a matter of seconds, something peeks through the soil and surges upward. It grows fast, stretching higher and higher until it brushes the dining hall's ceiling. I crane my neck to see it properly.

It's a tree, similar to the one in the back garden, except its branches bloom with flowers of every colour instead of leaves. They move as if alive, reaching across the hall and hovering inches above our heads. Petals drift down like snow.

Lukas shields his plate of waffles as a few petals land in my hair—blue, green, pink, yellow.

It's beautiful.

My gaze sweeps the room, and Alatar comes into view. He's watching me. Our eyes meet, and he grins, nodding once in acknowledgment. I return the smile before looking away.

As quickly as Elyon created the tree, he destroys it. The petals shrivel, drying to black, and the branches retreat into the pot until nothing remains. With a snap of his fingers, the fallen petals vanish, leaving the dining hall spotless, as if none of it ever happened.

Applause erupts.

Blade is no longer sitting with Nathan and Rex. He must have left during the demonstration.

"Thank you," Elyon says, raising his voice above the noise. The room quiets. "I hope this motivates you to work as hard as you can. Any one of you could win this tournament, and the power that comes with it is like no other."

With that, Elyon exits the dais alongside Alatar and Mykel's father. Mykel stands and follows them.

"Well," Lukas says, "that was something."

"People shouldn't have that much power," Celie says. "Especially people like him."

I linger on her expression, noting the anger burning behind her eyes.

Blade didn't tell me much about his father, but what he did say was enough for me to conclude that Elyon is a terrible person. It seems unfair that he possesses that much power. It's also a little terrifying.

I finish my breakfast and try to get Elyon's face out of my head, so similar to Blade's, despite the wrinkles around his eyes and the sheer dominance of his demeanour.

Then I head to the practice rooms.

I've heard there's a door that leads to a place in the sky, above the clouds, where you can practice spells or simply exist in peace. Time moves slower there; hours inside amount to only about one outside.

I have to see it for myself.

When I step through the door, the sky steals my breath. Lavender melts into amethyst in a soft ombré, deepening as it stretches outward. A clear crescent moon hangs overhead, luminous against the purple sky. The stars are enormous, constellations close enough to touch, twinkling rose gold.

I inhale deeply, letting the soft wind brush my hair from my face.

It's the most magnificent sight I've ever seen.

When I glance down at the surface beneath me, panic flares, and I expect to fall straight through. Instead, my feet sink slightly into the soft white clouds stretching endlessly in every direction. Once I realize I'm safe, my body relaxes.

There's no sound. No scent beyond fresh air. But the quiet isn't empty—it's peaceful. And slowly, I let the worries crowding my mind drift away.

Then I remember why I came.

I clasp my hands. "*Cito.*"

Moments later, Halo is flying toward me in the purple sky, glowing. He lands right in front of me as the glow fades, and he sits obediently. Since I last saw him, he's grown to the size of a full-grown wolf.

I thought this would be a nice place to train with him, which I haven't had the chance to do yet. I've been told that training with your familiar is personal, especially for the first time, so I figured this would be the perfect place to do it.

I pet his soft fur, and he responds with an enthusiastic lick, wings flapping and tail wagging.

"Okay, Halo. Let's see what you can do."

Eager to show me his new skill, Halo launches into the air, circling once before firing two silver blasts of radiant energy from his eyes.

"Wow! Good boy!"

He howls proudly and lands again.

"Let's test your healing," I say, before using a spell to create a small cut across the palm of my hand. It stings as blood beads at the surface. It's only a minor injury, so it shouldn't be too difficult to heal.

Halo trots over, tail wagging, and places his paw against my hand, like he's doing a trick. He releases a low howl. When he lifts his paw, my skin is healed.

"Very good," I say, scratching his side.

We train for a while, practicing his healing powers and learning how to control his radiant blasts, and all I can think about is how lucky I am that he chose me.

Eventually, I lie back on the clouds, smiling as Halo soars overhead, howling at the moon. He lands beside me, pressing close, and I wrap an arm around him, kissing the top of his head. I giggle as he licks my nose.

"Can we stay here forever?"

He barks in response.

I sigh. "I know, I know…"

I talk to him for hours—about Blade, Mykel, my birth parents, everything. About how surreal it is that this is my life now. Studying magic, having a group of friends… lying on a bed of clouds with a winged wolf.

Before I know it, it's time for my lesson with Mrs. Patrickson. Halo gives me one more slobbery lick on the cheek before flying away.

"Aria, welcome back! How did the trial go?" Mrs. Patrickson asks as I step into her office.

"I think it went well!" I say, taking a seat. "I was nervous going into it, but you really prepared me."

She stacks a few papers on her desk and flips through her notes. "I'm so glad to hear that. What did you think of Elyon's demonstration today? Pretty cool, right?"

His face flashes through my mind, and I immediately miss the calm I felt on the clouds.

"Yeah," I say, though it sounds insincere even to my own ears. If Mrs. Patrickson notices, she doesn't comment.

"Today's lesson is on mimicry magic," she says. "Mimicry allows you to copy features and attributes from people or creatures onto yourself. Are you taking notes?"

"Yes, sorry," I say, opening my notebook and scribbling quickly.

"The more powerful the person or creature, the harder it is to mimic their attributes," she explains. "For example, copying the voice of an ordinary human may be simple, but mimicking any trait of a powerful demon would be nearly impossible. It's also much easier when the subject allows it. If they resist, you'll feel the strain."

"So how do I do it?"

"So eager, I love it," Mrs. Patrickson says with a smile. "See my eyes? I want you to copy them. Don't worry, you can change them back whenever you want. You have gorgeous eyes." She winks.

Mrs. Patrickson walks to the board and writes a single word in all caps: EXEMPLUM.

"This is the incantation," she says. "Focus on what you want to copy and say *'Exemplum'*, followed by the attribute. Look straight into my eyes and repeat it a few times."

I stand and do as she instructs, meeting her gaze. "*Exemplum eyes.*"

Nothing happens. Of course, it doesn't work the first time.

I try again, focusing harder, channelling the magic inside me. After several attempts—though I don't feel any different—Mrs. Patrickson steps back with a pleased expression.

I turn toward the mirror across the room.

My reflection stares back at me, eyes no longer emerald green, but a rich chestnut brown.

CHAPTER NINETEEN

I find Mykel sitting on the stairs, a book resting open in his hands. When he sees me approaching, his face lights up. He closes the book and stands.

"I was waiting for you," he says, brushing off the back of his pants.

When I reach him, his eyebrows furrow, and something in my chest swells.

His face really is perfect.

"Are your eyes brown?" he asks.

"Yeah," I say. "Mrs. Patrickson taught me about mimicry magic. She showed me how to change them back, but I thought I'd leave it for a bit."

"You'd look pretty with any coloured eyes..." He cringes and pinches the bridge of his nose.

"Smooth," I say, laughing. "So, you were waiting for me?"

He chuckles. "I was. Every time the tournament takes place, there's a ball after the first trial. It's sort of a tradition. They just announced it'll be happening in a few weeks." He runs a nervous finger along my arm, sending a wave of chills through me, then takes my hand. "I was wondering, Aria Knight, if you'd do me the pleasure of being my date."

He's asking me to be his date.

To a ball.

Mykel.

My heart feels like it might burst through my chest.

Jesus Christ, Aria. Stay calm.

He scratches the back of his neck. "I mean—like, as friends," he adds quickly. "It could be fun."

Oh.

The word lands heavily. *Friends.* My heart sinks, but I force my expression to stay light. "Right. Yeah. That sounds great."

His expression turns unreadable, and I hate that I don't know what he's thinking. An awkward pause stretches between us before he pastes on a dimpled grin.

We start up the stairs together.

"I'm gonna have the prettiest date there," he says. "Everyone's gonna be so jealous."

"Shut up," I say, heat rushing to my face. I'm very ready to change the subject. "So, did you talk to your dad?"

Mykel nods. "He said he was glad to see me, apologized for not giving me a heads up that he was coming, and then said something along the lines of, 'I expect you to be studying and training every second of every day so you can win the tournament.'"

"Nice," I say flatly.

"He means well."

We reach my dorm room, and Mykel sighs. "Okay. I've got a lesson to get to. I signed up for more optional classes to brush up on some stuff. My dad's idea. I'll see you later."

He flashes his signature smile, and butterflies erupt in my stomach. Even when he turns away, the feeling lingers.

He asked me to be his date to the ball.

Granted, as friends. But he still asked me.

To a ball.

Do I get to wear a fancy gown? Excitement sparks at the thought.

I can't say I even remotely understand where Mykel's head is at. I don't think I'm imagining the attraction between us, but something is holding him back. I just wish I knew what it was.

I sigh and open the door—

And this is definitely not my dorm room.

I'm standing in an open field. Darkness stretches in every direction, the sky thick with rolling grey clouds.

I know I didn't accidentally teleport myself here. *That tool is definitely not in my wheelhouse.* Someone must have done this. But *why*? Who?

Thunder roars overhead, making me jump. At least, I think it's thunder—until a massive, dragon-like silhouette glides through the clouds above.

A few feet away stands a cabin, a single light glowing inside. The wood is dark and weathered, brittle with age. I slip off my shoe and wedge it into the open door behind me, making sure I have a clear way back, then creep toward the cabin.

Voices drift from inside.

"—don't you understand?"

"I do, but—"

"Clearly, you don't appreciate the severity of this issue. We're not young like them. We grow weaker with each passing day. We need his power."

That voice. Deep and familiar. Rough and calculated with every word. It's a voice I've heard many times since arriving at Silver Key.

Alatar.

Another voice speaks. "But this is wrong. If we do this, we'll be endangering humanity. Humans without magic. People who can't defend themselves. And what about the kids? This is too dangerous."

Footsteps shuffle across the floor.

"We have to make sure they're prepared," Alatar says. "We need to test their strength, their ability to think on their feet. Otherwise, how will we know who's capable of succeeding?"

"I get that, but—"

"We're doing this for the kids," a third male voice says. "They'll thank us one day."

Silence settles before Alatar speaks again.

"They have to be the ones to do it. The third trial has to happen. We're not strong enough anymore to do it ourselves. End of discussion. And if I hear even a word of this spreading around the manor, there will be consequences. The fewer people who know, the better."

What the hell?

My heart slams against my ribs. I force myself to breathe quietly and edge closer to the window—but my foot crunches down on a pile of dried leaves.

"What was that?" one of the men asks.

I press myself against the wall beneath the windowsill and squeeze my eyes shut, willing my heartbeat to slow.

Footsteps approach.

I sense Alatar's presence. He's staring out the window, directly at the door, where my shoe is wedged.

I hold my breath.

"I have a feeling this conversation is no longer private," Alatar says.

His footsteps retreat.

I don't wait. I back away carefully, then turn and sprint through the door. I grab my shoe, slam the door shut—

And I'm standing in the hallway outside my dorm room.

"Aria?" Celie says, rushing toward me. "Are you okay?"

I stare at her, trying to process what just happened.

"Aria?"

"C-cabin... Alatar... he was—there was something—"

"Hey, slow down."

I run through the conversation in my head, trying to cling to every word.

"Let's go inside and talk," she says, reaching for the doorknob.

"No don't—"

The door opens to our dorm room, just as it was before.

We step inside, and Celie shuts the door. "What is going on?"

"I don't know how, but I was teleported to an abandoned cabin. I heard Alatar and two other men talking. One of them was trying to stop whatever they're planning—they said their magic is weaker now. That *we're* the only ones who can do it." My voice shakes. "Whatever *it* is… it's dangerous."

"Aria—"

"I think they were talking about us," I say. "I think they're planning to make us do something, and it could put everyone in danger."

"Are you sure it was Alatar?"

"One hundred percent."

But who were the other men? And what are they hiding?

"There's something seriously wrong going on here," I say.

Celie groans. "We cannot have a crisis right now. My schedule is already insane."

I try to laugh, but nothing comes out. The unease settles deep in my stomach. Whatever they were discussing in that cabin, it can't be good.

We meet Mykel and Lukas at our usual spot in the library and tell them everything.

"What?" Mykel says. "Aria, are you sure? My parents know Alatar. They trust him. They wouldn't let him put me in danger."

"I don't think many people know," I say. "The way he talked, it sounded like only a few are in on it."

"In on *what* exactly?" Lukas asks.

"I'm not sure. I only heard part of it, but it sounded like the trials are meant to prepare us for something. Something they're too weak to do themselves."

"That could explain why the trials are longer and more intense this year," Celie says. "They're training us to do something that is potentially very dangerous."

I nod. "That makes sense. I wish I'd heard more."

"No," Mykel says. "It's good you got out before they saw you."

"But how did you get there?" Celie asks. "Someone had to create that portal."

"I have no idea."

"We need to figure out what they're planning," Lukas says. "If it's bad, we can't just go along with it."

"Especially if it puts people in danger," Celie adds.

Mykel nods. "Okay. We gather information—*carefully*. They can't know we're suspicious, so act normal. And we don't tell *anyone* about this."

CHAPTER TWENTY

"A fate worse than death."

"They're burnt cupcakes, Lukas," Mykel says.

I glance down at the tragic, hard-as-rock cupcakes. "I thought you said it would be easy?"

"I *thought* it would be!" Celie says defensively.

Note to self: never trust Celie when she says a spell will be easy.

I just tried baking cupcakes using a fire spell and managed to burn the entire batch. I also exploded a blueberry muffin earlier, but I'd rather not think about that.

"Look, next time, try—"

"Oh, there will *not* be a next time," Lukas says. "I will not sacrifice any more food."

I bob my head in agreement. I just wanted to eat some cupcakes.

I defeatedly toss the burnt remains into the trash when a black-haired kid I recognize as Alaric bursts into the room.

"There's a challenge in the back garden!" he says before sprinting out, leaving us to follow.

What the hell is a challenge?

By the time we reach the garden, a crowd has formed, students packed into a tight circle, shouting at whatever's happening in the centre. We push our way forward, and though maybe I shouldn't be, I'm shocked to see Blade fighting Nathan.

I've only spoken to Nathan once before, and it was such a *lovely* conversation. Let's just say I'm not exactly upset to see him getting the shit beaten out of him.

"What's going on?" I ask to no one in particular.

"Blade challenged Nathan, and Nathan accepted," Sherry says, eyes locked on the fight. I hadn't even noticed she was beside me.

I turn to Celie. "Where are the teachers? Shouldn't they stop this?"

Nathan pins Blade to the ground, and I wince as he lands a punch to Blade's face. Blade barely reacts. A flash of light bursts between them as his spell throws Nathan off, followed by a surge of magic that slams Nathan into the dirt.

"They can't interfere," Celie says. "A magical challenge doesn't allow it. The fight ends when someone wins. Or if they call a truce."

"That's horrible!" I say. "So much could go wrong."

Mykel shrugs. "They know the risks."

Blade drives another punch into Nathan's face. Blood pours freely now, and one of Nathan's eyes is swollen shut. Blade has a few cuts and bruises but is clearly holding his own.

"Okay!" Nathan gasps. "Okay—you win!"

Blade smirks and steps away, leaving Nathan sprawled and panting on the ground. The crowd slowly disperses. A few students rush to Nathan's side. A teacher appears and orders a group of sorcerers to escort him to the medical wing.

Blade approaches us. "Enjoy the show?"

"Blade, that's enough," Celie says. The sharpness in her voice catches me off guard.

"Celie—"

"No. This isn't you."

Mykel scoffs, turning to Celie. "Are you really surprised? This is exactly something Blade would do."

"At last, Griffin, we agree," Blade says.

Celie exhales and storms off.

I watch her go, then turn back to Blade. "Why did you challenge him?"

"He threatened something important to me."

I narrow my eyes, trying to peel back the layers of his answer, but I don't push. Instead, I follow after Celie. I find her sitting on the floor by the manor entrance, her back against the wall. I slide down beside her.

"What was that about?" I ask.

She takes a shaky breath and wipes at her eye. "I'm sorry I never told you, Aria. I hate thinking about it. And I hate talking about it even more."

"Told me what?"

She sighs. "Blade and I used to be friends. When we were kids. Best friends."

Blade and Celie. Best friends.

"We were in all the same classes—"

"I thought you were a year older?" I say.

"I am. He was too advanced in magical studies, so they moved him up for those classes."

I roll my eyes. *Smartass.*

"We were inseparable," she continues. "Then he grew up. He built walls around himself and stopped letting anyone see who he really was. His father taught him to be tough. To show no weakness. He taught him it's better to be a bully than to be bullied. And we grew apart."

I've never heard Celie talk about Blade like this. And Blade has never talked about Celie. I try to picture a little Blade running around with a little Celie, and I simply can't.

"When he was young, he wanted to be friends with everyone," she says softly. "He was kind. A little reckless, sure. But what kid isn't?"

I smile despite myself, imagining tiny Blade causing chaos.

"I'll never forget the day we met," she says. "I was sitting alone at the playground, drawing circles in the sand. Lukas was sick that day. I guess Blade noticed because suddenly the sand started lifting, spiralling into the air. When it fell back into the sandbox, he was standing there."

She smiles at the memory.

I try to picture it—the laughter, the floating sand, a younger Blade. Was his hair the same silver-blond? Were his eyes the same shade of blue?

"Mykel has always hated Blade," Celie says. "But I know that good kid is still in there somewhere, even if Mykel doesn't see it. Blade isn't a bad person. He's just... misunderstood. Even by himself."

I don't know what to say. This means Celie knew Blade long before she knew Mykel, and I can't wrap my head around it.

"How do you go from being that close to barely acknowledging each other?" I say.

"He forced himself to change," she says bitterly. "He insulted everyone. Put on this tough-guy act. It's his father's fault." Her voice tightens. I've never seen her this angry.

"That's how he got the scar," she adds. "He mispronounced a spell during training. His father threw a glass at him from across the room. He was ten."

My chest aches at the image she's describing.

"His mom left when he was two. He's never known her. All he had was Elyon, filling his head with cruelty and fear." She pauses. "After we grew apart, I'd still see flashes of the old Blade. But eventually, this version of him took over. He let it."

I sit with her words, thinking not just about the Blade she knew, but the one I'm starting to know. And how uncomfortably similar they feel.

"I stopped trying to save him a long time ago," Celie says. "But seeing him fight Nathan... it hurt. It really hurt to see him like that."

Silence settles between us.

I almost tell her about my conversation with Blade but decide against it. He's only just begun to warm up to me. I wouldn't want to jeopardize the trust we're building.

It breaks my heart to see Celie upset, so I pull her to her feet and drag her back to our room. After an hour of talking and studying—because this *is* Celie—we're both feeling a little lighter.

Still, I can't stop thinking about Blade.

After a few uneventful days, I'm going to meet Mykel in his dorm room. Celie wants to talk to us about something, and I was told to get Mykel—*only* Mykel—and bring him to our room. This is suspicious, since Lukas was explicitly not invited.

When I arrive at Mykel's room, he isn't there, but Lukas is. He's lying on his bed, staring at the wall, and it looks like he's been that way for a while.

"Lukas? I was looking for Mykel. Do you know where he is?"

He jumps upright. "Oh, hey, Aria. No, I haven't seen him." He smiles, but not like he usually does. It's tight-lipped, forced. Not right.

"Are you okay?" I ask, sitting on the edge of his bed.

He lets out a deep breath and shakes his head.

"Hey, what's wrong?"

He hesitates, torn over whether to tell me. Finally, he says, "Ten years ago today... my parents died."

My heart drops to my stomach.

I'm not sure what to say, but my heart sinks a little further when I see the twisted expression on his face, conflict and heartbreak mixed together.

I move to place my hand over his but stop short, letting it rest on the bed a few inches away. "Do you want to talk about it?"

He puffs out a breath of air. "I feel like I don't talk about it enough."

But he doesn't continue. I let him take his time.

The room is dark, the blinds shielding us from the bright sunlight outside. A single candle flickers on his dresser, wax nearly melted away.

Lukas rubs his face. "I try not to think about it... them and that night. It all just gets pushed to the back of my mind. But that only makes days like this ten times harder."

I want to comfort him, but I'm not sure how. I shift closer and give him my full attention.

"I hardly even remember them... just bits and pieces of who they were. I was so young. But not having them gets really hard sometimes. I..." His voice falters.

We hear voices outside. Boys walking past, their chatter and laughter filling the hallway before fading.

"It was always the three of us," Lukas says. "We did everything together. I even slept in their bed most nights. I knew I was old enough to sleep in my own bed, and they tried to make me, but sometimes I'd get scared and crawl in with them. They'd be too tired to care."

I laugh quietly, but it's almost a sob.

"Sometimes they even brought me to work," he says, a small smile tugging at his lips. "I loved going to excavation sites with my dad."

The smile fades. "I was eight when it happened. I was asleep when I woke in the middle of the night, scared, so I went to their room. On the way, I heard a loud noise downstairs.

When I reached the living room... there were four men in long black cloaks, hoods shadowing their faces. Broken glass everywhere—they must have come through the window. They were looking for something... an ancient magical artifact my dad had discovered at work. He was so excited when he got home from work that day. I'll never forget the smile on his face. I don't remember exactly what it was, only that it was green, it made my dad really happy, and it's the reason my parents are dead."

He squeezes his eyes shut, inhales shakily. "My parents came down when they heard the noise. They saw the men... and then they saw me." He wraps his arms around himself, chin on his arm. "My mom grabbed me by the shoulders, tried to stay calm for me. She told me to go upstairs and hide. *Hide*... I mean, hide and seek was my favourite game when I was little, but it was strange being told to hide like that. I went anyway, under my bed."

He exhales. "I heard shouting, things breaking, a few screams... it felt like it was happening right in front of me. And then... nothing. I couldn't move. The sun came up and went down, and I stayed under the bed. Until Celie found me. Her parents were worried since they hadn't heard from us. She crawled under the bed, held me... begged her parents to let me stay with them. I've been living there ever since."

My eyes sting, but I don't let the tears fall. "Lukas..."

Since I've known him, Lukas has been vibrant, funny, always trying to make others smile. I realize maybe it's a way to lighten the weight of his grief, to mask the sadness. I want to tell him how sorry I am, how I wish he didn't have to go through that. Instead, I gently place my hand over his.

His eyes meet mine—pain and grief shine there, yes, but also gratitude. He's thankful for the friends he has. Friends who care. And for me, here, listening.

He chuckles lightly. "It feels oddly freeing to talk about this. Like a weight has lifted off my chest."

"You don't have to bottle things up. You're allowed to be sad." I keep my hand over his, and he rests his head on my shoulder. "You can be real with me, Celie, and Mykel. You know that, right?"

He's silent, then whispers, "Thank you."

He pulls away, walks to the window, opens the blinds. Sunlight floods the room.

"I should find Celie," he says. "She knows what day it is. I told her to give me space, but she's probably spiralling. You're right—I should be able to open up with you guys. I trust you. I know you won't like me any less just because I'm not cracking jokes."

I open my mouth to mention Celie's original reason for summoning Mykel and me, but instead say, "I love how close you and Celie are."

His smile warms the room. "She's like a sister to me. I love her more than anyone."

He walks out of his room. I stand, blow out the candle, and follow him.

"Is this really necessary?"

"Yes, it is. Come on," Mykel says.

Dancing is a skill I've always wished I had but never possessed. I tried classes as a kid, and all I got from them was embarrassment.

"I don't think you'll want me to be your date after this," I mutter.

Mykel smiles. "You can't be that bad. Besides, waltzing is easy. It doesn't have to be perfect. Just know the steps and follow the beat."

I can do that. I think.

The ball is only a few days away, and I was just informed that I would be waltzing at it.

Mykel positions my hand on his shoulder and places his hand on my waist. "It's mainly a simple box step," he says, taking my other hand in his. "Step forward with your left foot, then right, back, left."

I follow along. Forward, right, back, left. Maybe this won't be so embarrassing—

I trip over my own feet and step on his. He catches me against his chest.

"I'm so sorry," I say.

He laughs. "It's okay. That actually wasn't too bad... until you tripped."

I roll my eyes and step back—but he pulls me closer. My breath hitches as I look up at him. His expression is unreadable.

Don't pull away. Don't pull away.

"Should we go again?" he asks, stepping back.

I sigh in frustration, and he furrows his brows at me.

"What's happening here, Mykel?" I blurt, immediately regretting it.

He looks taken aback. "What do you mean?"

"You keep pulling away. I don't get it..."

He takes a step closer, but this time *I* back away.

"Aria—"

"No," I interrupt, shaking my head. "Shit. Sorry. I shouldn't have said anything."

I turn toward the door.

"Wait! Aria!"

I spin back to face him. "Just... pretend this conversation didn't happen. I'll see you later, Mykel."

I march through the door and don't look back.

CHAPTER TWENTY-ONE

My dress is perfect. It hugs my chest and midriff before flowing to the floor in a wave of pale pink. Silver and rose-gold roses form two thin straps, blooming across the top of the dress and branching down toward the middle. My dark hair falls over my shoulders in elegant waves.

Celie taught me how to use magic to transform one item into another, which is how my one and only floral dress became a ball gown. I'm certainly questioning why I'm learning this spell only now, considering I have seven outfits at the manor—but bottom line, I love this dress.

I've never been to a ball before. Boring high school dances are all I know. Walking into the ballroom, I'm struck by its beauty. It's unlike anything I've ever seen. The room where the first trial's party took place looks completely different now. White and silver Renaissance art covers the high, domed ceiling, and a massive crystal chandelier hangs above the dance floor. Silver glitter floats across the room, shimmering magically in the light. Round tables are scattered around the floor, each topped with ceramic vases of those violet, petunia-like flowers from the back garden.

From the balcony, everything looks so luxurious, and I feel so... out of place. Until Mykel's warm hand finds mine.

"Crazy, right?" he says.

"It's all so beautiful."

"It is beautiful," he says, already looking at me when I turn to him, a spark in his eyes. My cheeks warm as I smile.

Mykel is wearing a dark maroon suit with a white shirt and matching tie. The way it fits his body, showing off his arms and broad shoulders, makes me want to just stare. His wavy hair falls perfectly across his forehead.

"I'm sorry about the other day," I say.

"No, no. I'm sorry."

Linking my arm through his, we carefully descend the long marble staircase and cross the dance floor.

"Hello, Aria," Alatar says from behind me. We turn to face him. His black suit fits perfectly, and I tense at the sight of him.

Mykel notices and rests a hand on my arm.

"No sneakers tonight?" Alatar asks, nodding to my silver heels.

I freeze, then realize silence would be more suspicious. "They don't match the dress."

His eyes narrow slightly, a small smile forming. "You know, you look just like your mother."

I keep my gaze on him, saying nothing. He lets his smile widen. "Have a good night." And just like that, he walks away.

I exhale. "He knows."

Mykel squeezes my shoulder. "Did he see you at the cabin?"

I shake my head. "But he saw my shoe in the door. I wedged it to keep it open. I'm such an idiot."

"No, it's fine. Could've been anyone's shoe. Just don't wear them again."

I nod, not entirely convinced.

We join Celie and Lukas at a table. I bury my uneasy thoughts as we take our seats. Jakson, Clarity, and Sarah are also there.

"Hey Jakson," I say. "I never got to see you after the trial. How are you feeling?"

"I'm alright, thanks Aria. They fixed me up right away. The pain was agonizing."

"I'm glad you're okay," I say.

"Did you guys hear?" Sherry joins us, taking a seat next to Jakson. "Diana, Rex, and Jess got sent home." Her bright yellow gown compliments her dark skin beautifully.

"Grace and Dean too," Sarah says.

I don't know them well, but it must sting to be sent home. Still, I feel a thrill at being here. To know that my hard work is paying off. Whatever Alatar is planning, I need to make sure I'm here long enough to stop it, and that means making it to the third trial.

"I kind of feel bad," Jakson says. "You've seen the way weaker sorcerers are treated."

I frown and look at Mykel.

"Being a weak sorcerer doesn't get you far," Mykel explains. "Harder to get jobs, harder to make friends. Getting kicked out of the tournament will only set them back."

I hadn't realized how much power and status affect a sorcerer's life. It makes me realize that, outside of Silver Key, I know close to nothing about how the world of magic works.

"I'm sure they'll manage," Sarah says.

"Yeah," Celie agrees. "We're young. They can still go to school and improve."

The music echoing through the room fades, and people make their way to the centre of the ballroom with their partners.

"Looks like it's time for the dance," Celie says.

Mykel stands and offers me his hand. "Ready to kill it on the dance floor?"

I place my palm in his. "Ready as I'll ever be."

He leads me across the floor. Everyone is paired up, Blade included. He's with a girl I've never met, wearing black with his blazer unbuttoned, running a hand through his silver hair. For a moment, his striking eyes meet mine. He winks, then focuses back on his partner.

The live orchestra begins their piece. The sound of violin fills every inch of the ballroom, and I follow Mykel's steps to the best of my ability.

"You've been practicing," he says, impressed.

"I didn't want to mess up!"

What he doesn't know is that I dragged Celie to the empty ballroom every day last week to practice. I *may* have been a little insufferable, but Celie is a great dancer, and I think she was proud of my improvement in the end.

We dance at a steady pace, one of his hands resting at my waist, the other clasped in mine. My free hand rests on his shoulder.

"Are you having fun?" Mykel says. "I'm sure this is different from the dances you're used to."

"It is, but I like this better. Back home, high school dances are awful. We just talk and eat snacks the whole time. Once, Violet and I filled three plates with cookies and spent the night eating them, betting on who would dance with who."

"Who won?"

"That depends on who you ask. You'll have to meet Violet when the tournament is over. I think you guys would get along."

"Can't wait."

The orchestra continues to play. The music, so warm and refined, fills my ears. I take a second to admire my surroundings, the glitter floating in the air. "This is amazing. Magical—"

"Literally."

I chuckle, admiring the scene. "So elegant and old-school. I love it. Decorations, dresses... I wish we had dances like this back home."

"It just makes this moment even more special," Mykel says.

When it's time to switch partners, I get nervous.

Mykel smiles reassuringly. "Ready? I'm gonna spin you like we practiced."

I nod, and he twirls me out of his arms. I spin once, twice. This isn't so bad. *Yeah*, I'm worried I won't be able to dance as well with someone else. And *yeah*, it's possible they aren't good at dancing at all, and we both make giant fools out of ourselves because of how stupid we look trying to do the proper steps, but—

I slam directly into someone else's arms. Looking up, I stare into a pair of beautiful blue eyes. There's something so dangerous and exciting hidden in their depths. Time seems to slow as he gazes down at me. I'm hit with a wave of déjà vu as I recall the day we met.

Blade smirks. "Hey."

I can't speak.

Aria, this is where you respond.

But his hand is resting on my waist, and suddenly it's all I'm aware of. I lose track of the people around us, the music, the dance. Even the glitter floating through the air seems to move in slow motion. His warm hand on my waist is all my attention seems to focus on.

Snap out of it.

"Hey," I say.

The world comes back into focus, music blaring in my ears once again. Mykel is dancing with Celie, her gold ball gown flowing gracefully as she moves. They laugh as they dance in sync, and I try to look anywhere but Blade's eyes. That spot on my waist feels like it's on fire.

I shake that thought away, quickly getting back into the rhythm of the song.

"I went back to the room—" Blade starts.

"You what? By yourself?"

"Yes. Listen. I translated the wall. *If it is the truth you seek, it is the truth you shall find.* That's what the symbols mean. I think it's the password—what?"

If it is the truth you seek, it is the truth you shall find.

"I've heard that before. Well, read it."

"Where?"

"My jewellery box back home. It's engraved on the front. Could it be a coincidence?"

"Maybe. But we should find out."

"How? We're not allowed to go back home. Could I summon it?"

"No, the magic protecting the manor won't let you summon something from the outside."

"There's no way around it?" I ask.

"Not that I know of. Especially not when you're summoning something from the ordinary world."

"So, what do we do?"

"I may have an idea," he says. "But there's something else. We need an energy source. The door won't open with only the spoken password—I'm gonna spin you."

I do a clean twirl and place my hand back on his shoulder.

"What do you mean?"

"If we don't have something to draw energy from, something powerful, then just saying the password won't work."

"What kind of something are we talking about?"

"I was doing research, and there are these stones. They're emerald green and supposedly hold a lot of energy—I'm talking, like, more energy than the sun, which is why they're called energy stones. They're also pretty rare and difficult to find, *of course*," Blade says.

"Well... if they need this green stone to open the door, there must be one somewhere close."

He grins. "Exactly what I was thinking. It's something they would have to carry with them at all times. They wouldn't leave it lying around."

Green stone, green stone, green stone... Where have I seen a green stone?

Then it hits me.

"Alatar's ring," I say. "I remember... it has a green stone in it."

"That could be it."

"But we can't take it. He'll know it's missing."

"You're right," he says. "We have to switch partners again. Let's talk later."

Blade spins me again, and I'm back in Mykel's arms.

He grins down at me. "Missed me?"

"Of course," I say.

But whether it's the excitement in getting closer to finding out what's behind the silver door or the way Blade's hand felt on my waist, I'm not entirely sure it's the truth.

When the song ends, I excuse myself to the balcony. As soon as I step outside, I'm refreshed by the chilly breeze that hits my hot skin.

I grip the railing—and pause, genuinely taken aback by my line of sight. The balcony itself is stunning, with white and silver railings that shimmer in the moonlight and twist in an intricate design, but it's nothing compared to the view. It's dark, so I can't see much below me, but above... the night sky is beautiful. I've grown used to looking up at night and admiring how the stars scatter across the sky, how the moon seems to actually glow in the darkness. It's a view that I never tire of staring at. But tonight, the sky is even more striking. Indigo streaked with deep shades of purple and pink, like a painting come to life. I find myself unable to peel my gaze away.

That is, until someone joins me. I turn to find Sarah.

She smiles. "Hey, Aria. I needed some air. You alright?"

"I'm fine," I reply. "This view is insane."

"It is."

Sarah leans her arms on the railing of the balcony and looks out at the view. I do the same, and we stand in silence for a few moments, allowing ourselves to soak up the fresh air, the stillness—the sound of music and chatter that fills the ballroom muffled.

Breaking the quiet, I say, "I love your dress, by the way."

I really do. It's navy blue with thin straps, and it fits her form beautifully, hugging her body before flowing out at the waist.

"Thanks! I love yours, too." She looks like she wants to say more, but right before she speaks, she stops herself. Looking back at the view, she says, "You were great in the trial."

I chuckle. "It was pretty intense, right?"

"Yeah, but you held your own, even though you're so new to magic. It's inspiring."

I shake my head. "Honestly, I was terrified."

"We were all terrified, but you took charge. It was really cool."

A silence falls between us again as I take in her words. It feels good to be acknowledged like this after all the hard work I put into learning magic and preparing for the first trial. I may still be pretty far behind everyone else, but... I feel like I'm starting to catch up.

"I should get back to the ballroom," Sarah says. "You coming?"

"I think I'll stay out here a little longer. It was nice talking to you, Sarah."

She nods before walking away, and I turn my attention back to the sky.

Later that night, I'm sitting with Mykel at an empty table, watching Lukas and Celie go wild on the dance floor.

"Did they choreograph this?" I ask, barely able to contain my laughter.

Mykel laughs too. "They must have."

Eventually, they tire out and join us at our table, and we talk about their performance.

"Hey, that was impressive, you have to admit," Lukas says. "Did you see my backflip? Do you know how long it took me to perfect that?"

"Yeah, and what about my pirouette?" Celie adds.

"Your form was perfect. Both of you," I say.

The opening notes of a slow song echo across the ballroom.

"I'm gonna go get that hot guy over there to dance with me. I'd say wish me luck, but I don't need it," Lukas says, striding toward the other side of the room.

We watch him from afar. He says something, the guy laughs, and leans in closer. Lukas has definitely got game.

Seconds later, Alaric Grimm walks over and asks Celie to dance. I can't hide my excitement as she accepts, and they glide onto the dance floor together. Celie has had a little crush on Alaric for a while now.

"Aria, shall we?" Mykel says.

"Ye—"

"Knight, can we talk?" Blade interrupts. I hadn't even noticed him approach.

Mykel stands. "What do you want, Casteel?"

"Chill, asshole. I'm here to talk to Knight," Blade says.

"And why would you need to talk to Aria?"

"That's between me and her."

Mykel's face hardens with determination. "Blade, I don't care what you have to say to her. We're having a great time, and we don't need you ruining it." Then he turns to me. "Aria, let's go dance."

"Why don't you let Aria speak for herself?" Blade says. "You're always protecting her like she's some innocent little girl who can't take care of herself."

"I'm looking out for her—"

"I'm right here, you know?" I interrupt, standing.

"Aria, you know I just want to keep you safe, right?" Mykel says.

Blade laughs. "What, from *me*?"

"Yes. From *you*. I'm not sure if you've ever heard yourself speak, but you're not a good guy. I don't want whatever you need to talk to her about ruining her night."

"Mykel, it's okay."

"No, Aria, it's not," Mykel says.

"I can take care of myself. Blade won't pull anything, and if he does, I can handle him. I'll be right back, okay?"

Blade smirks, which makes Mykel's jaw clench before he lets out a frustrated sigh and sits back down.

"Let's go outside," Blade says.

I follow him out of the ballroom, and we sit by a large arched window.

"On a scale of one to ten, how badly do you want to kill me right now?" Blade says.

"I'm hovering somewhere in the high thirties."

"Look, about Mykel—"

"I don't want to talk about it," I cut him off.

"Okay. So those stones. I looked them up. There are only two places they can originate from: somewhere cold—like *freezing* cold—or underwater, deep in the ocean."

"So to get one, we'd either freeze to death or drown," I say.

"Pretty much, yeah."

I sigh. "So what do we do?"

"Tomorrow, we'll go to your house and see if your jewellery box is somehow connected to the manor. There's a fountain in the forest behind the back garden. Rumour has it there's a magic coin in the water that grants wishes. If you can find it, you can make a wish. It'll transport us to your house without notifying Alatar, giving us time to investigate."

"Okay, and what happens if we can't find the coin?"

"Plan B," he says.

"And what does Plan B entail?"

"Don't worry about it."

I narrow my eyes. "Yeah... I don't think I want to know."

Sitting back down with Mykel, I can tell he isn't happy.

"What was that about?" he asks.

"Nothing. It's not important."

"Seriously? You're not going to tell me what you were talking to Blade about?"

"I told him I wouldn't tell anyone, okay? I'm sorry. Can't you trust me?"

"Whatever, Aria," Mykel says, standing and walking away.

Celie and Lukas have clearly caught the end of the conversation, because they're now standing in front of me, looking awkward.

"I'll go talk to him," Lukas offers.

My face burns with anger. Why is Mykel so upset with me over this? I get that he and Blade don't get along, but seriously...

I'm allowed to talk to whoever I want. I don't know exactly what Mykel and I have, but it should've earned me some trust. The fact that he reacted like this only emphasizes the lack of it.

"Are you okay?" Celie asks softly.

"I don't have to tell him every single thing," I say. "He should be able to hear me and just trust me. Right?"

"Mykel gets really sensitive when it comes to Blade, Aria," Celie says.

"Should I talk to him? He's pissed."

"No, let him cool off."

I've noticed Mykel can be overprotective. Although I recognize he's doing it because he cares, I can't deny it gets on my nerves sometimes.

But *should* Mykel have a reason to be mad? Should I feel guilty for whatever feelings stirred in me when I was dancing with Blade?

No. It was nothing. He caught me off guard, that's all. If anything, my brain was just adjusting to the fact that I no longer hate Blade. I sort of... want to be his friend. Either way, Mykel had no right to be angry at me just for talking to him.

There may be something between Mykel and me. He may even have my loyalty—but he does not own me.

CHAPTER TWENTY-TWO

Standing in front of room 17 of the boys' dormitories, I take a deep breath and knock. Two seconds later, Blade opens the door. Shirtless.

"Hey, Knight. Gimme a sec."

I avert my gaze, hoping he doesn't notice the flush rising in my cheeks. When he turns around, I relax—until my eyes catch the silver key tattoo on his back. Bigger than mine, it rests on his middle back just below his neck. He grabs a T-shirt off his bed and pulls it over his head.

Mykel hasn't spoken to me since the ball. Guilt gnaws at me, but I promised Blade I wouldn't tell anyone about our little adventure. I like Blade—I genuinely want to be his friend. If Mykel knew that, would he ever forgive me for even thinking it? The fact that I'm here with Blade, and Mykel doesn't know, eats at me. I probably have "guilt" written all over my face as we make our way to the back garden.

"So... Mykel's still pissed?" Blade asks.

I nod. "He hasn't spoken to me."

"He can be immature and sensitive sometimes, but he'll get over it."

I let out a breath. "I'd rather not talk about Mykel with you."

I have a feeling whatever Blade has to say about Mykel's and my relationship will only make me feel worse.

"That's fair," he says, but if he senses my discomfort, he doesn't care because he continues anyway. "But if we *were* talking about Mykel, I would warn you that he can be possessive and competitive, and a dick. So watch out for that."

We walk outside. I shoot him a glare. "God, Blade, you are such an asshole."

He stops walking. "Knight... are you flirting with me?"

"I called you an *asshole*."

He smirks. "Maybe I'm into that. Or maybe... I just like seeing you blush."

I roll my eyes and hide my face. "Just keep walking."

It's early, and the back garden is empty except for us. The fresh air brushes my skin as the morning sun warms my face, and we make our way to the fountain, a little farther from the manor, through the woods.

When we arrive, I pause to admire it. Tall, elegant, crowned with a statue of Astalon Ellfire, founder of Silver Key. Water shoots from the sides of the statue into the clear pool below. Blade is already digging his hands into the fountain, searching for the coin.

When I peer into the fountain, I understand what Blade meant when he said this would be tricky. The bottom of the fountain is completely covered in coins.

"The one we're looking for is silver, with a symbol on it," Blade says. He grabs my hand, flips it palm-up, and drags his cold, wet finger across it, slowly tracing the symbol until it glows: two inverted triangles overlapping, encircled, with a tiny star inside.

Blade places his palm over mine before lifting it into the air, the rings on his fingers gleaming in the sunlight. The symbol is no longer on my hand but floating in the air in front of us. The star at the centre sparkles.

"For reference," he says.

I plunge my hand into the water, but the coins are slippery, and the water is painfully cold. I can only keep my hand submerged for a few seconds at a time.

"So... enjoying being a sorcerer?" Blade asks, breaking the silence.

"Right now? Not so much," I say. "But overall... yeah. I think I made the right choice by staying. I do miss home, though."

"Good thing you're visiting then."

"Yeah... When we go, um, you might see some things—or hear some things. I've changed a lot since Silver Key."

"What is that supposed to mean?"

"Well, I kind of used to be super uptight. I would never even consider breaking the rules. I wouldn't do anything without a well-thought-out plan first."

"What changed?"

"I guess I realized life is more fun when you take risks."

I can't believe I just said that.

"Finding out I'm a sorcerer and that magic is real... it kind of changed my perspective on life."

"Well, Knight, I'm looking forward to seeing a glimpse of the old you."

I catch his eye for a moment. The morning sun hits his face, making the blue of his eyes glisten. I look away, sticking my hand back into the water.

About an hour later, Blade and I are soaked. His shirt clings to his chest, my hair drips, and I'm sore from searching every inch of this stupid fountain.

Then Blade pulls a coin out, holding it up to the light. "Holy shit, I think I found it."

"Thank God," I say, shaking water from my arms.

"*Lautus*," Blade says, and in a second, he's perfectly clean and dry. I follow suit, grateful to no longer be drenched, though still sore.

He hands me the coin. "Make a wish."

"Wait... is this one of those things where I have to be careful, or it'll backfire?"

"No. Intention is key. Know what you mean, and the coin will understand. And make sure to mention that no one will notice we're gone. Otherwise, our tattoos will alert Alatar as soon as we leave the manor."

I hold the coin, close my eyes, and think clearly. "I wish for Blade and me to be at my home without anyone noticing we're gone."

When I open my eyes, I'm standing in my bedroom. I've missed it more than I realized, and just being here makes me feel safer than I have in a while.

Blade is sitting on my bed. My face heats instantly at the sudden realization that *Blade* is in my *bedroom*.

"Nice room." He smirks, picking up a stuffed teddy bear. I snatch it and shove it into my closet.

"How long do we have until the wish wears off?" I ask.

"About twenty minutes. We'd better get to it."

I walk over to my dresser and grab the brown wooden jewellery box. Engraved on the front are the words: *If it is the truth you seek, it is the truth you shall find.* I hand it to Blade, and he runs his thumb across the words.

"Where did you get it?" he says.

"Not sure. I've had it for as long as I can remember."

"Are your parents home? Maybe you could ask them."

It's Saturday, so they should be. But will they freak out if they see me? Since the last time I saw them, I learned I was adopted, discovered I'm a sorcerer, and got sort of romantically involved with a guy they've never even met—Mykel. Who's mad at me because of Blade and would probably never speak to me again if he knew I was here and who I was with.

"It should be in her room," my mom calls from the kitchen. Then footsteps approach—closer and closer.

I snap my head toward Blade, panicked. He just seems purely amused. "Should I hide?"

I want to wipe that smug grin off his perfectly chiseled face. Honestly, I'm more afraid of my parents finding me alone in my room with a boy than of them finding me here when I'm not supposed to be. It's funny to think about having typical teen problems, but before I can dwell on that thought—or do literally anything—the door to my room flies open.

And there stands Violet.

"Don't scream," I say.

"*Aria?* You scared the crap out of me!" she whisper-shouts, closing the door behind her. "Oh my goodness, I missed you so much!"

She tackles me in a hug, and I nearly lose my balance, but a huge grin spreads across my face.

"I missed you too," I say, inhaling her scent—flowery, sweet, and familiar.

She pulls back. "Your parents told me you went to a boarding school?"

I turn to Blade. Should I tell Violet the truth? I don't know if I can lie to her. She has an unhealthy obsession with all things fantasy, and part of me thinks she'd be kind of relieved—maybe even excited—to know magic is real and that I'm a sorcerer. On the other hand, my mind flashes back to my dream. If I tell her and she doesn't take it well... I'll be heartbroken. I don't want to lose her.

I search Blade's face for guidance. He shrugs. *Great help, asshole.*

"Violet, there's something I want to tell you," I say, sitting her down.

"Is it about this attractive man in your room?"

I literally facepalm. That's going straight to his head.

Sure enough, he winks at Violet, a devilish smirk spreading across his face. I ignore him and turn back to Violet.

"His name is Blade—"

Violet snorts. Blade narrows his eyes, pretending to be offended, though there's a glimmer of amusement in them. I glare at her, silently pleading for her to be quiet. She ignores me.

"Your name is Blade?"

"*Violet*," I scold.

She studies him for a moment, ignoring me. "It's kinda hot."

"Jesus Christ. As I was saying, it's about the boarding school. Well... it's not exactly a boarding school. It's a magic school, and there's a magic tournament I'm competing in... because I have magic."

"*What?*" she says. Blade stifles a laugh. "Are you messing with me?"

"She's not," Blade says. "Show her."

I ball my hand into a fist. "*Lumen.*" A bright orb of light hovers above my palm, illuminating the room.

"*Whoa*," Violet breathes, eyes wide.

I lower my hand, and the room dims. "Not messing with you."

Violet is quiet for a moment, processing the news. Then she says, "I *knew* magic is real."

Relief washes over me. "Somehow, I thought you might say that."

"This is so cool..." Her voice trails off, and then she punches me in the arm.

"Ow!"

"I like her," Blade murmurs.

"What was that for?" I ask.

"That was for not telling me sooner. Have you always known?"

"No. I found out the day I got pulled out of school."

"Still! You should've told me the second you found out!"

"I'm sorry!"

She sighs. "It's okay. Conveniently for you, this is way too cool for me to stay mad."

"I'm glad you know."

Blade steps between us. "Sorry to ruin the moment. Is there a bathroom close by? I'll be quiet."

"Down the hall to the left," I say.

He leaves my room, carefully closing the door behind him.

As soon as the door shuts, Violet squeals, "Oh. My. Goodness. Aria Amelia Knight!"

"What?"

"He's so hot! Please tell me you guys are dating."

Here we go.

"No, oh my gosh, shut up," I whisper. "We're not dating."

"But you want to."

"No. I mean—*No*. I don't. I can barely even tolerate him most of the time."

"Well, he sure as hell wants to."

"What makes you say that?" I ask, intrigued.

"The way he looks at you. And the sexual tension in the air. What's stopping you?"

I'm silent.

"There's no reason you wouldn't—unless... is there another boy you're not telling me about?"

More silence.

"No way. He better be hot if you're turning *him* down."

"His name is Mykel, and yes, he's very handsome, but we're not dating either. I mean... we kissed once, but we're not official. I think he likes me, and I like him, but he hasn't asked me out or anything. Unless you count the ball as a date, though he asked me to go as friends... I don't know. It feels good to talk to you about this."

"Okay, first of all—ball? And second, what happened to '*I don't do relationships, Violet. I don't have time for relationships, Violet*'?" she mocks.

I roll my eyes and shrug. "I guess I've changed."

Violet nods, processing, then says, "My best friend, *Aria freaking Knight*, is caught in a love triangle, and I didn't even know. The only thing that could make this juicier is if they were related."

Silence.

"*They're related?!*"

"Violet, be quiet! But yes. They're cousins. And they hate each other."

"You really are living the dream."

"It's not as great as it sounds."

"Right. Two attractive guys fighting over you. Must be terrible."

I roll my eyes and pace. "I'm serious. I like Mykel. A lot. I don't know how I feel about Blade."

"Go on."

"It's just... Mykel is sweet and romantic, and I know he cares about me. Blade is arrogant and was such a jerk when we first met. But now... I see there's more to him than that."

"I love a good morally grey bad boy."

"That doesn't sound healthy."

"It's probably not. Continue."

I flop onto my bed, resting my head on my pillow. "Actually liking Blade as a person is new to me. I hated him when we first met... and I think I just want to be his friend. But the more I talk to him, the more I second-guess myself. And I don't want to hurt Mykel's feelings. He's pissed at me as it is—which is another annoying, frustrating story—but... I really, really like Mykel."

I say it, and the realization hits like a slap to the face. Nobody's perfect. Everyone has that one thing. That thing they do that other people may not really like. Mykel's thing happens to be his overprotectiveness. But Mykel is pretty close to perfect. He's sweet, kind, and charming. He's smart, and makes me laugh. He always knows what to say, and when I'm with him, I feel good. No, great. He makes me feel *great*. He's everything I've ever wanted in a guy. So if I have to move past one small thing, which he only does *because* of how much he cares about me, I can do that. Mykel is incredible, and I'd be a complete dumbass to walk away.

"To me, it sounds like you know what you want," Violet says.

"Mykel," I say, and it feels so good to say aloud. "But if we both like each other, why hasn't he asked me out yet?"

"You think he's leading you on?"

"No. I don't think he would. I think it has something to do with Eliza."

"Eliza?"

"His ex," I say, sitting up.

"Do you think he still has feelings for her?"

"I don't know. Maybe."

Mykel acts weird whenever Eliza is around. Celie told me their breakup was hard on him. When I asked him before, he said he didn't have feelings anymore, and I believed him... but maybe he still does. That could explain why he's hesitant to jump into a relationship with me, why he keeps pulling away.

"But you're right, Violet. I do know what I want. I want Mykel. And I'm willing to fight for him."

"What are you going to do about Blade?"

"Blade and I are just friends. If you could even call us that. That's what we'll continue to be."

"You guys talking about me?" Blade's voice cuts in as he opens my door.

"No," I say way too fast.

"Well, I met your mom."

Wait—*what?*

CHAPTER TWENTY-THREE

"You *met* my *mom?*"

Blade opens the door further, and there she is. My mom. Her light hair is curled into perfect waves, and she's wearing a floral blouse and jeans. I remember going to the mall with her, helping her pick out that blouse. She tried it on, and I knew she had to have it, so I bought it for her as a Mother's Day gift.

She grins at me and, before I can react, pulls me into a tight hug.

"You didn't tell me you'd be visiting!"

"That's because I shouldn't be."

She pulls back. "You're breaking the rules?"

"That was my thought," Violet chimes in.

"Your daughter's become quite the rebel," Blade says, and I want to shove him out of the room.

"Also, Rebecca, I would've appreciated a heads-up on your magical daughter," Violet says.

My mom sighs. "I'm sorry we lied, Violet. We were told not to tell anyone."

Violet nods understandingly.

"We can't stay long," I say. "We actually came for a specific reason." I pick up the wooden jewellery box. "Where did I get this?"

My mom examines it. "Your birth mother, when she gave you to us. It was the only thing she left for you."

Amelia.

"She left this for me?"

My mom rubs my back soothingly. "I'm sorry we never told you, Aria."

"It's okay, Mom." I can't get into this with her without crying, and I definitely do not want to cry in front of Blade. "Do you know what this means?" I gesture to the engraving.

She reads it over. "It's something Amelia used to say. Sort of a catchphrase."

"Why would something she said be the password to the door?" I ask Blade. "Unless it's just a coincidence."

"Maybe she and Alatar were close? They competed in the same year."

"Um... someone want to fill me in?" Violet says.

"No time. Blade and I are only here temporarily."

Blade nods. "We'll disappear back to the manor any minute now."

"Already?" My mom says. "I hardly got to see you. Your dad and brother aren't even home."

"I wish I could see them, but we don't control when we go back. There's a time limit," I explain.

"Let me look at you," she says, grabbing my face in her hands. I glance at Blade and flush at his entertained grin. "Are you eating? You look like you've lost weight. Sleeping well? Eight hours a night?"

I pull away. "Mom, I'm fine."

"You know I worry." She turns to Blade. "Take care of her, will you?"

"You got it, Mrs. Knight."

She seems pleased enough by his response.

"The second trial is starting soon, so you may not hear from me for a while," I say.

"Okay." My mom squeezes my hand. "Please be careful."

Then, without a proper goodbye, Blade and I are once again standing in front of the fountain at Silver Key.

"That was fun," he says, lips twitching like he's holding back a grin.

"It was so embarrassing." No point in hiding it now.

"Knight, you had five notebook planners on your desk, a calendar on your wall, a to-do list on your bedside table... and why so many pens?" He laughs at my reaction, so hard his shoulders shake.

"Blade—"

"But I think my favourite part was the pink polka dot bra hanging on your chair."

Heat rushes to my face. I must've forgotten to put it away. And how was I supposed to know I'd be teleported to a magical mansion with zero time to tidy my room? Blade is clearly enjoying himself as we walk back to the manor.

"Violet seems fun. Is she single?"

I stop walking. "Touch her, and I will personally castrate you."

He gasps dramatically. "Knight, are you flirting with me again?"

"You are impossible," I mutter as we continue walking.

"One of my many great qualities."

"Hey, what did you and my mom talk about?"

"I think that's between Rebecca and me," he says, grinning as I watch him walk away.

I spend the rest of the week practicing spells with Celie and Lukas. Mykel has barely spoken to me, and I'm starting to think there's something else bothering him—or that Blade was right, and he's being incredibly immature about this. I'm sitting in the library alone when I spot Celie and Lukas striding toward me.

"Where have you guys been?" I ask.

"Eavesdropping on Alatar," Lukas says.

"*What?* Are you serious?"

"Yes," Celie says. "And we overheard something."

"You can't just sneak around eavesdropping on him. Do you know how dangerous that is? He's obviously up to something, and we have no clue what he's capable of. If he were to catch you—"

"Aria," Celie interrupts. "Just listen."

I swallow and nod.

"Okay, so we couldn't see who he was talking to, but he said something about secret evidence... proof of what 'he's' done," Lukas says.

"Who's *he*?"

"We don't know. And we didn't get a chance to find out what *he* did either, but the secret proof... it's hidden here, at the manor."

"Our hypothesis is that it's in that room Mrs. Patrickson showed us on the tour, the one she said is off-limits," Celie says.

So that's what's in there. Some sort of proof, evidence of something Alatar's hiding. Something bad.

"Wow," I say.

Celie sits down next to me. "Crazy, right? There's definitely something suspicious going on. We have to figure it out."

I bite my lip. *I have to tell Blade.*

But I can't. Celie, Mykel, Lukas, and I promised we wouldn't tell anyone what we've discovered about Alatar, not until we know exactly what it is.

"After the trial," I say. "We *will* get to the bottom of this. After the trial."

I'm a naturally anxious person. But I don't think I've ever felt this much anxiety in my entire life, and that's saying something.

Alatar's conversation in the cabin made it clear: this tournament could actually be dangerous, despite what we've been told. We have to be careful going into the second trial.

Like the first trial, we're given a uniform. Still all black, still sporting the Silver Key emblem on the top left corner, but this time, the fabric is thicker, stronger, like spandex but not. Probably some magical clothing material I've never heard of. The biggest change? It's a one-piece suit, tight against every curve of my body, plastered to my skin.

"You two are looking sexy," Lukas says as Celie and I reach room 113, where the trial begins. At least we're in the same groups as before, so I won't be alone.

"Doesn't she?" Celie says.

Lukas pretends to check us out. "Both of you."

I wink, and his hand flies to his chest over his heart. He stumbles back a step as if struck, and Celie and I burst out laughing.

The guys look good too. I almost lose my breath when Mykel walks over. Every curve of his toned shoulders, arms, and abs is outlined through the material. I had no idea he was this in shape. I've seen him working out a few times, but damn...

Then I remember. He's still mad at me.

I look up and notice his eyes roaming my body, just as mine did to his. Neither of us says anything, but when we make eye contact, we both smile. Maybe he isn't as angry as before.

"In this trial, your goal is to locate a magical pearl with your name engraved on it. The same rules as the previous trial apply," Alatar says.

No one has any last-minute questions, so Alatar opens the door, and we walk through.

I'm immediately alarmed by my surroundings.

The scent of seawater hits me first. We're on a tiny rock in the middle of the ocean. Even shoulder to shoulder, the rock barely fits all of us. Waves crash below, and wind whips against our faces. Dolphins leap gracefully in the distance. There's not a speck of land in sight.

"We're gonna have to go in, aren't we," Lukas says.

"I don't see what other option—" I begin, but Kara interrupts.

"There could be anything in there! I don't like this. I really, really don't like this."

"Wait, look!" Celie says.

I follow her finger as she points at something moving in the water near the dolphins.

"What is that?" I squint.

Mykel steps forward. "I think it's a mermaid."

"Oh my gosh, I can't do this," Kara says.

Sarah places a hand on her shoulder. "Kara, you'll be fine."

"I'm terrified of the ocean! You know that!"

"Well, I'm going in," Blade says. "If we can get to the mermaid, maybe she can help us." He perches at the rock's edge and jumps. "Fuck, that's cold."

"So we're doing this?" I ask Celie, Mykel, and Lukas. They nod hesitantly, and we follow Blade into the water, a few people hopping in after us.

As soon as I'm in, I'm convinced it was a terrible idea. The water is so cold it hurts. Our uniform seems to help a bit, but not nearly enough. The water rests below my chin, and I tread water to stay afloat. The mermaid isn't too far away. Hopefully, we don't have to stay in this freezing water for long.

"I don't know if I can do this," I say, gasping against the cold.

"We have to," Mykel says, grabbing my hand. "It'll be quick. If it gets too much, swim back."

I nod. Then he says softly, "I'm sorry I overreacted."

"I'm sorry too. I know how you feel about Blade, and I can see how what I did might strike a nerve."

"Wow," Lukas says. "First fight didn't last long, huh, love-birds?"

Mykel rolls his eyes, a hint of a smile on his lips.

We swim toward the mermaid, teeth chattering, bodies shivering.

"The water's too cold. We'll get hypothermia if we stay much longer," Celie says. "Depending on the temperature, it can happen within minutes."

"*What?* Why didn't you mention this before?" I say.

"Come on, guys, it's not *that* cold," Lukas says through shivers, lips turning purple.

Celie stares at him. "We're going to freeze to death."

"No, we're not," Blade calls from farther out.

"Do you see her?" I shout.

He doesn't answer, so we pick up speed and reach him. That's when I see her. She's a few metres away, swimming closer. Her long blue and green tail splashes in and out of the water, glistening despite the lack of sunlight.

"Hello. My name is Amatheia," she says when she reaches us. Her voice is smooth and enchanting, and I notice her bra made of shells is also a bluish-green, matching her tail. Her wine-red hair falls off her bare shoulders in waves and reaches her waist. She has deep green eyes and smooth, flawless skin that sparkles. "You must be the sorcerers. We were told to expect you."

"Can you help us?" I ask, teeth chattering. "We need to find these magical pearls for our trial."

"I cannot aid you directly," Amatheia says. "But I can lead you to our home, Atlantis, if you wish."

Atlantis? As in, way down there in the ocean where I won't be able to breathe?

"As you are creatures of the land, you must find a way to join me safely. You must each make a decision on your own about how that will be done. If you are ready, I will lead you away one by one."

Think, Aria. I need a spell that allows me to breathe under-water.

I don't know any spells like that!

I panic as Amatheia brings Eliza out further into the water. Eliza utters some sort of incantation and submerges into the ocean. She doesn't come back up. Celie gives me an encouraging look.

One at a time, Amatheia leads my friends away. They say their spell and disappear under the water, until it's just Blade and me. He looks at me, eyes trying to tell me what to do.

That's when it hits me.

Amatheia takes Blade away, and I practice the incantation in my head.

"Are you ready?" she says to me.

"I think so." I place my hands on her shoulders and concentrate hard on what I want. *"Exemplum abilities."*

"A mimicry spell. Excellent."

Taking a deep breath, I submerge under the water and—

I can breathe.

I can breathe as easily as I can above water. My lungs feel normal. My eyes don't sting. I'm no longer freezing. I swim forward, and it's effortless, as natural as walking. The water feels like air on my skin, and the smell... it's an overpowering scent of seaweed and fish, and I can't move past the strangeness of this entire situation.

"Aria!" Mykel calls, and I hear him perfectly.

I follow his voice, meeting up with Celie, Mykel, and Lukas.

"That was stressful," I say.

I just spoke. Underwater.

Celie smiles. "I knew you could do it."

Lukas rests a hand on my shoulder. "I had very little faith in you, Aria. Not gonna lie."

"*Thanks,*" I say. "This spell won't wear off, right?"

It would be quite tragic if I was at the bottom of the ocean and suddenly found I couldn't breathe.

"No. Mimicry spells never just wear off. You need an anti-spell to remove them," Celie says.

Like Mrs. Patrickson taught me during our lesson on mimicry magic.

I exhale, bubbles clouding my view.

This is going to take some getting used to.

CHAPTER TWENTY-FOUR

"Everyone, follow me!" Amatheia says.

Most of us used some sort of mimicry spell to breathe underwater, though a few now sport actual mermaid tails or gills along their necks. We swim for a long time, descending deeper and deeper into the ocean. The light fades the farther we go, but luminescent fish and glowing algae swirl around us, casting an eerie glow. Mermaids sing as they swim, their voices enchanting and enticing. Schools of fish dart past—some small and delicate, others large and spiked. A shark glides by, and I tense, but it pays us no mind.

Somewhere along the journey to Atlantis, two other mermaids join us.

"Sorcerers, this is Sirena," Amatheia says, gesturing to the mermaid on her right. "And this is Nadia." The other mermaid gives us a small wave.

"We are pleased to accompany you," Sirena says. Her long blond hair is tied back in a high ponytail with a strand of seaweed.

My eyes drift to their tails. I worry they'll catch me staring, but I'm too fascinated to look away. The way they move... Each tail is long and powerful, tapering into smooth, curved fins. Scales shimmer in perfect patterns, the colours so vibrant they could probably be seen from miles away. They move with effortless grace, each flick strong enough to propel them forward at a startling speed. Sirena's tail is periwinkle purple, the tips of her fins more pointed than Amatheia's and Nadia's. Nadia's tail is a soft pink that matches her hair.

"Is there anything we should watch out for down here?" Mykel asks.

"Sirens, as you may be aware, are quite dangerous," Sirena replies. "Other marine life can also pose a threat. Most do not enter Atlantis, though some occasionally stray inside. There are warning signs near hazardous areas; those places are off-limits. Outside of Atlantis, however, you are fair game."

"Sirena, do not frighten them," Amatheia says.

"I am only warning them. These waters are not entirely safe. Caution is wise."

Nadia runs a hand through her hair. "You may also come across empty caves and abandoned ruins. You never know what might be hiding inside, so be careful."

Fantastic.

Not only do we have to find our own magical pearls, but we also have to avoid killer sirens and whatever else lurks down here. Between this conversation, Alatar's secretive plans, and the possibility of facing real danger during the trials, unease coils in my chest.

We continue descending until we reach the ocean floor. Pebbles and rocks scatter across the seabed, tangled with clusters of red algae. A low hum fills the water, accompanied by distant, echoing calls of marine life. We pass coral reefs and shadowed caves, along with giant clams I deliberately avoid. A long, dark tunnel yawns to my left, and I quickly swim past it.

"We have arrived!" Amatheia calls, surging ahead. "Before we enter Atlantis, I must warn you—it is quite large. It was once even larger, but much of our land has been lost over the years."

We pass through into a bustling underwater city filled with merpeople. Shops carved into coral and stone display seashell necklaces and gleaming trinkets. I feel like a tourist entering a city I've only heard about in stories, with Amatheia as our trusted guide. Vibrant lights shimmer from buildings and hanging decorations. Neon jellyfish—pink, green, blue, and purple—float above us, illuminating the streets and enhancing the city's lively glow.

We turn down a quieter stretch where the chatter fades to a distant murmur. Small coves line the streets, serving as cozy homes. Once we leave that district, the noise swells again. Mermaids and mermen, fish, dolphins, and marine life of all sorts weave through the currents around us.

"Lukas, is that your familiar?" Celie asks, pointing to a dolphin-like creature swimming toward us.

"Dot!" Lukas calls.

The dolphin nudges up against Lukas and squeals in excitement. His smooth, rubbery skin is violet, and where his fin and flippers should be, tiny white feathered wings flutter. He's adorable in a slightly goofy way. He bumps into Mykel next, who laughs and pats his head. After greeting Celie, Dot swims over to me and rubs against my neck. A surge of warmth floods through me, as if his touch carries pure joy.

"I think he likes you, Aria," Lukas says.

Amatheia, Sirena, and Nadia slow to a stop and turn to face us.

"We will now take you to King Neptune, ruler of Atlantis," Amatheia says.

"Wait—King Neptune as in the literal god of the sea?" I ask.

Amatheia smiles. "Not quite, though he is named after him. The King Neptune I speak of is no god. He rules Atlantis, and Atlantis alone."

I exhale, relieved, but the thought of meeting King Neptune still makes my stomach twist. I glance at Celie and find comfort in seeing she's just as nervous as I am.

Dot swims beside us, staying close to Lukas as we follow Amatheia down a well-guarded path. We reach a tall fence, and Amatheia speaks briefly with one of the mermen guards on duty. After a moment, he swims aside to let us pass.

"Welcome to the palace," Amatheia announces as we enter.

It isn't small like the caves we passed on the way. The palace is enormous—like an underwater cathedral. Massive columns frame the entrance; some roofs are pointed, others domed. Inside, the space stretches higher and wider than I expected. Ornate decorations line the walls, and stone statues of mermaids and mermen, each holding a trident and wearing a crown, stand scattered throughout the room.

A throne sits atop a towering rock in the centre. Someone who I can only assume is King Neptune sits there, a long trident in his right hand.

We swim closer, and I get a proper look at him. His dark grey hair, almost the same shade as his eyes, flows behind him in the water beneath a gold crown. He wears no shirt, revealing a well-defined chest, and his tail shimmers navy blue. He exudes confidence—back straight, chin high—as if he were born to rule.

Two mermen guards float on either side of him, tall and proud, each wielding a trident of their own, though smaller than the one in King Neptune's grip.

One steps forward. "You are in the presence of King Tiberius Orwell Caspian Neptune, ruler and mighty king of Atlantis, 300th grandson of King Neptune, god of the sea, and second son of Queen Cordelia and King Caspian III."

I swallow. *That has to be the longest title I've ever heard.*

"I think I'll stick with Neptune," Blade mutters behind me. I'm equally as tempted to agree as I am to elbow him in the side—this merman is clearly a big deal—but thankfully, King Neptune doesn't seem to hear.

"Welcome to Atlantis," the king says, his deep voice booming. "It is a pleasure to meet you all. I hope your stay here is enjoyable."

A wide grin softens his features as we all thank him, and suddenly, he doesn't feel quite as intimidating.

My eyes drift to his golden trident, mainly to admire how beautiful it is. And then I see it—an emerald stone embedded in the trident right where three pointed prongs fan out from the shaft.

"As this is a trial, neither I nor the merfolk may aid you in your quest. I will, however, advise caution. The Undersea can be dangerous, even here, despite our security," King Neptune says.

"Are there rules we must follow while we're here?" Celie asks.

He smiles. "Yes. Though sometimes, to find what you are seeking, you must break the rules." His gaze lingers on me for a moment before he turns to the group. "Food is available in the next room. Please help yourselves. Good luck."

We disperse, but I stick close to Celie, Mykel, and Lukas.

Celie looks lost in thought. I tap her shoulder. "You okay?"

"Yeah," she says, voice quiet. "Just thinking about what King Neptune said."

I nod, still hung up on his words as well. *Sometimes, to find what you are seeking, you must break the rules.*

"I'm starving," Lukas announces, yanking me from my thoughts.

Curious, we follow him to the next room. Two long tables hold a buffet of dishes. I wouldn't call any of it *appetizing*, but it's there.

"How many days can we survive without food?" Lukas asks, staring at the spread as if it has personally offended him.

"Technically, if only food is deprived, people can survive weeks depending on several factors such as age and weight," Celie says.

Raw fish, scales intact, fill several bowls. Other dishes contain strange sea creatures with long, thin, slimy tentacles. I peer into a nearby bowl and relax briefly, mistaking its contents for pasta—then remember merpeople probably don't eat pasta.

The tentacles.

"Is there a vegan option?" Celie asks.

Mykel, visibly disturbed by the main offerings, points to another table piled high with many kinds of seaweed.

"I guess that's slightly more appetizing," I say, then watch a merman bite the head off a fish like it's a hotdog and nearly gag. "On second thought... I've lost my appetite. Forever."

We exit the dining room and follow a sign that says "Lodging," the arrow pointing up a set of stairs. Swimming upward, we reach a landing. Three rooms line the floor, each guarded by a pair of mermen. The door at the end reads, "King Neptune: Office."

One of the guards sizes us up. "Are you here to speak with His Majesty?"

"Um, no," Celie says.

"Entrance is not permitted," he replies, clearly unamused.

Mykel swims forward. "We're looking for the spare rooms. We're here for the Silver Key Tournament."

"One floor up. Do you have proper payment?"

"Um... how much?" I ask.

"Four hundred erchings per night."

My eyes widen. "You're serious?"

The merman stifles a smile. "Quite."

"We don't have any... erchings," Celie says.

"Then you must find somewhere else to stay."

We leave Neptune's palace and surface onto the busy streets of Atlantis. Merchants are selling all sorts of food, trinkets, and services, while shoppers swim in every direction.

Celie pulls her hair over her right shoulder and smooths it out. "We should find somewhere safe to sleep before doing anything else."

"Good idea," Mykel agrees. "But I have a feeling we're not going to find anywhere that'll let us stay for free."

"True," I say.

"Guys, hear me out," Lukas whispers, leaning in. "We steal."

"Lukas!" Celie scolds, smacking his arm.

"What? He did tell us to break the rules!"

"We are *not* stealing!"

Lukas frowns, rubbing his arm, and we swim off to explore the area. Blade is nearby with Nathan and a few others I've never spoken to. I need to tell him about the stone. King Neptune seems... approachable. Maybe he wouldn't mind giving it to us?

"Should we split up?" I ask.

"I don't see why not," Celie says. "It should be safe if we stay near this area. The sooner we find somewhere to sleep, the sooner we can plan how to search for our pearls."

"Okay, let's meet back here in a bit," Mykel says.

We all agree and turn in different directions. I swim over to Blade.

"Hey, can we talk for a sec?"

Nathan scowls. "What does *she* want?"

"Are you and Mykel fighting? Now you wanna come crying to Blade?" another guy jeers.

"Shut up, guys," Blade says. They fall silent instantly. "Of course we can talk. Let's go."

Blade and I swim off to the side.

"King Neptune," I say. "Did you see his trident?"

"Yeah, what about it—"

"There's a green stone on it. Like the one you described. It looks exactly like the one Alatar has in his ring."

"Seriously?" he says.

"I mean, it makes sense. Underwater? That was one place they originate from, right?"

"Yeah. So... do we ask him for it?"

"I don't know. I guess we have to try. But not now. Let's focus on completing the trial first. Then, before we leave, we ask him."

"Sounds like a plan." He smirks. "I like this. Us working together."

"Yeah... I think I do too."

I swim around but can't find a place for the four of us to stay. Every cave I enter is already occupied by a family of merfolk who aren't willing to let us crash for the duration of the trial. Frustrated, I swim back to our meeting spot.

"You guys find anything?" I ask.

"I did," Mykel says.

We glide to a quieter part of Atlantis and slip into a cave. It's small—more like a deep crack in the wall—but it'll do for now.

"Guys?" Celie breaks the silence. "What do you think Alatar is planning? I know we're supposed to focus on the trial, but I can't stop worrying about it."

"I feel the same way," I admit.

Since the day I teleported to that abandoned cabin and overheard Alatar's conversation—how I managed that still baffles me—I haven't been able to shake this bad feeling. Something big is coming... and it won't be good.

CHAPTER TWENTY-FIVE

"So, ready to go pearl hunting, ladies and Mykel?" Lukas asks the next morning.

How he has any energy is astonishing. Last night was terrible. I'd never thought about what sleeping underwater would be like, but now I know—it's awful. Every time I got comfortable, the current dragged me away. When I finally dozed off, I woke up on the other side of Atlantis and spent far too long finding my way back to that crack in the wall. Celie had tied a long piece of seaweed around her wrist, anchoring herself to a thick rock to stop herself from drifting. Lukas and Mykel were nowhere in sight.

"Let's do this!" Celie exclaims, her good night's sleep evident in her excitement.

Mykel and I yawn.

We leave our little cave and swim through Atlantis. It must be early; there are hardly any merpeople bustling around yet.

Before bed last night, we hadn't come up with a strategy for finding the pearls, too preoccupied with our living situation.

"We could try summoning them?" I suggest.

"We could," Celie says, "but I don't think it'll work. We don't even know what the pearls look like. Summoning blindly is difficult."

We try anyway. As expected, nothing happens. Wherever the pearls are, they're going to be well hidden, probably in a place designed to challenge us.

We swim for a while, peeking in dark spaces and empty corners. We even ask around to see if anyone could point us in the right direction, but everyone says they can't help us.

Then we stop at a flower shop. The space is lovely, filled with bouquets of plants I've never seen, artfully displayed on wooden shelves. One catches my eye: a cluster of light pink flowers with round, glowing petals.

"What are these?" I ask, pointing to the bouquet.

"Opinias," the mermaid replies. "They represent trust and connection."

"They're beautiful," I say.

She nods, a friendly smile on her flawless face.

Celie floats next to me. "Would you happen to know of any hidden places in Atlantis? Areas where we might find a specific item we're searching for?"

The mermaid thinks for a moment, then leans closer. In a hushed tone, she says, "There is a place called Beliren on the outskirts of Atlantis. Few know of it, but there is treasure there if you know where to look."

I turn to Celie, considering her words.

She continues, "It's dangerous and forbidden. If you go, be extremely careful."

"Thank you," Mykel says. "How do we get there?"

The mermaid gives us directions, and we thank her again before swimming a few feet away.

"It's probably going to take a while to get there. We should get moving," I say.

Celie nods. "And we'll have to be really careful."

We've been warned that the outskirts of the city are less heavily guarded and more dangerous, but this lead seems too good to pass up.

Lukas waves off our concern. "We'll be fine."

Celie shakes her head, muttering something about him being the reason we get eaten by a giant shark. I stop paying attention when I realize Mykel is missing.

"Hey, where'd Mykel go—" I start.

"Aria," he says, swimming up behind me.

"Where were you…"

He holds out his hand, and I lose my train of thought. He's holding a single opinia flower, a shy smile on his face.

"For me?"

He chuckles. "Of course, for you."

Warmth blooms in my chest. I grin, noticing the faint blush on his cheeks.

"How did you even pay for this?"

"I didn't. She gave it to me when I explained our situation."

"I love it."

He places the flower in my hair, and it latches in place.

"You guys are adorable," Celie says, just as Lukas blurts, "You guys are disgusting."

Mykel and I roll our eyes in unison, and we set off on our journey to Beliren.

It takes hours of swimming before we arrive. This place is dead compared to the busy streets near the palace and the entrance to Atlantis. A few merfolk sleep in the streets, scattered along sidewalks and down dark alleyways, but otherwise, there's no one here. The plants growing from the ground are withered and grey. Even the water feels off—more grey-brown than the bright blue of the city.

We swim through the area, lit only by a few dim orbs of light, until a large cave comes into view. Before we reach it, we spot a sign that says, "*Danger. Do not enter.*"

"We should probably turn around," I say.

But Celie stops us. "Wait."

"What is it?" Mykel asks.

"I can't stop thinking about what King Neptune said yesterday about breaking the rules," she says. "Maybe the pearls are hidden somewhere and we have to go against the rules to find them."

I nod. "That makes sense. Since we met Amatheia yesterday, we've been warned about the dangers we might face. We've been told to avoid certain places. Maybe those are exactly the places we need to check for the pearls."

"Okay," Mykel says. "Let's stick close together."

We link arms and enter the cave.

"This looks ominous enough," Lukas mutters.

It's dark—so dark that I can barely see my hand in front of me.

"*Lumen,*" Mykel says, and a bright orb of light hovers above his hand. He gives it a soft push, and it floats forward. Celie, Lukas, and I follow his lead, and soon the cave is shining so brightly, it's hard to believe we're this deep in the ocean.

The cave is tall, with the roof many metres above us, but otherwise, it's empty. Just a few plants and scattered rocks. Circular holes puncture the walls like windows.

"Over there," Celie points. "Another entrance."

I shrug. "Let's go."

We swim toward the entrance when a loud sound startles us. I turn—

And a giant octopus tentacle shoots through one of the holes in the wall. Slimy, dark purple, almost black, and unnaturally long. It reaches for something—

Scratch that. It's reaching for *us*.

"What the hell?" Mykel says.

Then more tentacles appear. First three, then seven, then at least fifteen, darting in every direction. I lose my grip on Mykel, then Lukas. I thrash, trying to swim away, but they're everywhere.

"Guys! Get to that entrance! It won't reach there!" Mykel shouts.

Lukas swears to my left. Celie screams. Mykel calls my name desperately, but their voices are getting farther and farther away. I think I hear them shouting a spell. There's a loud squeal, but the tentacles don't retract. I feel a tight pressure against my waist. Looking down, I find a thick tentacle wrapped around me.

I'm caught.

"Can you see her?" Celie yells.

"No, I can't! *Shit!*" Mykel says.

"Mykel, watch out!" That was Lukas.

I can't tell what's happening. Tentacles circle my limbs, constricting one by one.

"Aria! Send up a flare!" Celie shouts.

"No!" I shout back. I need to think. *I can get out of this.* "You guys have to go!"

"We're not leaving you!" Mykel says.

"Get through the entrance! I'll be fine!"

A tentacle tightens around my chest. I'm being pulled in every direction, like this *thing* is trying to rip me apart.

"Let's go! She said she's got this!" Lukas says.

I catch a glimpse of them struggling. Mykel is attacking the tentacles, but it's useless. "There are too many! I cut one down, and another takes its place!"

"Come on, Mykel! If you don't move, you'll get caught too! Think!" Celie says as she and Lukas drag him toward safety. He swears in frustration, letting them pull him away.

It's up to me now. I have to do this, but I can't *think*. It's getting harder and harder to breathe. My mind is blank. I try to summon a weapon, but I can't think straight. I can't concentrate. I'm grabbing at the tentacles. Hitting them as hard as I can, digging my nails into them, kicking, trying to squirm free, but nothing is working. *Nothing is working.*

Then I hear it—my name. Someone's calling me, but I can't see where it's coming from.

Did Mykel come back for me?

The octopus-like creature lets out a piercing squeal, and its tentacles loosen around me. I twist and kick until I'm free, the slick limbs retracting into the walls

My breathing comes in uneven bursts, refusing to steady. I press a hand to my chest and feel it—the sharp rise and fall, the frantic pounding of my heart.

"Aria, are you alright? Can you breathe? Are you hurt?"

It's Blade.

Concern floods his face as he grips my shoulder, scanning me for injuries.

"I-I'm okay," I say. "What are you doing here?"

"I was swimming nearby when I saw a giant octopus circling the cave. Then I heard shouting—and I saw you." His jaw tightens. "I hit it from behind with a sleep spell. It swam off. It's probably unconscious somewhere."

"Thank you," I whisper.

We're hovering in the middle of a dark cave where I nearly died. My body is still trembling, but as I look at Blade, something inside me eases. Before I can second-guess myself, I throw my arms around him.

He stiffens in surprise as I press against him, my arms sliding around his waist. A second later, he hugs me back. His arms are strong and steady, his warmth grounding me. I cling tighter, burying my face in his chest, praying he can't feel how violently my heart is racing.

After a moment, Blade gently pulls away and grabs hold of my hand. "I'm glad you're okay."

His gaze flicks to the flower in my hair before returning to my face.

"Were you actually that worried about me?" I tease, trying to cut through the thick tension.

He studies me, his eyes a blue ocean of uncertainty. He opens his mouth, hesitates, then exhales. Finally, he says, "Look... I care about you, Knight. I don't know when it happened—when I started feeling this way." He shakes his head slightly. "That night, I was a mess. I'm glad it was you who found me. What I told you... you were patient. You didn't push." He closes his eyes briefly. "I don't even know what I'm saying."

When he looks at me again, there's no uncertainty left. "You're important to me. I need you to know that. I would never let anything—or anyone—hurt you."

"Blade... I don't know what to say—"

"You don't have to say anything. I just want you to know."

Mykel calls my name before I can respond. Blade releases my hand as Mykel, Celie, and Lukas swim toward us.

"What the hell are you doing here?" Mykel says.

"Saving your girlfriend's life," Blade says. "Where were you?"

I try not to react to the word girlfriend. Or to the fact that Mykel doesn't correct him.

"We couldn't stop it," Mykel says. "There were too many—"

"I told them to get to safety," I cut in. "Mykel was trying to help."

The look on Mykel's face makes my chest ache. I want to defend him, reassure him.

"Obviously not trying hard enough," Blade mutters.

Lukas exhales. "Can we not do this right now?"

Darkness settles over Mykel's hazel eyes. The heartbreak shifts into anger—at Blade, at himself.

"Aria," Mykel says. "I should've been the one to save you. I'm sorry. I—"

"Mykel, stop. I told you to go. You were going to get caught."

Blade scoffs under his breath.

"Aria's right," Celie says. "You did the right thing. Don't beat yourself up." She sends Blade a pointed look. He just shrugs.

"Did you find anything through that entrance?" I ask, desperate to change the subject.

Lukas shakes his head. "Nothing."

No pearls. No clues.

"Well," Blade says. "I should probably go."

"Yeah," Mykel says. "You probably should."

Blade bristles instantly. "You know, Mykel, since we got to Silver Key, all you've done is act like an ass."

"Like you haven't?"

"I've tried to put our differences aside—"

Mykel crosses his arms and gives Blade a doubtful look.

"Fine, maybe not. But I've tried to avoid you so we wouldn't spend the entire year fighting. Every time I'm near you, you throw out some unnecessary remark." His voice sharpens. "I saved Aria's life. You could stop being a jerk for two seconds and acknowledge that."

Blade turns to me, softening. "I'm glad you're okay, Knight."

I give him a small smile. He returns it. Then he swims away.

"The flower," Celie says, pulling the opinia out of my hair.

Frowning, I look at it. Its petals are torn apart.

I glance at Mykel, but he's silent, shoulders rigid. I try to tell him again that he did the right thing, but he won't hear it. He hates that he couldn't save me. And he hates even more that it was Blade who did.

CHAPTER TWENTY-SIX

Several days pass as we search through abandoned boats, hidden alleyways, and empty caves, but it all feels like a waste of time. Atlantis is huge, and we've taken our time searching anywhere and everywhere—twice—yet we've found nothing. This trial is starting to feel impossible. There has to be a secret place, maybe somewhere only certain people know about, like King Neptune, but—

"Knight!" Blade calls.

I'm digging through a wooden treasure chest beside an imposing boulder. I'm pretty sure we've already checked it, but it doesn't hurt to look again, right? I turn as Blade swims over.

"Did you find something?" I say.

"No. I was gonna ask if you want to come talk to Neptune with me about the stone. I know we said we'd wait, but I'm so fucking bored down here. I need something to do other than search another empty cave."

"Let's go," I say.

Side by side, we head toward the palace.

"So," Blade says, "about what I said the other day—after I saved you—"

"You're never gonna let that go."

"Never. Anyway, I got sappy, and that's not me. Heat of the moment. I said some stuff..." He shrugs. "I do care about you, don't get me wrong. But you're dating Mykel, and I think I'd rather kill myself than listen to him keep bitching about how much you mean to him and how I need to back off—"

"Wait. He said that?"

"Yeah. After I saved you, he saw us hug," Blade says. "Later, he came up to me and confronted me about it. I told him I care about you and enjoy spending time with you. Then he tried to punch me in the face—failed miserably, no surprise. I mean, seriously? After all these years, he still thinks he could beat me in a fight?" He snorts. "Anyway, I told him I can do whatever the hell I want, and so can you. That was that."

Thoughts race through my mind.

Mykel saw us.

He got jealous.

Blade thinks Mykel and I are dating.

Does Mykel think we're dating? Does he *want* us to be official? And if he does... why hasn't he asked me?

I wish Violet were here. She'd know exactly what to say.

"He didn't tell me," I tell Blade, avoiding the millions of questions spinning through my mind.

"Probably because he was embarrassed. I could've kicked his ass if I wanted to."

"Why can't you guys get along?"

I've grown close to Blade. Yes, I may be slightly attracted to his annoying smirks and irritatingly handsome face, but we're friends. Just friends. And I have really strong feelings for Mykel. Things would be so much easier if they liked each other.

"We tried. It didn't work. He thinks I'm a terrible person—which, I'll admit, isn't a total lie—but he'll never see me as anything else. He can't."

I know that good kid is still in there somewhere, even if Mykel doesn't see it.

Celie said it herself. Maybe Mykel just isn't capable of seeing Blade as anything other than his rival. Seeing him as a good person would mean he has no reason to keep hating him, and sadly, hatred is the only way Mykel has ever known him. They have their family to blame.

"But you're trying to be better. I can tell. I don't think you're a bad person. Anymore."

Blade chuckles. "Thanks."

"I'm serious. When I first met you, you were a bully. You made rude comments for no reason. I understood why Mykel despised you—"

"This is supposed to make me feel better?"

I shake my head. "Let me finish. You've shown me another side of you, and I think that's the real you. You're not a bad guy. In fact... I'd even go as far as to call you my friend."

He smiles. "Huh. Friends. Who would've seen that coming?"

"Definitely not me," I say, and he rolls his eyes playfully. "But I mean it."

"You know, you're the only person I can be this way with," he says. "Honest. Myself. I don't have to put up a front with you. I can say what I want, feel what I feel, and you'll accept me. You won't use my weaknesses against me or stab me in the back."

He looks at me, serious now. "I trust you. I think you're the only person on this planet who's ever made me feel that way."

"What about Celie?"

"She told you?" he asks. When I nod, he sighs. "I guess I felt like that with her when we were little. But then I grew up and... pushed her away. We drifted apart. I couldn't confide in her anymore. Not like I can with you."

Part of me wants to be mad at him for putting me in this position—stuck between him and Mykel. But another part of me wants to hug him for being honest with me. For trusting me.

"Crap," he mutters. "I got sappy again."

We both laugh, and I notice how nice his smile is. His usual smirk is attractive, sure, but his genuine smile is even better.

We reach the underwater palace where King Neptune lives and swim toward his throne.

Does he just sit there all day?

"Hi... Your Majesty...?" I say, unsure how to address him.

Blade stifles a laugh beside me, and I elbow him in the side.

King Neptune has a bright grin on his face. "How may I help you two?"

My gaze drifts to the tall trident gripped firmly in his hand. The green stone is practically glowing.

"We were wondering about your trident," Blade says. "More specifically, the green stone in it. It's an energy stone, right?"

"Very astute. Yes, it is," Neptune says. "And you want it?"

"Well... we kind of need it. It's important. We know they're rare, and we wouldn't ask if we didn't truly need it," I say.

"I cannot give you this stone," Neptune says. "However, I can tell you where there may be others."

"So there are more of them?" Blade asks.

"Oh yes. Certainly."

I frown. "But I thought they were super rare."

"They are if you walk the dry land. Down here, they manifest in several places, though only one of them is safely accessible. Of course, only those who live here would know that."

Blade's arm brushes mine as he floats next to me. "Where can we find them?"

"Just outside Atlantis there is a tunnel," Neptune says. "It will take you deeper into the sea, and once you reach the bottom, you will find a path to your right. The path leads to an old ruin—the remains of a sunken city—where you will find a crumbling stone staircase. At the end of the staircase, you will enter a cave, and... well, you two are resourceful enough. What fun would it be if I gave you all the answers?"

I sigh. "This sounds dangerous."

"It can be. And outside Atlantis, you will be beyond our protection. This is a risk you must take if you want these stones."

I turn to Blade. "We have to do it."

The corner of his mouth lifts into a devilish smirk. "Glad to know we're on the same page, Knight."

"Please," Neptune says, "do be careful."

We nod our thanks and swim out of the safe confines of Atlantis.

CHAPTER TWENTY-SEVEN

Blade and I enter a dark tunnel. It's the same one I noticed when Amatheia brought us to Atlantis. Although I'm terrified about what could happen to us out here beyond the city's protection, I'm reassured by the fact that I'm with Blade.

We each cast a light spell, and two bright white orbs illuminate the path ahead, following us deeper into the tunnel. The chilling sounds of marine life echo around us, disturbing the quiet, and I stick close to Blade as we move through the narrow passage. I brush my fingers along the walls as we swim—cold and rough against my skin. This tunnel must have been here for a long time.

A moment later, a group of fish races past us. I nearly have a heart attack while Blade gasps and lets out a string of colourful curse words, which causes me to laugh at him.

We reach the end of the tunnel, and I get the sense that we're much deeper in the ocean now than before.

"Okay, so there should be a path to the right," Blade says.

Seconds later, we spot it. We swim along the path for a long time, grateful we haven't encountered any danger yet. But the longer we're gone, the more I worry about not giving Mykel, Celie, and Lukas a heads-up that I'd be missing for a while. I don't want them worrying about where I disappeared to.

Shaking the thought from my mind, I continue down the path with Blade until he abruptly stops.

"Did you hear that?" he asks.

"No. What did you hear?"

"It was probably nothing."

"You can't just say that! Whenever someone says that, it's usually *not* nothing."

Then I hear it. A high-pitched screech unlike anything I've ever heard. It's so terrifying I feel it in my bones, and I instinctively grab Blade's arm.

"We're fine. Let's keep moving," he says.

"We're *fine*? Did you not hear the same sound I just heard?"

"I heard it, but it's farther away than it sounds. I'm pretty sure it's a lyri. Its voice can travel up to ten thousand miles underwater."

"Since when are you a fish expert?" I tease.

He shrugs. "I've always been fascinated with marine life."

The slightest blush tints his cheeks, and I bite my lip to hide my smile.

"Huh," I say as we continue on.

We reach the old ruin. Little remains of the sunken city, only broken pieces of buildings and scattered debris. We swim beneath a tall stone archway and find a steep set of decaying stairs that disappears into a hole in the rocky wall.

"This must be the staircase, right?" I say.

Blade nods, and we swim toward it. The staircase is short, and soon we arrive at the cave King Neptune described. It's deep, but not too deep. Stalactites hang from the ceiling, and I carefully swim beneath them, searching for cracks in the walls or holes in the rocky ground where the stones could be hiding.

Eventually, I spot an opening in the ground, as if the rock has been split in two.

"Blade, over here!" I call.

He swims over. I move the orb of light above the crack and try to peer inside, but if there's an energy stone down there, I can't see it.

"Can we crack it open a bit more?" I say.

He nods. "Back up."

I do, and he raises his hands over the opening.

"*Destruo.*"

A loud cracking noise echoes through the cave. The water ripples outward with a force strong enough to knock us back a few feet, and the ground splits further apart, widening the crack. When I peer inside again, two small green stones gleam in the light.

I glance up at Blade. He winks before pulling one stone from the hole. The moment I touch the second one, a rush of energy shoots through me, starting at my fingertips and racing all the way down to my toes. Power ignites inside my body.

"*Whoa,*" I say.

"Right? This stuff is powerful."

We did it. Now all we need to open that door is a key. I hope what Celie and Lukas heard about the room is true. If there's proof of what Alatar is planning, it should be in there. And once we know his plans, we can figure out how to stop him.

"Let's get out of here," Blade says.

We exit the same way we came. As we approach the tunnel entrance, we hear the same screech again. Only this time, it's much closer.

We both freeze.

"Crap," Blade mutters.

"Come again?"

"It's close."

"It's *close*?"

"Yes, Knight. It's close."

"Well, what do we do?"

I realize I'm being completely useless right now, but Blade is the supposed underwater creature expert here, and quite frankly, I'm terrified of what could be lurking this deep in the ocean.

"We should go before it gets even closer. Maybe we can make it back to Atlantis before it—"

Another ear-splitting screech cuts him off.

"Let's move," he says.

We swim through the tunnel much faster this time.

"What does this lyri thing look like exactly?" I ask.

"Think a humpback whale mixed with a shark. But five times bigger. And completely red."

"Holy *shit*," I say, panic rising in my chest.

"It's ruthless. Eats anything in its path. Kills for fun. It could probably smell us from ten thousand miles away, which is why it's heading this way."

"What is *wrong* with you? Why would you tell me that?"

He laughs. "Relax, Knight. I'll protect you."

"Shut up, asshole. If it gets close and we can't stop it with magic, I'm sacrificing you."

Blade suddenly stops swimming and grabs my hand. His expression turns serious, all traces of laughter gone. "I won't let anything happen to you, Aria. I promise."

His eyes lock onto mine, and I feel the pure honesty in his words.

I nod. Any attempt at a sentence gets trapped in my throat.

We exit the tunnel, and I scan the ocean in every direction. Atlantis is close—just a little farther ahead. We could make it before the lyri reaches us—

It screeches again. Louder than ever.

"Knight, don't turn around," Blade says.

"You've got to be kidding me," I mutter before slowly turning.

It's enormous. The creature towers over us, filling my entire field of vision. It's so long I can't even see the end of its body. Its red skin glows in the dark water, and massive shark-like teeth jut from its mouth as it stares at us.

"Will magic even work on that thing?" I ask.

"Normally I'd say no. But we have these." Blade pulls the emerald energy stone from his pocket.

I pull mine out too, energy immediately surging through me.

"We can't kill it—we'd need a special weapon for that—but we can blast it hard enough to knock it unconscious," Blade says.

"I know the spell."

On the count of three, we clutch the stones and shout, "*Obtundo!*"

The power creates a violent maelstrom around us, blocking my view of the lyri. Red flashes through the swirling water as sand, bubbles, and seaweed whip past me. Blue magic pours from my hands, surging toward the creature.

Slowly, the vortex fades. When the water finally clears, the lyri lies unconscious on the sandy ocean floor.

Blade and I exchange a look of relief before swimming quickly back toward Atlantis.

"That was fun," he says as we pass through the gates.

"We almost *died*."

"Did we, though? We totally had that. Besides, I told you I wouldn't let anything happen to you. I keep my promises."

"Blade," I say. He stops and looks at me. "Thank you."

"No need to thank me, Knight. I'll talk to you later."

I find Celie, Mykel, and Lukas near the palace.

"Where have you been, Aria?" Mykel asks when he spots me approaching.

"I'm sorry. I was checking out a cave and lost track of time." Guilt swirls in my chest as I say it. I hate lying to them.

Celie studies me, suspicion in her eyes, but only says, "We were worried."

I send her an apologetic look.

"Did you at least find something?" Lukas asks.

"No. Not really."

They're disappointed, but I understand. Now that Blade and I are back, I'm reminded of the pearls we're supposed to be searching for and dread settles in my stomach. None of us have the slightest idea where they could be. This trial is only getting more frustrating. I guess we'll just have to keep looking and hope we stumble across a clue that points us in the right direction.

And hopefully avoid any more near-death experiences along the way.

CHAPTER TWENTY-EIGHT

I'm with Celie when I hear the screams.

A frantic blur of tails and fins rushes past us as merpeople swim for their lives, shouting in a sea of chaos.

"Sirens! They're coming for us! Hide!" someone cries.

My heart hammers in my chest as I watch the sirens attack. With scaly grey skin and arms covered in gills, they chase the merfolk through Atlantis, swimming in sharp, precise movements and baring their jagged teeth. Their slimy, eel-like tails and lidless serpentine eyes are a menacing contrast to their merfolk counterparts.

I know sirens lure their victims, specifically men, and *then* kill them. So why are these sirens chasing everyone?

Unless...

Unless it's a distraction.

My heart drops into my stomach.

Mykel. I don't see him anywhere. I search for Blade, and he's nowhere to be seen, either.

Celie is panicking. We duck behind a corner, far enough away from the sirens to stay hidden.

"What do we do?" she says.

We watch the slaughter unfolding before us as the sirens mercilessly kill the merfolk. Some are strangled to death. Others clamp their hands over their ears as the sirens sing their bone-chilling song—but they all collapse anyway, one after another.

"We have to find the others," I say. "Lukas, Mykel, Blade—"

"Celie! Aria!"

It's Lukas. He's frantic, his breathing uneven. I've never been so relieved to see him... and Dot, who follows close behind.

"Where's Mykel?" Celie asks.

"He's swimming toward them. They're luring him with their voice."

"*What?*" I say. "Wh-Why didn't it work on you?"

"I'm *gay*," he replies, like it's the most obvious thing in the world.

"So they only lure people attracted to women?"

"Yes! Get with the times, Aria!"

I would laugh if everything weren't so insane right now. Instead, panic floods my body. Mykel is swimming toward them. Toward *death*. And Blade most likely is too.

I have to find them.

I swim out from behind the corner. Most of the sirens have moved deeper into Atlantis, though a few remain, searching the bloodied streets for anyone still hiding.

One of them finds someone behind the flower shop we had visited. The bouquets are destroyed, flowers scattered across the ground.

The siren grabs the girl by the hair—

Clarity.

Before I can react, the siren's hand clamps around her throat, squeezing. Its sharp nails dig into her skin as she thrashes helplessly. Blood seeps from each puncture as the claws press deeper.

I watch as the light drains from Clarity's eyes.

As she stops fighting.

As her body goes limp.

My heart shatters as she drifts down to the ocean floor.

"Aria, get back here!" Celie says, grabbing my arm and yanking me back. "What are you doing? Have you lost your mind?"

"We have to save them!"

"If we go out there, we're dead," Lukas says.

"I have to try. I *have* to." My mind races as I try to form a plan. "Are you coming or not?"

They hesitate. I can practically see the gears turning in their heads. This is dangerous, and I wouldn't blame them if they chose to stay hidden.

They exchange a quick look.

"*Crap!* Okay, we're coming," Lukas finally says.

The siren that killed Clarity swims away. Once the coast is clear, Celie, Lukas, Dot, and I slip through the streets toward where the sirens came from, careful not to be seen.

Atlantis fades into the distance as we spot a group of people swimming in a single direction, their movements slow and mindless.

We follow them. It's dark now, with only a few dim orbs of light scattered through the water. The tension feels thick and suffocating as we trail behind the enchanted merfolk and sorcerers, watching them drift like zombies toward their doom.

Mykel and Blade aren't among them, but that doesn't mean we're too late. If we can—

Lukas lets out a strangled yell as he's yanked away from Celie.

"Lukas!" Celie shouts—but she's jerked away by another siren.

The sirens hold Celie and Lukas suspended in front of me, long claws pressed against their throats.

"Don't!" I shout.

My heart pounds violently in my ears. Dot squeals anxiously but doesn't move closer.

Then I see Sarah behind the sirens.

"Please," I say to the sirens, trying to keep their attention on me. "Don't kill them."

The sirens remain eerily silent. Maybe that's a good thing. Their voices seem just as deadly as their claws.

Sarah is only inches away now, but she can only strike one of them. We lock eyes. Without a word, we understand each other. I give the slightest nod.

Sarah swings her arm in a sharp slicing motion. *"Segmentum Gladio!"*

At the same time, I thrust my hand forward. *"Impetus!"*

Celie is freed first. The siren holding her arches back as if slashed by an invisible blade. Black blood spills from its back, mixing into the water.

My spell slams into the other siren, knocking it backward.

Lukas tears free from its grasp and rushes to Celie. "Are you okay?" he asks as Dot nudges him.

I don't hear her answer. One of the sirens is already charging toward me. It's unbelievably fast. I barely have time to react before it reaches me—

"Flagellum!" Sarah shouts.

Purple and gold magic bursts from her hand, twisting together to form a glowing rope. It snaps around the siren's neck just before it reaches me, and Sarah yanks it backward.

I take the opportunity. *"Obtundo!"*

My spell blasts the second siren that's racing toward Sarah.

Now clear, Sarah swims over and hovers beside me. We brace ourselves, ready to strike again—

A melodic tune echoes in the distance. The sirens freeze. Then they turn and swim away.

I release a breath of relief, bubbles escaping my lips. "Thanks," I say to Sarah.

"Don't mention it." She glances around. "Have you seen Clarity, by the way? I can't find her anywhere."

My chest tightens. "Sarah…"

She bites her lip and turns away. "She's dead?"

"I saw it happen. I'm so sorry."

She looks at me, and her expression says everything—the grief she's trying so desperately to hold back.

"There's an abandoned ship nearby," she says. "I saw people swim there. You guys go check on them. I'm going to see if there are any survivors left in Atlantis."

"Okay."

She places a hand on my shoulder. "Be careful, Aria."

"You too."

She hesitates before swimming away.

"That was close," Lukas says.

I take a deep breath, trying to steady myself. "Are you guys okay?"

"We're fine," Celie says. "Let's go."

We arrive at the abandoned ship. It's enormous—broken masts rising like jagged spears into the dark water, sails shredded and drifting. It must have been down here for ages. Unable to decay, the wooden hull rests on the pebbled seabed, splintered beams jutting out in every direction.

A group of people drifts mindlessly toward the entrance.

"Dot, can you keep them from entering the ship?" Lukas says. "Take them as far away as you can. Maybe if they're far enough, the trance will break."

Dot chirps a cute dolphin noise.

"Be careful, okay?" Lukas says.

Dot makes another funny noise and swims toward the five or so people we followed here. Before they can enter the ship, Dot extends his wings. I thought they were small, but they grow a few metres in length as he stretches them. He beats them powerfully, pushing the enchanted merfolk and sorcerers backward through the water.

Lukas watches nervously. With sirens still roaming the area, anything could happen.

I notice a large crack in the side of the ship—an opening. We slip inside. At first, I can't see much. The ship is dark and long, with splintered stairs leading below deck.

"So, what's the plan?" Lukas whispers.

I press my face against a gap in the wooden floor and peer through. Three sirens are below. They watch eagerly as more victims drift toward them, lured by their haunting melody. They're excited, waiting to kill them—

And there he is.

Blade.

His wrists are tied to the wall, his body floating limply in the water. He's unconscious, eyes closed as if peacefully asleep. Mykel is beside him, in the same state as Blade.

The sirens must be keeping them unconscious until they're ready to kill them. Maybe waiting for the other sirens to return.

"I see them," I whisper. "They're unconscious."

"We could try a freeze spell?" Lukas suggests.

"That won't work on the sirens. Their voices act as a protective barrier. As long as they keep singing, our magic won't work on them—at least not the kind of magic we have. We're not strong enough to break through it," Celie says. "And if we can't stop their singing, they"—she gestures to Mykel, Blade, and the others—"will remain unconscious."

Lukas peeks into the hole before looking back at us. "So what do we do?"

Everything I've learned at Silver Key so far has led to this moment—the moment where I can prove that all my tireless training and studying has paid off. I'm a *sorcerer*. I can do this. I just need to think.

Think, Aria. Think...

I pull the energy stone from my pocket. It glows in my hand.

"Where did you get that?" Celie asks.

"I got it from this place King Neptune—never mind, that doesn't matter right now. Will this give us enough power to break their spell?"

"It should."

We're about to creep down the stairs when the sirens stop singing. We freeze.

Mykel, Blade, and the others stir slightly. Blade's eyes open a crack, but he's still in a trance, not even trying to free his hands.

"*Shit.* Do they know we're here?" I say.

One siren peers up to the ceiling, looking through the cracks. Any second now, we'll be caught.

I turn to Celie and Lukas. "We have to attack. Now."

They nod, and we swim down the short set of stairs. The sirens resume their chilling tune. We aren't fully visible yet, but we're close enough to see the room clearly.

Everyone is tied up. I spot Jakson lying unconscious on the floor. I wonder if Sherry made it out alive. I hope Sarah and Eliza are okay.

Shaking the thoughts from my head, I clutch the stone and glance at Mykel's and Blade's dazed, helpless faces.

I have to save them. I *have* to.

These sirens will not take them from me.

I focus on that thought—on the fierce need to protect them—and use it to fuel my magic. I feel it rise inside me, surging to the surface. "*Irritum Facere.*"

Instantly, the stone flashes a blinding green. Its energy churns through the water, whipping into a swirling vortex of seaweed and sand and—silence.

They've stopped singing.

We look at the sirens. They're dumbstruck, confused, unsure what just happened. That's when we reveal ourselves.

"You fools," one of them says.

I smirk. "I wouldn't be so sure about that."

Still holding the stone, I thrust my hands forward and shout, "*Confuto!*"

The sirens freeze where they stand, motionless as statues.

"That might be one of my favourites," I say.

I glance at Lukas, who laughs. Celie is already untying people.

Lukas and I swim over to Blade and Mykel. Lukas unties Mykel's hands while I work on Blade's. They both look confused and disoriented for a moment but slowly come to.

"Aria?" Mykel says. "What happened?"

"We saved your asses. That's what happened," Lukas says.

Blade looks up at me. "I guess we're even."

I roll my eyes and glance over at Mykel, who forces a small smile.

Celie finishes untying the last of the merfolk. "I'm glad you're all okay, but we need to get out of here. With the energy we used, the spell should hold for a while, but it won't last forever."

We leave the ship together. The mermaids and mermen thank us and swim away, leaving only the sorcerers to figure out what we'll do next. There aren't many of us left.

"I don't know about you guys, but I'm over this trial. I have no idea what the hell Alatar and the other teachers were thinking, but we almost died here. I'm done," Jakson says. He shoots a red flare from his hand.

A few others mumble their agreement and do the same. One by one, they disappear until only Celie, Lukas, Mykel, Blade, and I remain.

"I'm staying," Blade says.

I nod. "Me too."

"I'm staying too. There's no way I'm leaving until I find that stupid pearl," Mykel says.

Celie and Lukas nod in agreement.

There's a moment of silence before Celie suddenly says, "Holy shit." Her eyes are wide, like she's just had a revelation.

"What?" Blade says.

"I know where the pearls are."

She takes off, and the four of us race after her.

CHAPTER TWENTY-NINE

We follow Celie back to King Neptune's palace, doing our best to avoid the dead bodies along the way.

The streets are eerily quiet, the distant sobs of people mourning their loved ones the only sound. The once-busy shops lining the streets are destroyed—windows smashed, signs torn down. We swim past homes and spot merpeople peeking through seaweed blinds, fear written across their faces. The colourful jellyfish are nowhere to be seen, leaving Atlantis dim and grey—red where blood still mixes with the water.

As soon as we enter the palace, Amatheia swims up to us in a panic.

"Amatheia, are you okay?" Mykel says.

She struggles to respond, and I realize she's crying. A long, thin gash runs across her cheek, and several scrapes and bruises cover her arms.

This can't be good.

She silently leads us into King Neptune's office. I haven't been in here yet, and I'm a little surprised by the decor. Seaweed is neatly draped along one wall, while empty picture frames hang on the other. Neptune's shelves overflow with books, small figures, and statues—items that were discarded or abandoned in the ocean.

My thoughts are interrupted when I see King Neptune sprawled on the ground. At first, I think he's asleep. I can't even fathom someone as important as him being killed. But he doesn't move. Cuts and bruises cover his once-flawless skin. Strangulation marks line his neck, and blood drips from his ears.

"Oh my God," Celie says.

"Is he…" Lukas trails off, unable to finish the sentence.

Amatheia nods, another sob escaping her throat.

I gently place a hand on her arm. "I'm so sorry."

"He was the best king we ever had," she cries. "I do not know what we will do now."

"Is there anything we can do to help?" Mykel asks.

"No, I—I must think. I am glad you sorcerers are alright. I hope you find what you are looking for soon."

She swims away, leaving us alone with King Neptune's body. As she leaves, Dot enters.

"Dot!" Lukas shouts, pulling his familiar into a hug.

We all fall silent for a moment, unsure what to say as we stare down at Neptune's corpse.

Then Celie starts searching the office. She checks under the desk, inside drawers, behind a picture frame, under the carpets.

"Um… Celie?" Lukas says.

She pauses. "I think the pearls are in this room somewhere. Think about it—think about what King Neptune said when we arrived."

Sometimes, to find what you are seeking, you must break the rules.

"The day we got here, that guard told us we weren't allowed in his office," I say.

Mykel nods. "None of us have been in here."

"This is the only place we haven't searched," Celie says.

"They have to be here," Blade agrees.

We each begin frantically searching the room. It's much smaller than the rest of the palace, almost like a normal office. We dig through desk drawers and look under tables. I pick up a small statue resting on a bookshelf. The wall behind it swings open like a door. My eyebrows rise in surprise, and the others freeze at the sound of the wall shifting.

"*Cool,*" Lukas says.

I grab the edge of the wall and pull the door open farther. On the other side is another room. The walls are covered from top to bottom with hundreds of pearls. They're large—about the size of my hand—and they glimmer in the sunlight filtering through a hole in the ceiling.

Each pearl has a different name written on it.

"You have *got* to be kidding me," Celie says.

Mykel lets out an exasperated sigh. "Let's get looking."

We search through the pearls one by one. At least five frustrating minutes pass before I find mine.

Aria Knight.

My name is written in bold cursive across a metallic, rose-gold pearl.

Blade finds Celie's pearl, then his own a moment later, and Mykel finds Lukas's. We decide to wait before grabbing them so we can all be transported back to Silver Key together.

Eventually, Mykel locates his pearl on the other end of the room.

"Finally," Blade says, earning an exaggerated eye roll from Mykel.

"On the count of three," I say.

I count down, and we each grab our pearls from the shelves. It's heavier than I expected. The moment I touch it, my name begins to glow, growing brighter and brighter until the light nearly blinds me.

I turn away from it, my gaze landing on another pearl.

Clarity Hearthfire.
The name fades, but the pearl remains.
The death of a friend, lost in the vicious lands of the Under-sea.

CHAPTER THIRTY

"Congratulations," Alatar says.

Standing in Alatar's office, I look around and am grateful to find Celie, Lukas, Mykel, and Blade here too. I'm disoriented. It feels strange to stand on dry land again. Afraid I might tip over and fall, I grab the wall beside me for support.

Alatar looks at each of us, an impressed expression on his face. "As of yet, you five are the only ones to complete this trial."

"Yeah, well, it wasn't easy," Lukas says.

"You know some of us died, right? Clarity? I saw a siren kill her. I thought you said we'd be safe?" I say.

"Yes, I must admit, things did not go as planned."

"That's it? That's all you have to say?" Blade says, taking a step toward Alatar. "We could have all died down there. We don't even know how many made it out alive, and that's all you have to say?"

"Mr. Casteel, you of all people should know to show me some respect. What would your father say if I told him you spoke to me like this?"

Blade averts his gaze and takes a step back. A glimmer of satisfaction sparks in Alatar's eyes.

I push myself off the wall. "No, Blade's right. You don't give a shit about any of us, do you?"

"I would advise you to calm down," Alatar says. "All of you have proven your strength and determination in this trial. You have shown us your ability to defend yourselves, fight for each other, and think on your feet. That is exactly what these trials are about. Yes, this trial had casualties, and I am not taking the situation lightly. It was unexpected, but it happened, and now I—along with the reputation of Silver Key—will have to deal with the consequences. You are all dismissed."

The door behind us flies open, and I jump at the sudden movement. We walk out of his office. The door slams shut behind us.

"Can I please burn this place to the ground?" I say.

"Seeing as it's a giant manor reinforced with magical protection, I don't think fire will do much damage," Lukas replies.

"But trying would make me feel a bit better."

Blade snickers.

"Has he ever lashed out like that before?" Celie asks.

Blade shakes his head. "Not that I've seen."

Mykel nods in agreement.

Lukas sighs. "Well, I'm gonna go lie down. Mykel, you coming?"

"Yeah, I'm exhausted," Mykel says, grabbing my hand. "I'll see you tomorrow?"

I nod. He squeezes my hand before following Lukas toward their room.

"Knight, can we talk?" Blade says.

"Yeah, sure." Turning to Celie, I say, "I'll meet you back in our room later."

She gives me a curious look, then glances at Blade with the same expression. "Okay," she mutters before walking away.

We move to a secluded area. The second we're sure we're alone, Blade says, "We need to find that key."

"I know... Blade, I think I need to tell them about the door."

He shakes his head. "If it gets out that we're trying to sneak in there, we're done. We'll get expelled, and then we'll never find out what's inside."

"They won't tell anyone! They'll want to help. Please, I trust them."

"Knight—"

"And there's something I need to tell you, too."

Blade stares at me, waiting for me to continue.

I tell him about getting teleported to the cabin and describe the conversation I overheard. "It sounded like he was planning something. Something dangerous involving us. They said something about them not being strong enough... I don't know."

I pause, waiting to hear what Blade has to say, but he stays silent, so I continue.

"And then Celie and Lukas heard Alatar talking about some proof in the manor of what he's done. Which—I'm not sure what that means—but the proof they're talking about has to be behind that door. It has to."

"Why didn't you tell me this sooner?" Blade says.

"I'm sorry. I know I should have. But I promised Celie, Mykel, and Lukas I would keep it between us."

"But don't you think this concerns me? Considering I'm the one who's been trying to find out what's behind that door since the beginning, and you wouldn't be this close to finding out if it weren't for me?"

He doesn't seem too angry, but... hurt. Because I kept this from him.

"You're right," I say. "I should've told you."

We're both silent until Blade finally says, "It's fine. Just don't hide anything important like this from me again, okay?"

"I won't. If it makes you feel any better, Mykel, Celie, and Lukas are going to hate me for keeping what we've been doing a secret."

Blade laughs. "Mykel's gonna kill you."

"Hey, you don't know that! It's possible he'll understand. You did, right?"

"Mykel is not me. He's going to be pissed."

"*Great*," I say.

"Good luck. You're gonna need it."

I laugh. "Shut *up*."

I shove him playfully, and he smirks before walking away.

I make it back to my dorm room to find Celie. Might as well tell them all now and get it over with.

I grab her and, without explanation, take her down to Mykel and Lukas's dorm room.

"What's up?" Mykel says, letting us in.

"She won't tell me. She keeps saying she needs to tell us together," Celie replies, sitting next to Lukas on his bed.

I take a deep breath. "Okay. First of all, please don't be mad at me."

"This is off to a great start," Lukas says.

"So, you know the silver door?" They nod. "I've kinda been trying to sneak into it with Blade, and we've gotten pretty close to getting all the way through. The only thing we're missing is a key, which is probably also hidden in Alatar's office, but that's just a guess. I'm actually not sure at all. But once we get that key, Blade and I can get through the door and find out what Alatar is hiding from all of us."

I say it so fast I have to stop to catch my breath.

"*What?*" Mykel says.

I'm not sure what I was thinking. Maybe if I explain it really fast and ramble on, they won't be as shocked—or betrayed—by me not telling them?

Celie stands. "Aria, are you serious? That's so dangerous."

"I know, I just—I saw Blade sneaking around there, and then he told me what he was trying to do, and I—I told him I'd help him."

"How long has this been going on?" Mykel asks.

"Since the first few weeks we've been here..." I cringe as I say it.

Lukas grabs Celie's hand. "Maybe we should go." They both head out the door.

Mykel crosses his arms. "So you've been lying to us this whole time?"

"No. I told him I wouldn't tell anyone. We'd be in so much trouble if we got caught, and we really wanted to see what's in there."

"Oh, I see. You promised Blade you wouldn't tell us. You wouldn't tell *me*. And you've, what, been sneaking around with him this whole time?"

"Mykel, you're making it sound worse than it is—"

"Am I, though? Aria, not only have you been lying about something this important, but you've been lying about spending time with Blade. You knew how that would make me feel, and you did it anyway."

"Mykel, I—"

"You think I haven't noticed how you are with him?"

"What's that supposed to mean?"

"I see the way you look at him. You care about him, and I don't understand why."

"He's not that bad, Mykel. We're friends!"

"*Friends?* With *Blade*?"

"Yes! Is that really so bad?"

Mykel looks at me like I'm crazy. Like he can't even begin to comprehend how my mind works.

"Are you seriously trying to defend him to me right now?"

"I just—"

"Just what? You've known us for what, seven months now? I've known Blade my whole life. You have no idea the kind of person he is, and you have no right to come in here and try to tell me you do."

"He's different with me, okay?"

"You're naive as hell if you truly believe that."

His words feel like a slap across the face.

"You know what? It's my life, Mykel. I'm allowed to be friends with whoever I want! Just because we're—whatever we are—doesn't mean you can control who I can and can't spend time with."

"You know this is different. This is Blade we're talking about. Did I ever tell you about the time he stole a magical artifact from our grandfather? It was priceless—something our grandfather won—and Blade stole it from him. And when I told on him, he blamed the whole thing on me, and I lost my magic for a month. You know what he did? He didn't come clean or apologize. He laughed. Because that's the kind of person he is."

"Mykel—"

"Or what about when he cast a spell on some poor, innocent kid, causing him to fall and hit his head? His injuries were so serious that after he got out of the hospital, his parents sent him to another school just to keep him as far away from Blade as possible. Blade is not a good guy, Aria. You have to see that. He doesn't change, and you're blind if you think he's changing for you."

I shake my head in disbelief, trying to process the words he's throwing at me. But they hurt, and this isn't him. This isn't the Mykel who trained with me, who kissed me beneath the fireworks.

"What is wrong with you? I don't even know you right now."

"That's right, Aria. You don't know me! You got thrown into our lives, and now you think you know everyone better than they know themselves."

"Of course I know you guys. You spend every day with someone for seven months straight, and you get to know them. And I know this isn't you. Blade brings out the worst in you. You're jealous and angry, and it's taking over your ability to think before you speak."

"Of course I'm jealous and angry! I'm in love with you, and you have feelings for Blade!"

In love?

Since I came to Silver Key, since I got to know Mykel, all I've wanted was to be with him. To hear him say those words to me.

I'm in love with you.

But not like this.

Not like this.

"Mykel, I chose you. I was willing to fight for you. But every time we get close, you pull away! You haven't even asked me to be your girlfriend yet," I say.

A tortured look clouds his eyes. "I was afraid, Aria. And with the trials, I didn't think it was the right time."

"Why were you afraid?"

"Because I—" He sighs. "I'm sure you've heard about my relationship with Eliza."

I know he and Eliza used to date, but little else. I know he was hurt after their breakup, but I didn't think she was that important. Especially after he told me nothing was going on between them anymore.

"Is that what this is about? Do you still have feelings for her? Is that why you keep pushing me away?"

"No! *No*. Look—Eliza and I met at a party and started dating pretty soon after that. We were together for eight months, and then she broke up with me out of the blue. I didn't even know why. I was crushed." There's pain in his eyes as he says it.

"When she pulled me aside in the library that day, she was coming clean. She told me she broke up with me because I was too competitive. Too jealous. Too overprotective. And then I realized you were feeling the same way—that I was being too overprotective—so I took a step back," he says, running a nervous hand through his hair. "I couldn't handle another heartbreak like that. Especially not with you, Aria, because the way I feel about you is more than I ever felt for Eliza.

"I tried to change. I thought maybe we could work if I watched myself. But at the ball, I got so angry seeing you talk to Blade and realized changing is hard. I tried again during the second trial, but every time I saw you with him, that competitive, jealous side of me came out. I tried to use Blade as an excuse to push you away, but I shouldn't have. I know it was wrong, and I'm sorry. I do want to be with you. I can work on my issues—but I know I want to be with you."

I've officially lost my ability to speak. Nothing comes out. Thoughts race through my mind so fast I can barely keep up.

I think about the day Mykel and I met. All the times we trained together. When we went to the ball. That kiss. Every romantic gesture.

My feelings for Mykel are real.

But then I think about Blade. When we danced. When we hugged. Through every annoying argument, I've felt there was something more there, even though I tried to suppress it.

So I say the one thing I know for certain, no matter how hard it is.

"Mykel... you were right, though. I... I think I do have feelings for Blade."

The hurt that flashes across his face cuts into me like a knife. Like a sharpened blade, it digs deep into my heart—and if this is how I feel, he must feel so much worse.

My words, that confession, it hangs in the air between us like poisonous gas.

All he says is, "Whatever we had... it's over."

"Mykel—"

"No. You led me on, Aria, and you lied to me. I can't even look at you right now."

He wanted to avoid getting his heart broken. But I broke his heart anyway.

CHAPTER THIRTY-ONE

My heart aches as I walk out of Mykel's room, his words echoing in my mind.

I wasn't expecting it—the heartbreak. It snuck up on me and left my chest hurting, like something inside me is trying to claw its way out. Because yes, he broke my heart, just as I broke his. But the worst part is I can't even blame him. He's right. I lied to him about something that matters.

I do have feelings for Blade.

They're new and confusing. I don't even fully understand them myself. But they're there. Maybe they've been there longer than I want to admit.

"Aria!" Celie calls from behind me.

Footsteps echo in the hallway as she runs to catch up. I don't stop. I barely notice where I'm going, just moving forward through the dim corridor, past doors and flickering lantern light.

Mykel has been there for me since my first day at Silver Key. Every moment since then, I've felt myself falling harder for him. So why does some part of me keep pulling toward Blade?

And how could Mykel say those things to me? Each sharp utterance like an arrow to the heart. I can still feel them lingering, piercing.

But he's in love with me.

What am I supposed to do with that now?

Celie catches up and grabs my shoulder, spinning me around. The moment I see the concern in her eyes, something inside me finally cracks. Tears spill down my face before I can stop them. Everything hits me all at once. Mykel's voice. The look on his face when I told him the truth. The hurt in his eyes.

Celie pulls me into a hug, one hand rubbing slow circles on my back.

"I've got you," she murmurs.

And that's it. I break.

I cry harder than I have in months, the kind of crying that makes your chest hurt and your throat burn.

Images flash through my mind—home, my parents, my brother. The life I left behind.

Violet.

God, I wish she were here. She'd know exactly what to say to make this feel less impossible.

Then another thought creeps in, quiet but heavy.

My biological parents. Questions I've buried for months push to the surface.

Why didn't they want me?

Where are they now?

I just want my mom. I want to cry in her arms and feel her soothing hand on my back.

But the thoughts dissolve as quickly as they come, swallowed by the ache in my chest.

Mykel.

He looked so hurt. And I hate that I'm the reason.

We reach our dorm room, and I sink down onto the edge of my bed, suddenly exhausted. Celie sits beside me.

"I didn't mean to hurt him," I whisper.

"I know."

"But he's right," I say, my voice shaking. "I shouldn't have lied to him. I do care about him. I really do."

Celie pulls back, studying my face. "But?"

I wipe my eyes with the sleeve of my shirt. "But I can't pretend Blade means nothing to me."

Celie doesn't look surprised. That almost makes it worse.

"You like him," she says.

My head snaps up. "What?"

"Aria." She gives me a small, sympathetic smile. "I've seen the way you look at him from across the room when you think no one's paying attention."

I stare at the floor.

"I noticed it at the ball too," she continues. "When you danced with him. The way you talk about Blade... it's more than just friendship between you two."

"And you didn't say anything?" I ask, letting out a weak, watery laugh.

Celie smiles. "It's not my place to tell you how you feel. That was something you had to figure out on your own."

"I swear I never meant for this to happen," I say. "I really like Mykel. I never wanted to hurt him. But everything feels so... tangled."

Celie is quiet for a moment before asking, "Does it feel the same?"

"What?"

"The way you feel about them."

I open my mouth to answer, but nothing comes out. The truth hits me before the words do.

Mykel feels like safety. Like warmth. Like the kind of future that makes sense.

Blade...

Blade feels like standing too close to the edge of a cliff. Dangerous and unpredictable. But impossible to walk away from.

He challenges me, pushes me to take risks, to do things I never would have done before. With him, there's a sense of danger and mystery, and for some reason, I can't help being drawn to it.

The realization sends a ripple of unease through me.

"I don't know," I admit.

But that's not true. I do know. And that's the part that scares me.

When I was younger, my mom used to warn me about guys like Blade. The charming ones. The reckless ones.

"They're easy to fall for," she'd say. "But they'll break your heart."

Most people at the manor seem to agree; Blade has a reputation for being difficult. Cold. Not exactly the nicest person. But when I'm with him, that's not what I see. I see someone guarded. Someone who's been through more than he lets on. Someone who's finally starting to let me see the real version of him. And the real him isn't bad at all.

Celie nudges my shoulder. "We should get some sleep." She stands and climbs into her bed. "Tomorrow's going to be a long day."

A cold knot forms in my stomach. I'd almost forgotten. Tomorrow we're finding the key and finally finding out what Alatar's been hiding.

For a moment, Mykel and Blade fade into the background. Whatever is behind that door... I can't deny I'm a little scared to find out. But I'm just as worried that when I do, I'll wish I hadn't.

CHAPTER THIRTY-TWO

"Celie and I have called you here bright and early to discuss how we're going to steal the key from Alatar," Lukas says.

This morning, Celie and Lukas dragged all of us out of bed and told us to meet in the library.

I glance around the room. It's eerily quiet. I don't think I've ever seen the library this empty—no books levitating through the air, no sorcerers chatting near the fireplace. Just towering shelves and long shadows stretching across the floor.

Through the tall windows, the rising sun spills golden light over the manor grounds, the sky streaked with soft pinks and oranges. The warmth of it barely reaches me. A chill sits heavy in my chest as I think about what we're about to do.

We're standing in a secluded corner beside a towering bookshelf. Celie, Mykel, Lukas, Blade, and I. *Yes*, Blade. You can probably guess how well this is going.

"Why is he here?" Mykel says.

Blade smirks. "Really feeling the family love, Griffin."

"Shut it, Casteel, before I—"

"Okay!" Lukas cuts in quickly. "Clearly it's not too early in the morning for arguments."

Celie crosses her arms with a sigh. "Blade is here because, whether you like it or not, Mykel, he plays a big part in this."

Mykel stands stiffly to my right, his jaw tight, fists clenched. Blade leans against the bookshelf on my left, looking far too entertained.

How I ended up standing between these two, I have no idea.

"Can we just try to get along for five minutes?" I say.

The second the words leave my mouth, I regret them.

Mykel turns toward me. "You must enjoy having Blade around."

Well... at least he's talking to me.

"Jesus Christ, just shut up, Mykel," Blade snaps. "You're acting like a child. All Aria did was keep a promise. If you're too insecure to handle that, that's your problem. Stop taking it out on her."

"If only that were true," Mykel says, his eyes flicking back to me. "Right, Aria?"

I shake my head, annoyed.

"I bet you're looking forward to the next time you two sneak off together," he adds. "Especially now that whatever we had is over."

Blade straightens. "You broke up?"

"Last night," Celie answers quietly.

"Ohhh," Lukas says, nodding slowly. "That explains a lot." We all turn to him.

"What?" he says defensively. "Mykel wouldn't tell me what happened."

Mykel rolls his eyes and looks back at Blade. "I'm not stupid. I know exactly what you're doing."

Blade raises an eyebrow. "And what's that, smartass?"

"You're using Aria to get back at me. You want to prove you're better than me, and you'll do it however you can." He turns to me again. "Don't you see that, Aria?"

"That's bullshit, and Aria knows it," Blade says. He steps forward. "I know I may come off as an asshole a lot of the time, but that doesn't mean I'm incapable of having actual feelings."

"Would you all shut up?" Celie snaps.

The room goes silent.

She rubs her temples, looking exhausted. "Please. I'm already nervous enough about this."

Lukas rests a hand on her shoulder, then looks at the rest of us. "Yeah, sorry if I'm not reacting properly to this dramatic revelation, but I'm currently more focused on the fact that we're about to rob one of the most powerful sorcerers ever." He pauses. "I'm also a little hungry."

"Fine," Mykel says at last. "Here's the plan. Blade distracts Alatar. Celie, Aria, and I use an invisibility spell and search Alatar's office for the key. Lukas keeps watch."

Lukas nods. "Simple. Illegal. Potentially life-ruining. I like it."

"How long will the invisibility last?" I ask.

"Not long," Mykel says. "None of us are that experienced with it."

"What about the energy stones?" I say.

"What energy stones?"

Blade pulls the emerald stone from his pocket. It catches the morning light, glowing faintly. "These. They help power the door we're trying to open."

"That'll definitely help," Celie says.

I pull the second stone from my pocket. "But we only have two."

"You and Celie should use them," Mykel says. "I'll manage."

Celie shakes her head. "No. You take one. I'm the most experienced with the spell. I should be able to hold it longer."

"Great," Lukas says. "Decided. Let's go steal this key."

We leave the library and make our way through the quiet hallways of the manor. A few minutes later, we're standing outside Alatar's office. He should still be in a faculty meeting right now.

Blade waits down the hall near the conference room door, ready to intercept him when the meeting ends.

"If I hear Blade and Alatar coming, I'll knock three times," Lukas says.

Mykel steps up to the office door and tries the handle. It's locked. He places his hand on the doorknob. "*Recludo.*"

A burst of white light flashes across the metal. The lock clicks open.

We slip inside.

The office looks exactly as I remember.

Almost.

Alatar's desk is a mess: papers scattered everywhere, an empty mug with a dried ring of coffee at the bottom, books stacked unevenly. Alatar has always been meticulous. Perfectly put together.

This... isn't. It's wrong.

Mykel pulls the energy stone from his pocket. I do the same. "*Indespectus,*" the three of us say.

In an instant, Mykel and Celie vanish.

That is incredibly cool.

"Okay," Mykel's voice says somewhere to my left. "Let's search."

We move quickly through the room, looking through desk drawers, under carpets, behind curtains, being mindful to place everything back to where it belongs so there's not even a frame angled out of place.

After searching through every book on the bookshelf, frustration creeps in. For all we know, it might not even be in here.

"Where the *hell* is it?" I say.

Mykel lets out a frustrated breath. "I don't know. It's not like the office is that big."

"Maybe we're trying too hard," Celie says. "We need to take a step back, look in plain sight."

I take a deep breath and glance around the room, searching for anything that might seem out of place.

"There," Celie says.

I can't see her, but suddenly a medium-sized picture frame levitates into the air.

I walk over to it. It's a portrait, but not of anyone I've ever seen. Or *anything* I've ever seen. It appears to be a portrait of a demon. But I've studied demons, and I've never encountered one like this. His skin is pitch black with a crimson tint beneath it. Long, blade-sharp horns curve from his skull. Massive wings fold behind his back, their membranes blood-red. His eyes are pure black. They seem to stare straight through me. Something about him feels... familiar. I can't figure out how.

Then I see it. A small silver key is tattooed over his heart. It blends perfectly into the painting, nearly invisible. The key slowly peels away from the canvas, leaving a dark hole where the demon's heart should be.

I stare at the key floating in mid-air. It's small and old, but shining with bright silver light. It looks identical to my silver key tattoo.

"Holy shit," Mykel breathes. "You found it."

"Aria," Celie says. "Put it in your pocket and let's go. I can't hold the spell much longer."

I grab the key and shove it deep into my pocket.

"Okay, let's—"

Knock knock knock.

"Crap."

I hurry to the door and ease it open. Down the hall, Blade's voice echoes.

"Sir, you have to come with me right now. My father—"

"Perhaps later, Blade," Alatar says. "I have matters to attend to."

"Sir, I received a letter from him. It's urgent. We need to go now or—"

I don't wait to hear the rest. I slip out of the office and turn the corner. Lukas is peeking around the wall.

"Everyone out?" he says.

"I'm here," I say.

"Celie said she'd fix the painting," Mykel says. "So Alatar wouldn't notice the key missing."

Lukas freezes. "She's still in there?"

I glance over the wall, waiting to see or hear any sign of Celie joining us. Alatar is at his office now, about to walk in. Blade has nothing else to say. He anxiously runs a hand through his hair, hoping we all got out in time.

"Celie?" I whisper.

Nothing.

Until Alatar's voice cuts through the silence. "Miss Solano?"

My stomach drops. Every nerve in my body tightens.

"I hope there's an excellent reason you're in here right now," Alatar says. "Talk."

I run over to the door and contemplate showing myself. But what good would that do? Mykel's presence at my side gives me a sliver of courage. I pray Celie can talk herself out of this.

"I-I was looking for you—"

"Where is it?" Alatar blurts the question, eyes darting to the portrait. The key is gone.

"Sir!" Blade steps forward, trying to interrupt, but the door slams shut. Right in my face.

"Shit," Blade mutters, pressing against the wood. Nothing.

"Where is the key?!" Alatar shouts, the sound carrying through the door.

"I don't know!" Celie's voice cracks.

"Do you think I'm an idiot, Solano? Come on. You're smart enough to know better. Where are your friends? They've no doubt had a hand in this."

The Alatar I know—calm, composed, controlled—is gone. In his place stands someone wild and terrifying. The mask has fallen, and the man beneath it is far darker than anyone could have guessed.

"They're not here. I don't know!" Celie says.

"What do we do?" I say to no one in particular.

"Aria. Thank God." Blade says at the sound of my voice, relief flickering in his eyes.

Lukas jogs up beside us. "We have to do something!"

"Is there a spell to break the door?" Mykel says. "The stones—we could use them, right?"

"I'm sorry, Celie," Alatar says, almost mournfully. "You were a good kid—"

"No, sir, *please*! I don't know anything!" Celie says through tears.

"I cannot let you leave here," Alatar snaps. "Dammit, Celie! Why did you go sneaking around?"

"I swear I don't know anything—"

"*Cito*," Alatar says.

The familiar summoning spell.

"*Obtundo*—" Celie tries, but Alatar laughs—mocking, almost gentle in the way he praises her failure.

"Good try," he says. "Hestia, you know what to do."

I try to break open the door with a spell, but nothing happens.

Blade shouts Celie's name, bangs on the wood, casts spells of his own. Each strike, each attempt, yields nothing.

Then—a scream.

And silence.

I freeze. My breath catches as I wait for her to say something. *Something. Anything. Please.*

A heavy sigh, a curse from Alatar, and the door swings open. He steps out, calm again, his mask back in place, hiding whatever darkness had slipped through.

Alatar binds the door shut before turning to Blade.

"Are you gonna kill me, too?" Blade says, voice wavering.

"No. But I will do this." He grabs the back of Blade's neck with his rough hand. "*Secretum Silentium.*"

Blade steps back, stunned by Alatar's work. "What did you just do?"

"A vow of silence. You are now incapable of speaking or writing any truth of what you just witnessed."

Rage washes over Blade's face. His fists clench, knuckles white, but he knows better than to do anything.

Alatar takes a deep breath, composes himself. Then he marches down the hallway, turns the corner, and is out of sight.

As soon as he's gone, Blade rushes to the door, shaking, pressing every ounce of energy against the spell keeping the door locked.

Blade is panicking. I've never seen him like this.

"Aria?" he says, without turning around. "Are you still here?"

I let my invisibility fade, but I don't move, too afraid to see what's happened to Celie on the other side of this door.

Blade rushes over to me. He grabs my hand and squeezes. "She might still be alive." Then he goes back to the door.

Mykel materializes beside him, helping Blade undo the spell sealing the door shut. It must be strong because even together, they're struggling.

My attention turns to Lukas, who is just as stunned as I am. Just as scared.

Finally, with a violent snap, the door bursts open.

Celie lies on the floor. Head lolled to the right. Her body is burning, leaving a pile of ash on the ground beneath her. Her legs from the knees down are already burned away. The silver key tattoo below her inner elbow turns to ash.

Lukas rushes into the room and kneels next to his best friend. He grabs her and pulls her onto his lap.

"Celie..." I whisper, my voice barely my own.

Blade is the first to check her pulse. He doesn't need to say she's not breathing for me to know she's dead.

"*Fuck,*" he says, sitting on the ground next to her.

"Celie? *Please, Celie*. Oh my God, please open your eyes," Lukas cries. "I-I can't lose you, okay? I'm here. I'm right here. I need you, Celie, please. *God*, I can't—*I can't*... I need you."

Mykel's shoulders shake. Tears streak his face.

I kneel on the ground and grab her limp hand in mine. It's hot to the touch, like an open flame. But I don't care. I don't notice I'm crying until my vision blurs and I feel a tear slide down my cheek.

I feel like someone ripped my heart out. Like everything that makes the world bright just got sucked out, leaving in its wake an empty shadow.

All I can think is this... *this* is what heartbreak feels like. This is what it feels like to be completely and utterly shattered.

CHAPTER THIRTY-THREE

I never feared death. I never had a reason to. Sure, I've wondered what happens after... but I never paid it much mind.

I've always been consumed by the minutiae of everyday life, yet every little thing I've ever done now feels meaningless in the grand scheme of things.

What happens when we die?

I have all this knowledge laid out in front of me—demons, celestial beings. I've encountered them, spoken to them. Heaven and Hell—surely that's what happens. But what does it matter if I don't know for certain? If I don't know where Celie is?

I never feared death.

Until now.

I don't fear it because I don't know what comes after. I fear it because I don't want it to take anyone else from me.

I can't lose anyone else.

"As many of you may have heard, Celie Solano has passed away," Alatar says.

The dining hall goes silent. Only the quiet sniffles of mourning students and Alatar's deep voice echo across the room.

I feel heavy, like I'm lugging her loss around with me.

"We are unsure of the cause of death at the moment but are working hard to find out." Alatar pauses, clearing his throat. "Celie was a bright girl—smart, friendly, kind. She touched the hearts of many here at Silver Key Manor. It is truly a tragedy that she is no longer with us."

My vision blurs as hot tears of rage cloud my eyes. I tremble with fury while he speaks.

Blade keeps his gaze forward but places his hand on my thigh under the table, trying to calm me. It does nothing to soothe the fire in my chest.

"In light of this tragedy, we have decided to move the date of the last trial up. It will commence in two weeks. As the Silver Key Tournament rules state, we cannot postpone the trial or cancel the tournament. However, nothing prevents us from moving the trial earlier. We thought it best to get it done sooner and send everyone home. If anyone wishes to drop out before then, that is understandable. Let me know right away, and you will be sent home.

"We'll hold a memorial for Celie tomorrow night in the back garden. Please come and pay your respects. Celie will be missed. Thank you."

"I'm going to kill him," I mutter as he walks off the dais.

Mykel looks at me, his worried expression softening into sadness. Lukas has barely spoken since we left Alatar's office. Blade is trying to hold us all together, but I can see the grief lurking behind his calm. I remind myself that, although he and Celie grew apart, Blade was once her best friend, and he's probably so angry at himself for pushing her away.

Then, as if a switch is flipped, my heart and brain connect, and they decide I can feel sad later. I can grieve later. Right now, I'm angry.

And I want revenge.

Blade and I stand in the hallway leading up to the silver door. We decided it would be best if it were just the two of us. We've made it this far before, and fewer people means a lower chance of getting caught.

Blade quickly deactivates the wards and opens the door. The room looks the same as the first time we were here—dark, lit only by a dim gold glow. Blade murmurs a spell, and the same ancient inscriptions from before appear, crawling across the walls. I pull the energy stone from my pocket, feeling its power surge through me as I hold it in my palm.

"If it is the truth you seek, it is the truth you shall find," Blade says.

We stare at the door. Nothing happens.

I frown. "Why didn't it work?"

"How should I know?" Blade says, frustrated. "That's the password. I triple-checked."

Could Blade have translated the walls wrong? That seems unlikely. Maybe—

"Will you be quiet?" Blade says.

"I didn't say anything!

"Well, stop thinking so loud!"

I sigh. "Let me try. I'm holding the stone, maybe I have to say the password."

Blade nods. I close my hand around the stone and stare at the door. *"If it is the truth you seek, it is the truth you shall find."*

For a long moment, nothing happens. Blade looks like he's about to punch a decent-sized hole into the wall when—a soft click. The stone blazes green, and it's as if a veil has been lifted from the door. The keyhole glimmers, begging for its key. Blade takes it, inserts it.

It's a perfect fit.

He twists, another click, and the door is open.

I spin toward him so fast I almost give myself whiplash.

"For Celie," he says.

"For Celie."

We step inside together. Glowing red walls light up the darkness, but besides that, it's a plain room lined floor to ceiling with shelves. Boxes, filing cabinets, and stacks of papers fill every surface.

"You start on that end," Blade says. "Tell me if you find anything."

I move to the farthest row on the right side, overwhelmed by the sheer volume of documents. I pull out a folder and flip through some papers—they're all blank.

"They used a spell to hide the writing," Blade says from across the room. "Try *Detego*."

I place my hand over the paper. "*Detego*."

Slowly, black text blooms across the page, starting in the centre and spreading outward. I scan it. It's a news article about four men breaking into a family's home at night in search of an artifact. They wore black coats and hoods, faces hidden. They didn't find what they wanted. Two people died; one survived—a little boy.

Lukas.

My pulse quickens as I turn the next sheet. The name Nicholas Prince is listed at the top, with objects and their locations underneath. Lukas told me his father discovered magical artifacts at work. This must be a record of his discoveries.

I flip the page, and one object is circled in thick red ink: a green energy stone.

The following sheets are wanted posters of the four men and notes on possible sightings. On the last sheet, a note in the margin catches my eye: *They want to use the stone, and other magical artifacts, to gain enough power to bring him to their realm.*

It doesn't make sense. I grab the next file, desperate for clarity. My frustration mounts as I flip through endless sheets—until a folder labelled "Amelia & Peter Drake" makes my heart skip.

"Knight? You need to see this," Blade calls. "Aria?"

I can't respond. My chest tightens. Words fail me.

"Aria?" Blade says again, next to me now. "Are you okay?"

I look at him, and worry floods his eyes at the sight of my expression.

"What are those?" He takes a sheet from my hand. "Death certificates? Died of natural causes... Who are these people? Aria, talk to me."

"My birth parents," I say. "They're dead."

CHAPTER THIRTY-FOUR

eath... there it is again.

My birth parents are dead. I never even got to meet them. I'll never get the chance to know the people who gave me life.

They're *dead.*

Blade cups my cheeks, lifting my face toward his, but I don't meet his eyes. I stare at the wall instead, the image of those death certificates—their names printed across the pages—burned in my head.

"Aria," he says. "Aria, look at me."

I meet his gaze. The red light darkens his eyes, but I can still see the faint blue beneath it, and it's more comforting than I could have imagined.

"I'm so sorry," he says. "I can't imagine how shitty this feels. I'm sorry."

"Let's keep looking," I say. "We shouldn't stay here too long."

Before I can reach for the next paper, Blade pulls me into a hug. His long arms wrap around me, warm and tight, and my whole body relaxes as his scent surrounds me—pine and sandalwood with a hint of something softer... vanilla.

I press my face against his chest and stay there, breathing him in, not wanting to move. For the first time in a while, I feel safe. Tears threaten to spill over. I swallow the lump in my throat.

Don't cry. Don't cry. Don't cry.

Now isn't the time. I can cry later.

"I meant to do this earlier," Blade murmurs, his breath warm against my ear. "Things have just been... crazy."

"Thanks," I say, pulling away.

"I'm bad at comforting people."

I force a smile, but when I look up at him, it doesn't feel so forced anymore. "You're not. Not at all."

I take a steadying breath and return to the papers. "Wait, there's more about their deaths here."

The piece of paper looks like it was ripped from a notebook. At the top is a title: *Alatar's Notes — For the Records.*

It was around 8 p.m. when I caught Peter and Amelia. They had discovered the truth about Astalon and planned to trap him in Hell. By the time I realized what they were doing, they were already in the Underworld. I went down to stop them, but I was too late. They had already trapped Astalon in the cage and were finishing the sealing incantation when they saw me. I tried to interrupt their spell, but every attack I cast was deflected. They were seconds from finishing the sealing, and I knew I had to stop them.

Amelia was speaking the incantation. I pulled the knife from my back pocket and stabbed her in the back. She bled out quickly. Peter was outraged and cast a spell so powerful it nearly killed me. It knocked me to the ground. I could barely move. My familiar—an emppeta—healed me. I think Peter believed I was dead. He went back to Amelia and tried to save her, but she was already gone. I managed to sneak up behind him and slit his throat.

I had to dispose of the bodies, so I pushed them off the cliff and watched them disappear into the lava. I am working on a way to free Astalon from the cage. The sealing was incomplete, so that is a positive. I will do everything in my power to see that Astalon is

The note cuts off there.

"He killed them," I whisper. "Alatar killed my parents."

First Celie. Now this.

All three of them—gone. Handed over to death by the same person.

Death is cruel. And so is Alatar.

"I need you to read this," Blade says, holding out a folder. "I found it back there." He gestures to the other side of the room.

I open it. Inside are records—natural disasters, plagues, wars. Pages and pages of historical tragedies, each one listing the death toll.

"Look at the title," Blade says.

I close the folder and read the words on the cover. "Astalon Casualties." My hand flies to my mouth. "Does this mean... did he cause all of these?"

"Looks like it." Blade flips through another file. "I found records on Astalon himself. It says he's the most powerful demon and *the* source of magic. Apparently, as sorcerers age, their magic weakens. They need his energy in this realm to maintain their power."

"Astalon—as in the founder of Silver Key?" I ask.

Blade nods.

They want to use the stone, and other magical artifacts, to gain enough power to bring him to their realm.

The four men who attacked Lukas' parents must have wanted the energy stone to free Astalon—to bring him back and strengthen themselves.

"So my parents found out about the destruction Astalon caused," I say slowly, "and they trapped him. To stop him."

"But if he's trapped in Hell, the link to our source of magic weakens," Blade says. "Which is why Alatar wanted to stop them."

Cold dread settles in my stomach.

"That must be the last trial," I say. "Alatar wants us to help Astalon escape Hell and return here."

Blade hands me another set of papers and flips to the third page. "It says that when Astalon is on Earth, it's like he infects the planet," Blade explains. "People commit mass genocide. Viruses spread. Natural disasters increase. Think about it—since Astalon's been in Hell, have we seen anything like the events on this list?"

No. Nothing close to this scale.

We can't let Alatar free him.

"Curfew's in ten minutes," Blade says. "They're doing routine checks now since Celie..."

I nod. "We have to go. Let's meet in the back garden tomorrow morning at nine. I'll tell Mykel and Lukas."

We leave the room. The door seals shut behind us.

"And Knight," Blade says. "Be careful."

"Yeah," I say quietly. "You too."

I head toward my dorm room. I want to be alone. I want to sleep and stop thinking about everything eating away at my brain.

"Aria?" a voice calls from behind me. I'm halfway up the staircase when I turn and see Mrs. Patrickson a few steps below. "Can we talk for a moment?"

"I don't know, Mrs. Patrickson. I'm not really in the mood. Besides, there's curfew, so..."

She climbs the steps and places a gentle hand on my arm. "Please, Aria. Let's talk in my office."

Her voice is calm, careful. She's choosing her words cautiously, like she's afraid of upsetting me. The worry in her eyes is genuine, so I follow her.

When we reach her office, she closes the door behind us and sits down.

"I won't ask if you're alright, because I know the answer," she begins. "But I want you to know I'm here if you need to talk."

I don't want to talk about Celie. And I definitely can't tell Mrs. Patrickson about what we discovered tonight, considering I wasn't supposed to be in that room in the first place. I can't help but wonder if she knows about what's hidden there. Everything written on those pages. Everything locked away.

No.

Mrs. Patrickson would never support Alatar bringing Astalon into our realm, not if it put innocent lives at risk. The little girl in the framed photo on her desk... I don't know much about her, but I know Mrs. Patrickson loves her like a daughter. She would never endanger her for power.

"I don't want to talk about it," I finally say.

It's the truth. If I start talking about Celie, I'll start crying, and I'm afraid I won't be able to stop.

Mrs. Patrickson nods and glances at the photo on her desk.

"You said she's like a daughter to you?" I ask.

It's selfish, maybe, but I want to change the subject. Anything to take the focus off me—anything so I don't have to acknowledge the ache in my chest.

Mrs. Patrickson gives me a sad smile. "She's my friend's daughter. Her name is Lila. My friend passed away a few years ago, and I've been taking care of her since."

I offer her a sympathetic look but stay silent.

"A year ago, Lila was diagnosed with leukaemia," she continues. "Chemo isn't working. If she were a sorcerer, she never would have gotten sick. And even if she had, there are healing potions. But they don't work on people without magic."

"I'm sorry," I say.

Mrs. Patrickson shakes her head and wipes away a tear. "I don't want to burden you with my problems, Aria. You already have enough on your shoulders. I'm okay. Really."

I don't entirely believe her, but I nod anyway.

"What I want to know," she says, "is whether you'll be okay."

I sigh and stand. "I'm not sure."

She rises and takes my hand before I can walk away. "You're always there for other people, Aria. I've noticed that about you. But you have to let people be there for you, too."

I stare up at the ceiling, forcing back my tears.

"You push your feelings away like ignoring them will make them disappear. But it only makes things worse."

I want to deny it, but I can't. That's exactly what I've been doing since I arrived at Silver Key. Ignoring the fact that I'm adopted. Ignoring the lies. Pretending it didn't bother me that the people I love most kept the truth from me my whole life. I thought I'd moved past it, but maybe I didn't. Maybe I just buried it.

"I love my parents. But I'm angry that they lied to me. They've known my whole life, and they never told me." Guilt knots in my chest as the words leave my mouth. "I know they love me. I know they were trying to do the right thing, but..."

My voice trails off. I don't even know how to finish that sentence.

"Sometimes we adults make choices we don't fully understand," she says. "Even if it seems like we do, we don't have all the answers. A mother may believe she's making the right decision, only to realize later that she was wrong." She pauses. "We all make mistakes, but the beauty of it is we're loved enough to be forgiven for those mistakes. Just as your parents forgive you for yours, try to find it in your heart to forgive them."

Her words settle into my mind. She's right. I know she is. I love my parents, and they love me. That should be enough.

"Thank you, Mrs. Patrickson."

"You can always talk to me, Aria. About anything."

I know she means Celie. And while I'm grateful for the offer, losing Celie isn't something I'm ready to talk about yet.

With that, I leave her office and drag myself up several flights of stairs. When I reach the dorm hallway, I stop in front of the door. My hand rests on the doorknob.

For a moment, I hesitate.

Then I take a deep breath and open the door to my quiet, empty room.

CHAPTER THIRTY-FIVE

The weight on my chest makes it impossible to sleep.

The room feels hollow, and I fight the urge to scream just to fill the silence. I try to force out tears. I feel like I should be crying, but I can't.

I look at the foot of my bed, and she's there, gently smacking me with a book to wake me up so we can train. I glance toward her bed, and we're sitting there, giggling about something Lukas said earlier that day. I look at the window, and she's standing there, staring out at the view, the sun warm on her face.

Then she fades. Disintegrates into ashes and drifts into the moonlight.

I can't stop hearing her scream. I can't stop seeing her body slowly burning.

Celie brought so much light into my life. She helped me through difficult times, and we bonded over it. I'm so grateful for our friendship.

Ever since I was little, I've had a hard time making friends. Violet always told me I needed to open up more. She practically dragged me out of my shell, and because of that, I wasn't as scared to open up to Celie.

Celie wanted to help me find my parents.

Alatar's written confession burns in my mind. We were going to search for them together after the tournament ended. Now, in the span of a day, I've lost all three of them for good.

And Mykel won't speak to me. It doesn't seem like as significant a loss compared to everything else we're going through, but it still hurts. I feel like I'm losing everyone. How can everything be going so wrong?

I thought this was a gift—at least once I moved past the initial shock of being adopted. Discovering I'm a sorcerer, competing in a magical tournament... what girl my age wouldn't want that? I thought I'd made the right decision choosing to compete, choosing this life.

But I was right from the start.

It's better to have a plan. It's better to know what lies ahead, to have structure in your life. Because this... this is not a gift.

It's four o'clock in the morning, and I've given up all hope of getting any sleep. I drag myself out of bed and decide to walk through the manor. My feet guide the way as my mind spirals through dark, depressing thoughts. Somehow, I end up in the boys' dormitories.

I need company. Staying in that room alone was torture.

I start toward Lukas and Mykel's room but stop myself. Mykel wants nothing to do with me.

Everything feels strange with Mykel and Lukas now. With Celie gone and Mykel and me on bad terms, I don't feel like I belong anymore. And Lukas... Lukas hasn't been himself. I can't blame him, but I miss his smile.

I knock on Blade's door. A few seconds later, he opens it. He's shirtless and wide awake. He clearly hasn't slept either. His eyes are red and puffy, like he's been crying. Mine probably look the same. He doesn't say anything when he sees me, just opens the door wider and lets me in, closing it quietly behind me.

When I step inside, I realize he's alone. Then I remember he's had this room to himself ever since Rex was eliminated after the first trial.

"I couldn't sleep in there," I say.

He nods in understanding and sits on his bed. I lower myself to the floor, leaning my back against the mattress and pulling my knees to my chest.

"I can't stop thinking about everything," he says.

I tilt my head back to look at him. He stares straight ahead, a defeated expression on his face.

"Do you think my father knew about all this?" he asks. "He and Alatar are so close."

I look away. "I don't know. Maybe. Do you?"

He doesn't answer. Instead, he slides off the bed and sits on the floor beside me. Just like that time in the hallway, we sit side by side, pain and sorrow hanging heavily in the air between us. The only sound is the rain tapping against the window.

I turn to him. "Can I stay here tonight?"

"You can sleep in here for as long as you need to."

"Do you want me to take the other bed?" I ask, pointing toward Rex's empty one.

"No."

My face flushes as we both stand and crawl into his bed. I lie back, grateful for the darkness.

Shoulder to shoulder, Blade and I lie beside each other. His hand brushes mine. Our fingers intertwine.

"Aria?" he says.

"Yeah?"

"I didn't want to be alone tonight either."

I wake up a few hours later.

Blade's arm is draped over my shoulder, and my head rests gently against his bare chest. I tilt my head up to look at him. He's peacefully asleep, his silver hair falling over one eye. It's gotten longer. I move to brush it away but stop myself and—

That's when I realize... I realize that this is what I want. To wake up next to him and see his handsome face this close to mine. I trace the sharp line of his jaw with my eyes, the softness of his slightly parted lips, the length of his dark eyelashes, the small scar above his left eyebrow.

Normally, this would be the moment he wakes up and makes some snarky comment about how I'm admiring his beauty—which, to be fair, I am. But he's still sound asleep.

I carefully slip out of bed and wipe a hand across my face. I should've stayed there. Stayed in that moment with Blade. I don't want to deal with life again—Celie, Mykel, Alatar, my parents... I don't want to think about any of it.

With a heavy sigh, I head for the door. But when I step through it, instead of entering the hallway, I walk straight into another dorm room.

I freeze. My eyes widen, confusion creeping in.

This seriously needs to stop happening to me.

I know it's a girl's room. It smells like perfume, the bedsheets are purple, and makeup is scattered across the bedside table.

And Sarah is standing in front of me.

I've only spoken to her a handful of times. I've always liked her, but this is...

"Hi, Aria," she says.

"Hey, Sarah? Um..."

"Sorry. I thought it would be easier to teleport you here. I don't want anyone to know we're talking."

"Why?"

"Because I'm about to tell you something, and it's important that no one finds out."

"What's going on, Sarah?"

"I guess I might as well just say it." She exhales, hesitates. "You and I are... biologically sisters."

CHAPTER THIRTY-SIX

S*isters.*

Just when I thought there was nothing else that could surprise me... I have a *sister*.

Peter and Amelia had two children: Sarah and me. Sarah was born first, three years before I was. She tells me I was born right before our parents went to the Underworld to trap Astalon. They didn't know if they would survive, and they wanted me to live a normal life, far away from the darkness of the magical world, with two perfectly normal parents and a perfectly normal home. They wanted me to go to a normal school, have normal friends, and be safe.

They wanted me to be safe.

They knew what they were doing was dangerous, and if they succeeded, I could be in danger too. That's why they gave me up.

They sent Sarah to live with our grandparents, secluded from the rest of the world, hidden under protective magic. Sarah grew up alone. She only had a few friends who visited occasionally. Our grandparents taught her magic, and when she was old enough, they told her the truth about everything. Since then, Sarah has made it her life's mission to avenge our parents' deaths. She wants to make sure Astalon stays trapped in Hell forever and that Alatar pays for what he did to them.

"Wow," is all I can manage.

I'm drowning in questions, yet somehow, I ask none of them.

"I know it's a lot," she says, "but I had to tell you for this to work. I want to take Alatar down, but I need you and your friends' help."

"Wait. Were you the one who teleported me to that creepy cabin when I overheard Alatar's conversation?"

"I had to clue you in somehow," she says. "And it was too soon to reveal that we're sisters. If word got out, Alatar would kick me out of the manor. Then I'd never get the chance to kill him."

"Right. Um... I'm sorry. This is a lot to process."

Her voice softens. "I know. And I know you're already going through a lot with Celie and finding out all this messed-up shit. But can I count on you to help?"

"Why me? I get that we're sisters, but you hardly even know me."

Sarah smiles. "You take after our mother. She was incredibly strong. And you have just as much reason to hate Alatar as I do. He's taken something important from you—several things—just like he has from me."

I barely know her. And what I thought I knew about her was a lie. I know I shouldn't trust her so quickly, but something in my gut tells me she's telling the truth.

The more I study her, the more I see the resemblance. Her eyes are grey, and her hair is dirty blond like our father's. She looks a lot like our mother too. The same round face and full lips. I can easily believe we're sisters.

She watches me hopefully, but beneath that hope I see something else: anger, frustration... desperation she's trying to hide.

She isn't lying. We *are* sisters. And it's clear she wants nothing more than to make Alatar pay for what he's done.

That's something else we share.

"I'm in," I say. "Do you have a plan?"

She lets out a breath of relief. "I do. It's going to require a little extra help, though."

"I'll get Mykel, Lukas, and Blade on board."

I glance at the clock on the wall. 8:37 a.m. I have to change and meet Mykel, Blade, and Lukas in the back garden.

"I'm going to meet up with them now," I say. "I'll let you know how it goes."

"Here." She hands me a small, clear ring. "It's charmed—kind of like a walkie-talkie."

I slide the ring onto my finger. "How does it work?"

"Just talk into it and I'll hear you. I have one too." She raises her hand, showing the same clear ring on her index finger.

"Thanks," I say, opening the door.

"Hey, Aria."

I spin back around.

"I'm glad I could finally tell you. It's been tough keeping this in."

I give her a genuine smile. "I'm glad I know."

The sun hides behind the clouds, casting a blanket of shade over the back garden. It's as if Celie's death drained the world of its light. The roses that were blooming just days ago droop toward the ground in despair, and even the soft breeze that usually ripples across the lake seems still in its grief.

I sit in silence beneath the willow tree. It's not long before Blade joins me, followed a few minutes later by Mykel and Lukas.

None of us speak as we wait for someone who isn't coming, unsure what to say. Finally, Mykel clears his throat and turns to Blade and me. "What did you guys find?"

"Before we talk about that," I say, "something else happened this morning."

They all look at me. *Where do I even start?*

I tell them about Sarah and our parents. How we're sisters, and how she was the one who sent me to that cabin the night I overheard Alatar. How she's been planning her revenge against him for almost her entire life.

They listen intently, not interrupting once. When I finish, they look just as stunned as I felt.

"*Sarah?* The plot thickens," Lukas says. For a moment, I glimpse a piece of the real him still buried beneath the grief. But it disappears just as quickly when he drops his gaze to his lap.

I rub a hand over my face, feeling strangely calm about everything. Maybe I've had so many bombs dropped on me that I'm numb to it now.

"So she wants our help killing Alatar," Blade says. "Do you know her plan?"

"No. She hasn't told me yet. But she said she'll need all of us. She can't do it alone. I totally understand if you guys don't want to get involved. It's probably going to be dangerous and—"

"I'm in," Lukas says. "I'm ready to risk my life if it means avenging Celie's death. I don't care. I just want him to pay."

Blade studies Lukas, worry in his eyes, before he turns to me. "Knight, you know I'm in."

Mykel looks at Blade for a moment, thinking, then begrudgingly sighs. "I'm in too."

Blade doesn't say anything at Mykel's reluctance to work with him. He just gives Mykel the finger.

I roll my eyes and raise my finger with the ring to my mouth. "They're in," I say.

A second later, Sarah's voice echoes in my mind. *Great. I'll meet you guys at dinner tomorrow night.*

Tomorrow night.

I can't lie—I'm curious to see what Sarah has planned. I'm so eager to take Alatar down, it's all I can think about. Part of me is scared to think about anything else.

Blade and I fill Mykel and Lukas in on everything we discovered about Alatar, my parents, and Astalon. They're shocked, to say the least. When we finish, the conversation fades into an uncomfortable silence.

Then, clearly trying to break it, Mykel turns to me. "Do you have lessons today?"

Although normal classes were cancelled due to... recent events, I still had the option of continuing private lessons with Mrs. Patrickson.

"No. I cancelled them," I say. "I literally can't focus on anything right now."

"Yeah," he says quietly.

And then more silence.

"Well," Blade says, standing. "This is awkward, so I'm gonna go."

He heads back toward the manor. Lukas gets up a moment later and walks away without saying a word.

I let out a breath. "This is so unfair. Why did all of this have to happen?"

Mykel looks at me, guilt written all over his face. "Aria, I shouldn't have said all those things to you. I'm really sorry."

I look up at him, my expression softening. Mykel did say some hurtful things during our argument, but I still want him in my life, even if it's only as a friend. With everything going on, we need each other. We all do.

"No, you shouldn't have," I say. "But I get it. You were angry. And you were right. Plus, I kind of deserved it."

His eyes snap up to mine.

"I tried to deny my feelings for Blade because I felt guilty about them," I continue. "But they're there. And I should've told you sooner."

"I know," he says. "And as angry as I am—and even though I still think he's going to hurt you—you can't help how you feel. Just be careful."

I nod, unsure what to say.

Mykel stands to leave.

"Hey," I call after him. "I hope you know my feelings for you were real. I really did like you, Mykel. I still do."

"I know," he says. "But you don't love me the same way I love you. And that's what hurts the most."

That night, I go to the memorial being held for Celie. Alatar says a few words. People cry and stand in silence. We light candles, and people share stories about how Celie impacted their lives. How she inspired them, how she helped them when they were down. I hadn't realized how many lives Celie had touched until now. There are people here crying over this loss who I've never even spoken to.

But that's just who Celie was. She cared about people. She was kind to everyone.

"Celie was my best friend," Lukas starts.

Most people have already left the memorial, but a small group remains.

"I didn't want to speak tonight because I wasn't sure I could get through it without crying," he says. "And I don't think any words I have could express how deeply heartbroken I am."

He shakes his head and looks down at the candles, photos, and flowers.

"Celie, you were the best person on earth. You were selfless and kind and smart, and... I could go on for hours about how great of a person you are—were."

His words bring a heavy lump to my throat, and I swallow hard, forcing back tears.

His voice softens as he continues. "When we were little, we used to sneak out and go to this place in the forest near your house. There's a lake there. We liked to think we were the only ones who knew it existed, and it became our spot." He smiles faintly. "We'd go there to talk, hang out, have picnics, play games. We never stopped going. That's where I came out to you. That's where we cried over boys together." He picks up a flower and twirls it between his fingers. "That place is special. It's ours.

"The last time we were there was right before we left for Silver Key. We promised each other that as soon as the tournament was over, we'd go back for a picnic. Just like we used to."

His voice breaks. He stops fighting the tears and lets them fall. Once they start, he can't stop them.

"I'm sorry," he says.

Then he walks away.

I'm about to follow him, but Mykel tells me he's got it and runs after Lukas.

Lukas once told me he had nowhere to go after his parents died. He's been living with Celie ever since. The two of them were inseparable. For Lukas, losing Celie means losing the most important person in his life.

I stay at the memorial long after everyone leaves. I sit on the cold grass, staring at the flowers, candles, and photos. Darkness has fallen, and the full moon hangs low above me.

I hear rustling and notice movement in the distance. I strain my eyes, trying to see what made the sound. A small bunny with a unicorn horn hops toward me and lands in my lap. Soft and warm, she nuzzles against my stomach before looking up at me, grief mirrored in her brown eyes.

And I cry.

CHAPTER THIRTY-SEVEN

The next day at dinner, I sit at a table on the far end of the dining hall with Blade, Mykel, and Lukas as we wait for Sarah to join us.

"Is she coming?" Mykel asks, biting into a slice of pizza.

I glance toward the entrance. "She said she's on her way."

"So what happens if her plan is, like, awful?" Lukas says.

"Let's hope it's not," Blade replies.

A minute later, Sarah approaches. I squeeze closer to Blade to make room for her.

"Before I say anything, no one can find out about this," she says. "Seriously. If I find out you told someone, I will kill you."

"Lovely," Lukas mutters.

"We won't tell anyone," Mykel says. "Trust us. We want Alatar to suffer as much as you do."

"Okay," Sarah says. "Astalon is loose in the Underworld right now. He escaped his cage, but he can't leave Hell on his own. He'll need powerful sorcerers to help him. That's the third trial. We're supposed to be tricked into helping him."

"How do you know for sure that's the trial?" Mykel asks.

"I have my sources."

Lukas narrows his eyes. "Mysterious."

"I've been preparing for this my whole life," Sarah says. "Of course I had to know what Alatar was planning if I wanted to figure out how to beat him. I met with a demon a while back. In exchange for one of my deepest secrets, it answered two questions I had."

"A kaldin demon?" Blade says.

"That's the one," Sarah confirms. "It told me Alatar plans to use the trial to free Astalon from the Underworld, and that it would be the sorcerers competing in the tournament who would help him."

I grab another slice of pizza and plop it on my plate. "How did it know? Can we trust a demon?"

"Kaldins are all-knowing," Mykel says.

"That can't be good. An all-knowing demon?"

"Kaldins are all-knowing, but they only reveal what they know when asked the right questions," Blade says.

Mykel nods. "And in exchange for one's deepest secret, they have to answer that person's questions truthfully."

"Exactly," Sarah says.

"Plus, they mostly keep to themselves and are hard to find," Blade adds. "The most common place to find one is in the Underworld."

"I heard they're pretty creepy," Lukas says.

Sarah picks up a slice of pizza. "I can attest to that. The one I tracked down looked almost human, but its body was outlined in mist. Charcoal-grey smoke hovered around it, and its eyes were pure white—the only thing I could see clearly through the dark."

I shudder.

"Anyway," Sarah continues, "what the demon told me has to be true. The only advantage we have is that Alatar doesn't know we know. We can go down there, trap Astalon, and seal him for good."

"But won't Alatar see what we're doing?" Blade says. "The trials are monitored."

"Yes," Sarah says. "The trials are normally monitored using magic, but the demon said Alatar will be watching the third trial closely. He'll want to stop us if he sees what we're up to. He can't enter the Underworld alone; he's not strong enough. That makes me think something in the trial will unlock the door for him. I just don't know what. Either way, we get a head start. If he catches us, we'll have to fight him. He's weaker right now, but still a powerful sorcerer. And his power will only increase if he makes it into Hell, in close proximity to Astalon. Be ready to call on your familiars—they could help in a fight."

"Is it weird that I'm kind of excited?" Lukas says.

"Yes," Blade and Mykel say in unison. They glance at each other, then quickly look away.

I stifle a laugh and take a deep breath, my mind returning to the task at hand. I'm ready to risk my life to take down Alatar and Astalon once and for all. Maybe that says a lot about how I'm coping. Either way, I'd rather feel this than grieve. I know I'll have to face my feelings eventually, but that time is not now.

"I'm assuming you know the spell to seal Astalon in the cage?" Blade says.

Sarah smirks. "Of course."

"So, Aria, when you blast a spell at Astalon, Blade will sneak up behind him and hit him with the spell to trap him in the cage. Then Mykel will repeat it, shooting from the right or left. Once he's weak enough, the cage will hold him. Lukas and I will either help with the spell or handle Alatar if he catches up to us. After that, all five of us will say the incantation to seal him in the cage. Once it's done, we get out by shooting a flare."

"Got it," I say.

"Okay, we'll go over this more tomorrow."

I turn to leave with the boys, but Sarah stops me. "Hey, Aria, can I talk to you for a sec?"

"Of course. What's up?"

She hesitates. "I just... Sorry. I practiced how I'd tell you this so many times, and now that I'm here, I can't remember a thing."

"You can tell me. Whatever it is, I won't freak out. Probably."

She takes a deep breath. "All my life... I always wanted to find you and tell you. About Mom, Dad... about me. I dreamt about it—having my sister with me, growing up together, doing whatever it is sisters do. I wanted to tell you so badly, but I was never allowed. I was told it was for our own good. So we could be safe. Sometimes I wish I'd reached out anyway."

"It's okay. I understand why you didn't. And yeah, it sucks. It's so unfair... I'm just really sorry you had to grow up alone. I wish we could have grown up together."

"So do I," she says, sighing. "They took you out of my life when I was three. You had just been born, but I loved you so much. My grandmother told me I spent every second with you—from the moment you came home to the moment you were gone. She said that before my parents gave you up, they put an enchantment on us. It's a tradition in magical families: a spell that bonds two siblings, creating a connection deeper than any other. The bond can't be broken, but it can weaken. The more time we spent apart, the weaker it got. I don't know if you've ever felt it. You were just a baby, but I was old enough to feel that bond... and feel it weakening every day we weren't together."

"Wow. I guess I did feel something when you first introduced yourself. I felt like I could trust you, even though I barely knew you."

"I felt it too. That bond. Like a little spark inside me, igniting after so long."

That's exactly what it felt like. A spark.

"I'm glad we have each other now," I say.

I've always wanted a sister. Don't get me wrong, I love Ashton to death. But he would never help me pick an outfit for a date, teach me makeup tricks, or do anything girly for that matter. After I met Violet, she became like my sister, the one I do those things with. But I've always felt like something was missing. Sarah is that missing piece. The bonding spell explains that feeling.

And then it hits me—how excited I am to get to know Sarah, to introduce her to Violet. I just hope they get along. It may take time for Sarah and me to develop a sisterly relationship, but there's no doubt in my mind we'll get there eventually. Just like Violet and I did. Just like Celie and I did.

The following weeks are filled with anxiety and anticipation. I spend most of my time with Blade, going over spells and training. I only see Mykel when it's to discuss the trial, and even then, we barely speak. It's awkward between us, and neither of us is sure how to proceed. I hope we can be friends again—that is, if we survive the third trial—but I understand he needs time.

Lukas is doing a bit better. He's gradually becoming himself again. I think he's in the same boat as me: motivation to avenge Celie consuming every other emotion. It's strange to think how much a person can change because of what they experience. I know I've changed. I'm afraid I've changed so much that my old life wouldn't recognize me.

Now that the last trial is here, I realize I'll have to go back home soon. Surprisingly, the thought scares me. What if I really don't fit in with my own life anymore? And what about the friends I've made here? Will I ever see them again? Will we go weeks without speaking until we finally move on?

That's not what I want.

The relationships I've made at Silver Key are some of the strongest I've ever had. We've been through so much together. I can't imagine not seeing these people every day.

"Hey," Blade says, stealing me from my thoughts.

"Hey."

"What were you thinking about?"

A sigh escapes me. "I was thinking about how I don't want this to end."

Blade doesn't respond, and I take it as a sign to elaborate.

"I've been the happiest I've ever been and met the most amazing people here. I went on adventures, learned things, saw and did things I never thought I would. And I experienced heartbreak. In so many ways. I've felt lost, conflicted, angry, betrayed. I'm a completely different person than I was before I came here. I don't know if that's good or bad—but I'm not ready to go back to my old life. I'm not ready to leave this place, my friends... you."

Blade smiles. "Knight, just because you leave Silver Key doesn't mean it has to end. You don't have to go back to your old life if you don't want to."

"What do you mean? Of course I do. I have friends back home. Family. I haven't seen my little brother in almost a year."

"What I'm saying is, you can go back to the same place, but you don't have to go back to the same life. You can keep learning magic, and we can still see each other." He grabs my hand. "Honestly, the thought of not seeing you scares the shit out of me."

"I don't know where you're going with this," I say.

"There's a school of magic near you, in New York. I'm thinking of transferring there next year. You could too."

"Are you serious?"

"One hundred percent."

"But—I know next to nothing about the magical world. How society works, the rules… transportation? Do we just teleport through doors?"

"Some do, but most of us just drive," Blade says, and I release a shaky breath. "You'll learn, Knight. You'll adapt. I'll be there to help you every step of the way."

"What about *your* life before Silver Key?"

"You mean Rex and Nathan, my only friends, and my abusive dad? Moving to a different state is something I should've done a while ago. Now I have a reason."

It sounds too good to be true. A school of magic… with Blade. I'd be able to be with my family and still see him every day.

"Are you crying?" he says, a hint of laughter in his voice.

"Shut up," I chuckle. "I'm happy. That… that sounds amazing."

He brushes a stray tear from my cheek and rests his hand there. That one simple touch sets my whole body alight, and suddenly, the mood shifts.

"Aria," he says, barely a whisper. My name on his lips feels intimate, electric.

I look up. Our eyes meet. I swear I can see the ocean in them—the perfect shade of blue, deep yet bright, mesmerizing. I used to think his eyes were so cold and closed off. But now I gaze into them and am met with an overwhelming sensation of warmth and… safety.

The way he looks at me is intense, like he can see my soul, every thought, every feeling.

His gaze drops to my lips. A haze of desire clouds his eyes. They trace every feature—my lips, my eyebrows, the flecks in my green eyes—committing each little detail to memory.

He leans in slowly. We're inches apart. I feel his breath on my lips. Peppermint clouds my senses. Our lips brush, sending a chill through me. My heart has never beaten this fast—

"Oh shit," someone says.

Blade and I fly apart.

"So sorry."

Lukas.

"I came to get you guys," he says. He's trying not to laugh. I can see it. He's clearly amused. "We have to meet in the dining hall in, like, two minutes."

"Please leave," Blade says. "We're right behind you."

"Right," Lukas says. "Yeah, I should let you guys finish."

He winks at me. Blade flips him off.

"By the way," Lukas says, turning back, "I totally saw this coming. From the start. Something about the way you two bickered... the tension... I didn't want to say anything because, you know, Mykel, but—"

"Leave!" I shout, shoving him out the door.

Blade and I enter the dining hall, which is filled with people. Food is laid out on every table, but none of us have an appetite—or a voice, apparently—as our footsteps echo through the silent room.

I sit next to Lukas. He gives me a knowing look, and I lightly punch his arm. Mykel, sitting across from us, frowns in confusion, but becomes distracted as Blade slides into the empty seat beside him. He opens his mouth to speak, but Alatar's voice cuts him off.

"By now, you all know the drill," Alatar begins, standing on the dais. "You know where to go and what to expect. Normally,

I would give you a hint for the trial, but... you've made it this far. I'm sure you can figure it out yourselves." A glimmer of mischief lights his eyes as he smirks at the audience. "As this is the last time we'll all gather in this room together, I want to thank you for your hard work and dedication this year. It's inspiring to see such young, powerful sorcerers strive to succeed in this competition. If you make it to the end of this final trial, you will teleport back here, where your accumulated points will be totalled, and the winner revealed. The winner will receive the magical grimoire and be granted the Sight of their choice." He pauses for effect. "Good luck to all of you."

I can't hold back my eye roll any longer.

We're given the same style of uniform as the first trial and change into it before approaching the entrance.

"So... do we have any idea what to expect when we enter?" Mykel says.

Blade shrugs. "Hopefully we're right, and as soon as we step in, we're in the Underworld."

"How are we going to find Astalon once we get there?" I ask, a flicker of worry in my voice. This is usually the point where I panic.

"I've got it figured out. We just need to stick together," Sarah says, joining us. She hands each of us a golden dagger. "Take these. They're made for killing demons. They'll come in handy."

I slide the dagger into its sheath strapped tightly to my thigh, and we approach the entrance.

"We can do this, right?" I say.

Sarah smiles at me. "Of course we can. We have to."

CHAPTER THIRTY-EIGHT

I step into the darkness.

I'm vaguely aware of the door shutting behind me—the soft click the last sound I hear before silence engulfs me. I can't make out any of my surroundings.

"Blade?" I call.

No answer.

I'm alone. My pulse spikes, heart hammering, as I scramble to think.

"*Lumen.*" A bright orb illuminates the space.

I look around and see nothing. Absolutely nothing but this black empty void.

I'm afraid to move. Afraid to speak. Solitude seeps into me like poison. My breaths grow shallow. My hands shake. My mind fixates on the loneliness, consuming everything else.

"Aria," a voice calls. It's a whisper. I almost miss it over the roar of my thoughts.

"Hello?" My voice comes out quieter than I intended.

"Aria!"

I move forward, careful with each step.

"ARIA!" The voice screams, louder this time. Hoarse, desperate, urgent. "ARIA! ARIA! ARIA!" It repeats my name again and again—

I follow it, running as fast as I can through the pitch black.

Until I see a light. It draws me in like a moth to a flame.

Someone lies in the distance, under the spotlight. They don't move as I inch toward them—

My blood runs cold.

Celie.

The metallic stench of blood hits me as pools of it seep from her chest, her mouth, her eyes... like tears of blood.

"Oh my God, Celie!" I kneel, pressing my hands against her wound, trying to stop the bleeding.

My hands. They won't stop shaking. I pull them away, clenching my fists, nails digging into my palms. There's blood under my fingernails. It seeps into every crease, staining my palms scarlet.

Her eyes are wide and unblinking, but she's not dead. I feel the rise and fall of her chest as I place my hands back on her wound.

"Celie, what's—stay calm, just—I'm gonna get us out of here. H-How is this—"

"Aria!" someone calls from behind me. I turn, and when I look back, Celie is gone.

"What is happening," I whisper.

Not a speck of blood remains.

"Aria, hurry!" It sounds like my mom. My adoptive mom.

I scramble toward her voice. She's on the floor. No blood like Celie, but her eyes are lifeless.

"Mom?" I say, barely a breath.

I apprehensively bring my hand down to caress her cheek. It's cold to the touch.

She's dead.

I fight the urge to be sick, resting my hands on my knees, taking shallow breaths. Once calm, I close my eyes, trying to quiet my thoughts.

Silence.

There are no sounds, not even the sound of my own breathing—

Until a drop. Like a raindrop falling into a puddle. But it's not rain, it's a tear. I realize I'm crying. The drop echoes in the void, blurring my vision.

Someone kneels before me and tilts my chin up.

"It's okay, Aria," Mykel says, dimpled grin on his face. But blood coats his teeth. It drips down his chin, and he falls unconscious in front of me.

I scramble to my feet in shock and—

Behind him, Blade hangs by the neck.

"No!" I stumble back, collapse to my knees. "I can't—"

I crawl backward, away from Mykel, away from Blade, until my back hits a wall. I bring my knees up to my chest and bury my face in my arms.

This isn't right. *This isn't real.*

I have to get out of here.

I take a deep breath, force myself up, and run.

Vision blurred, tears streaming, legs burning, head pounding—I run. And run. And run.

And then I'm on the edge of a cliff.

I halt, rocks crumbling beneath my feet, falling down down down to the ground below. I step back from the edge, get on my hands and knees, and peer over—

Below me is everyone I love and care for... dead.

My mom, dad, brother, Violet, Blade, Mykel, Celie, Lukas, Amelia, Peter, even Sarah. A pile of dead loved ones.

Nausea crawls up my throat. I turn away, retching.

There has to be a way out.

But everywhere I turn is pure darkness.

The cliff disappears, and I'm back in the black void.

"You're alone, Aria," Violet's voice says. "We're all dead because of you."

I squeeze my eyes shut, hands on my head. "This isn't real!"

"You couldn't save me," Celie says. "You just stood there and did *nothing*!"

"I'm sorry," I sob, head to the ground. "I'm sorry."

"Fucking pathetic," Blade says. "You think I'd change for *you*?"

"*Please*, stop." I cradle my head, cover my ears, but it doesn't help. The words invade my mind, no matter if they're real or imagined.

"You're weak," Mykel says.

I can't breathe.

"You aren't enough, Aria." This from a woman's voice that I somehow know is her. Amelia. "You're *weak*."

The voices multiply, taunting, overlapping, screaming every fear, every self-doubt I've ever had.

I can't breathe. I can't breathe. I can't breathe.

I feel suffocated, trapped in this inescapable hell.

I sob. Pull at my hair. Bang my forehead against the floor. Again. And again. And again.

Then I stop.

Giving in to this living nightmare won't help me escape. I need to be brave. I need to stand against my fears.

I know this isn't real, no matter how real it feels. I *know* I can save myself.

So I stand and do the only thing that feels right.

I scream.

The loudest, most powerful scream to ever escape my lungs. It shatters the darkness around me. A surge of energy bursts forth—bold, bright, electric purple—enveloping me like a protective force field. It glows, lighting up the void.

I scream, and I feel everything: anger and relief, sadness and joy. Every emotion I've ever felt crashes through me at once, sending every ounce of magic in my body into overdrive.

Suddenly, I feel stronger. I gain control over my emotions. When I finally stop screaming, I fall back to my knees. The light fades, but even in the fractured darkness, I can see far better than before. My mind is clear—a clarity I thought I'd never regain. I am no longer scared, no longer sad, no longer angry. In this moment, I am entirely composed.

A faint purple trail shimmers in front of me. I rise and follow it. Eventually, it leads to a white door. I open it, and step outside.

I'm on a cliff. Relief floods me at no longer being trapped in that hell—but fear creeps in for whatever place this is.

The world here is drained of colour, muted and dusty. Everything that makes the world beautiful has been sucked away. The sky hangs heavy and grey. The wind whips my hair across my face, and a thick fog obscures my view.

It's quiet. I don't see anyone around me—until I notice a figure moving through the fog.

"Hello?" I call.

The figure moves toward me. Though we're still far, I can make out who it is, and I've never been so relieved to see someone in my entire life. I don't know how one person's presence can make me feel so overjoyed. So overcome with a painful need to be close to them.

He sees me and runs. All I can think is that I would give anything to be in his arms.

I move. The distance feels endless.

Finally, we meet in the middle. He locks his arms around me in a hug, clutching me to him, and I hug back with the same urgency. He buries his face in my neck, trembling, as if afraid I'll let go. Neither of us speaks. Neither of us moves.

When we finally pull away from the hug, we don't pull away from each other.

He gazes down at me, inches from my face. His breath brushes my lips, sending a shiver through me. I search his eyes, waiting.

Then he cups my cheeks and presses his lips to mine.

My hair whips around us in the wind, but I don't care. All I feel is him. All I feel is how right this is.

Blade.

He's so different from the day I met him. Before, all I saw was an arrogant boy... but I was wrong. Blade is kind and gentle—yet so strong. Every glance, every shared moment brought us closer, peeling back the layers we'd built between us. And as much as I could say I helped break down his walls, I know it was him who had to push himself. Who had to trust me, no matter how difficult it was to finally let someone in.

And I had to trust him. Blade showed me he was more than just some asshole. He showed me it was okay to open up, to trust that if I did, he wouldn't hurt me. That's what makes this so special. When you trust someone, you can open your heart fully, show them every part of yourself, and not worry about the consequences.

Being with Blade makes me happy. He melts away my inhibitions. With him, I'm not afraid to just... be myself. I hate that it took me this long to realize it. It's all-consuming, this realization, and all the feelings that come with it.

And now, as his lips press hungrily against mine, we both, *finally*, lay ourselves bare. We let these feelings, this moment, engulf us. Drown out the world. Nothing else matters. Nothing but this. Us.

His hands are warm on my cheeks, sliding down to rest at my waist, leaving a trail of heat in their wake. My arms wrap around his neck. He pulls me closer, pressing our bodies together, craving a closeness beyond the physical. All I can focus on is how perfectly he fits against me, how he invades every sense in the best possible way.

When he pulls back, I'm breathless, lips cold without his. Despite the incomprehensible things I just experienced in that void, I've never felt better.

He runs his thumb over my lip and presses his forehead to mine. "Your eyes are purple."

"What?"

He chuckles and kisses me again. His lips are like magic. As they meet mine, time disappears. My thoughts vanish.

"Are you serious right now?" a voice says behind me.

I pull back and turn to see Mykel and Lukas approaching. Mykel is seething.

"Mykel—" I start, but he cuts me off, punching Blade in the face.

"What the hell!" I shout as Lukas pulls Mykel away.

"It's been, what, two weeks since Aria and I split, and you're already trying to get with her?" Mykel snarls.

"Mykel, what is wrong with you?" I say, making sure Blade is okay.

When I look at Mykel again, he's... different. His eyes are darker, filled with a raw, uncontrollable anger—the angriest I've ever seen him.

"He's been acting weird since I found him," Lukas says. "I think the realm is affecting him. We're definitely in some kind of purgatory."

"Aria, the mere sight of you right now makes me want to jump off this cliff," Mykel says.

I try not to take offense. Or at least, not too much.

"Why didn't it affect me?" Blade asks.

"It only heightens negative emotions—anger, sadness... If you came in feeling any of those, they'd be magnified. Maybe that's why I feel so depressed right now," Lukas says.

"Well, can we hurry and fix it?" Blade says. "Mykel's about to murder me."

Lukas shrugs. "The only thing I can think of is a warding spell. It should block the negative energy."

"Okay, let's do it," I say.

"But... do I really want to?" Lukas says. "What's the point? Life will just disappoint me anyway. Might as well be miserable."

Mykel struggles in Lukas's arms. "Blade, I'm going to slit your throat and—"

"Okay! I'll take Mykel, you take Lukas," I say to Blade.

I pull Mykel away from Lukas and place a hand on his chest. He struggles, but I speak firmly: "*Custos.*"

My hand glows against his chest, and then Mykel gasps like being snapped awake.

"Holy shit," he mutters.

"Are you okay?"

"I'm... yeah, I'm fine." He rubs a hand over his face, through his hair. "I've never been so furious. Every thought in my head was pure anger." Then realization hits him, panic and regret washing over his face. "I'm so sorry."

"It's okay. You weren't yourself."

"You should be apologizing to me, asshole," Blade grumbles, pointing at his bruised cheek.

"I would, but honestly, I don't feel bad about that at all."

"Aria, why are your eyes purple?" Lukas asks.

"Great question," I say. "I have no idea. Something weird happened before I got here. I was trapped in this... endless darkness, and I—I saw things. Terrible things. I screamed, and this burst of purple magic exploded out of me. After that, everything stopped, and I found my way out."

"I think when we entered the Underworld, we all had to go through our own personal Hell," Blade says. "It takes the thing you fear most and traps you inside it."

"Why? What did you see?" Mykel asks.

"None of your business. What did you see?" Blade shoots back.

"None of *your* business."

"You two are worse than children," I say. "But if we all went through our own Hell and made it out, why am I the only one with purple eyes?"

"I have no idea," Blade says. "But it's hot."

He winks. My face heats instantly. Mykel swings at Blade again, but Blade dodges.

"I'm too quick for you, Griffin."

Mykel rolls his eyes. "You're intolerable."

We walk toward the edge of the cliff.

"So, where do we go from here?" Lukas says.

"We need to find Sarah," I say.

Blade shrugs. "I guess we pick a direction and start walking."

We head left and walk for what feels like ages until we reach a set of stone stairs descending into the fog.

"Why do I feel like I'm descending straight to my death?" Lukas mutters.

I try to laugh, but the sound never comes. He might not be wrong.

CHAPTER THIRTY-NINE

I'm not sure when our descent to the Underworld went from black and white purgatory to fiery red and orange flames, but here we are.

"Well, this is a delightful change of scenery," Lukas says.

We're standing on a bridge over a sea of molten lava, with a perfect view of towering volcanoes and jagged, rocky mountains. The bridge is made of old bones—human or otherwise, I'm not sure. Maybe all of the above. The smell of smoke and fire burns my lungs, and I feel like I'm standing in the hottest sauna imaginable.

Demons screech as they circle the dark red sky. I hear the heavy flap of their wings as they soar through the grey clouds. In the distance, a never-ending symphony of screams echoes across the landscape.

Everything about this place is terrifying.

We quickly make our way across the bridge, afraid it might break at any moment. I grip the railing as it creaks and sways with each step. When we reach the other side, I'm only slightly relieved. The land is just as unsettling. Bones litter the ground among dead trees and scattered ashes, some of which still drift through the air. The rocks are stained with blood, and countless dark caverns gape open all around us.

I don't even want to know what's inside them.

There's a group of sorcerers wandering around in the near distance, but besides them, no one else is in sight.

Until Sarah runs up to us.

"You made it!" she says.

I acknowledge her but keep scanning our surroundings. "This place is awful."

"Aria, your eyes…"

I turn toward her. "Yeah. They're purple, I know."

She stares at me with a knowing smile. "I knew it."

"Knew what?"

"You have the Sight," she says. "Purple eyes mean the Sight of Emotion."

I have the Sight… but how?

When I came to Silver Key, I was told the Sight is one of the prizes for winning the tournament. The only other way to get it is if—

"You're worthy," Mykel says.

"But how?"

"Whatever happened to you in your personal Hell must have triggered it," Blade says.

"Why me?"

"Aria, to be worthy of the Sight, you have to be a true hero," Sarah says. "Someone selfless. Someone willing to risk their life to do the right thing. Someone brave, kind, and smart. A leader. Someone who doesn't back down—someone who can survive life's toughest obstacles. In the time I've known you, I've watched you grow. Maybe from a distance, but I've been watching since our first day at Silver Key. Life kept throwing obstacles at you. Your entire world was flipped upside down. You lost your friend, and you lost your birth parents without ever getting the chance to know them. And yet you're here. In the Underworld. Ready to face the most powerful demon in existence and risk your life to stop him. To save the world. You're a hero."

For a moment, I don't know what to say. I never would have thought of myself as a hero. Someone worthy of a power so many people dream of.

Blade watches me with the faintest hint of a smirk, pride shining in his eyes, as if he isn't surprised at all. I turn to Mykel, who's looking at me with that same expression.

"Can I control it?" I ask.

"It should be fairly easy," Sarah says. "You just need to concentrate. Close your eyes, count to five, and focus on turning it off."

I do as she says. As I count, I feel the power sink back into the depths of my mind. Like a memory saved for later, it settles there, waiting for the next time it's called.

When I open my eyes again, I feel different. Weaker, almost. When the Sight was active, I felt stronger. Sharper. More in control.

"Good job," Sarah says. "I've heard leaving it on all the time can be draining, so only use it when you need to."

"Noted."

"Oh, and our mom was worthy too. My grandma told me she had the Sight of Emotion, just like you."

I smile at the thought.

"Sorry to interrupt this lovely sister bonding moment, but we should probably get moving," Lukas says. "Alatar could be right behind us for all we know."

"Any idea which way we're going?" Mykel asks.

"I know exactly where we're going." Sarah turns and starts walking. "This isn't my first time down here. Follow me."

Lukas hesitates before trailing after us. "Are we supposed to gloss over that?"

"Astalon likes to stay near the Pit," Sarah says. "That's where the lost souls are trapped—the souls of people who died and ended up here but don't actually deserve to be in Hell."

"That's terrible," I say.

"They don't always end up in the Pit," Sarah explains, "but if they're trapped in the Underworld for too long, their body dies and their soul goes to the Pit."

"There's nothing they can do?" Mykel says.

"No. Honestly, going to the Pit is probably their best option. Otherwise, they're just stuck here, being tortured constantly."

"Is there any way for them to speed up the process?" Blade asks.

"If they stop fighting their death, they can go straight to the Pit."

We descend a set of stairs made of crumbling red stone as Sarah continues. "Anyway, there are a lot of lost souls down there, and their despair makes Astalon more powerful."

I let out a slow breath, thinking about the torture people must endure down here. Another scream shatters the air—much closer this time. Blade grabs my hand and squeezes it.

We walk for a while until Lukas stops so abruptly that I nearly crash into him.

"Is that..." he says, trailing off.

"What?" I ask, following his gaze.

My eyes land on a lineup of four people. Prisoners. Their clothes are torn, their hair tangled, and they're covered in dirt. They kneel on the ground with their hands tied behind their backs.

And then my heart nearly stops because kneeling in that line is someone I never thought I'd see again.

CHAPTER FORTY

She's there. A few feet away from us. My voice is barely a breath when I say her name.

"Celie."

My heart feels like it's going to explode with joy. Celie is here! She's... *here.*

"We have to go get her," Lukas says, already starting toward her.

"Wait." Blade grabs his arm and yanks him back. "We have to be smart about this. I'm sure there's a demon watching them."

"I hate to say it, but Blade is right," Mykel says. "We have to be careful."

"I'm not waiting. One of us better come up with a plan right now, or I'm going over there," Lukas says. "Look at her. They're torturing her!"

I shake my head. "Celie is the nicest person I've ever met. She shouldn't even be here. *Why* is she here?"

"How did you say she died?" Sarah says.

Mykel clenches his jaw. "Alatar killed her with his familiar."

"An emppeta," Sarah says. "If you're killed by one, you're automatically sent to Hell. It's part of its curse."

"So she's been getting tortured in Hell for two weeks... and we didn't know." Lukas looks like he's about to be sick.

"But if we save her, we can take her back home with us, right?" I ask.

Sarah's eyes soften. "I'm sorry, but no. She's dead and tied to this realm now. She wouldn't survive if we tried to take her back."

"There has to be another way," Blade says. "She's coming back with us."

The confidence in his voice brings a small sense of relief.

"The only way is for Alatar's familiar to break the curse and revive her," Sarah explains. "But that'll never happen. Alatar has to command it, and you know he won't."

"He will," Mykel says, voice hard with determination. "We'll make him."

"In the meantime, we need to figure out how to get to Celie. Fast. There's a demon over there, and if it lays a hand on her, I won't be able to wait," Lukas says.

I catch a glimpse of it. Its eyes are black, hollow pits, and it has the long, sharp tail of a scorpion.

"It looks like a duraaz. It shouldn't be too difficult to defeat," Mykel says. "They usually stay in groups, though, so there are probably a few. Maybe four or five."

"Perfect. One for each of us," I say.

We creep closer for a better look. Mykel was right. There are five of them. They surround the prisoners, deciding what to do with them next. One of their long scorpion tails skims the top of Celie's head, and she squeezes her eyes shut.

When she opens them again, she spots us in the distance. She tries to hide her happiness, but I see it in her eyes—a glimmer of hope. I give her a small, reassuring smile.

"Okay, so... attack on three?" Lukas says.

He counts down, and we all spring from our hiding spot. When the demons see us, they growl and hiss, baring their pointed teeth. But they weren't expecting us.

I take the duraaz closest to Celie. It tries to claw at me, to sting me with its tail, but I dodge.

"*Gravitas,*" I say.

As if dragged by gravity, the duraaz slams into the red, dusty ground, unable to rise.

"You," it spits in a rough, raspy voice. "You're the ones who sent us back here."

I ignore it. It lashes its scorpion tail toward my leg. I hop over it, pulling my dagger from its sheath. I bring the blade down through the tail, slicing it clean off.

The demon lets out a bloodcurdling screech. Thick, black blood coats my dagger before I drive the blade through its neck. The rotten stench of the demon's blood fills the air as the duraaz dissolves into red ash and scatters into the air.

Blade sends his demon flying into the cave wall. It slams into the rock so hard it leaves a dent before Blade drives his blade where its heart would be. I turn just in time to see Mykel stab his duraaz through the stomach.

Once Lukas and Sarah finish theirs off, Lukas runs straight to Celie. He unties her, hands shaking as he checks her for injuries.

Unable to wait another second, I wrap my arms around her. When her hands are free, she wraps them around my waist. Happy tears roll down my cheeks.

I pull back, and Lukas tackles her to the ground in a hug. She laughs, and it's the most beautiful sound I've ever heard.

I didn't know it was possible to feel this happy—this relieved. It's kind of ironic that we're in Hell right now.

"Thank God," Lukas says when he pulls away.

"I'm so sorry this happened, Celie," Mykel says, wrapping her in his arms. "Are you okay?"

"I will be." She pulls away from the hug. "I'm so glad to see you guys."

"You're coming back with us," Blade says. "I don't care what we have to do. We're not leaving you here."

Celie looks at him, and something unspoken passes between them. She nods.

"Sorry to ruin the moment, but we should get going," Sarah says.

"What about the other prisoners?" I ask, gesturing to the three other people curled up on the floor.

"There's nothing we can do for them. They're dead, and whatever life led them here, their souls are tied to the Underworld now."

"That's it?" Mykel says. "We leave them here to be tortured?"

"Yes. Now we have to go."

I spare another glance at them. Fear fills their eyes as they stare blankly at the world around them. Blade takes my hand and leads me away. With a pang in my chest, I let him.

We walk for what feels like hours. Lukas stays at Celie's side the whole time, filling her in on what she's missed, but she doesn't say much. Whatever happened to her down here wasn't good, and it hurts to think about what she must have gone through.

We reach the edge of a cliff. A narrow path leads off to the right, presumably toward the Pit of Lost Souls where Astalon should be.

"How much longer?" Lukas asks, peering over the cliff at the deep, steaming lava below.

Sarah studies the surrounding terrain. "Just a little longer. It should be up ahead—"

"Where do you think you're going?"

A few feet ahead of us stands Alatar Blight.

We knew he might follow us here once he realized what we were planning, but we'd hoped we would've done what we came to do before that.

He strolls toward us. "You kids are clever, I'll give you that."

Blade steps forward protectively, and Mykel does the same.

"Sarah Belmont—oh, I'm sorry. Sarah *Drake*. How I didn't realize it was you this whole time is beyond me. You look just like your parents."

"So I've been told," Sarah says. "Too bad they never got to see that for themselves."

Alatar smirks. "Yes, that is a shame."

Sarah steps forward. She's trying to keep her composure, but I can tell she's furious. She said she's been preparing for this moment her whole life, but I don't think anything could truly prepare her for this—the moment she finally stands face to face with her enemy. The man she's made it her life's mission to destroy.

"You know I'm going to kill you for what you did to them, right?" she says. "For what you did to me."

"You can try," he replies. "You won't succeed, but you can certainly try."

Those words shift something inside her. I see it on her face: the exact moment her mindset changes from careful strategy to reckless anger.

"We'll see about that," she says. "Why don't we make this formal?"

"Are you challenging me?" he asks, amused.

"Sarah, no," I say. "This wasn't part of the plan."

She ignores me. "I am. Do you accept?"

"Of course."

"Good. I've been waiting for this for a long time."

Sarah lets out a scream and charges toward Alatar. "*Mortem!*"

Alatar deflects the spell, but before he can recover, she throws a punch that lands squarely on his jaw, sending him stumbling backward.

"*Impetus!*" he shouts, striking the air like he's hitting an invisible wall.

Sarah is thrown to the ground, clutching her stomach. Alatar lets out a cruel laugh.

"There has to be a way to help her," I say, rushing forward, but Blade grabs my arm and pulls me back.

"We can't," Mykel says. "It's an official challenge. No one can intervene."

"He's going to kill her!"

"We physically can't do anything, even if we wanted to," Blade says. "The fight is protected by the magic of the challenge, like when I fought Nathan. There are no loopholes."

"That's bullshit."

There must be something I can do.

Breaking free from Blade's grip, I run toward Sarah and Alatar—but before I reach them, a magical force slams into me and throws me several feet back. I hit the ground hard, the impact knocking the wind out of my lungs, leaving me coughing and gasping for air.

"Aria!" Blade calls, rushing to my side. "Shit—are you okay?"

"I'm fine," I manage between breaths.

He sighs in relief and helps me to my feet. "There's nothing we can do. We just have to hope she pulls through."

I let out a frustrated huff and turn back to the fight.

Sarah swings at Alatar, and he dodges.

"*Obtundo!*" she shouts.

Alatar is sent flying backward, but he recovers quickly. In a flash of movement, he lifts his arm as if drawing an arrow, then pulls it down so it's outstretched in front of him. Purple magic trails through the air in the wake of his movement. He holds an invisible bow and arrow, readying his shot.

"Sagitta," he says.

The purple magic forms a thin arrow that shoots straight toward Sarah. It sinks into her shoulder, and she stumbles back.

The magic fades, but she clutches her shoulder as blood seeps through her fingers. Shaking it off, she marches toward Alatar and thrusts her hands forward. Golden magic bursts from her palms and blasts into his legs, knocking him to the ground.

She kicks him while he's down, then kneels on his chest. Pulling a long dagger from the sheath strapped to her thigh, she raises it high. Seconds before she drives the blade home, Alatar kicks her off him.

I curse under my breath.

She rolls across the ground, and Alatar seizes the opportunity. He grabs her by the front of her shirt and slams her back against the ground. He snatches her dagger from where it fell a few inches away.

"No!" I shout.

But it's too late. He plunges the dagger deep into her side. She cries out in pain. Blood fills her mouth, and she coughs it up.

"You were naive to think you could beat me," he says, hand still wrapped around the dagger's hilt as he twists it.

She gasps, eyes wide.

Then, in one swift motion, Alatar yanks the blade free. The dagger drips scarlet as Sarah bleeds out, staining her clothes and the ground beneath her.

A tear slips from the corner of her eye as her last breath escapes her lungs. Her body goes still, and I don't know how much more heartbreak I can take.

I may have gotten my best friend back, but I lost my sister.

CHAPTER FORTY-ONE

I can't stop staring at her body.

I'm vaguely aware of Blade's hand on my back. Of Lukas, Celie, and Mykel standing beside us. Of the single tear rolling down my cheek.

"Celie is coming back with us," Lukas says.

Alatar's eyes glimmer with amusement. "What makes you think that?"

"You're going to summon your familiar, and you're going to command it to revive Celie so she can come home."

"And why, exactly, would I do that? Are you going to try to kill me? We all saw how that went for your friend."

I glance down at Sarah again. "If he doesn't, I will."

Alatar laughs. "You? *You*, Aria? The amateur sorceress? You know, my magic is strong right now, this close to Astalon. I'm more powerful than I've been in a while. And you've known magic for what, less than a year?"

I'm about to defend myself when Lukas steps forward. "*Magicis Affligo!*"

In a blaze of orange, magic sparks in Lukas's hands and shoots outward. It strikes Alatar from above, slamming him into the ground and crushing the dirt and rock beneath him.

But Alatar recovers quickly, shaking it off. "*Segmentum Gladio!*"

The spell hits Lukas instantly—a glittering slice of icy blue across his stomach. He collapses to the ground. Dark blood pools in the wound before spilling out.

Celie drops beside him. "Oh my God! Lukas, are you hurt?"

"No, I normally spurt blood from my ribcage," he says, panting.

Mykel presses his hands against the wound. "We have to do something. Fast. It's not too late—we can save him."

And then a brilliant idea pops into my head.

Folding my hands together, I say, "*Cito.*"

A moment later, a handsome white wolf with large angel wings descends from the sky. When he lands, he runs straight toward us.

"Good boy, Halo," I say, patting his head.

He's grown even more since our practice session on the clouds, now larger than a normal wolf.

"I need you to heal Lukas."

Halo walks over to Lukas and licks his face. Then he rests his chin on Lukas's chest. An angelic silver ring forms above Halo's head, and his wings wrap around Lukas in a warm, glowing embrace.

"We'll be okay," Celie says, turning to me. "Go get that son of a bitch."

I wipe the tears from my face and give her a firm nod.

Then I turn toward Alatar. He's further away now, running to Astalon. He used Lukas as a distraction to reach him first, but he hasn't made it to the path yet.

I run after him, Blade and Mykel right behind me.

"*Iter,*" I say.

A vibrant pink blast shoots from my hands, slithering after Alatar like a snake chasing its prey. It coils around his legs and yanks him to the ground.

I stand over him, Blade and Mykel on either side of me, and I just want to scream.

Celie! My parents! Sarah! Who else, Alatar? Who else?

I want to ask why. *Why can't you see that what you're doing is wrong? You're the villain, and you don't even realize it!*

But all I say is, "Summon your familiar and command it to revive Celie. Now."

Alatar doesn't answer. Instead, his gaze shifts past me. And he laughs.

I turn. A giant lion, its fur as white as snow, charges toward us. Its eyes glow blue, and strips of green light zigzag along its sides.

Someone is riding on its back. He has short blond hair and wears a long black cloak.

"Dad?" Blade says.

A low roar rumbles through the sky. I look up just in time to see a massive red dragon descending toward us. Its tail is lined with spikes, and it exhales a deep breath of fire as it lands.

"Dad?" Mykel says.

The two men dismount their familiars and land gracefully on the ground. I'm so distracted that I don't even notice Alatar slipping away to join them.

As they approach, I see their faces more clearly. When I saw them at Silver Key, it was from a distance. Now I can study them up close. Blade shares his father's sharp jaw and arrogant smirk. Mykel has his father's bright hazel eyes, but none of the cowardice behind them.

"Elyon, Jakob. Glad you could make it," Alatar says, raking a hand through his hair. His familiar now hovers behind him, its fiery wings beating slowly as it waits for a command.

I step closer to Blade. He grabs my hand and squeezes it. I squeeze back.

Blade inhales sharply, looking at his father. "What are you doing here?"

"I came to stop you before you do something you'll regret," Elyon says, his familiar standing beside him like a silent guard.

"We know exactly what we're doing."

"I'm with Blade on this," Mykel says, stepping toward his father. "Dad, do you know how many tragedies Astalon has caused? How many innocent lives have been lost because of him?"

"I know, Son," Jakob says. "But Elyon and Alatar are right."

Mykel shakes his head. "How can you say that?"

"You're too young to understand. One day you'll thank me."

Mykel takes another step forward. "For allowing countless people to die? Because that's what's going to happen if Astalon is freed."

"Mykel, I don't want to fight you."

"You don't have to! You just have to see that what we're doing is right. You can help us."

"No. I can't. If you don't back down, you've made your decision."

"Dad—"

"All I've ever wanted for you is the best, Mykel. I've given everything up for you. Risked everything so you could be the best."

"I didn't ask you to! I never wanted to be the best!" Mykel says, voice cracking. "All my life you've pressured me to be better than everyone. I lost my friends at school because they couldn't deal with it. I lost Eliza. Blade and I hate each other because of the pressure you and Elyon put on us. When will anything I do be enough? I thought you'd be proud of me—for standing up, for being brave, for trying to save the world. But all you care about is power. You're just like Elyon."

"How dare you," Jakob says.

"Don't sound so offended," Elyon comments.

Jakob takes a step toward his son. "I do care about you, Mykel."

Mykel lets out a bitter laugh, though tears shine in his eyes. "Right. You just care about your power more." He shakes his head. "I'm done trying to impress you. I'm done trying to live up to your expectations."

He takes a step back, toward Blade. They stand together, side by side. Blade is still holding my hand, but he turns to Mykel, and something silent passes between them. Mykel gives a single nod.

All Mykel and Blade have ever wanted was to make their fathers proud—an impossible task they've chased their entire lives. It's a cruel thing to realize that the person you looked up to is standing on the wrong side.

They both know what they have to do.

"Blade," Elyon says. "You're pathetic if you think you can stand against us. Against your own father. Join us now, or you'll regret it."

I glance up at Blade beside me. He stares at his father in disbelief, a flicker of apprehension in his eyes. But he doesn't move.

I place my free hand on Blade's forearm. Elyon's gaze drops to our interlocked fingers, and the faintest smirk curls his lips.

"I see. You're doing this for a girl?" His eyes sweep over me, assessing. I scowl back in disgust. "You could do so much better."

I open my mouth to fire back, but when I see the unreadable look on Blade's face, I decide against it.

Elyon walks closer. "You're worthless, Blade. You always have been. You always will be." He leans into Blade's space. "Don't think for a second I won't do what's necessary if you get in my way."

But Blade doesn't break. He stares at the man in front of him—his father, the man who made his life a living hell—with absolute loathing.

"I'm not scared of you anymore," Blade says. He gives my hand one last squeeze and lets go. Then he steps back and folds his hands together. "*Cito.*"

A moment later, a black nine-tailed fox streaks across the ground and skids to a stop beside him. Each tail is traced with lines of fiery orange.

"So if we're going to fight," Blade says coolly, "let's get it over with."

"You're willing to fight me?" Elyon scoffs. "You know you don't stand a chance. I trained you, Blade. You may be powerful, but I will always be more powerful than you."

Blade steps closer to him. "Fuck. You."

Elyon stares at his son, momentarily speechless. The flash of shock on his face vanishes almost instantly, replaced by blazing fury. His face reddens with rage.

I stand frozen, unsure what to do.

But when Elyon says, "*Impetus,*" and a red ripple of magic slams into Blade's stomach—sending him staggering back with a gasp—I know exactly what's about to happen.

"Okay," I mutter. "So we're doing this."

"*Incendo!*" Mykel shouts.

Two balls of fire flare into existence above his palms. He thrusts them forward. The flames streak toward Jakob, barely missing him. Jakob recoils in surprise, but recovers quickly and charges. Mykel throws a punch. Jakob dodges and drives a fist into Mykel's gut. Mykel doubles over, hurt in more ways than one.

He looks up at his father, heartbreak in his eyes. "I don't want to fight you."

"You don't have to, Son."

"Yes," Mykel says. "I do."

He lunges again.

Blade attacks with his dagger, slashing at his father. Elyon dodges easily and fires off a spell. Blade blocks it, deflecting the magic before countering with one of his own. A burst of harsh silver light slams into Elyon's chest.

But this time he's ready.

When Blade casts again, Elyon shouts, "*Regero!*" and catches the silver magical energy in his right hand.

For a moment it stays there. Then it sinks into him. The light travels through his body, crawling up his arm beneath the skin. A split second later, it erupts from his left hand, firing straight back at Blade. It strikes his side and sends him stumbling.

Blade's eyes flash with anger. He raises his dagger and throws it. The blade flies with deadly precision. Elyon tries to twist aside, but he's too slow. The dagger sinks deep into his shoulder.

Elyon cries out in pain. Blade freezes for half a second, stunned by what he's done. But the moment of surprise is gone before Elyon can see it.

Elyon recovers. The wound isn't enough to stop him, and he—

"Aria, watch out!" Mykel shouts.

I turn.

Alatar is running at me.

I throw my hands forward. "*Obtundo!*"

My magic hits its mark. Alatar flies backward and slams into the ground.

Close your eyes. Count to five. Focus.

Sarah's words echo back to me. I reach for it—the Sight—buried deep in the back of my mind. When I feel it there, waiting, I grab hold and let it rise to the surface. As I open my eyes, clarity floods every inch of my body.

Everything sharpens.

Everything slows.

I focus on a single emotion. The one that will carry me through this.

Anger.

Alatar pushes himself back to his feet. Before he makes his move, magic builds around his hands. It's a glimmering purple, faint at first but quickly growing brighter. I know he's about to cast a spell.

"*Intersaepio,*" I say.

A violet-tinted shield snaps into existence in front of me just as his spell fires. The magic crashes into the barrier and dissipates.

He stares at me in bewilderment. "You have the Sight."

I smirk and clasp my hands together. Somehow, using this power feels natural, like it's always been part of me. I know exactly what to do.

I meet Alatar's gaze. A flicker of fear crosses his face as an electric-purple dome forms around me, crackling with energy—just like in the darkness of my Hell. I throw my hands forward. The dome collapses inward, rushing through my body before exploding outward from my palms.

The blast hits Alatar in the chest. He crashes to the ground. He's unconscious for only a few moments, but by the time he wakes, I'm standing over him.

We're dangerously close to the cliff's edge. Heat from the lava below warms my face. Sweat trickles down my back, my hair sticking to my neck, but I ignore it.

Alatar looks up at me with a wild expression. His black hair hangs in messy tangles across his face. A deep red cut runs across his cheek, and his shirt is torn open where his chest is badly bruised.

I grab him by the collar and drag him closer to the edge until his head hangs over it.

"Aria," he says. He's trying to sound calm, but his voice waivers. "You aren't going to kill me."

The rocky edge crumbles slightly beneath his head, pebbles tumbling down into the lava. I can feel the fear in his eyes. Can taste it.

"Oh, I'm not?" I tilt my head. "Huh."

"Please. You can't do this."

"I can, Alatar. You killed my parents. You killed my best friend. You killed my sister. All those people are dead because of *you*." Every word drips with venom. "And right now? All I feel is anger."

"Aria, you're not yourself. You'll regret it if you kill me!"

"I won't." My grip tightens on his shirt. "You deserve to die. You deserve to be tied to this realm for eternity." My voice drops, cold and steady. "So if I have to use this anger—this horrible, repulsive hatred—to do what needs to be done, then I will." I lean closer. "My anger is more useful than my grief."

"Aria—"

"Command your familiar to revive Celie," I say. "This is the last time I'll ask."

He hesitates. I see the calculation in his eyes. He raises his hand to cast a spell, but before the magic even leaves his fingertips, I say, "*Confodere*."

My spell sharpens into a thin blade and pins his hand to the ground.

He lets out a strangled cry and jerks back, breathing in short, ragged gasps through his teeth.

"Okay," he pants. "Okay."

His familiar is battling Halo nearby, launching bursts of fire while Halo dodges each one. Halo howls and silver blasts of radiant energy shoot from his eyes toward the emppeta.

The creature dodges, but instead of attacking again, it flies toward us, as if responding to a silent command.

Alatar orders it to revive Celie, and the emppeta darts away to obey its master. I release my grip on Alatar. He scrambles away from the edge, collapsing on the ground.

Across the battlefield, Blade and Mykel are still fighting their fathers—spell after spell, blow after blow.

Blade's fox is locked in combat with Elyon's white lion. The fox summons nine massive balls of fire that hover around it before launching toward the lion. The creature roars as the flames strike. Enraged, the lion lunges forward, claws slashing. It narrowly misses the fox's face but tears a long, glowing green gash across its side.

High above us, two dragons battle in the sky.

Mykel must have summoned his familiar as well—a silvery-white ice dragon, jagged shards of ice protruding from its body like frozen spears, fights Jakob's dragon. They roar, unleashing breath that collides in a violent clash of fire and ice. Their massive wings beat against the crimson sky as they struggle for dominance.

"I knew you couldn't kill me," Alatar says, slowly catching his breath. "You think you're so smart. You and your little friends. You think you know everything." He laughs. "You know nothing."

"Oh, we know a lot more than you think," I say.

He smirks. "Right. Then I guess you already know I orchestrated the siren attack in Atlantis." He watches my face carefully. "Judging by that expression... I'd say you didn't."

"Why would you—"

"You really thought the trial was about finding those useless pearls?" He laughs. "No. The real trial was the attack. To see how you sorcerers would react under pressure. Who would survive. Who might actually be strong enough to help us rescue Astalon."

My hands clench into fists. My voice shakes with rage. "So many people died."

"If Astalon is saved," Alatar replies calmly, "it will have been worth it."

I'm about to respond when I hear Celie say, "It worked!"

I turn to find her walking toward me. "I feel better now," she says. "Stronger. I feel... alive again." Disbelief flickers across her face.

"I did what you asked," Alatar says from the ground. "Now you can let us go, and we can all go home."

I look down at him, into those black eyes. I don't want to grieve anymore. I don't want fear or uncertainty. I want to be strong. Hard. I want to do what needs to be done.

"No," I say.

"Aria—"

I cut him off with a punch to the face. Blood spills from his nose.

"That was for Celie. This is for my parents."

I drive my foot into his ribs. He cries out in pain.

The world is a big, terrifying place full of endless possibilities. You can have everything one moment and lose it all the next. It's painful. Cruel.

But it's also beautiful. And it's worth fighting for.

I have the power to save people—to give them the chance to experience the hardships and the beauty of *living*. I can't let fear or guilt stand in the way of that.

I know if I don't kill Alatar, he will kill me. Then he'll kill my friends. And then he'll help Astalon escape and doom the world to an eternity of war, hate, and destruction. Power like Astalon's was never meant to exist on Earth. It was meant to destroy it.

So I focus on the rage burning inside me. I let it grow. I feed it until there's nothing else left.

"And this," I say, raising my dagger, "is for Sarah."

The blade hovers inches from his chest when he speaks. "Your mother would never have been so ruthless."

I freeze, dagger mid-air. "What did you just say?"

"Your mother," he says. "She was a good person. Even with the Sight, she would never have used it to take another life."

"You don't get to talk about my mother," I say, voice trembling. "Not after what you did."

A smirk creeps onto his bloodied lips.

I slowly shake my head. "You pretend to be so calculated. So controlled. But it's all an act. You're reckless, Alatar. Greedy. Selfish. Heartless. My mother was your friend. She trusted you, and you killed her." My grip tightens on the dagger. "All you do is betray people. *Hurt* people. But do you know what your biggest mistake was?"

His smirk fades. He looks at me with what appears to be regret in his eyes, but it's not. I see him now. Truly see him. He can't hide his true self from me anymore.

"Your biggest mistake," I say quietly, "was underestimating the power that can come from the pain *you* caused."

Without hesitation, I drive the dagger straight through Alatar's heart.

He cries out. Then, still staring into my eyes, he lifts his hands and grips mine—gripping the dagger buried in his chest.

We stay like that until his hold begins to loosen. He glares into my eyes with shock, sadness... and then nothing as the life leaves his eyes.

I pull the dagger free. In one swift motion, he collapses to the ground.

Other emotions try to fight their way to the surface. Sadness, fear, grief, *guilt*. But I force them back down. Anger is the only thing holding me together.

Sarah wanted him dead. She died trying to make it happen. I finished the job for her.

It's what she would have wanted.

314

CHAPTER FORTY-TWO

Alatar's corpse lies at my feet.

Blade takes a step toward me. "Knight—"

"What have you done?!" Elyon shouts, cutting his son off as he rushes to Alatar's side. "You little bitch! You killed him!"

Blade moves to defend me, but before he can speak, I say, "He's lucky that's all I did. He deserved so much worse."

Elyon ignores me. He kneels beside Alatar's body, checks his pulse, and mutters curse after curse under his breath.

Mykel comes over and stands beside Blade and Celie. They all stare at me, unsure what to say. They're worried about me—worried that the guilt of taking someone's life will destroy me.

Maybe it will.

Right now, all I feel is a lingering rage. And as I think about what comes next, that rage only intensifies.

I killed Alatar. Now to take care of Astalon.

"I'm fine," I tell them.

Blade places his hands on my shoulders and looks into my eyes. "It's okay if you're not."

"I'm fine," I repeat.

Uncertainty flickers in his eyes. He hesitates, searching my face for something. But then he backs away. "Okay. You and Celie go take care of Astalon. Mykel and I have to finish this."

I nod. As Celie and I turn to head down the path, Elyon stands and faces Blade.

"You care for her," he says. "I'm sorry I have to do this."

I barely process what's happening before Elyon shouts, "*Scintilliam!*" just as I turn my back to him.

There's a deafening bang, like explosives going off—but somehow, I'm fine. Not even a scratch.

Then I hear a thud.

I turn to find Blade on the ground, blood pouring from his side, arm, shoulder, stomach, leg—

He jumped in front of Elyon's spell.

The blood spills out of him fast, pooling beneath his body. For a moment, I just stare in distant shock. The Sight within me shifts. Worry for Blade creeps to the forefront of my mind, pushing past the anger.

And I let it.

Fear and panic crash over me. At first, I'm in denial. I can't lose anyone else. The thought of losing Blade hits me like a punch to the gut, and I nearly lose my balance.

"Blade," I whisper, dropping to my knees beside him.

I grab his bloodstained hand and look into his eyes. He's still alive. He struggles to breathe and coughs up blood.

"I—I didn't mean to..." Elyon says from behind me.

Mykel steps closer to him. "You did this. Look what you did!"

Elyon—whether from fear, shock, or both—stumbles back.

Mykel turns to his father. "You really want to work with him? Look what he just did to his own fucking son!"

"I was aiming for *her*..." Elyon says weakly.

Jakob grabs Elyon by the collar and pulls him back. "Elyon. We should go."

"Knight," Blade says.

I turn back to him and... seeing him like this is torture. His black Silver Key uniform is soaked through with blood. His arm hangs at a terrible angle, barely attached, and a massive gash splits his leg open.

There's so much blood.

It's terrifying.

"You're alright." Tears blur my vision. "Halo can save you."

I call Halo over and tell him to heal Blade. He obeys, wrapping his white wings around Blade just like he did when he healed Lukas. I pray it works. That Blade isn't already too far gone. That the damage can be undone.

Please.

"Knight," he says again.

"Don't talk. You're fine. You're going to be okay."

"You have to stop Astalon," he forces out, his voice barely audible. "You can't let him escape. You have to go."

"I'm not leaving, Blade."

"Aria," he says with what little strength he has left. "You have to—"

"No. Halo's healing you. When I know you're okay, I'll go."

I look at Halo. *What's taking so long?* He's whimpering. I stroke his back, and his body trembles beneath my hand.

"Halo?" I say. "Halo, what's wrong?"

"It's not working," Mykel says.

I turn to him. "What do you mean it's not working? Mykel, it has to work."

He shakes his head. He looks just as lost as Celie and me.

I gaze into Halo's aqua-coloured eyes and watch as the light slowly drains from them, leaving only dull grey.

"His eyes..." A sob escapes me. "What's happening?"

"It's taking too much energy," Celie says, tears silently streaming down her cheeks.

"But he healed Lukas," I say.

"Aria... Lukas's injuries weren't nearly this severe," she replies softly.

"But—"

I look down at Blade, who's fighting so hard to keep his eyes open. To stay with us. With me.

"It's okay," he says, forcing a smile.

My heart sinks.

I shake my head. "No. Don't say that. You can't—I can't—"

Tears fall from my face onto the blood-soaked ground.

"You know what my personal Hell was?" he says.

"Blade don't—"

"I saw my father. He was saying horrible things…" He takes a shaky breath. "That I'm worthless. A pathetic excuse for a son. A weak sorcerer. Unworthy of people's love."

I squeeze his hand tighter. "It's not true. None of that is true. You're a good person. You're brave and strong," I cry. "You're amazing, Blade. You're so special. Please believe that."

He squeezes my hand back. "Thanks, Knight." His eyes shine with tears, his lips stained red. His skin is so pale. "I think that's what I've always needed to hear."

"It's the truth."

"That's not all I saw," he says, blinking away tears. "Mykel was there. And Celie. And you." He meets my eyes. "It was overwhelming; these terrible words coming from every direction." He gasps for breath. "I felt like I was suffocating. And then… hearing you call me an awful person. Saying you could never love me. That you'd never be with me…"

"God, Blade, I would never say those things. You know that, right?"

"I do. That's what snapped me out of it. Made me realize it wasn't real. I thought about the real you. How good you are. How you see the best in me. It gave me hope… and I got out."

I can't stop crying.

"You need to be brave now, Knight. You need to leave me and go save the world."

"I can't," I say. "Mykel and Celie can go after Astalon. I can't leave you like this."

He shakes his head weakly. "It has to be you. Sarah knew. She knew you had the Sight. You're the only one strong enough to defeat him." He coughs up more blood, and it spills down his chin. "You can do it... but you have to go now."

No.

No, this can't be happening. I can't lose him. I can't leave him. I—

"What the hell is that?" Mykel says, stumbling back.

I look up. Two blue-grey figures hover a few feet away from us. Small. Moving through the air with eerie speed.

"I think they're souls... from the Pit," Celie says.

Halo lets out a strangled howl as the souls approach. Somehow, they seem to make his condition worse.

Another sob rips from my chest.

"Astalon is at the Pit. There has to be a connection, right?" Mykel says, his eyes red with tears.

"Wait," Celie says, realization dawning. "It's Astalon."

"What?" I ask.

"The souls are filled with fear. Astalon is the source of magic—and the most powerful demon to exist. His influence is so strong that just by being on Earth, he infects it. The souls near the Pit... they're reacting to him." She glances at Halo. "Halo is an angelic creature. Astalon's presence is counteracting his abilities."

Mykel nods. "That makes sense. I read about it once—how demonic presences can weaken angelic powers. That has to be what's happening."

"So if we trap Astalon in the cage—contain his power—Halo might be able to save Blade," Celie says.

"Knight," Blade says. "I'll be okay."

"I don't want to leave you."

"I know." He lifts his hand and rests it against my cheek. I grab it, holding it there. "But I need you to go, Aria. Save me."

Closing my eyes, I let the tears fall. After a moment, I take a deep breath and nod.

I kiss his hand before leaning down to press a kiss to his forehead. "I'm coming back."

Then I stand and run toward Astalon, not daring to look back.

CHAPTER FORTY-THREE

I run toward the Pit of Lost Souls. Toward Astalon.

Tears stream down my face as I try to push my worry and fear for Blade out of my mind, but it's hard. Those emotions are so strong, and the more I think about him, the stronger they become. I try to breathe, take deep breaths. I have to do this. I can save Blade if I just focus.

When I reach the end of the path, the Pit becomes visible in the distance. Behind it rises a tall throne made of jagged rock, molten lava bubbling and dripping down its sides. Sitting on the throne is the same demon from the portrait in Alatar's office.

Astalon Ellfire.

He sits with absolute confidence, clearly comfortable in his position of power. Not even a hint of worry or unease touches his face.

He's in his demon form—his true form. His sharp horns look even longer in person, and his enormous scarlet wings, riddled with rips and tears, spread wide behind him. The thick black skeletal structure of the wings is exposed, each tip razor sharp. His black, opaque eyes are completely soulless. Even from this distance, I know looking into them for more than a moment would be unbearable. He's the kind of thing born in nightmares.

This form is so different from the other one—the one I saw in the book at Silver Key or in his statue at the fountain. Yet I can still glimpse pieces of his human form in certain features: the sharp line of his jaw, the shape of his dark, hooded eyes.

Two people stand beside him.

Is that...

No.

When we discovered Alatar's plan, I hadn't even thought about who else might be involved. Standing on either side of Astalon are Mr. Johnson and Mrs. Patrickson.

I push the rising sense of betrayal back down. I can use a paralysis spell on them long enough to deal with Astalon, but I need to prepare for the possibility that they might fight back.

As I approach the Pit, particles of magic shimmer in the air. Most of it pours from the Pit itself, brimming with countless tortured souls. Their deafening screams are like knives stabbing into my ears. The glittering blue magic streams toward Astalon, fusing into him—fuelling him.

I focus on the anger I felt earlier, push every other emotion aside. When Astalon spots me, he looks down and grins.

"You're just in time," he says, sending a chill down my spine.

His voice is a deep, booming baritone. Each word carries a low undercurrent of rage, sharpened by absolute confidence. He knows he can beat me.

"I was about to make my escape," he says.

The blue-grey souls continue to feed him their energy.

"I'm not letting that happen," I say.

Astalon smirks and leans back in his massive throne. Lava bubbles onto his shoulders and drips down his arm, but he doesn't react in the slightest.

"Aria, no," Mrs. Patrickson says. "Alatar's plan has to succeed. We're saving the world. Don't you see?"

"How can you say that? Astalon's presence in our realm will destroy it. People who have nothing to do with magic will suffer. How can you believe any of this is right?"

Something flickers in her eyes: doubt. Still, she shakes her head. "You don't understand. Helping Astalon will save our world. Alatar told me himself. He said Astalon's power can heal—even the incurable. He's the most powerful being in the universe. With him, we can help people." Her voice cracks slightly. "He could save Lila, Aria."

A sharp pang hits my chest. "I'm so sorry, Mrs. Patrickson… but Alatar lied to you. Astalon will destroy the world if we let him escape. You need to listen to me—"

"No… Aria, no." She shakes her head harder now. "I trust Alatar. He would never lie to me about something this serious."

But it sounds like she's trying to convince herself more than me.

"Tell her, Mr. Johnson," I say.

He's been far too quiet.

"She's lying," he replies instantly.

The lie is so obvious on his face that I can only hope Mrs. Patrickson sees it.

I look at her pleadingly. She hesitates, conflict twisting across her expression. "I'm sorry, Aria."

My heart sinks as she steps in front of the throne and grabs Mr. Johnson's hands. Together, they begin chanting a spell I don't recognize. Immediately, the blue magic thickens, growing stronger, denser—before surging straight into Astalon.

I take a step forward, and as I do, Astalon rises.

With a thunderous whoosh, his wings spread even wider, and he leaps into the air. He hovers far above me, out of reach. Then he raises his arms above his head, palms to the sky—and pushes.

A firm layer of magic appears in the sky above him. He pushes harder, trying to break through. The barrier cracks like ice. It shines so brightly it blinds me, forcing me to look away. The red sky around us crackles violently as the grey clouds darken to black.

I force my legs to move. One foot in front of the other. I run around the Pit, dirt kicking up beneath my feet as I sprint and stumble forward. My arms pump desperately as I push myself faster.

I can't let him escape. *I can't.*

I'm screaming now, shouting frantically at Mrs. Patrickson and Mr. Johnson to stop the spell. I'd think they couldn't hear me if I hadn't seen Mrs. Patrickson flinch. If I paralyze them like I planned, the spell should stop long enough for me to trap Astalon and seal the cage.

"Mrs. Patrickson, please!" I shout one last time—

I trip. My knees slam against the rocky ground, scraping painfully as I fall. I scramble to my feet again—and that's when I hear it.

A song.

The melodic tune wraps around me like the warmth of a blanket. Like a mother embracing her child, it soothes the worry in my chest. It calms my racing heart. It blocks out the horrific screams from the Pit. The song is so beautiful that a tear slides down my cheek, and a soft smile forms on my lips.

I look up. In the sky, a bird circles above me. I've seen it before. As it glides through the air, a feather drifts gently to the ground in front of me. A perfect, vibrant blend of colour.

Mrs. Patrickson's familiar.

The realization snaps me out of the enchantment just before it fully takes hold of my mind.

Mrs. Patrickson looks straight at me. I know I have to act now, before it's too late. Before her familiar charms me completely and forces me to obey her.

I push myself to my feet. Without hesitation, I thrust my right palm toward Mrs. Patrickson and my left toward Mr. Johnson. "*Confuto!*"

A second later, they both freeze.

At first, nothing happens. Then the blinding light in the sky fades. Astalon glides back down to the ground with the same eerie grace as the falling feather. If he was angry before, he's furious now. The careless confidence from earlier has vanished. His face has hardened completely as he stares down at me. There's pure rage in his eyes.

It makes me feel powerful.

"I told you," I say. "I'm not letting that happen."

Astalon lets out a deafening roar that echoes across the Underworld.

"Was that supposed to be intimidating?"

"You're not scared," Astalon says, almost intrigued.

"Please," I reply. "I've had worse nightmares about failing biology."

If I wasn't so in control of my emotions right now, I probably wouldn't have said that. But fear has been completely shoved aside, and if I can use that to my advantage, I will.

If Astalon is surprised by my lack of fear, he doesn't show it. "You can't stop me. Your parents failed, and you think *you* can succeed?" He laughs. "You're weak."

I glare at the demon in front of me, jaw clenched. "I am *not* weak."

I thrust both hands forward, unleashing a blast of magical energy. Purple light erupts from my palms and surges toward Astalon. He blocks it with a spell of his own. His magic is a deep crimson red. The two forces collide mid-air, purple and red slamming together as the colours twist and fuse in the space between us.

Although I may not feel fear, I still recognize who it is that I'm fighting. Astalon is *the* source of magic. The most powerful being in the universe—and I'm trying to beat him. I'm not weak, but the longer this goes on, the more doubt weaves its way into my mind. It's a good thing I'm only trying to trap him and not kill him, because I'm not sure I could do it if I had to.

I force the thought away and focus on the magic leaving my body. I shout as I pour all my force and energy against Astalon's defensive spell. My throat burns, and I gasp for air, each inhale coming in short, painful, uneven breaths.

Astalon doesn't even budge.

I cling desperately to my anger, trying to use it to fuel me like I did with Alatar, but it isn't working. Astalon doesn't seem fazed at all. Meanwhile, I'm clinging to the last bit of strength I have.

It's getting harder and harder to breathe. I'm drained of energy. My legs are giving out. My whole body aches. And Astalon is as strong as ever.

No... he's somehow stronger.

Why did I think I would be strong enough? Why did I let myself believe I could beat him?

Even with the Sight, my emotions are slipping away, becoming harder to control. I feel like crying, but the tears won't come. I'm empty. *Hollow.*

My magic grows thinner. The purple is nothing compared to Astalon's overpowering red. It's inches from me now. My arms bend inward. I push as hard as I can, but *I can't do this.*

I crouch down, using my legs for leverage to push my magic forward and keep my balance—

Astalon's magic breaks through.

It slams into my chest, propelling me backward. The wind is knocked out of me as I hit the ground . I gasp for air.

Astalon laughs and walks to the edge of the Pit. He raises his arms, and the trapped souls rise from it. There are so many.

One by one, they float toward him and recede into his mouth. He consumes them like a midday snack. It makes him visibly stronger. Bigger.

He's feeding off their despair. Their fear.

Another crackle splits the sky, followed by a flash of black lightning. Like giant black veins striking the Underworld, the lightning hits to my left, then to my right. Each crack is deafening, startling me every time it strikes.

Then it stops, and Astalon looks more powerful than ever.

I feel defeated. I can't breathe. I can't think. Pain pulses through every part of my body, and my energy is completely gone.

It's over.

I'm going to die here.

Astalon is going to kill me. I was a fool to believe I could overpower him. That I could win.

That I could save Blade.

Blade.

I thought I was out of tears, but there they are. I close my eyes and see him lying there, dying.

You need to be brave now, Knight. You need to leave me and go save the world.

He believed in me, and I failed him. I failed all of them. I failed the *world.*

Astalon refocuses his attention on me. He smirks at the defeat on my face and starts walking toward me.

I'm sorry, Blade. I couldn't save you. I'm so sorry—

Then Astalon flinches. At least, I think he does. It happens so quickly I might have imagined it.

He's standing above me, towering over me.

This is it. This is the end.

He wraps his hand around my throat and squeezes.

I close my eyes and wait for death to take me, like it's taken so many before me. I don't want the last thing I see to be Astalon. Instead, I think about Blade. But not about him dying. I think about how much I care about him. Every moment we've spent together. Every moment that's made me fall for him more and more. His blue eyes are so vivid in my mind. His smile. His soft lips. His arrogant remarks. His cocky attitude. His bravery. His strength. His *kindness*.

I think about our kiss—somehow more magical than anything I've experienced this year—and I realize it wasn't just the kiss itself that made it so magical. It was who I was kissing. Because I loved that kiss. I loved it so much. But I love the person I was kissing even more.

I love Blade.

Astalon's grip on my neck loosens.

My hands fly to my throat as I cough and gasp for air. Astalon growls, and when I look up, I see he's backed away.

Why?

Why hasn't he killed me yet? Why did he step back?

He looks stunned. His wings are folded behind his back, and he's shrunk from his unnaturally large, soul-fuelled form to his regular size.

But *why*?

Then it hits me, and a sliver of hope creeps into my mind.

When Astalon flinched earlier, I was thinking about Blade—about how much I want to save him. About how badly I don't want to fail him. Realizing I love him... that emotion seemed to hurt Astalon. Maybe even weaken him.

Astalon feeds off negative emotions. So maybe, if I want to beat him, I have to focus on something else, something positive, and use those emotions against him.

I close my eyes and concentrate. I think about Blade again, about how much I love him.

And I amplify that love.

I feel it in every inch of my being. Every cell in my body. It's so strong it brings tears to my eyes. I thrust my hands forward and blast my magic at Astalon. Before it reaches him, the souls from the Pit form a shield in front of him. He's controlling them somehow, but it doesn't matter.

I hold on to the spell. I hold on to the image of Blade in my mind. To the feeling of love and empathy—feelings Astalon is incapable of.

Celie. Mykel. Lukas. Blade. I love them all. I have to make sure they're safe. I have to make sure Blade survives.

The souls melt to the ground, and Astalon curses. Then they move toward me. I take a step back in fear, but when they reach me, they form a barrier around me, as if... *shielding* me. Until one of them floats forward and touches me. The contact is brief. I feel it on my face, a warm hand pressed against my cheek.

I close my eyes, leaning into it, and I see her.

My mother... *Amelia.*

A tear escapes my eye and rolls down my cheek.

Behind her is my father, his hand resting on her shoulder, tears in his eyes. And beside him...

Sarah.

She looks at me with a smile on her face, her arm around our mother's shoulder. There's light in her eyes. Hope. She seems happy to be reunited with our parents.

As I look at them—my family together again—the tightness in my chest finally loosens.

Behind them are countless other faces I've never seen before. As I stare out at this sea of souls, I suddenly feel heavy. Heavy with emotion. Heavy with love, as if I'm carrying the love of these people in my heart.

Then, in a soothing voice that will forever linger in my mind, my mother whispers, "Let go."

So I do.

And as I let go, I release every soul trapped in this pit.

I open my eyes, and one by one, the souls disappear in flashes of bright light. As they vanish, one of them grows larger and forms into the shape of a human.

The shape of my mother.

My biological mother… she's standing right in front of me. I know it's her, even though she looks older than she did in the photos.

"It's you," I say, unable to form any other words.

She smiles. Her eyes are purple, reflecting my own. "I'm so proud of you. You can do this, Aria. The love you feel is your greatest power. Use it."

"Will I ever see you again?" I ask through tears.

"No, but I'll always be with you," she replies, and I know it's true. "I love you so much, Aria. Always remember that."

She walks closer until we're inches apart. She kisses my forehead, and I feel her love—amplified by the Sight—melt into me.

And then she's gone.

As the last of the souls disappear, my protective barrier fades with them. Astalon stands before me.

He wastes no time, blasting a spell at me like before. But this time is different, and he knows it. I'm not fuelled by anger; I'm fuelled by love. And not just my love. I feel my mother's love within me as well.

Adrenaline surges through my veins as I blast my spell forward, screaming through my tears.

Astalon loses his balance. He's getting weaker. It's working. *Maybe I can do this.*

I push my spell further, using every last ounce of energy in my body. I'm exhausted. My hands shake as I force my magic out.

But I won't give up.

I'm breathing uncontrollably, but my spell is overpowering his.

Not when I think I've figured it out.

He's being forced to the ground.

Not when I'm so close to saving him. Saving everyone.

Astalon's magic is barely visible now, almost completely swallowed by my own. He's weaker, struggling to hold on.

I yell as I force out one final surge of magic.

Astalon falls to his knees. The colour drains from his skin, and his eyes turn grey. My magic surrounds him, forming an electric purple dome.

He gives up, collapsing to the ground.

The dome surrounding him strengthens and glows. I've trapped him in the cage. Now I need to seal it.

I take a few seconds to catch my breath and calm my racing heart. Then I say, "*Sigillum Daemonium Infernum. Sigillum Astalon Decipula.*"

I repeat the incantation, remembering how Sarah taught us. My body is worn out. I'm so tired, but I force myself to stay steady.

I take a deep breath in.

A deep breath out.

And a surge of energy washes over the cage. There's a burst of light as the dome solidifies into a shell.

Everything goes quiet. Tiny particles of purple magic—the remnants of my spell—float through the Underworld before settling to the ground.

"Did... did it work?" I whisper to myself.

"It worked."

I spin around. The fidolus from the first trial stands before me. She still looks identical to my adoptive mother. "Don't worry. I'll keep an eye on the cage. There's no way he's getting out."

I collapse to the ground, lying on my back. I'm panting, crying, struggling to breathe between sobs. I'm drained. There's nothing left.

The Sight inside me flickers, settles in my core and retreats to the back of my mind. My emotions crash into me like a tidal wave. I gasp as if I've been held underwater and am finally coming up for air—

Except I'm *drowning*. Drowning in my emotions.

Blade.

Maybe he'll make it. Maybe...

I force myself to stand, dragging myself to my feet. It takes everything in me, but I have to get back to them. I have to make sure Blade is okay.

I try to run, but I'm limping. Every step feels like a thousand. My legs threaten to give out, but I keep moving.

When I reach them, I stop short. Blade lies on the ground, unmoving, surrounded by a pool of blood. Celie cradles his head in her lap. Lukas kneels beside her. Mykel sits on the ground with his head in his hands. Halo lies beside them, wings folded against his back.

I force myself forward. Halo senses my presence, lifting his head to look at me. He tries to stand but collapses back down.

When I reach them, the words barely leave my mouth. "Is he...?"

Celie looks up at me and shakes her head. "Not yet."

I drop to my knees beside Blade, rocks stabbing into them. I grab his hand and squeeze.

He doesn't squeeze back. He doesn't move at all. His eyes are closed, but he's still alive. I stare at the slow rise and fall of his chest, blocking out every other sound so I can hear the faint rhythm of his breathing.

"He just... stopped responding," Mykel says. "We didn't know what to do."

I let out a shaky breath. "I trapped Astalon in the cage. It's sealed."

All three of them look up at me.

"I did it," I say. "So why isn't Halo able to heal him?"

"Maybe he just needs time to regain some strength," Celie suggests.

"We don't have time."

I turn to Halo and gently pet his head. He lifts it again, looking up at me. When I meet his grey eyes, I notice faint specks of aqua within them. It's not much. But it's something.

"Halo," I say, "I need you to try to heal Blade again. I need you to give us more time."

Halo forces himself up. It doesn't seem quite as difficult as before, but he's still trembling. He walks over to Blade, extends his wings, and wraps them around him like he did earlier. My heart is racing. I'm still exhausted from my encounter with Astalon. I'm trying so hard not to pass out, but I feel like I might at any second.

I place a comforting hand on Halo's side, and he stops shaking. A halo flickers above his head. Then it solidifies into a thin, perfect circle that glows with blinding light. The grey in Halo's eyes gradually fades, replaced by that familiar aqua. They're small signs, but I cling to them.

Halo unwraps his wings and steps back. He looks exhausted, even though his features have returned to normal. He's done his best. We have to hope it was enough—

Blade's injuries begin to heal. It happens so slowly that if it weren't the only thing I could focus on, I would have missed it.

I try not to get my hopes up, but I can't help it. I can't hold back the feeling in my chest telling me Blade will be okay.

And then he squeezes my hand.

"Blade?" I say.

His eyes open—just a crack—but it's enough to fill every inch of my body with relief. I bend forward and rest my head against his chest, feeling his heartbeat beneath me. Then I lift my head and brush a strand of wet, matted hair away from his forehead.

"Knight," he says.

His voice is hoarse, barely above a whisper, but he spoke, and he's alive, and that's all I care about right now.

He tries to sit up, but I stop him and guide him back down so his head rests in my lap. "Don't move. You're still really weak."

He exhales and looks up at me. When our eyes meet, he forces his lips into a smile. "I knew you could do it."

I smile through my tears as Celie, Mykel, and Lukas stand nearby, relieved that Blade is doing better.

Then Lukas says, "Holy shit. Aria. You just defeated Astalon."

"I did," I say, still a little in disbelief.

"By yourself," he adds.

I nod.

"That's so hot," Blade forces out.

"Don't talk. You're going to hurt yourself," I say.

Mykel rolls his eyes. "Look at him. He'll be fine."

Celie scoffs. "Don't pretend like you weren't just crying over the fact that he might be dead literally less than five minutes ago."

Mykel narrows his eyes at her, his lips parting slightly in betrayal.

"Griffin, you cried for me?" Blade says. "I'm touched."

Mykel shakes his head. "Shut it, Casteel."

"You know what?" Lukas says. "I think this calls for a group hug. Come on, everyone on the ground."

"Please be careful," Blade mutters as Celie and Lukas wrap their arms around us. Mykel hesitates, so Lukas grabs his wrist and yanks him down.

We stay like that for a minute. I close my eyes, take a deep breath, and let myself enjoy the moment.

When we finally pull away, Lukas jumps to his feet and shouts, "We fucking did it!"

It takes me a second to laugh, because I'm pretty sure that's the first time I've ever heard Lukas say that word. But once I start, I can't stop.

We laugh and cheer. Even Blade laughs, though his is followed by a pained, "Fuck, that hurt."

Honestly, I think we're all a little hysterical. Mykel and Blade watch Celie, Lukas, and me laugh and cry at the same time with genuine concern. I'm so overwhelmed with emotions I don't know what to do with myself. I'm happy that I defeated Astalon, but...

In the distance, I see Sarah's body lying on the ground. I'm sad she isn't here with us. But at least I know she's in a better place. Still, I can't deny the part of me that feels guilty for killing Alatar. And I'm so tired I think adrenaline is the only thing keeping me upright.

"Okay, so..." Lukas says. "Can we get the hell out of Hell now?"

Celie grabs his hand. "Yes. Yes, we can."

We lift our arms into the air, and five bright red flares shoot from the palms of our hands. Moments later, we're back at Silver Key Manor.

CHAPTER FORTY-FOUR

"We need to contact the Emergency Sorcerers' Authorities."

We're in the Silver Key library. Blade groans in pain as I help him lie down on the couch in front of the fireplace. He's still bleeding more than he should be. Halo did the best he could, but he hasn't fully recovered his powers yet.

Celie nods. "Aria's right. Blade is still in critical condition. He needs medical attention immediately."

"Guys, I'm fine—" Blade starts.

"No, you're not." I sit on the edge of the couch and lay his head on my lap. "But you will be."

"I'll contact the ESA," Mykel says, tracing the number 829 on his palm and whispering, "*Subitis.*"

Five seconds pass before a man and woman appear before us. They don't make a sound. The only evidence of their arrival is a shimmer of red magic fading into the air. Both wear red-and-white uniforms. The white forms a round symbol on their chest with *ESA* etched into the centre.

The woman steps forward. "I'm Officer Alva. Are you in immediate danger?"

"My cousin," Mykel says, guiding the officers to the couch where Blade lies pale and sweating. When I touch his face, it's ice cold.

"What happened?" the male officer asks. Officer Ruston, according to his nametag.

"We were competing in the third trial of the Silver Key Tournament. He was injured badly. Aria's familiar tried to heal him, but this was the best he could do," Celie explains.

"What happened during the trial?" Officer Alva says.

Mykel summarizes the trial, focusing only on the most critical details, while Celie nervously paces the room, and Lukas sits in front of the fireplace.

As he speaks, Officer Ruston approaches Blade and me. He places a hand on Blade's chest. "*Iniurias.*" He scans Blade's body, assessing the injuries.

"They tried to kill us," Mykel finishes. "They were willing to do anything to stop us."

Officer Ruston steps back and turns to his partner. "His injuries are severe. I need to transport him to Rahasia's."

"Meanwhile, you all need to be under twenty-four-hour surveillance," Officer Alva says, turning to Mykel and Blade. "Until we locate your fathers, you cannot return home. The rest of you will have a security team keeping watch at all times."

Officer Ruston places a hand on Blade's shoulder and looks at me. "You need to let him go, ma'am."

"What?" I tighten my grip on Blade's hand.

"He needs medical attention now. I'm taking him to a healer. If we don't move immediately, he may not survive."

"I'll go with him," I say. "I don't want to leave him."

"That's not possible—"

"*Please,*" I plead, tears brimming.

"It's against protocol. You need to let go so I can teleport him," he says firmly.

"Knight, it's okay," Blade says.

"When will I see you again?"

Officer Alva places a comforting hand on my shoulder. "If he survives, he will be taken into protective custody with Mykel. You'll be able to see him when we deem it safe."

"*What?* How long?"

"We don't know."

"Aria, it'll be okay," Celie says, helping me off the couch.

I shake my head. "No—"

"Knight," Blade murmurs.

"Why can't I go with you?"

"Rules," he says.

"Screw the rules."

Blade sighs. "I've been such a shitty influence on you."

I laugh through my tears.

"I'll see you soon," he says.

I take a deep breath. "Okay."

He'll be alright. That's all that matters.

Blade looks at me, and through his eyes, he tells me what I need to hear. *Everything will be okay.*

With that, Blade and Officer Ruston disappear. I collapse onto the couch, resting my elbows on my knees and burying my face in my hands. I don't even realize how much they're shaking until I press my palms against my eyes. They're covered in blood—but so am I, so it doesn't matter.

"Mykel, we have to go," Officer Alva says. "I'll contact the station and alert them that the tournament is over." She turns to Celie, Lukas, and me. "You three will be teleported home. You may not see them, but there will be eyes on you at all times."

The tension leaves Celie's body as she nods. I don't think I can process everything yet. Celie runs to Mykel and embraces him. He tightens his arms around her and whispers something before they pull away. Lukas and Mykel fist-bump before Lukas rolls his eyes and hugs him.

"Aria," Mykel says, sitting next to me on the couch, wrapping me in his arms. "He's going to be okay." We pull apart, and he wipes a tear from my cheek. "I'll keep an eye on him. We'll be living together, after all."

"Yeah, good luck with that," Lukas mutters.

I force out a small chuckle.

Mykel stands, walks over to Officer Alva, and nods in confirmation. She places a hand on his shoulder. A moment later, they vanish, leaving only faint particles of magic behind.

Lukas exhales deeply. "And then there were three."

Soon there'll be one. Once I teleport home, I'll be away from them all.

As if reading my thoughts, Celie says, "We know where you live—"

"That sounds creepy," Lukas interrupts.

Celie ignores him. "We'll teleport to you every single day."

"Promise?" I say.

"Promise," they reply.

We smile at each other. I feel a faint tingle on my wrist. Before we can speak, the silver key tattoo glows, and I'm suddenly in my bedroom at home. I take a deep breath, trying to steady myself. Fatigue from defeating Astalon hits me harder than before. I fall onto my bed.

"Aria?" someone asks from outside my room.

I register it, but I'm too tired to respond. Exhaustion overtakes me, and I finally welcome it.

"Let's let her rest. She looks exhausted."

"I'll make her some food. She'll be hungry when she wakes up."

Footsteps leave the room, and I feel the bed dip as someone sits. Something damp and cold presses against my forehead.

"What happened, sweetie?" my mom whispers. "You're covered in blood."

I can't open my eyes. Sleep presses in and the world fades away again.

"Aria, can you just eat a little bit?"

I open my eyes just a crack. My mom's face hovers above me. *I'm so tired.*

I wake up, and I'm in my bed.

Not my bed at Silver Key, in my dorm room with Celie. I'm in my bed at home. The scent of fresh peony mixed with honey and caramel—my mom's signature fragrance—wraps around me, and I let out a small sigh.

"Oh, thank God you're awake." It's my mom's voice, reaching the side of my bed.

I try to remember what happened... I remember defeating Astalon. I was so tired. I remember the fidolus, looking exactly like my mother, reassuring me that Astalon would never escape that cage. I turn to my real mother and am comforted by her loving eyes. The demon didn't have that. I feel myself relax, but only for a second, because then I remember... Blade.

He was in bad condition. They took him to a healer. Even if I can't see him, I need to know he's okay.

My feelings must be written across my face, because my dad says, "Aria, you're okay."

Hearing those words breaks something inside me. I let out a sob—out of worry, confusion, fear... and longing. I missed my dad so much. I haven't seen him or Ashton in almost a year. I hop out of bed and embrace my father.

"I missed you so much," he murmurs into my hair.

"I missed you too, Dad."

"Aria!" Ashton shouts, running into my room.

"Ash, I thought I told you to wait," Mom says. "Your sister's been through a lot. She needs time to—"

"No, it's okay," I say. "I missed you, Ash!"

He runs into my arms. God, I really did miss him. When we pull away, he looks at me with a mix of happiness and sadness in his eyes. I'm hit with a wave of guilt.

"I'm sorry I was gone for so long," I say. "I'll never leave you again. I promise."

He smiles, relieved, then masks it with a cringe. "I didn't miss you *that* much."

I roll my eyes. "Yes, you did. Don't lie."

"I'm not lying."

"Come on, Ash, admit it."

"Did not."

"Ash—"

"Already, you two?" Dad interjects.

We both laugh, and I pull Ashton into another hug. He hugs back just as tight. When we pull away, my emotions dart in every direction. I'm thrilled to be reunited with my family, but terrified for Blade. I'm sad I'm not with my friends.

"How long was I asleep?"

"You've been in and out for five days," Mom says.

"*Five* days?"

She nods. "You showed up in your room out of the blue. You were a mess, sweetie—tangled hair, dirt and blood all over you.

I was so worried. You were exhausted, could barely stand... then you collapsed onto your bed and fell asleep."

"Do you remember what happened?" Dad asks.

"I..." I'm unable to form words. I don't even know how to begin to explain everything that happened during my time at Silver Key. Or how to explain what happened in the Underworld.

Yeah, Mom and Dad, I thought my best friend was dead, but she got revived by a fire butterfly, and then my long-lost sister was killed. I murdered the headmaster of the manor and sealed the most powerful demon in the universe in a cage in Hell so he can't escape to this realm and infect the world with his evilness. Oh, and the guy I'm in love with might be dead.

"We'll give you time to process everything," Mom says. "Let us know if you need anything."

They begin to leave, but I call out, "Wait."

It's like my mom can read my face. She tells Ashton to go to the living room, then closes the door. None of us know how to start... how to address the unspoken issue lingering in the air.

Finally, Mom says, "We love you so much, Aria, and we never wanted you to find out the way you did."

Dad places a hand on her shoulder. "We should have told you sooner. We're so sorry, and we just hope you can find it in your heart to forgive us."

I close my eyes. I've held anger toward them since I first arrived at Silver Key and learned about the adoption and magic. I suppressed it because I know they love me. I felt guilty being angry when they've done so much for me—raised me, cared for me, loved me. Now, looking into their eyes and seeing that love, that regret...

We all make mistakes, but the beauty of it is we're loved enough to be forgiven for those mistakes. Just as your parents forgive you for yours, try to find it in your heart to forgive them.

I sigh with relief and pull my parents into a hug. "I love you guys."

"We love you too," they say.

When we pull away, both of them have tears in their eyes. My dad's grin stretches across his face.

"We're so glad you're okay," Mom says, tucking a loose strand of hair behind my ear.

"I'm okay."

It feels good to say it out loud. Despite everything, I *am* okay. We won. And I know in my heart, an inexplicable feeling in my chest, that Blade is okay too.

"Oh, and these two kids around your age keep showing up, asking to see you. Celie and Lukas?"

I smile.

"They usually come around this time, so I'll tell them you're up when they arrive."

"Thanks," I say.

My parents leave, closing the door behind them. The backpack I brought to Silver Key leans against the wall. I think about pulling out my phone and contacting Violet, but instead, I strip off my dirty, bloodstained clothes and take a much-needed shower.

Warm water hits my bare skin, relaxing my aching muscles and washing away the blood. I try not to focus on the cuts and bruises scattered over my body. I comb my hand through my knotted hair, trying to rid the tangles.

I reach for the shampoo bottle—it slips, hitting the tub. The lid pops open, and shampoo oozes onto the floor. My heart races.

Blade, lying in a pool of his own blood. The way it oozed out of him and onto the dusty red ground of the Underworld. There was so much of it, so much blood.

I bring my hands to my face, shaking myself out of it. The sound of water splashing against my skin snaps me back. My pulse slows slightly. I bend down and pick up the bottle, my hands trembling as I set it back on the shelf.

No matter how hard I try, my mind drifts back to the third trial: Sarah falling still on the ground, Alatar pleading beneath me, the way it felt to plunge the dagger into his chest. I can't stop thinking about it. I know I did what was necessary, but the memory still makes me sick with guilt.

Opening my eyes, I force the thought away. What's done is done. And I wouldn't take it back, even if I could. I have to remind myself that, in the end, I did what needed to be done.

After my shower, I dry off, change into clean clothes, and return to my room. Celie is sitting on my bed, and Lukas is lying on the floor, balancing a pen on his nose.

The sight fills me with joy. I run onto the bed, startling Lukas. He—rather than drop the pen like a normal person—throws it at me, missing by an inch, as I wrap Celie in my arms.

"Jesus, Lukas! You could've hurt her," Celie laughs, pulling away.

"Is Blade okay?" I ask, desperate.

Celie grabs my hand. Her lips stretch into a grin, and she nods. "He's perfectly fine. Officer Alva contacted us but couldn't reach you, so she asked us to tell you when you woke up."

I collapse onto my bed in relief. "Thank God."

Celie looks at me for a moment. "You really love him."

"I really do."

She hands me a ring, identical to the one Sarah and I used at Silver Key to communicate. "Maybe you should tell him."

I stare at her in confusion.

She chuckles. "When the officers were explaining everything at Silver Key, I summoned them and slipped one to Blade before he and Officer Ruston teleported away. You won't be able to use it all the time—the enchantment wears off after a week of regular use—but I thought you'd want to hear his voice."

I throw myself into Celie's arms, hugging her tight. She doesn't protest. "Thank you so much."

When we pull away, she says, "Go talk to him. We'll wait here."

I leave my bedroom, my feet dragging me to the bathroom. I sit on the edge of the bathtub, lifting the ring to my lips.

"Blade?" I say, but it comes out as no more than a whisper.

Can't get rid of me that easily.

I exhale in relief. His voice is smooth, warm, and laced with the usual arrogance I've come to love.

I roll my eyes, but smile. "You're okay?"

Of course I am, he says. *All healed up, as perfectly handsome as always.* There's a pause. Then he says, *Mykel's telling me to shut up.*

I chuckle.

I missed hearing that laugh, he says.

"I'm so happy to hear your voice."

Not as happy as I am to hear yours. Celie is a lifesaver.

I nod, even though he can't see me. "Do you know when we'll be able to see each other?"

No. But I'm trying to convince them to let us go to school when the new term starts if we aren't already released from protective custody.

"I believe in you," I say.

I can be very persuasive.

"I wish you could see the smile on my face right now."

So do I. But it's okay. I can picture it. Anyway, we should go. If we don't talk long, we can probably stretch the rings' use for about two weeks.

"Okay." I take a shaky breath. "But I need to tell you something first. I—"

I know. Tell me when you see me.

I sigh. "Fine. But you suck for ruining the moment."

I was trying to make it romantic. And I didn't want you to say it first.

My heart feels like it's about to burst out of my chest. "We'll talk tomorrow?"

Of course, he replies. *And Aria?*

"Yeah?"

I love you.

"You asshole!" I shout, and I hear the echo of his laugh in my head, fading until there's nothing left but my own thoughts.

I compose myself before leaving the bathroom. When I enter my room, Celie and Lukas are sitting at the edge of my bed, pretending to act normal.

I narrow my eyes at them, and Lukas breaks. "We were eavesdropping."

Celie punches him in the arm. "Lukas!"

"It was obvious," he says.

Celie rolls her eyes, then stands and hugs me. "Did he say it?"

I nod, and she pulls away, grinning.

"Thank you for this, Celie," I say, gesturing to the ring.

She waves her hand. "It was nothing. I'm happy for you guys."

We sit on my bed.

"And we know you're probably feeling a little overwhelmed with everything we've been through, and now having to get used to living here with magic," Lukas says. "Just know we're here for you. We'll help you adapt. You're not alone."

When did I get so lucky? I'm surrounded by so many people who care about me, and I couldn't be more grateful.

I send him a small, appreciative smile, but before I can reply, my bedroom door flies open, banging against the wall. The three of us jump.

"*Aria. Amelia. Knight.*" Violet stands in the doorway, her hand still resting on the door. "How long have you been awake?"

I shrug. "Maybe an hour."

"A whole hour and not once did my phone vibrate."

"I was going to call you, Violet. I promise."

"Uh-huh," she says, stepping into my room.

"So this is Violet?" Celie asks, standing. She walks over and hugs Violet. Violet's face softens instantly, as if she's forgotten all about me. "It's so good to finally meet you. I'm Celie."

As Celie pulls away, Violet asks, "How do you get your hair so soft?"

"Magic."

Violet's eyes go wide. "Can you do mine?"

Celie grins. "Sure."

Violet hugs Celie again. "I love you already."

When they let go of the embrace, Lukas joins them. "I'm Lukas. Nice to meet you—is that a Lemon Rain T-shirt?"

"It is," Violet says. "Wait, you like their music?"

"Of course!" Lukas practically shouts. "I've been a fan since their first album!"

Violet literally jumps in excitement. "No way! Me too! You're the first person I've met who listens to them."

"Same here!"

The two of them launch into a tangent about the band—their last album, favourite songs—while Celie chimes in occasionally. I watch them, grinning.

When they catch me staring, they stop talking.

"Aria?" Celie says.

Violet chuckles. "Are you okay?"

I nod. "I'm just... so happy."

CHAPTER FORTY-FIVE
One Month Later

I wake up to the loud blaring of my alarm clock.

Violet slept over last night, and we're sitting at the dining room table, eating the breakfast my mom so graciously made. Well... she *started* to make it. It was taking too long, and none of us wanted to be late, so she asked me to help speed things up. I didn't burn anything this time. Turns out Celie was right; it is pretty easy. The blueberry pancakes are mouth-watering, and between my parents, Violet, Ashton, and me, they disappear way too fast.

Today is my first day at Blakeworth: New York School of Magic. Needless to say, I'm a nervous wreck.

Blade and I haven't spoken in weeks since our magic rings stopped working, but I think about him every day. A part of me hopes he'll show up at school today. Another part knows I shouldn't get my hopes up.

Violet hands me my backpack. "Let's go, Aria! Wouldn't want to be late for your first day at magic school, would you?"

Since Blakeworth is on the way to my old school, Violet agreed to drive me every morning.

"I'm gonna miss you so freaking much at school. How will I get through every boring-ass day without my bestie?" she pouts.

"Trust me, I'm gonna miss you, too."

We say goodbye to my parents and Halo, who's sound asleep on the couch. I pet his head, and he lets out a huff of acknowledgment. Then we walk out.

I step through the front doors of the massive school.

"School" doesn't feel right. Castle is more like it.

I sigh as I take in my surroundings and attempt to find my way through the building. The Victorian-esque decor immediately reminds me of the manor, polished floors gleaming under the light pouring in from tall, arched windows, every surface pristine in a way that feels almost too perfect. Walking down the hallway, I can't help but think of my first day at Silver Key—the uncertainty, the novelty, the anxiety.

Violet had to drop me off a block away from the school because, first, it sits atop a hill and the narrow path to the entrance is long; second, bringing a non-sorcerer inside would get us in trouble; and third, the school is magically hidden—only those with magic can see it. She was utterly pissed, muttering under her breath and glaring up at the hill like it had personally offended her.

Even though Celie cast a spell on Violet so she can see magical things—like Halo—some places and creatures still elude her sight.

As I walk alone through the long hallway, passing arched windows and student achievement plaques that hang along the walls, people stare at me. I guess they know who I am now.

Awesome.

Honestly, so many rumours swirl around me that I've stopped keeping track. I can't tell who likes me and who doesn't.

My phone buzzes in my pocket. It's a text from Violet.

Violet: You better tell me every single detail about what that school is like so I can live vicariously through you. And text me after every period.

I reply with a quick *lol, will do.*

And then I continue on in a sad attempt to find my way through the school. I glance at my timetable.

Am I even on the right floor?

This place is insane. If high schools look like this, I can't imagine college. Do sorcerers even have post-secondary schools? I make a mental note to ask Celie and Lukas later. Apparently, most sorcerers don't finish "high school" until they're twenty-three.

The bell rings, and I'm surprised by how similar it sounds to my old school's bell, all things considered.

As I make my way to my first class of the day, desperately trying to block out the whispers and stares around me, I feel something hit the back of my head and look down to find a balled-up piece of paper by my feet.

Someone seriously just threw a paper ball at my head.

Oh, *hell* no.

"Do you have a problem—" I turn around, and my heart nearly stops at the sight of two perfect blue eyes staring back at me.

"Blade."

He smirks. "Hey, Knight."

EPILOGUE

"Thank God it's almost winter break."

"Only three more periods to go," Blade says, wrapping his arms around my waist.

I bring my arms around his neck, and he leans down, planting a soft kiss on my lips.

"Come on, I already told you two—if I'm going to be spending time with you guys, that can't be happening in front of me," Mykel says. "At least for a little while."

"Sorry," I murmur, but I don't remove my arms from Blade's neck, and he doesn't remove his hands from my waist.

"Right, you definitely seem sorry," he says.

I think he's finally getting used to seeing Blade and me together. At first, I felt guilty. But I was also so happy to see Blade that I couldn't keep my hands off him.

Though Mykel's and Blade's fathers have yet to be found, the ESA allowed them to attend school so as not to "hinder their education." Blade told me those were the exact words he used to convince them.

There's still a security team watching each of us at all times. Initially, I thought it would be annoying, but now, I hardly notice they're there. I'm just glad Blade is okay and that he and Mykel are here.

Seeing Blade on that first day of school was incredible. Those eyes. That smirk. For a moment, I couldn't believe he was real. And then I realized he was—he was really standing in front of me. I couldn't waste another second. I basically catapulted myself into his arms. His familiar scent, his warm embrace... it was real, and I could finally breathe again.

Then he told me that he and Mykel were now living in a loft a few blocks from my house.

Blade and Mykel. *Living together*. By choice. They still fight sometimes—it's a work in progress—but they're trying, and it warms my heart.

Even though Celie and Lukas don't live here, I still see them every day, just like they promised. They often teleport to my room, and sometimes pop downstairs unannounced. My mom and dad weren't thrilled at first, but they've grown used to it, especially since Celie and Lukas come over for dinner so often that my mom sets a plate for them most nights. One night, Celie teleported to my room in the middle of the night and scared the hell out of me.

The bell rings, snapping me from my thoughts. Blade, Mykel, and I gather our things and make our way to our shared class of the day.

After school, Blade and I head back to my house. My dad greets us at the door.

"Hey, Mr. Knight," Blade says.

"Please, Blade, I told you—call me Kevin," my dad replies with a friendly smile.

"Right—"

"Blade!" Ashton calls, racing down the stairs.

"Hey, buddy!" Blade says as my brother wraps him in a tight hug.

I smile at the sight. I love seeing how much my brother admires Blade. And Blade is always so good with him.

"How was school?" Blade asks as Ashton leads him toward the living room to play.

Dad turns to me. "Learn any new magic tricks today?"

I shake my head at him. I told him not to refer to them as *magic tricks*... it is what it is.

"I learned a few new spells, yeah," I say. "But honestly, a lot of it was review from Silver Key. Blade said we'll get into new stuff next semester. I'm still not thrilled about having a math class, though. Thank goodness this semester's almost over."

Dad gives me a teasing look. "Never was your strong suit, huh?"

I squint at him, then shrug and nod in agreement.

There's a knock on the door, and I open it to find Mykel standing there. I let him in and lead him to the living room where Blade is playing video games with Ash.

"I'm totally beating your ass," Blade says.

"No, I'm beating *your* ass!" Ashton fires back.

Blade's eyes go wide. "Don't say that around your parents. And also, don't tell Aria."

I smirk, leaning against the wall. "Don't tell Aria, huh?"

Blade cringes and turns around. "It's only 'ass'. It's not like I said fu—"

"Dude!" Mykel interrupts, and I chuckle.

Blade and Ashton finish their game—Ashton wins, though Blade claims he let him. I highly doubt it. And then Celie and Lukas descend the stairs.

"Who's ready to get their escape room on!" Celie announces, hopping off the last step.

"You're here!" I shout, running over to hug them.

"Violet should be here any minute—" I start, but the door-bell cuts me off. My mom goes to answer, and moments later, Violet waltzes in.

"Ash, come eat your snack," my mom calls.

Ashton darts to the kitchen. I take his spot on the couch next to Blade, and he wraps an arm around me.

Since it's everyone's first escape room except Violet and me, we give them a quick rundown.

"So they lock us in a room, and we have to solve clues to get out? Is this what normal people do for fun?" Blade says.

I flick him on the arm. "It will be fun, asshole."

He kisses my cheek playfully.

"And remember," Violet says, "no phones."

"And no magic," I add.

Lukas rolls his eyes. "Yeah, yeah."

"And no losing," Violet warns. "If we don't escape, our friendship is over."

Mykel chuckles.

Violet looks at him. "You'll be first to go."

"That sounds slightly terrifying," he mutters

Violet smirks and winks at him, and then we all head out of the house.

"Shotgun!" Lukas shouts, hopping into the passenger seat of Violet's car.

Once we're settled in, Violet turns on her Bluetooth, and music blares through the speakers.

"I'm changing the song," Mykel says, reaching for her phone.

Violet scoffs. "What, you don't like indie rock?"

He laughs. "Violet, this is not indie rock."

"Fine, if your music taste is so much better, be my guest."

"I will, thanks," Mykel says with a teasing grin.

She narrows her eyes at him. "You know what? I take that back. Celie, I trust you more."

Mykel sighs and sits back in his seat.

"Yeah..." Violet says.

Mykel looks at her. "Huh?"

"You're definitely the weakest link."

He rolls his eyes, but the smile doesn't leave his lips. "Okay, Celie. Pick something good."

"You should not trust Celie to pick the music," Lukas says, "unless you're really into hip-hop. I'm talking, like, explicit rap."

Blade chuckles. "Celie?"

"It's expressive," she says defensively with a half shrug.

"Hip-hop it is!"

I can't contain the grin that spreads across my face as I rest my head on Blade's shoulder.

I stare out the window at my hometown, and as I watch the houses pass by, I consider the fact that life is not about planning out every little thing. It's not about making do with what you're given. Making spontaneous decisions and accepting the unexpected with open arms is what leads to the biggest adventures. And yes, sometimes things may go terribly wrong, but other times it can go incredibly right.

I glance down at the silver key on my wrist and run my thumb over it. I never expected my life to change so drastically. I've always been content living how I was, but now I realize that before, I wasn't really *living*.

And now, hanging out with some of the people I love most in the world, laughing about Celie's choice of music and Lukas's enthusiasm to successfully escape the escape room, I can still feel the magic coursing through my veins, and I've never felt more alive.

ACKNOWLEDGEMENTS

I can't believe it's finally out!!! Writing this book has been a long, difficult journey. But I had fun, I learned so much, and I have so many people to thank.

Firstly, thank you to my brother, Matteo. You inspired so many parts of this book, helped me come up with amazing ideas when I was stuck, and were the first person to read the book. You always understood exactly what my intentions with the story and characters were, and you gave me incredible feedback. This book would not be the same without your help. Writing this book was very overwhelming at times, and you were always able to calm me down and give me advice when I needed it the most. I am so grateful for your support. Thank you for being the best brother I could ever ask for.

I'd also like to thank Mark Whitbread, who not only took the time to read and edit the book but who created the AMAZING cover. I know I'm a bit of a perfectionist, so thank you for having the patience to listen to my suggestions. I appreciate your help so much and am so grateful for the time you spent working on this with me.

A HUGE thank you to one of my best friends, Erin. You spent hours going through the book with me, editing, leaving notes, and providing me with invaluable feedback. I am so appreciative of the time you took to help me make this book as great as possible, so thank you so so much.

Of course, Mom and Dad, thank you so much for all the support! This is the first book I've ever written, and it was a struggle, but whenever I felt discouraged, I had you guys cheering me on. You encouraged me throughout this whole process, and I want you to know that I am so blessed to have such amazing, supportive parents. You were some of the first people to read this story when it was in the early stages of editing. You motivated me and helped me believe that I really have something worth working on, so thank you and I love you so so much.

MANY thanks to my beta readers/proofreaders: Christy, Justine, Max, Griffin, Cj, Ethan, Chloe, and Heather. Your notes and opinions were a tremendous help, and I am genuinely so thankful for you guys.

Thank you to everyone who supported me during the writing/editing process, who expressed their excitement about the book, and continued to encourage me to push through and finish this. It took a while, but it's finally here!

And lastly, I want to thank anyone and everyone who gives this book a chance. Seriously, THANK YOU. It means so much to me. Aria Knight has such a special place in my heart, and I hope you all enjoyed her crazy journey!

ABOUT THE AUTHOR

Alyssa L. Bertinato was born and raised in Ottawa, Ontario, and holds a Criminology degree with a concentration in Psychology from Carleton University. Her love of reading began in childhood, and she has since dedicated herself to crafting worlds full of romance, magic, and adventure. *Silver Key* is her debut novel.

alyssalbertinato.com   @alyssalbertinato   @authoralyssalbertinato   @alyssalbertinato